Forbidden Hollywood

Forbidden Hollywood

By
William Prendergast

Cole Dixon Publishing
Minnesota

Published by Cole Dixon Publishing Company

First Edition, 2002

LIBRARY OF CONGRESS
CATALOGING-IN-PUBLICATION DATA

Prendergast, William.
Forbidden Hollywood / by William Prendergast. – 1st ed.
p. cm.
LCCN 20011118936
ISBN 0-9714739-2-7

1. Hollywood (Los Angeles, Calif.)– Fiction.
2. Mystery fiction. I. Title

PS3616.R455F67 2002 813'.6
QBI33-165

Thank you:
Mimi Zarsky, Dr. John Levine, Sister Rita, Steve Brown, Marchel Hardin, Shauna O'Connor, Dan Baum, Randy Mason, and Peter Esmonde.

Printed in the United States of America.
Distributed by Cole Dixon Publishing, 92 Mahtomedi Ave., Mahtomedi, Minnesota, 55115. Telephone: (651) 334 8165.

For Kit
a beautiful and patient woman

They found him, in the end; it sure took 'em long enough. It wasn't until after the Second World War; some government surveyors came across him when they were scouting out the Mojave for some kind of military project. He was nothing but bones by then, of course. But he was still chained to that great big cast-iron safe, and he still wore the rags of that silk kimono. It must have been pretty weird for those surveyors; finding something like that out in the middle of the deep desert, miles from anything.

The newspapers said that there was no violent disfigurement of the skeleton; no bullet holes or anything like that. Except around the chained wrist, some of the bones there were fractured. This indicated that the victim must have been alive when he was left out there; broken wrist bones obviously meant that he'd struggled to try and free himself before he died.

Another thing: whoever the dead man was, he'd known the combination of the safe. The door was still open, sand and dirt swirling around it. The cops figured maybe the dead guy opened the safe to try to crawl inside, get out of the sun. But he couldn't, the opening was just a little too small for that.

They never did figure out who he was. The whole thing looked like a gangland killing, of course; like he'd been left out there as punishment for stealing or something. Symbolic, you know? Being chained to an empty safe and left to die. And the safe was empty; if there had ever been anything inside it, it had long since dried up and blown away.

The only other clue was the little glass jar. It lay near the body; the skeleton held the lid to the jar in his bony hand. The sheriff's guess was that the heat had finally made this guy so crazy that he'd opened up the jar and drank or ate whatever was inside.

1

"Now come on, Mr. Boswell. Come on down off that window, you're not gonna jump. That's twelve stories straight down."

"You're filth! Nothing but filth!"

Okay, I thought, maybe I'm filth, but you're a goddamn screwball. I couldn't get to him at that window, I was still standing on the other side of his great big desk. He was a little guy, but fast; I'll give him that. He got up out of his swivel chair and hopped onto that window ledge before I even knew what he was doing; it was like he'd planned the whole thing even before I'd come in to his office.

Maybe he had. He'd had plenty of notice before I showed up that morning at the bank. It had been about a week since I'd taken the pictures; the pictures of him balling his fat Irish maid. I'd burst in on the two of them in the bedroom of Boswell's summer place in Cape Cod. I managed to get three good shots before Boswell wrapped himself up in a bed sheet and chased me out of the house; it was like he was Caesar's ghost or something.

So Boswell knew the score; he knew it was a shakedown and he knew that I'd show up on his doorstep sooner or later. He knew I wasn't a private detective, working for his wife, looking for evidence for a divorce. If that had been the case, I would have shown up in his bedroom with witnesses to the adultery. So he knew it was just a piece of money I was after; Boswell was a vice president at one of the oldest banks in Boston. I bet the only thing he couldn't figure was: why hadn't I made him write me out a check right there on the spot? Simple: I worked alone in those days, and if you worked alone you never made the pitch for the money right on the spot; there might be a gun around somewhere.

So I always gave my marks a few days to think things over first, cool off a little. Only in Boswell's case, it backfired. This guy didn't cool off; he came to a boil. And flipped his lid.

"Come down, now, Mr. Boswell, you don't want anybody on the street to see you standing up there, do ya? How's that going to look for the bank?"

Actually, it wasn't all that uncommon for a banker to be up on a ledge in those days; this was the Depression, the 'thirties, you know how it was if you've seen the old newsreels. Hard times all around, banks folding up all over the country. Boswell's bank was one of the ones that hadn't folded; that's why I figured he'd be a good prospect. I never blackmailed anybody who couldn't afford to pay off; that's just silly, and dangerous. And I mean, gimme a break, it was only five gees I was after; they'd spent more than that on the Italian marble in the lobby downstairs.

But this idiot has to make a whole goddamn opera out of the deal. I misjudged him. I had him down as a blue-blood businessman who'd see things reasonably, unemotionally, and pay off. In my experience these Boston Brahmin types never lost their cool; a Jew I knew in stir called them "God's Frozen People." But Mr. Boswell must have had some Italian blood in him, somewhere…

I was working my way around the desk, slow. I said: "Okay, look, maybe five thousand is too much." (Like hell it was.) "Come on down from there, have a seat, we'll talk about it."

"Don't come any closer!" He was hanging on to the curtains for balance now. I still wasn't convinced he meant to jump, but the whole situation was giving me the creeps. The guy was old enough to be my father, he shouldn't be pulling stunts like this.

"Look, you can have the pictures, okay? Here they are." I tossed the envelope on his desk. I had to get him down from there; and the pictures were absolutely no good to me if he jumped. They didn't have any, what do you call it, 'intrinsic worth.' Shots of him with that maid; she was almost as old as he was, they looked like a pair of Siamese walruses and it was a toss-up between 'em whose titties sagged the furthest. Useless as pornography, who wants to jerk off looking at that? And the quality of the photos wasn't anything to brag about either; I'm no Ansel Adams with the camera. All I care about is, are they good enough so that the wife can recognize the sucker's face?

So Boswell could have 'em, and good riddance. But that wasn't good enough for him, either:

"No!" he screeches. "No no no!" like a little kid. "You have the negatives, you'll send copies to my family!"

This guy's seen too many movies, I thought. He was right though; I did have the negatives, and I would make copies and send them to his wife, but that wouldn't cost him a cent—I'd do it out of spite, this guy was such a cheap, sissy, pain in the ass prick.

"The negatives are in there with the pictures," I lied. That made him turn his head to look at the envelope where it lay on the desk, and that's when I made my move: I jumped forward and tried to throw my arms around his legs. I was bigger than him, and young and strong in those days, so I figured I could just pull him back into the room, using the weight of my body. And then maybe I'd pound him on the head a couple of times for causing me such grief over a crummy five grand.

But he was fast, like I said. I barely managed to get a hold of one of his legs. His foot slipped and he lost his balance, the next second he was hanging out the window and screaming blue murder. He was still clutching at the curtains. He didn't want to die. I decided right then that the stupid son-of-a-bitch hadn't ever really meant to jump at all. It was just an act to beat me down on the price.

He wasn't acting now, though; hanging upside down, squirming like an eel and peeing up his shirt. I still had his leg, and I might have been able to hang on if he would have just kept still. I heard the curtains rip off the rod above us, and then they came down around my head, and I felt light all of the sudden—and then, when I got myself out from under those curtains, I was standing there, all alone in his office. Looking down out of the window, holding on to one of his shoes.

He'd already hit the sidewalk, of course. I could see him now; a tiny man stretched out down there, like he'd just decided to take a nap on the pavement. There were a couple of shouts and screams from below, tinny and small, and the little crowd was beginning to ad-lib a circle around him, keeping a respectful distance away from the body. It didn't look that gory from way up here, but I still felt a little sick. Already some of the itty-bitty faces were beginning to turn upward, to see where he'd come from. Then a police whistle blew somewhere, shrill and small and far away; the sound was so unpleasantly familiar to me that it snapped me right out of my trance.

I stepped back from the window, and let Mr. Boswell's shoe drop to the carpet. Let's see, I thought, what are my options? Should I stick around and try to explain my take on the situation to a bunch of Boston cops? Or should I just tuck this envelope under my arm, stroll out of the office, shut the door softly behind me, and give Mr. Boswell's secretary a polite smile on the way out?

A relatively easy decision, right?

California, here I come, I sighed, as I put my foot on the accelerator of my Dodge and headed west. I'd never been before, but it's as good a place as any when the cops are looking for you. Because I was hot now, and how. That guy's secretary probably gave them a real good description of me ("He was a handsome young fellow, in a sinister sort of way…well dressed, though a little flashy…not the sort of person that poor Mr. Boswell would normally see here at the office…") And 'poor Mr. Boswell' hadn't left a suicide note or anything--which would give some bright, ambitious young assistant district attorney the clever idea of hanging a murder rap around my neck.

And the worst part of it was, it wasn't even my fault. Not really. I mean, come on, over a lousy five thousand bucks, the moron starts getting dramatic on a twelfth-story windowsill! And him a millionaire, can you believe it? Throws away the precious life that God gave him, out the window, just like that. Over five thousand bucks. Christ, I bet my father never made five thousand bucks in his whole life. Do you think he killed himself? No such luck.

So even though that score hadn't panned out and I was down to my last hundred and fifty bucks, California sounded pretty good, basically because it was so far away from Boston. Also, I had a pal out in L.A.; he'd dropped me a line a month or so before and said we might get something going together if I came out to see him.

As if I needed another reason to get the hell out of there. I didn't want to go; there were plenty of marks in Boston and the cops were manageable. But that's the way things are: you finally get set up some place you think is perfect, and the very next day it's the most dangerous place in the world. So what do you do? You lam it, that's all you can do. It was like that ancient Greek philosopher said, Hercules, or whatever his name was: one should never step into one's own stream twice.

It's boring to drive cross-country. The scenery is nice 'til you're about half way through Ohio, then it's bone-ugly. Once you get out of Oklahoma it's nice again, but a mountain's a mountain, a tree's a tree, you know what I mean? My mind tends to wander, I get a little edgy when I spend that much time driving all by myself.

I wanted to stop at a roadhouse or something for a few drinks, and I was dying to get laid—but who was I kidding, I didn't have the dough to spare. A hundred and fifty dollars to get a guy like me from Boston to Los Angeles; that's pathetic.

Maybe a fella can get laid for less than five dollars in west Texas, but it would probably be with a cow or something. The smart thing for me to do was to keep on going, as fast as I could. I couldn't show up at my pal's place in Los Angeles completely broke; that's bad business, gotta have some kind of front.

So I promised myself, no distractions.

I almost made it, too. I think it was near the west Arizona border, just about sundown, when I first saw her. (Beautiful sunsets out there.) I remember saying to myself, just before she came into view, saying to myself out loud as I'm driving: "Friend, you have had a tough time of it this trip and you deserve a change of luck." And then there she was, my change of luck, standing at the side of a ridge by the highway, thumb stuck out into the air, suitcase in hand.

Sometimes you can tell if they're lookers or not even if you're still a ways off. I know I can. It's unusual for a hitchhiker to be good looking; then as now, most of the folks you'd see hitching a ride looked like they'd already been run over a few times by passing motorists. But right here, coming up fast in my windshield, was a breath of fresh air. One cute little number, nice shape, tight sweater, tight skirt, legs, all the necessaries. All dolled up to go traveling in her daywear from the mail-order catalog.

Blonde, too. As I closed in on her, I could see the careful little curls peeking out from under the cloche hat. I've never passed up a blonde in my life, not even a Golden Retriever. My luck *must* have changed, because she'd obviously just started hitching this minute; there wasn't a salesman or truck driver in the whole wide world who'd pass this one by.

I didn't pull right over, though. There's a lot of unethical people in the world—in those rough times, a pretty gal was occasionally the bait for a boyfriend or two, waiting out of sight by the side of the road with plans to tag along or maybe something worse. So I pulled off about a hundred feet or so beyond where she was standing, to make sure she was all alone. As she walked up to the car I could see that she was a little miffed that any guy would ever pass her up by even that much. The little lips were pouty, very kissable. I flashed my bandleader smile at her as she came up to the window.

"Hey there, beautiful."

"You going to California?" Gravelly, little girl voice; it was kind of sexy, but it didn't go with the big girl shape.

"As a matter of fact, I am. Hop in, it must be getting cold out there."

"You're right about that," she said, sliding in. I reached across her and slammed her door shut. Cheap perfume; that was a good sign, I wouldn't have to spend a lot on dinner.

I sped off with my new prize. Gosh, she was a cutie. Though a little scared of me, at first. I sympathized; it's tough being a good-looking gal out on the road. You never knew what you were going to draw as a ride.

We got across the California border like a breeze. They had guards on the roads in those days to keep folks out, because they already had enough guys standing in breadlines in California. But my car wasn't that old, it had Massachusetts plates, and we sure didn't look like Mexicans or broke Okies. So they hardly even slowed us down, they just waved us through the crossing.

I hadn't tried to chat her up yet, 'cause the top was down and it was a little noisy. It would have been pointless, anyway, because, like I said, this baby was hot; she'd probably already heard every cheap line there was to hear. So I played it cool, let her start the talking. She must have figured me for okay after the first twenty miles or so, because she finally spoke up first, loud enough to hear over the breeze.

"Where're you headed in California, mister?"

Mister? Uh oh. I took a glance at her sideways and felt a thrill of horror all the way down through my pants. She'd been standing in the shadows in front of a cliff when I'd first picked her up, and all I'd really seen was her tight sweater and the grown-up clothes. That was why I hadn't noticed—but now we were out in the open and driving into the red light of the setting sun. The wind was blowing the hair back from the made-up face, and I could see: she couldn't have been a day older than seventeen.

My heart was pounding again, and not because it was true love. You see, in those days, they had this thing called the Mann Act; it was a federal law which provided for criminal prosecution of any guy who took a woman across state lines for immoral purposes (as though there were any other reason to take a woman across state lines). Like every other single fellow of the day, I knew that this act was designed to protect the virtue of women. I wasn't sure whether the virtue of seventeen-year-old girls was also protected by this law, but it seemed the safe way to bet.

"Honey, exactly how old are you?"

She took the fifth, turning from me and staring straight out at the other side of the road. I couldn't believe it, she was actually offended by the question.

"Oh, Jesus." Not that it was any good calling on Him; even He wouldn't forgive anybody for being this stupid.

We were in the deep desert now, and it was turning to night. A million stars were coming out up above in the purple, but I didn't see any future for us in any of them. I was seriously considering ditching her, deep desert or no. Didn't want to do it, but I would if I didn't see lights of a filling station or a truck stop real soon. It was her own fault if she got stranded—by dolling herself up and playing on my lust and compromising me, this girl had put her own survival on the line. It's the law of the jungle out here in the desert, I told myself.

"Please don't make me get out of the car," she pleaded. Jeez, she's a mind reader. She turned towards me again and she scooted over close, putting her hands on my arm. I couldn't help it, spasms of pleasure began to shoot through me, piercing the fear of serious prison time. But I was good, I was firm:

"Next filling station. That's the end of your ticket."

"You won't call my father, willya?"

I sped up and shouted over the roar of the air, "Honey, the last thing in the world you have to worry about is me calling your father."

"Thank you, mister. He'd kill me if he caught me hitchhiking again—"

That sounded like a great idea to me. But she twisted in closer, and I felt softness and warmth beneath the silk blouse. I tried to shake her off, but not too hard.

There had been something wrong with the way she said that stuff about her dad. She hadn't taken her hands off my arm when she made that remark, and she'd been looking back over my shoulder—

A siren, way behind us. Getting closer. Without even thinking about it, I stepped down on the gas. She turned around in the seat again and was staring out the back down the dark highway behind us. I looked in the mirror and made out the single headlamp, tiny, but burning bright and angry and getting closer. A motorcycle cop.

"Oh boy," she said. "That's him."

"That's who?" I said. We both knew I knew the answer to that one, but I just had to be sure.

"My dad. He's an Arizona state trooper—"

I didn't know how much faster my Dodge could go without the bottom dropping out, but I made up my mind I was going to find out. An Arizona state trooper chasing me all the way into California, fancy that. Wonder what's buggin' him? Could it be something I did? Like maybe taking off across the border with his jailbait baby girl in my front seat, rubbing up against me for warmth? It was cold out, but I decided to sweat, anyway. I cut the car lights; I liked to think that would make us vanish instantly into the darkness, out of Daddy's view. Of course once I did that, we were invisible to any oncoming traffic; we'd end up as big smear on the highway if some truck—

"He can't arrest you," she says, "He's out of his jurisdiction."

"You be sure and tell him that if he catches us!" I yelled back, not taking my eyes off the road. I shouldn't really have been so short with her; she was trying to cheer me up. Sweet kid. I wondered if I popped open her car door and shoved her out at this speed, would her Dad forget about me for a moment and stop to scrape her up? I know I wouldn't.

I took a last glance at the little headlamp in my mirror and then I flipped it up; no reflection was going to give me away. My eyes were getting used to the dark now; I could take notice of my surroundings. Which were nothing, just more desert; not much scrub and the waves of sand that you see after you cross into California from Arizona. No cover, no hills, nothing; not even a billboard or a Burma Shave sign to hide behind.

So that was it for me. Done for. Her daddy might have already radio'd for help from the local force; either they'd run me down or he'd do it himself. A Dodge, in the final analysis, is just a Dodge. And then she'd get a spanking or go off to convent school or something, and I'd spend the next ten years or so babbling my sad story to a parade of smelly cellmates, nursing a broken skull. And the other guys in prison would probably make up a funny nickname for me, like 'Crack-head', or 'Ripple-head', or something. Because when her daddy caught up to us, his jurisdiction was going to be between my ears, with a billy club.

Well, screw that scenario.

I downshifted, slowing the car a bit. Not much, but enough.

"What are you doing?" she screamed.

"Hang on." I downshifted again, and the transmission objected. The police siren seemed to be wailing right in my ear now, and the light of the motorbike behind me was flooding the windshield in front of me so I couldn't see ahead. She screamed and I could see her terrified face in the reflected light; she really was very beautiful, she could be in the movies. I reached up for the mirror with my right hand and flipped it back down so I could see him. He was right on top of us. Practically in the rumble seat—

I stepped on the gas, putting it to the floor. The car jerked forward like Man O'War. I put both of my hands at the top of the wheel and pulled left and down as hard as I could, with my whole body. I felt us leave the ground for a moment, and I popped it out of gear as she grabbed me around the neck, and we returned to the road with a bang and a squeal.

As we did, he shot ahead of us. I saw the headlamp dip down dangerously towards the road—but he righted himself again—he was way out in front of us, getting his bearings.

I was already back in gear and underway; this was the plan. I took it up smooth and steady; we must have been doing fifty by the time he figured out where we were—right behind him, and headed straight for him.

Remember, our lights were out. That's why it took him a couple of seconds to realize he was about to get run down—and then he stepped on it, hard. He was fast and I was slow, but I stayed right on him, dogging him—he tried to edge over to either side, but I was wise to that. If he slowed, he was hamburger, so he kept speeding up.

How was his daughter taking this? Better than you might think. She was giggling like she was on the ferris wheel at the state fair. She and her dad probably weren't as close as father and daughter should be. He hadn't raised her right, that's for sure, and how much sharper than a serpent's tooth is a thankless—

He was reaching down for something, carefully. A radio? A gun? I didn't know, and I didn't want to know. I leaned on the horn and floored the pedal, veering off to the side so as not to mash him, and he nearly went over again—but dammit, he was good. He shot off the road and onto the desert, but that headlamp stayed up. I saw it rumbling, bouncing up and down across the rocks behind us. We were already a hundred yards ahead of him in the dark, two hundred yards—but then the tiny little headlamp was making its way back onto the highway behind us again. And then it was on the highway, coming after us, picking up speed.

Idiot.

I downshifted, slowed, taking it easy on my poor abused clutch. My seatmate said nothing; she was dying to see what I'd come up with next. So was I.

I fishtailed the car around and faced him. In the dark, he wouldn't be able to see me for another second or so. Then I kicked it in, and the Dodge picked up speed—

I was steering slowly for the center of the road, probably doing about thirty or so, when he realized that we were coming at him head-on. My lights were still off and he'd been building up speed, remember. And that's when I popped on the headlamps. It blinded him—his ugly old face was lit up for us to see. And, believe it or not, he nearly dodged me again, shearing off just to my left—but I was ready for him this time, turning into him and punching open my car door.

Nailed him with it. Pretty good, eh?

Actually, it just clipped him a bit, but he was moving so fast that it nearly came off from the impact. I guess he must have panicked at the loud noise and jerked the handlebars, and then he was out of control. Like father, like daughter—both of them screamed. The cop and his bike shot off the road and into the starry sky like he was Buck Rogers in the twenty-first century.

We had spun around and started to skid, but I managed to stop us. We could hear the motorcycle roaring, but we couldn't see it anymore—all I could see was that headlamp, arcing over the sky as the bike turned over in mid-air. Then there was a soft thump in the distance, and then a beautiful mechanical cough from the same direction—a motorcycle engine cutting out, dead.

"Daddy!" she screamed, looking back, tears in her eyes. Aw, she cared about the old man after all. Tugging at my heartstrings.

"He's dead!" she screamed. "You killed him!"

I hoped not, for her sake. She could identify me, so if he was dead—

I turned the car around slow and put it back on the highway. We cruised back the way we'd come, looking for skid marks. They were there, and so I took the Dodge off the road again. And there up ahead was the bike, spilled over and mussed up a bit, the disappointed headlamp gone dim. Too bad; such a beautiful bike, a great big Indian Chief. Looked fairly new, too.

About ten yards beyond was Daddy, a little worse off than the bike. I could see him laying on the ground, face down, making an "arghh" noise into the dust. So we knew he was alive. A broken leg or two, was my opinion. He probably would have been killed, though, if he'd been going any faster when I clipped him.

She hopped out of the car and got to him first. She could move pretty fast in that tight skirt. "Daddy! Daddy!" she wailed. Pitiful.

He was mumbling something, grumbling something to her as she knelt by him. "What is it, Daddy? What is it?" He was a lot bigger than she was, but in her panic she was strong enough to roll him over on his back so she could see his face. He let out an awful scream as she did so, and she instinctively skipped back from him and let go, allowing him to fall back down in the dirt again. This was too much for the old officer, and he passed out. It was just as well, I thought. He probably wouldn't have anything constructive to say to us anyway.

"We've got to get help!" she cried to me.

Boy, she was pretty.

"Yes," I said, trying to jam my poor old car door back into its slot. "That's a good idea you got there, honey. You wait here with him, and I'll drive to the next town and call a doctor." Or maybe not. I might just keep on going. It looked like the bastard would live, and she wouldn't have much of a problem getting a ride by morning. Kid or no, she had a terrific set of—

"No!" she cried. "We'll both go. We'll call my mother down in Yuma. And tell her where he is." She stepped over some sagebrush and came towards me.

"Sorry, babe. Can't take the chance. Anyway, you're better off with him than me. I do this kind of thing to cops all the time, honey. I'm trouble."

"I can't go back home now. I've tried to run away twice before. They'll kill me. I mean, they really will."

Hmm. She sounded serious. Everybody's got some sad story, I guess. But too bad, I got problems of my own. I ignored her, and tried to kick the car door back into its socket.

She reached into her blouse and brought out a roll of bills. "They'll kill me, mister. He knows I stole from them. I have a hundred dollars. I took it out of my folks' bedroom. I'll give you half if you take me along."

I looked at the roll. "Okay, get in," I said. Why the hell hadn't she told me about the money in the first place?

We were distracted by a noise; her old man had become conscious again at the mention of his hundred bucks and was fumbling for the gun in his belt.

I skipped over to him and pulled the revolver out of his clumsy, bleeding fingers. "We'll have no more of your shenanigans now, officer." I tossed the revolver off into the dunes, as far as I could.

I called over to the daughter: "You get in the car, baby, I'll be right with you." I watched her do so, and then I knelt down beside the fallen officer and spoke to him quietly. "Listen, copper. You just relax and stay right where you are and we'll send someone back to pick you up as soon as we hit the next town. Don't worry about your little girl, she's in good hands, I'm a professional. Anything you want me to tell her for you?"

He growled something horrible into the dirt.

"Attaboy. The old fighting spirit. Remember to keep an eye out for snakes while you're down there."

And, leaving him to mull that one over, I went over to his fallen bike and wobbled it back out onto the road. That would make it easier for other, more compassionate citizens to find him. Then I returned to the battered Dodge, climbed over my dented door and settled back into the driver's seat, next to that pretty little girl and her hundred dollars.

And as we drove off into the soft western night, beneath that canopy of a million stars, I felt hope for a better future.

And a good night to you, too, officer.

2

Her name was Vera, Vera Honecker. And, fellas, I don't know if there's a Nobel Prize for balling strangers who stop to give you a lift, but if there is, I vote for *Vera.* I rented us a cabin at a motor court in Glendale. It occurred to me from the easy way she got past the manager that, seventeen or no, she wasn't new to this. In the room, I found out that my suspicions were right; she sure showed me a thing or two. Very eager; she rocked the bedsprings so loud that the people all the way over in the next cabin started banging on the walls.

And it wasn't just the sex, either; once the cheap clothes were off her, she looked like the goddamn Garden of Eden—all peaches and cream, flat tummy set on top of those long lovely legs. Oh, yeah, I know it's not nice to talk about it, but I've led a hard life, give me a break, okay? Besides, it's relevant to the story.

She really did me in: afterwards, all I could do was lay there and stare at the cracks in the ceiling, with the steam still coming off of me. I couldn't have gotten up out of that bed if the joint had caught fire; if it did, I'd just lay back and watch it burn down around me, smiling all the way.

Vera lay beside me, smelling terrific and saying nothing. Using every last atom of strength left in my body, I gave her a little kiss on the forehead; show her I cared, see? She liked that, she snuggled closer and kissed my neck. She didn't seem worried about her broken-legged old daddy, lying back there in the desert somewhere. I'd pulled off the road and made one anonymous phone call to the local cops telling them where to look for him, and then we pretty much put him out of our minds for the rest of the evening. But I felt sympathy for him now that I knew her a little better; it must be tough trying to raise a handful like Vera. Under the circumstances, I guess all of us were better off with things the way they were.

I knew it had been the moral thing to do, to make that anonymous call for help after running him off the road. But it made me awful nervous, the way I get whenever I do anybody a good turn. What if they found him *too* soon? What if the old bastard was still conscious when they got to him? It wasn't likely, but if he was, he'd describe the Dodge and his daughter and there'd be California cops all over us any minute.

That's why I told Vera she'd have to ride the rest of the way in the trunk. She was a good sport about it. Didn't squawk. Just took her shoes off and hopped in; that's the sort of gal you want to be traveling with if you're in a tight spot. I didn't want the fumes to get to her, so I drove fast, to keep a little breeze going for her back there.

I gave her a break when we were about halfway to L.A. We parked in the shadows behind a truck stop and I let her out for a breath of fresh air; it was okay because there were no other cars there that late at night. She straightened herself up and inhaled a few times and then she looked as right as rain; smiling, even. I explained that I couldn't take her inside with me to eat; it was past four in the morning and she would look awful young under the lights in the diner. A bored short order cook might figure out what she was doing up so late, and cops come into truck stops all night. So I told her that I'd eat first and then bring breakfast out to her afterward. She kept smiling and nodded. What a trooper!

America needs more young girls like her, I thought to myself as I put away my first ham and eggs in three days. It was good; I ordered the same again. The knucklehead working the counter gave me a dirty look—okay, I hadn't shaved and he'd probably been stiffed before by a lot of bums who stopped by to stuff their faces without paying. But I couldn't help being offended by his attitude; I peeled a sawbuck off Vera's roll and flashed it at him with a superior smile. That sent him back to the grill, alright.

The second helping was as good as the first, and I got to thinking about Vera as I mopped up the last of the eggs. So far she'd been a major liability, but that didn't mean she couldn't be turned into an asset, now that we'd made it across the border. She was a hot number. Nah, I wasn't thinking about pimping; I've never had the character it takes to be a pimp. Too much slapping girls around, and too much bookkeeping.

No, I was thinking of running her in the old badger game, the favorite of blackmailers around the world. It's pretty damn easy: you find a good mark, see to it that he meets up with an irresistible cutie like Vera, and then you burst in on them when they're alone in the hotel room, making like you're the outraged husband or older brother.

It was a good gig; if the mark was a millionaire or something the payoff could be very high. Usually he'll write you a check on the spot, and that's one check a mark wouldn't dare to stop payment on—very hard to explain why his signature was on the bottom.

I'd worked the badger game before with a couple of different New York whores; but the problem was that those girls *looked* like New York whores. Any fellow stupid enough not to recognize them for what they were would also be too stupid to have a lot of liquid assets. This proved to be the case; they paid off every time, but it wasn't much. Certainly not enough to make it worth all the preparation and a split with some screechy tramp afterwards.

I thought it might be different with Vera. Get her out of those cheap rags and into something a little classier, and she could be a real hot property. Very up market, very fresh; she didn't have that faded look that working girls get after a while. The idea had promise. Better feed her.

I took out Vera's ten-dollar bill again and paid the cranky counterman. (No tip for that prick.) I got a donut and a cup of coffee to go for Vera; if she was going to work with me, she'd have to watch her figure.

And she seemed happy with her coffee and her donut when we pulled back onto the road; it really doesn't take all that much to please a chickie, just a little attention, that's all. But how was I going to put this partnership proposition to her? It doesn't pay to be straightforward with a young girl; they're full of ideals. I'd have to be subtle. She'd be more likely to go for it if she was already my girlfriend or something; they'll do almost anything if they think they're in love with you. But again, you have to be careful how you work it—a hot number like Vera was always getting come-ons, even if she had grown up in some cowflop town in Arizona. She probably wouldn't go for the direct approach.

So I decided: I'm gonna have to figure out a way to get *her* to seduce *me*. That way, she'd think the whole romance thing was her idea; she'd think she was in charge. It's not as stupid as it sounds; come on, I mean, look at the circumstances. She was a runaway, without a friend in the world, Daddy lying by the side of the road somewhere—she'd be vulnerable. And besides, I'm not bad-looking. In fact, in those days, I was pretty good-looking. I tried to stay in shape, I had a pencil-thin moustache like Clark Gable, and I practiced personal hygiene. I never had any trouble getting the babes, when I was flush.

I calculated the kind of pitch I thought she'd go for. Church. I'm a deacon, or something. Ministry. Going to California to buy Bibles for Negroes. What I did to your father back there was wrong. It was a sin and I have to atone for it. I will have to take you back to your mother and father.

I tried it out on her and she seemed to buy it. She looked real guilty and begged me not to call her folks. I told her that I had to give the whole thing some serious thought. For now, we'd get a room in the next town (Glendale) so she could freshen up and get a nap. "Then I'll decide whether to send you home or not," I said. She smiled at this news; just the trace of a secretive smile as she nibbled her donut and watched the darkened countryside drift by.

What she was thinking then, I couldn't guess.

I found out after we got into that cabin at the motor court. Once the door was shut, she'd grabbed me like I was the winning Irish sweepstakes ticket, desperate to convince me not to take her back home.

"What an imagination!" I thought afterwards, as I lay there beside her. Even if we did take some guy at the badger game for big bucks, at least he'd go home with some wonderful memories.

And it wasn't all sex, either; I enjoyed the warmth of her next to me, and the affection, I get so little of that. She was talking to me about something; the words began to drift in gradually.

"…So my mother said, 'Well, that's the way it's gonna be so long as you're living with us.' And I said, 'Well, maybe I'm not gonna be living with you much longer. And Daddy said, 'What the hell is that supposed to mean?' And I said, 'You're a policeman, why don't you see if you can figure out what it means, like one of those detectives on the radio.' And he slapped me right on the face."

The memory of the slap stopped her for a moment. Then she went on:

"Well, I didn't say anything, but I thought to myself, that's the last time either of you are gonna hit me, I swear it. I know how to get out of here now.

"The mistake I made the first time was taking a Greyhound, the man at the ticket office recognized me and called the patrol, and Daddy pulled over the bus about twenty miles out of town and pulled me off by the ear. I was mortified. I was never so embarrassed in my life. He took off his belt and whaled the tar out of me right there by the side of the road. That was a month ago and I've still got marks on the backs of my legs, see?"

I could see.

"I could have died, the bus driver and the passengers looking out the windows at us and laughing and calling out things as he beat me. And it took me most of the last year to save up for that bus ticket; I couldn't afford another one. I knew if I was gonna get to Hollywood I'd have to hitchhike my way.

"So I waited 'til Daddy was off on patrol and I headed out across the field in these clothes and I got to the highway, and I got a ride pretty fast, but of course, it was from Mr. Galloway. From the Agriculture Department. Our family is pretty well known around Payton County because Daddy's a cop, well, you know that. So, Mr. Galloway asks me, 'Vera, where're you going all dressed up like that?' and I told him I was going to visit my cousins out in Brinks, but I knew he didn't believe me because he asked if it was okay if he stopped off and called my mother to see if it was alright giving me a lift. And I couldn't think of what else to say, so I said, sure, that's fine with me, but when he pulled in towards the filling station, I got scared and I begged him not to call. So then he knew what I was doing, but he just smiled and pulled out of the filling station and up the county road instead of the highway. I was crying and telling him 'please don't tell my father, he'll beat me to death for sure.' And he was sayin' stuff like 'hush, child, now, don't get scared' and he put his arm around me, and I knew I'd have to let him screw me so he'd keep quiet, the fat old bastard. Got a cigarette?"

"I don't smoke."

"I'd kill for a cigarette," she said. "And would you believe it, that fat cocksucker told on me, anyway? After he took me back to town and let me off, he phoned up Daddy from his office and told him that he'd seen me hitching a ride and made me get into his car so he could take me back. That old liar Mr. Galloway!"

I made a mental note of the name, Galloway. Might come in handy if I was ever out that way again.

"Daddy was furious. He was so mad that the town knew, he hit me harder than he ever had. With his fist. I lost one of my back teeth, see?" She pulled a corner of her little mouth back to show me; she looked like a fish on a hook.

"And that's not all he did."

She stared at the ceiling.

"So this last time I'd figured out how to do it right. I figured I'd take some money with me this time whether it was mine or not, so I wouldn't have to screw any more jerks to get rides. I knew Mom had some money she'd got out of the bank before it failed; she kept it under a shingle out in the tool shed. A hundred dollars, that's about ten dollars for every time Daddy beat me up the last two years. I don't consider it stealing; I paid for it." She rolled over on top of me. "And I don't grudge giving it to you, baby. It's *worth* a hundred dollars to get out of that house, and you took care of Daddy for me, he won't be coming after me anytime soon.

"I figured on fooling him by hitching a ride into town but then going south instead of west. I asked one of the boys I knew from school, I knew he'd do anything I asked him, and I got him to drop me off way out of town, almost out of the county, where no one would be likely to drive by and recognize me. And it worked, too, that's when you came along."

She rolled on top of me again, and asked me, pleading, with the big blue eyes that welled up with tears:

"I know you don't have to, mister, but would you please take care of me? The money is yours, I gave it to you, but I've just got to get to Hollywood and I don't have a job or anything. Could you take care of me 'til I get some more money together? I know I could get a job in the movies, you said I was beautiful, right?"

"Hey, hey, take it easy," I said, all comforting. "I'm a sinner, and I know what we just did was wrong, but sure, honey, I'll take care of you, don't worry about it. A man doesn't just use a lovely young thing like yourself and then just toss her out on the street without a second glance. You've had some tough breaks, but I think you're something special. Worth keeping around."

"Oh, thank you, thanks, mister…"

"Call me Bob," I said. "Deacon Bob." It was as good a name as any. It would be easy for me to remember because I'd be reminded of how she made me bob up and down all night.

"I'll never forget you for helping me out, Deacon Bob." She was doing something with her hand. "I'm going to make it in the movies, I'll do anything I have to. And I won't forget that you helped me out when I needed a friend."

She sure knew how to treat a friend. Where does an Arizona girl learn to do the kind of stuff she did to me? It was like she had electricity running through her. She nearly killed me that next time; I'd sunk into a Polish coma by the time she got through.

And when I woke up just before noon the next day, with the chambermaid banging on the door and yelling about check out time and changing the linen—Vera was gone. My reflexes kicked in immediately; I leapt up out of the bed and grabbed for my wallet. I had hidden it the night before while Vera was out in the shared washroom, preparing for the evening's lovemaking. Very clever of me, eh? No teenage tramp is going to get over on me, I'd thought, heh, heh, heh.

But sure enough, little Vera had tracked down that wallet like a bloodhound while I'd snored away, wasted from sated lust. And sure enough, the wallet was empty, empty as a lawyer's heart. I thought I'd been quite the snake charmer with that gal, a real Svengali. But it was me, and me alone, who was left standing there in my underwear, staring stupidly into an empty wallet, with an angry chambermaid bitching at me through a locked door. Not only was Vera gone with everything she owned, including her hundred bucks—she was gone with everything *I* owned.

Including my hundred and fifty bucks, the money I'd started out with. Also my suit, the rest of my clothes, my treasured wristwatch, the knick-knacks I'd picked up from other people's places in my travels—my shoes, even. The girl knew how to pack. If I wanted to chase her through the streets of L.A. now, I'd have to do it in a stolen bath towel. Jesus, even the change was gone from the night table near the bed; this Vera hadn't left me so much as a nickel for a half a sandwich.

In the cold light of the morning, things were becoming all too clear. The early bird with the cute tail had flown, taking my worm with her. But then, what could I expect? Some bitches are just no damn good.

3

Yep, that's me, folks. The criminal mastermind. A regular Dr. Fu Manchu. Screwed, robbed and stranded in my underwear by a renegade Girl Scout. A cop's daughter, no less! How Ma would have laughed, if she coulda seen me right then. I was lucky Vera wasn't old enough to drive away with the Dodge.

Not a cent to pay for the room, of course. But even though I'm stupid, I'm not crazy—I kept a twenty tucked inside my hubcap in those days; always did, ever since I hit the road. I watched in my underwear from the window of my unpaid-for room while the manager pried the hubcap out of the wheel well.

He gave me a horrible look when I asked him if he had a pair of pants and a shirt I could buy off him, but now that I was a paying customer again he could hardly send me out into the streets in nothing but my shorts and a dented Dodge. He went through some luggage he'd seized from a previous defaulter and came up with the ugliest suit I've ever seen south of Canada. It was a red checked flannel job with high cuffs on the pants. What kind of guy would be caught dead in a get-up like that? Me, it turned out. I bought the whole suitcase from him for three bucks, which was three bucks more than he ever expected to get for it.

I drove south, and through the hills; Glendale to Los Angeles. It was kind of nice out there back then; lots of green all around, even in the city itself, and a fine fresh mist in the air early in the morning. I love to look at light. Different parts of the country have different light; and the colors in Los Angeles are saturated and intense. Like in the desert, but the difference is that in Los Angeles you're looking at the colors through this filter of mist, like a special lens on a camera. It smelled terrific, too—there's less cowshit when you get this far West, the farms out here were all orange groves. They were around everywhere back then, and they had a perfume.

The town itself was nothing, but it was the biggest nothing I ever saw. It just spread out from the foot of the hills and then went all over the place. I knew there was a downtown in it somewhere, and groups of tall buildings were clumped together here and there, every so often. But it wasn't like there was a skyline or anything; it was impossible to take in the whole thing at once. It seemed to me that you could fit seven or eight Manhattans into a space this big. The town wasn't about those clumps of office buildings; it was all about the bright yellow sun, the green hills, and the tree-lined roads running between pretty little bungalows and fancier Spanish houses.

And it was quiet, compared to New York or Chicago. The few people that were walking around the sunny streets seemed to be asleep on their feet. They already looked hot, and it was still early; they tended to be carrying things, like bundles of newspapers or sacks for delivery. They weren't going to work, I thought to myself, they were at work—doing things for bosses, people too important to come out in the sun.

There were lots of cars, though, mostly new-looking. It was odd because, times being what they were, most folks around the country tended to hang on to their old transportation and keep repairing it until it literally fell apart. Nobody had the bucks for a down payment for a new car. Here it was different. Automobiles shined new under the sun; some nice ones, too. I guess it was a point of pride with the people out here.

I pulled over to one side of a road to look at a map; it looked like I was on something called Alameda. I was now officially hunting for that friend of mine, old Sam. He'd told me where I could find him—out on the street. As usual.

We'd met years before, in a drunk tank in Indianapolis. Sam was a drunk. I was not. I was having a little trouble with one of my marks, a local hood who'd threatened to kill me for shaking him down. A drunk tank can be a good place to lay low for a couple of days. And it doesn't take much to get in there for the night on a drunk and disorderly; just stop shaving, down a few shots, speak with a foreign accent, and hit a bartender. Thugs like my mark don't like to come sniffing around county jails. Too many memories.

Sam was in the tank ahead of me. When I arrived he was already laid out like a dead man on the dirty little bunk, staring up at the ceiling, saying nothing. A leathery old bird with a buzzard nose and a silver moustache. I remember thinking he looked more like your basic Western desert rat type than one of the local Indiana yokels.

Our mutual cellmate was the real thing, though; a big farmboy, probably in for his first big bender in the city, obviously still loaded. It took him all of a half hour before he figured out that he was bigger than anybody else in the cell, and so was entitled to the bunk.

"Hey. Mister. Get offa that bed."

Sam turned his head. He was probably used to this, I figured. That old face has seen the insides of a lot of drunk tanks.

"I wanna lay down. Tired."

Sam said nothing.

"Get offa that bed."

Sam looked up for just a moment, as if to say, "You wouldn't be doin' this if I was twenty years younger." But he wasn't twenty years younger, not big or strong or young enough to keep his bunk. So he started to get up, slow. Too slow for the farmboy; he grabbed Sam by the collar and tossed him across the cell like a chewed-up bone.

I believe in minding my own business, usually. But Sam had yelled out an ugly word at the farmboy when he hit the cement, and the kid turned to Sam with murder in his eyes.

He took a step towards Sam, who cringed in the corner like an old dog. That seemed to provoke the kid all the more.

I wasn't much older than the farmboy, and he was much bigger than me. So fighting fair was not an option. (You know, I can't think of a time when fighting fair was ever an option.) As the kid took another step towards poor old Sam there on the floor, I drew my fist back and yelled in his ear.

He turned his head, and my knuckle caught him right on the temple. Which is a tricky thing, because I'm no weakling, and getting a good sock in the temple is enough to kill some people. Not a Scandinavian, though; the brain is not one of their vital areas.

Thank God the kid was tight. He was huge and if he got hold of me he probably could have squashed me like a ripe banana. The punch I'd thrown had simply puzzled him for a moment. He blinked a couple of times and started towards me—but I tackled him, pushing him backwards against the cell door. He lost balance, and I grabbed up at his hair and banged his head against the bars so hard they clanged. The farmboy sank down on his overall-ed ass and then settled in for the night down on the cement floor, dreaming sweet dreams of shiny tractors and high wheat prices.

"You ain't drunk," says a voice from the corner of the cell. I turned around and looked down at Sam, smiling an old buzzard smile at me.

"No e-speak Inglese," I said. And I took the bunk for myself.

"And you ain't no Eye-Tie, nor a Bohunk or nuthin' either," he says.

"I go sleep now. You shut up, hokay?" I closed my eyes.

"You ain't too good at accents, son. And you were at the cell door tonight, listenin' to the cops. I was watchin' you. You were listening to 'em pretty good for a while there."

I stared at the insides of my eyelids. The old bird was sharper than I first figured.

"And you took out this hayseed pretty good. Drunks don't punch that hard or move that fast."

I clasped my hands behind my head and looked over at him.

"What are you, mister, the shitkicker Sherlock Holmes or something?"

"No, I guess I ain't, 'cause I'm damned if I can figure out how the hell I could stop in for a beer at a bar in downtown Los Angeles and wind up in Indianapolis two weeks later." He coughed. "This is no town for any honest white man, drunk or sober."

He was right about that, and it's as true today as it was back then. We stayed up and talked for a while. He needed money to get back to Los Angeles, and I needed money to get the hell out of town. My gangster mark wasn't gonna pay off; not in money, anyway.

So Sam and I worked out a little dodge to raise some cash. After we were both released and the night shift at the jail had gone home, Sam went to see one of the local used car dealers. He made out to this car dealer that he was real interested in buying a used Ford farm truck; that he had ready cash and 'By gum, I'd go as high as a thousand dollars for one of them Ford farm trucks, in good condition.' The dealer tried to sell him on some of the other models he had on the lot; but no, Sam's heart was set on a Ford farm truck. He gave the number of a hotel in town where the dealer could reach him, and left.

Then Sam telephoned the sergeant's desk at the police station and pretended to be the father of our unconscious farmboy cellmate. Sam told the sergeant that he was sending 'another of his sons' down there to pick up the farmboy's Ford truck, which the cops had impounded the night before. I walked into the station a short while after that, pretending to be the farmboy's brother. The sergeant handed me the keys and told me my 'brother' was still sleeping it off in the cell; did I want to see him? I said, "No, thank you, sir, he's a mean drunk and sometimes he gets a little violent when he's hung over. You watch out for him when he wakes up; if he looks funny at you the best thing to do is give him a crack on the head before he gets really ornery."

Then I got out of there as fast as I could and drove the kid's Ford farm truck over to the used car dealer. I told the dealer I was interested in selling it or trading it in; he told me that there wasn't all that much call for that model these days, and things were pretty slow, etc. (The lying shit, just this morning Sam had come in here and offered this guy a thousand bucks for just this make and model. Some people.) He offered me peanuts, but I said no to everything until he coughed up five hundred bucks cash.

The proceeds from the transaction financed our way out of Indiana; and so far as I know, the used car dealer is still waiting for Sam to show up and pay a thousand bucks for that crappy old truck. (I don't know what happened to the big farmboy, but I like to think the whole experience taught him a valuable lesson that he'll never forget.)

Sam and I took a Greyhound out west together for a thousand miles or so. By the time I got off at Yuma, I got to know him pretty well. I could see he was what other people call a character; a colorful type, one of those lovable coots whose experiences provide much amusement to everyone except his family. Sam's family had disowned him.

Sam was a cowboy, a real one. He'd worked at ranches all over the West, but he'd come down to Los Angeles when he was in his forties and the movies were just getting started. This was way before the talkies. He came because he'd heard what these movie fellows were willing to pay for a man who knew how to handle horses, and Sam knew a lot about horses.

He must have, because in spite of the fact that there's never been any shortage of cowboys in Southern California, Sam got himself movie work right away with the biggest of the old cowboy stars. William S. Hart, remember him?

"Wrangling," they call it; handling the horses in between scenes, helping out the stunt riders. Sam didn't think of it as real work; I guess it wasn't, compared to ranch work. But it paid better than any job he'd ever had in his life, and that proved to be his downfall.

Sam was not used to making good money on a regular basis. When he was a kid rounding up cattle he'd work through the fall, put together a bankroll and blow the whole thing by the time spring rolled around—women, liquor, the usual. By that time, he'd be sober as a preacher and just as broke. Which was okay, because a young fellow who knew the craft could always find himself another job on another ranch.

A fine life for a young hellion, but Sam wasn't young anymore by the time he got his first horse work in Hollywood. And when he finally did start making that good studio money on a regular basis, he managed it with the same financial wizardry he'd displayed in the past.

At first it hadn't mattered so much; he was single and unobliged, and Hollywood was full of pretty gals, even back then. Not a bad deal for a balding, bow-legged wastrel. But then he made his next big mistake: he fell in love, for the first time, at age forty-five.

Not only that, he goes and marries her. I can't really blame him; I met her once, and you could tell she was a peach, alright. She was about twenty years younger than Sam, but that wasn't why he wanted her for a wife. She was a decent loving Christian sort who really cared what happened to him. So you see, it was doomed from the start.

They had three kids in as many years, as fast as they could make 'em—and all the while Sam was working, going out on location, drinking, and screwing anything that he was fast enough to catch. It was in his blood. He'd sober up, feel bad, and then start all over again. Word would get back to her, of course, and she'd throw him out. He'd take the pledge and she'd take him back for a while, for the sake of the kids. (I still don't see exactly how the kids benefited from having Sam around, even if he was their father.)

The finish was in 1925. He was cheating on her again; nothing unusual really, except that this last time, it was with a notorious local whore. And this last time, Sam had gotten himself so plastered that he'd actually brought this whore home with him. "Why, there's a clean bed back at my place," he'd told her. They drove out to his house together, surprising Sam's wife and children, who were just sitting down to Thanksgiving dinner. The atmosphere was chilly, Sam said; the wife and kids were already miffed that he'd broken his promise to return the previous evening with a holiday turkey. As he introduced his young lady friend around, the enormity of his faux pas began to penetrate.

Every woman has her limits. Sam admitted that even the whore was offended. Ugly words flew back and forth across the table, Sam and his friend walked out, and when he returned home the next day the wife and kids were gone. For good. He found them a few weeks later, in another state, but it was way too late. "She'd even turned the children against me," he said.

The experience didn't improve Sam's character or his drinking habits. He drank more than he worked. Then one day he took a tumble off a pony during a shoot, and that was the end of his movie wrangling. The old bones just didn't knit up the way they used to. He had lots of friends in pictures back then, so he was able to get by with some extra work for a while. But finally he sank to the lowest of lows, just to keep himself in booze. These days he was practicing that most dishonorable of California professions.

I spotted him as I was driving down Sunset Boulevard; you couldn't miss him. He was sitting out there in the sun, on a crappy folding deck chair, big old white trousers, fanning himself; his bald head burnt as red as a little old cowboy cherry tomato. Behind him was a sizable billboard, obviously of his own making: "GUIDED TOURS OF THE HOMES OF THE STARS! SEE THE FABULIS PALACES OF THE STARS! PERSONELIZED TOURS OF THE HOLLYWOOD HILLS. NO REASONABLE OFFER REFUSED."

I pulled the Dodge over to the roadside and put it into park, but I didn't get out. We regarded each other silently for a moment, taking notice. Neither of us smiled.

He had the same big walrus moustache as before, but something looked "wrong" about him. Old age? Fat? Then I realized with a shock that he was sober. He sat there cooling himself with a big, round woven fan; the Texan Mikado. Finally he nodded, acknowledging my presence.

I hopped out of the car, slamming the door and strolling over to his throne with my hands in my pockets. He was staring at me now through his crinkled, beady eyes; something about me seemed to disgust him a bit.

"Had an uncle once had a suit like that. He was with the circus."

"Things have been kind of thin, lately," I said.

"That why you dress like a clown, now, cheer yourself up a bit?"

He grinned, pleased with his own wit. His teeth were relatively white.

"Well," I said, nodding at the billboards behind him, "Not all of us are so fortunate these days that we own our own business. I see you paint the signs yourself. I recognized the spelling."

He stopped fanning himself, and looked at the sign, double-checking. Then to me:

"I ain't doin' so bad. Pays cash. Tips, too."

"Hmm."

"Maybe I could train you to show folks around, too. You could do your Eye-talian accent for the customers, tell 'em you're Rudolph Valentino."

"Dress me up like a sheik, or something, eh?"

"Beats what you got on now."

He rose and shook my hand.

"Pull up a chair over here in the shade."

I reached for a folding chair. "There isn't any shade," I observed.

"It'll be along presently. It's fine to see you anyhow, Wagner."

"It's not 'Wagner' these days, Sam. I lost that one some time back."

"Well, what is it, then? What should I call you, this time 'round?"

"I haven't given it much thought." A big, beautiful new Cadillac rolled along and passed us by, just like success. "What was the name of that cowboy fella, the movie guy you used to wrangle for?"

"William S. Hart."

"Yeah." Pretty girl walking by, chiffon sundress, looking straight ahead, not seeing us, that's for sure. "Why don't you call me that," I said. "That's a good name. Bill Hart."

"Pleased to meet ya," said Sam, watching the girl as she walked away. "You get my letter?"

"Yeah," I said. "Took a little while."

"Have a sody pop," he says, reaching into a watery bucket that sat by his chair.

"Thanks." Cripes, it was hot around here, once you stopped moving.

"Nickel," he says, holding out one pink empty palm. Then he waved it away. "Aw, hell," he says, "The first one's on me."

"Thanks. I'll never forget that." I popped off the top using both my thumbs. No spray. Flat.

"So what didja think?" asked Sam.

"What did I think of what?"

"My letter, stupid. You interested?"

"In what?"

"In my proposition."

"What proposition?"

"Didn't I tell you?"

"Tell me what?"

"My idea?"

"Look," I said, "the sun's going to go down in another few hours, and after that spring will turn to fall, so let's end this part of the conversation, okay?" I pulled his letter out of my pants pocket. "All it says in this letter is that if I ever want to make some 'real' money, I should come out to Hollywood and look for you at this address. That's all it says." I handed it to him. "So what's the deal?"

He examined the letter. "I was drunk when I wrote this," he says.

He rose from his chair, surveying the sun-drenched Boulevard; he might have been sizing up the herd. He sighed. "I think I've stood enough of this bullshit for today. Help me get this stuff into the back of my truck, behind the billboards there." He folded up his little chair and tucked his fan under his arm. "We'll go on back to my place and talk things over a bit."

I picked up the ice bucket and the cardboard display featuring maps to the movie stars' homes.

Sam turned around and spoke. "On second thought, you stay here. I'll drive around the front and you can follow me in your own car. I don't want folks to see us walking together. You're a sight in that outfit."

And with that he disappeared behind the big sign, leaving me standing in front of it, sweating under my hatband, holding the heavy ice bucket and the folding chair. A convertible full of high school kids came dashing by; girls in tight sweaters. They honked the horn at me as they flew past; one yelled out: "Hi, clown!"

As they sped away, I heard the others laughing.

Loud and long.

4

"So why'd you get me out here?"

We were in Sam's room; he rented by the week from a pal he knew from his movie days. The room was in one of the old wooden hotels you can still see around Los Angeles; a great big barn of a place that had once catered to drummers and traveling men, twenty or thirty years before. It had been turned into a boarding house and it needed a coat of paint. Sam told me that it had almost shaken itself to bits during the last big quake. But apparently that which would not kill this building made it stronger.

Sam's room was small, but it had a nice window and he kept it pretty clean, except for a few racing forms scattered around the bedside.

"I'll tell you why I got you out here," he says, "But first, take some advice from an old friend and go down the hall there and get yourself a bath. Nothing personal, but you'll be sharing this room with me, and I'm sure you don't want to offend me."

"No, I wouldn't want to do that."

"Leave that get-up outside the door and I'll see if I can't fix ya up with somethin' better."

"You're gonna buy me a suit?"

"Hell, no, I ain't gonna buy you jack shit. There's a Chinaman down the hall takes in laundry; he owes me a favor, he might have a coat and some pants he could spare."

"What makes you think he'll have something better looking than what I've got on now?"

"Everybody does," says Sam, and leaves.

The bath was hot, anyway. I lay there like a steeping teabag for the best part of a half an hour. Vera was still on my mind. I wondered how she was doing.

Better than me, I bet. It was probably better for both of us that we parted company; it's not good to be with any girl who's that wise to the ways of men. One of us would have ended up selling out the other; that's usually how a relationship between two dishonest people ends. An affair doesn't stand a chance unless at least one of the participants is honest. So much for me and Vera.

"You in there?" Sam's voice, behind the door.

"Yeah."

"Gotcha somethin' decent to wear, when you get out. And look at this—"

Something was sliding underneath the door, inch by inch. A magazine.

"See it?" called Sam.

It was a copy of *Photoplay* magazine; on the cover was a painted portrait of Stacey Tilden, the movie star.

"You gonna put me in the movies?"

"Read that, while you're in there."

"What, the whole thing?"

I reached over the edge of the tub and took it, splashing soapy water on the floor.

"The bit about the dame on the cover. I'm leavin' a clean towel out here with your new clothes."

The magazine was a few months old, and dog-eared; Sam or someone else had read it over many, many times. The spine was bent back and it practically fell open to the feature he'd meant me to read: "The Secret Sorrow of Stacey Tilden."

If you don't know who Stacey Tilden is, you're either eight years old or you've never been to the movies in your life. She was on top of the world, that year; still in her twenties and number one or two at the box office. She'd already won an Oscar; Joan Crawford and Bette Davis fought for the parts Stacey Tilden turned down. Marlene Dietrich once called her the most beautiful woman in the world.

Not that I ever cared for her pictures much, myself. I like a good western, the Three Stooges, something light. Stacey

Tilden did those "women's pictures"—you know, heavy romances and stuff. Or one of those big historical dramas where she's the Queen of Austria or something and guys are fencing and writing with feathers. Very high-tone, I guess. For Hollywood.

Anyway, she was famous, probably one of the most famous women in the world. And she really was top-shelf stuff, I thought as I looked at the photo of her that preceded the article. Very fine and dangerous-looking. That little Vera was sexy; but this Stacey Tilden was the big leagues of gorgeousness: so lovely it was unreal.

Okay, okay, so I'd been to see a couple of her pictures. Like I said, she was a big star, you couldn't avoid seeing her she was around so much, and girls like it when you take them to see a movie with Stacey Tilden in it, they think it means you've got a little class. So I'd seen her on screen, and like every guy who's ever seen a beautiful woman, I wondered what it would be like to, you know.

And, you know, she was a good actress. She could put that high-tone stuff over, that 'frustrated mistress' and 'feathery-pen' jazz they wrote for her. Take it from me, I hate those kind of pictures, but if she was in one I never had any problem staying awake all the way through. She was that good.

The lady who wrote the article seemed to think a lot of her, too. It was one of those 'star profile' articles where they tell the whole story of the career and the hard work and interview the star about all the heartache along the way and all that shit. The angle on this story was Stacey's recovery from the 'trauma of her recent divorce.' Unlike most movie stars, Stacey Tilden had only been married once in her life; to a producer at her studio named Jerry Fiske, and they'd just split up.

According to this article, Stacey and Jerry seemingly parted the best of friends. Still, Stacey nursed a 'secret, inner ache' for some months after the split, wondering if her failure to make the marriage work meant she had 'failed as a woman.'

(Christ.) That was her 'secret sorrow'; that and the fact that her mother had died the same year.

Stacey and her Mom had been real close. The biography part of the article told how Stacey's dad had passed away when she and her brother were still little kids. Her mom had to pull up stakes and re-locate to the Los Angeles area to run a rooming house. It was rough financially, so Mom had to send the little brother off to relatives in Colorado for a few years. And then *he* died, of heart disease or something. But Mom was able to tough it out and raise Stacey in Los Angeles single-handed, paying for her dance lessons and stuff.

Stacey turned out to be quite the little dancer, and when she got older she headed back east to take a crack at Broadway. Started out in the chorus, then teamed up with some cluck who did his own specialty bit in nightclubs; they put this act together, Hayes and Tilden. This was during the twenties, so they had to work the speakeasies, but all the same it was very classy stuff—a tuxedo and evening dress routine, no cooch, nothing vulgar. They ended up being the top dance team in Manhattan, when Fred Astaire and his sister were out of town.

But, it was hinted, her partner Hayes became something of a lush. 'A thwarted genius,' the writer called him. His boozing finally got in the way of the act, and Stacey ditched him in London, England—on stage at the Palladium. She took a boat back home, and he stayed in Europe and drank himself to death, a few years later. (Jeez, everyone who gets near this woman drops dead.)

At least he was spared from reading this crap, I thought, and turned the page. Stacey did a single for a while, and, against all odds, became a favorite of the café society types. The Gershwins were pals and helped her out by writing a revue based around her talents; it was a big hit, and suddenly 'Hollywood beckoned.' The talkies were coming in and all of the sudden movie stars actually had to have talent. She sang and danced in a couple of "okay" movie musicals, but then she got a straight dramatic part for a change, and—sensation, she could act.

The movie was called, "The Forgotten Woman." It was supposed to be a Marion Davies picture, starring Marion as a housewife who puts up with a cheating playboy husband. Tearjerker. But when the movie was over no one even remembered that Marion Davies was in it. Because Stacey Tilden was so good in the role of the mistress that she stole the whole picture. She even got herself nominated for an Oscar—not, to Marion Davies' chagrin, for Best Supporting Actress, but for Best Actress. This was a real phenomenon, because in the early days of the Academy Awards, the fix was in, real tight: the studio heads controlled the Oscars, who got nominated and who finally won. It was unheard of for a new-comer like Stacey to be nominated, and it was considered impossible for her to win.

But she did. The buzz about Stacey's work in the picture (from the public and the national press) was so strong that there was no denying her the award. An Academy Award, for her first dramatic role, at age twenty-two. Christ, I was twenty-five at the time and the biggest thing I'd ever won in my life was a gravy boat on Free Dish Night at the Cincinnati Rialto.

She celebrated by marrying the genius producer who brought her to Hollywood, Jerry Fiske. They'd had a thing going before she left New York, and he was the one who convinced her to try the pictures. His picture was there in the article, a studio headshot of the dashing young playboy; he looked like a smiling eel with a lit cigarette. I wondered if he'd have married her if she hadn't bagged that Oscar.

She was a very hot property, in demand, and Fiske managed to work out a sweetheart deal for her with Jack Roth, the head of Olympic Studios. Roth was paying her a small fortune and she could choose her own scripts; that was unusual in those days, because even the biggest stars tended to do what they were told. Here was a picture of Stacey grinning like the

Cheshire Cat, getting a peck on the cheek from Roth, a dapper little fellow in his late forties. He looked more like a small-time bootlegger than a studio chief.

I'd heard of this Jack Roth before I got to Hollywood. Apparently he was some sort of monster. Roth was a guy that even other movie producers considered unethical; a pretty horrifying assessment. But he was respected as well as loathed: at a time when the little studios were being eaten up by the big studios, Roth had fought off takeovers and kept Olympic for himself. I guess you'd have to be pretty tough and pretty smart to fight off Mayer and Thalberg and Zukor and those guys.

The main reason Roth was able to survive as an independent was Stacey Tilden. It was the bucks from her pictures that kept Olympic in the black when the Depression got serious. She and Fiske were good at picking out the projects; matching her with the right script and the right director. She didn't upstage leading men or co-stars; she gave them room to work and so turned out a better product. She often played a victimized beauty looking for revenge, but she hadn't made the mistake (noted the author of the article) of simply re-making the same hit picture over and over. She was just a little bit different in every picture, every setting, 'finding the nuance that made the difference.'

Maybe that's my problem, I thought, tossing the magazine over my shoulder onto the floor and pulling the plug out of the tub. I've never been good at finding that nuance that makes the difference; I gotta work on that.

I came back into Sam's room with the towel wrapped around me.

"Did you walk down the hall like that?" he said, flustered.

"Well, I didn't have the towel on," I replied as I closed the door.

"There's ladies who live on this floor," he said.

I farted and handed him his magazine. As I sat on his bed and began to dress myself, he went to the door and peered nervously out into the hall.

"I don't want to get thrown out of here 'cause you're walking around air-drying your pecker in front of old Mrs. Ferguson across the hall."

"No, you wouldn't want to lose a sweet deal like this, would you."

"Cheap room is hard to find, these days," he muttered, closing the door. "What did you think of that article?"

"Not my sort of thing, really. I'm more the Russian novel type."

He ignored this, all serious. "You seen her in the pictures, though, right?"

"Sure, who hasn't? What's the matter, you a fan or something?"

He sat at the little table across from me, turning the pages of the magazine. "She's worth a bundle," said Sam.

"I bet she is. Are you building up to making some kind of point, Sam?" The socks didn't match the suit, but they were clean.

He kept flipping through the pages.

"Did you see this?" He held the magazine open, and I leaned over and peered at it.

"That's her house."

It was an aerial shot of a kind of oriental palace set in the hills. The lawn looked as big as a golf course and there was a swimming pool out back the size of Lake Michigan.

"I been there," says Sam, looking significantly at me.

"Sure, you been there." I started doing up my shoes. "You drive hicks from out of town up into the hills for a gawk at the place, so what."

"I ain't talkin' about that shit," he says. "I was there one night, for a party."

"*You* were invited?"

"I was there to park cars," he said. He held up the picture again and pointed with his stubby leather finger. "See that road there?"

In the picture, a tiny dark path led from the palace to an ornamental stone gate out front. A road, on the estate.

"This was about a year back," says Sam. "She was throwin' one of those big Hollywood parties, you know? Big old-fashioned orgy or something. They needed fellas to park the limousines and sorta keep out the riff-raff, you know? Friend of mine called me up, says, 'Let's do it, it's twenty bucks for the night.'"

"Not bad."

"Damn right it ain't bad. I worked the gate out front there, checking the invites, undoing a great big chain to let the cars in and out. It ain't hard. I done it a buncha times since for the rich folks around town; I got my own chain now so I can rent it to 'em."

"That's a very inspiring story," I said. "But please don't tell me that you got me all the way out here to park cars."

"Shut up and listen. That night at the Tilden place, they paid us off in cash. It was around three, four in the morning. I never saw her up close; we got the pay from some Jap houseboy or something. But I saw her go by while we were waiting in the big hall. This was after the last guest had left." He flipped over the cover of the magazine and looked at it. "She's mighty pretty, gave us a wave and a smile as she walked by. She was well-oiled by that time, too, she had a champagne bottle in her hand, swingin' it as she crossed in front of us. 'Good night,' she calls out, and she's gone."

He leaned over the table and stared at me. "Funny thing, though. She ain't goin' up the great big stairs to some bedroom. She's going outside, through these big doors out back. Out into her yard."

"Why?"

"That's what I asked myself, I said, 'Now, why's a pretty young gal like that headed out to the garden at four in the morning all on her lonesome?' She sure as hell ain't fixin' to plant lilacs."

"Where was her husband, what's-his-name?"

"Fiske. He wasn't there. They divorced. Didn't you read this thing?" he says, wagging the magazine at me. "She hates his guts now, is the word. Anyway, it got me thinking about something you said once. You know, when we were riding out that time on the bus together, and you were tellin' me about how you'd operate, and about how whenever you saw somebody do something that looked a little odd, you might follow 'em around for a bit and sometimes you'd learn something useful—"

"You didn't follow her—"

"Naw, the Jap servants probably woulda bust my head for me if they caught me out there after hours. But I knew that there was this dirt road, way, way up the hill, behind her house." He tapped the magazine photo. "When I drove the truck outta there that night, I figured it wouldn't hurt to take a drive up and look the place over.

"So I did. I parked alongside this dirt road, way up on the hill; nobody lives that far up. And sure enough, I could see the whole damn place from up there, swimmin' pool and all, all the way out to the back. The only trouble was, it was dark, and the place looked so small. I couldn't see Miss Tilden. I was about to give it all up and go home, when these lights went on."

"What lights?"

"The lights in the bungalow. There's a shack out back, well, not a shack exactly, it's a pretty nice little house, but it ain't jack shit compared to the main house. It's behind the big pool, there, near the back wall and the gardens."

I picked up the magazine and took a look.

"You can't see it in that picture." Sam went on, "So I'm getting ready to call it a night, when I see these lights go on."

"She went in there?"

"Who else? This was about ten minutes after I saw her walk out into the garden. It takes about that long to walk from the main house, past the pool, to this little house out back.

"And I'm standing there, thinking to myself, that's a bit odd—a big movie star with more money than the governor's wife, going out to this flyspeck place in the back, and settin' there with a bottle of champagne. Why don't she drink inside, if she's gonna drink?

"So I stayed, though I was dog-tired, and I watched the place. And I was there 'til sunup, and I'll be damned if them lights didn't stay on the whole time.

"Around nine o'clock the next morning, one of the houseboys marches from the big house over to the little one, then goes *back* to the big house all by himself. I guess he was rousting her out, because I seen her come out about fifteen, twenty minutes later."

"Alone?"

"Yeah, she was by herself. And dressed the same as she was when she said good night to us the night before."

I lay back on the bed, and looked at the ceiling.

"She drinks, and she doesn't want people to know," I said.

"Nope," says Sam. "Don't make sense. The Jap houseboy knew where to find her; he was taking a tray out to her, like it was a regular thing. If it was just the drink, she could do the very same inside the house. Don't make sense, unless she built that little house just to store her empties."

"Go on."

"So like I said, I thought I was on to something. Over the next few nights, I took a drive up that mountain, up that road, and parked for a while. Different time each night. Nothing."

"You musta been bored."

"It's the kinda thing you end up doing if you quit drinking. Anyways, I'd put in an hour or two, every night, and about a month later—pay dirt. Them lights went on again."

"What time was this?"

"About one in the morning. Middle of the week, a Tuesday, I think. I went back the next night at the same time. No lights. The night after that, Thursday, I think it was, she was back. After that I had it down. She's sitting there every few nights or so, in that little place, drinking and doing something she don't want anybody to know about."

He tried to look real wise, at this point, and added: "Something she won't even do in the privacy of her own bedroom."

"You never saw anybody else go in or out of that building?"

"Nope."

I thought a moment. "Is there a phone line running from the main house to the little building?"

He smiled. "I thought of that, too. Nope. No phone out there, not as far as I could see. She ain't calling anybody."

I got off the bed, and walked to the window. Lovely day.

"Interesting," I said.

Sam chuckled. "I thought you might find it so."

"There's something out there."

Sam stretched and yawned. "And it must be something special. One morning I was there with binoculars and I seen her come out of the bungalow carrying some bottles and a couple of glasses. Guess what that means."

I thought a moment. "She won't let the houseboys or the maids clean the place."

He smiled and nodded.

"She's the only one who's allowed to go in," I added.

We said nothing for a minute or two.

"So whaddya think?" said Sam.

"I think you might have something. What are you gonna do with it, though?"

"Not me. You. You're gonna go down the back of that hill one fine evening real soon, and you—"

"Not a chance, Sam. Breaking and entering, burglary, that's not my line—"

"Now hear me out, son—"

"Let's not argue, please. The place is probably alarmed, and did you see those picture of her in the magazine, with the hunting rifle? Those big dogs?"

"That's only when she's huntin' down in Mexico," says Sam. "She goes there every weekend this time of year; she owns a big spread down there, too. Takes the dogs and the houseboys with her."

He leaned toward me. "Listen. Nobody's around all weekend, just a couple of store cops the locals pay to patrol the hills in the evening. And those guys couldn't find their own assholes without a compass and a Boy Scout to help 'em."

I shook my head. "It's not in my line. Let me think for a while, I might be able to come up with something else."

"There's nothing to think about, son. There's something of interest in that house and she's away all weekend."

I looked out the window again.

"Hell," said Sam, "I'd do it myself if I was a younger man, but I sure couldn't make it back up that hill. Not carrying out whatever it is she's got in there. You, you're in good shape, you've lived clean, you—"

"Aw, shut up."

"Well, I say it's worth a try. I bet she doesn't have that back building alarmed; she been drunk as a sailor every night I've seen her go out there, and never set it off once."

He put his hand on my shoulder, and looked up at me, sincere. It was ghastly.

"Young fella," he began, "There comes a time in every man's life when he must—"

"Cut that shit out!" I snapped, shaking off his dried-out old hand. "I said no," I added, reaching for my new hat and slipping on my new coat. They fit okay.

"Sorry, Sambo," I grumbled, "—but I haven't done any serious time yet, and I don't want to. It's not my line."

Sam stared at me, hurt. But then he nodded, and turned away.

"Don't worry. I'll think of something else," I said.

"It's up to you," he said. "But I should tell you, I can stake you to all of about five bucks, because you're a friend of mine. But after that you're on your own. I pay seven dollars and fifty cents a week for a room like this one, and they're scarce at that price."

He was taking my 'clown' suit off the hanger on the back of the door; the red checked coat and pants I'd been wearing up to now.

"And by the way," he said, "Them clothes you got on, they're just on loan. I told the Chinaman down the hall you'd sent your regular things out. You'll have to return that stuff to him tomorrow or pay for it; he'll be around about five."

He laid out the red checked coat and red checked pants neatly on the single bed in front of me.

"I'll just put out your old togs here for you, in case you don't get a big brainstorm tonight."

After that, there was nothing else to say. Sam went to his corner and kicked back with the racing form, and I just stood there in front of the bed. The golden sunlight streamed through the window, picking out the highlights of my clown suit.

5

At least Stacey Tilden has some style, I thought, as Sam and I sat in his truck that evening, looking over the tasteful old palace that she kept out in Bel Air. It was very dark, and very late at night, but you couldn't miss the huge stone façade spread out beyond the gates. This was not the home of some trashy 'noo-voh reesh' movie star, not one of those glitzy streamlined joints that East Coast longhairs were churning out back in the 'thirties. It really was an oriental palace; the kind of place you'd keep a princess in exile. Magnificent, romantic, splendid, exotic good taste coming out the wazoo, you know what I mean?

But you had to ooze good taste just to get into Bel Air, in those days. Most of the Hollywood types were still a little afraid to go there; it was a lot quieter and a lot less brassy than Beverly Hills. Bel Air had been designed as a sort of safe harbor for a more respectable sort of Californian, which was anybody who'd gotten rich more than twenty minutes ago and not from movies. Actually, they tried to keep *everybody* out of the neighborhood; not only were there great big iron gates in front of the biggest houses—there were great big gates and walls around the neighborhood itself. But after the Stock Market crashed, the nice folks who ran the place got less particular about who they sold to—"screen artistes" like Miss Tilden were now acceptable, though Jean Harlow would still probably be greeted by machine gun fire if she ever showed up at the gate. Another consequence of the Depression was: no more armed guards patrolling the borders to keep out the riff raff. Which was fine by Sam and me, because let's face it, that's what we were.

The estate that Stacey and her former husband had purchased was one of the first to be built in the development. According to the article in the magazine, it had been put together about twenty years earlier by one of those California oil barons who owned half of Los Angeles and twenty percent of Warren G. Harding. Stacey bought the place from the oilman's kids after he croaked; she added the swimming pool and arboreal gardens and stuff to make it a little snappier.

Sam put the truck into gear and drove along the frontage. The main house sat up high on the side of one of the hills, way back—maybe about a half a mile up behind the carved front gates. The designer had been what they call an "orientalist"; he liked that East Indian stuff, and it showed. It looked like the Taj Mahal, maybe a couple of Taj Mahals stuck together. With a bigger swimming pool.

We saw some lights on, but Sam said that was just for show; he knew for a fact that nobody was home that weekend. He started up the truck again and we drove back out of Bel Air through the big gate that led to the real world. Sam continued on down for a while and then he turned onto a different dark, palm-lined road. This was the way that wound back and up and around and to the part of the hill that was high above the neighborhood.

The road turned to dirt beneath us as we climbed higher into the hill. California nights are pretty, I was thinking; all those stars. I could get used to this.

We were now far above the mansion, looking down on it. Sam drove off the road apiece so the truck wouldn't be conspicuous to a cop passing by. A black Ford AA, a 1926 model, with a two-seat cab in front and a little platform back with rail posts running around the sides; it was way too shabby for this neighborhood. The only folks around here who drove anything like that were the rich people's gardeners and they sort of wore out their welcome in Bel Air after sundown. Sam maneuvered the Ford down into a gully in the side of a hill; a shadowy spot, with a scraggly old tree that provided some more cover.

It was down there, just like Sam said—a tiny old bungalow out in back of the main house. Compared to the showplace out front it was a matchbox; probably the original house on the property before the twin Taj Mahals went up. It didn't fit with the oriental splendor motif at all; I don't know why Tilden hadn't bothered to tear it down in the first place. She probably hadn't noticed it.

It was a steep drop down the side of the hill from where we were parked to that cottage. In fact, it was practically vertical.

The plan was for me to crawl down the side of the hill—slide was more like it, really—to the garden at the rear of the estate grounds, break into the bungalow, and take whatever Tilden had hidden out there. Sam's job was to keep an eye out for any cops or servants that might happen by. From up there he could see both the back of the estate and the road out front. If he blew the horn, I had two minutes to make it back up the hill. After that it was every man for himself.

I opened the passenger side door, taking one last look at Sam. "Two minutes!" he hissed at me, holding up two fingers for emphasis. As I began to slide down that hill towards the bungalow, it seemed to me that two minutes were not going to be enough. I was no mountain climber. Things improved a bit once I got further down, there was lots of cover from this landscaping she'd done—all sorts of, I don't know, ornamental shrubs and Japanese plantings and hanging vines and stuff. That would make it hard for anybody to see me. I hoped.

The last bit right behind the bungalow was the worst—a rock wall that dropped straight down, about ten feet. Sam hadn't told me about that, probably because he'd never seen it from up the hill; but there it was all of the sudden, a dead drop coming up as I broke through a bunch of ferns. I would have stepped out from that jungle into thin air and broken my neck if I hadn't panicked and grabbed a thick branch. I lost my balance and fell, clinging on to the big vine. I swung out into the yard with an awful noise, like an elephant bursting through the trees, and into the air. I must have looked like Tarzan until I hit the ground.

On the grass, thank God; I'd missed the concrete edge of the pool by a short foot. Which was quite a feat, because that pool was hard to miss. It was like something you see in the gardens of those French kings. Bigger than most homes I'd been in, not that that's saying much. If I'd landed in there it would have made a hell of a splash.

I rolled over and looked up at the back of the main house—no lights had come on. Good. But some of these ritzy places still contracted with private detective agencies to make a patrol once in a while, so you never knew who was around. I'd made so much noise swinging through the bush that I couldn't be sure that there wasn't someone out there now, watching me skulk.

I saw something-someone?-move against a darkened bedroom window on the upper floor of the main house. I stood up straight and waved at the window, smiling, friendly. It would be crazy to run; that's an invitation for someone inside to call the cops. Better to have them think I'm lost, drunk, or a kooky fan.

I stood there staring at the window for almost a minute; the shadow moved again—a curtain, shifting with the breeze. Feeling like an idiot, I moved back into the shadows by the little bungalow. I was here, I may as well get the job done.

Sam and I had already decided that if I spotted any signs that the bungalow was alarmed we'd call the whole thing off; I didn't know much about beating burglar alarms. I got close to the back of the little house and looked for the telltale metal stripping in the glazing of the windows—nothing there that I could see. I was feeling a bit more confident about the whole thing—if anyone was in the house they wouldn't see me now; the window I wanted to go through was on the back side of the bungalow, and covered by the wall and hill behind it. I took the driving gloves out of my coat pocket and put them on.

I had a bath towel rolled up tight and stuffed under my belt; I spread it out now and sniffed a corner of it—still wet. About a half an hour before, Sam and I had saturated one side of it with some wallpaper paste we'd mixed up. There was an empty trashcan nearby. I up-ended it and stood it on the soft earth behind the window of the bungalow. Then I got up on top of it, one knee at a time, very careful. I could feel the can sink a little into the moist dirt beneath me and with one hand I grabbed the windowsill for balance. In my other hand was the saturated towel; I turned carefully and pressed it against the window, sticky side to the glass, plastering it to the window like a great big postage stamp.

I let it set for almost a minute while I listened to the noises in the yard. Nothing, just the night. Good. I knocked at the center of the towel with the edge of my fist, like I was knocking gently on a door. Tap, tap, tap. Then a little harder—tap-tap—crack. Just a little crack, muffled by the towel and the paste.

And no alarm bell. Good.

I pressed, gently, and felt the glass give beneath my fingers. As the broken plate was pushed inward, I tried to get a grip on its edge through the towel, wiggling it back and forth. It gave; the glass came loose from the window frame. A big piece. I had to be careful now. Before I lifted it out I pulled down a corner of the towel from the top of the now-broken window, and was delighted to see that all the tiny and medium size pieces of glass had adhered to the paste, just like I'd hoped they would. I'd hardly heard the window break myself.

I picked out the bigger pieces of the window with my gloved hands and tossed them over my shoulder onto the grass. Using the towel, I kept breaking off more pieces of the broken window, bit by bit. It was kind of relaxing, like snapping peppermint sticks.

Finally, it was done. I covered the jagged bottom of the windowsill with the towel, and began to haul myself up.

And I was in. Not a scratch on me.

Of course, I couldn't see a damn thing; it was dark in there. But as my eyes got used to it, I could tell that Sam and I were in luck. It was, as he expected, a one-room affair, with open rafters, no attic. It wouldn't take long to search, to find what was here—if there was anything here.

I had to think like Stacey Tilden. If I could put myself in her place, I'd figure out where she usually kept whatever it was she came to see—and figure it out without having to tear up every floorboard in the bungalow with the little cat's paw I'd brought along. So this is your secret room, Stacey. The place you hide out in once or twice a week; all by yourself, no servants allowed. I stepped around, feeling my way. The place seemed to be used for storage; there were four or five nice old wooden chairs, like you'd find in a dining room. Big heavy boxes, nailed shut; hadn't been opened in years. Whatever I was looking for, it wasn't in those boxes; a big Hollywood movie star doesn't lock herself in a room to look at packing crates. A roll top desk; locked, of course. I'd have to get in there later. What was this on top? A kerosene lamp. Dusty.

Mostly junk. That's right. This was junk, which meant: memories. These were her things, from before she was a movie star. That's why the furniture looked like it was from the old days, like something you'd find on a farm. The rolltop desk was straight out of a Sears Catalog—

Did she grow up on a farm? Maybe. I couldn't remember that part of the *Photoplay* story. There was a heavy wardrobe in one corner: I rattled the door- it swung open. Dust again, no one had been in there for quite a while. Inside were a bunch of dresses, more like costumes than dresses, really—twenties stuff, a couple of short skirts, like the flappers used to wear. Oh, yeah—she'd started out as a dancer; half of a dance team in the Broadway clubs…

This was no good; nothing useful here. I had to think faster and come up with something good, soon. I pulled down a couple of hats from the top shelf, a headband, a cloche, one of those bell-shaped caps. No jewelry, no papers, no photos. I felt the bottom of the wardrobe; shoes, probably tap shoes. Christ.

I had been in there nearly five minutes and I didn't have a clue. Maybe there was something on top of the big wardrobe—I tiptoed up and reached—nothing, nothing but more dust on my gloves—

Dust. Aha. This was the room the servants weren't allowed to clean. Which meant, it got dusty. Except for the part of the room thatStacey Tilden was interested in, because Stacey used that part of the room, the same part, every single week. I slipped the flashlight out of my pocket and turned it on, muffling the light as best I could.

When I crouched down to the floorboards, I could see it. The path cut through the dust on the floor, leading from the front door of the bungalow to—

One of the dining room chairs, sitting upright against a wall. Not dusty. So Stacey would come in through the front door of the bungalow, turn, lock herself in, turn, walk the few steps to this chair, sit herself down, and face—

A wooden box, in a jumble of other boxes, but I knew this was the one, because it was fairly clean and required a key. I flicked off the flashlight, and let my eyes get used to the dark. The box was old-fashioned, made of some heavy wood, walnut or something. It was like the big carved box my grandma used to keep her silverware in. Jeez, I hope Sam hadn't got me all the way out here to steal some broad's silverware.

No key, but that was no problem. I slipped the glove back on my hand and reached into my pocket. A cat's paw, if you didn't know, is like a baby crowbar. Woodworkers use it to pull nails, pry open joints, whatever. It's also good for breaking into movie stars' silverware boxes, if you ever have to.

The lock must have been pure decoration, because it cracked open like a pistachio.

And there it was, all laid out before me in the top drawer of the box: photos. Old photos. I flipped through them with one hand, resting the other on top of a dusty trunk. Old postcards and photos, some of those tiny little, uh, daguerreotypes, like from before the Civil War.

The gloved hand that I'd been resting on the trunk next to the box was sticking to something. I squinted at it. A water stain, like when you don't use a coaster under your glass. Several of them, in fact. The silly bitch came out here once a week to get blotto and teary-eyed over her old family pictures. Sure enough, I reached down and there it was, a big fifth-size bottle of clear liquid—vodka, probably, the drink of the stars, the stuff you drank if you didn't want to reek. I ought to break it over Sam's head, I thought.

I rifled through the box again—more crappy old pictures of ugly, unsuccessful dead relatives. No jewelry, no earrings, not even any silverware, for Christ's sake—No, wait. There was more. There was a bigger drawer below the one on top. I took the top drawer out, real careful. And there, indeed, there was something I hadn't expected.

A scrapbook, filled with more photos.

"Shit," I said, out loud. That about summed it up, as far as I could see. An entire evening, wasted. I was still rummaging around the bottom drawer, muttering about Sam's senile old brain, when I felt—something small, and hard, like bakelite or glass. I pulled it out and held it up against the window… A jar, like a cold cream jar, only made of glass, filled with some kind of clear, syrupy liquid. And inside, God as my witness, was floating—a pickled frog. That's what it looked like to me. If I did get caught and sent up for this job, how was I ever going to explain to the other boys in San Quentin? That I broke into a movie star's home and stole her family album and her pickled frog?

I'd had it for this evening. It seemed that nothing else in the immediate area had been touched or moved for years, so I'd probably seen all there was to see. I was determined not to come away empty handed. Maybe Tilden would pay something for the photos—I wouldn't, but maybe she would. I put the stuff back in the box, the drawer, the jar, everything. Then I took off my belt and drew it tight around the box, cinching it good, and knotting it so I could—

Far away, a car horn sounded. At first it didn't register, it just seemed to be one of those peaceful, lonesome night sounds. But then I got the shakes as I realized that it was Sam and, turning and looking out the front window of the bungalow, towards the main house—a light had gone on in a bedroom on the second floor.

Don't panic. Two minutes. Okay. Don't make a sound. Just get out.

Now.

I slid out of the broken window legs first, probing the air for the trash can. My foot hit it, and I steadied myself, holding the heavy walnut box in front of me. (I thought about leaving the damn thing behind, but if I didn't bring something I'd only have that little cat's paw to brain Sam with.)

The weight of the box put me off balance. My feet slid off the trashcan and I hit the ground with a thud, getting the wind knocked out of me. I lay there a second, trying to get air into my lungs, and listening. Nothing. Then, the sound of a door opening, and from far, far off, a man's voice calling out: "Who's there?"

Time to get up. I was in the shadows and I scrabbled to my feet, clutching the box. Two alternatives: try to sneak out the front way, or climb the ten-foot wall at the back of the yard. No choice at all, really. The man's voice might have a gun attached to it, and my two minutes weren't up, yet.

Praise be to Jesus, the wall was made of limestone; no mortar between the big flat sandy stones, lots of great cracks and crevices, plenty of room for your fingers and feet to find purchase. Normally, climbing the thing with a big walnut silverware box wedged between my belly and the wall would have been a bit difficult, but to a person in my frame of mind, it might as well have been an escalator.

The box made a scraping noise as I went up; and now there were two voices behind me, a man's and a woman's. Stacey Tilden? Not that it mattered. I was up that wall like a gecko, and I flipped myself onto the ledge without even thinking about it.

It was a quiet night and I could hear the voices real good, now. They were getting closer, heading for the bungalow. The word "police" was mentioned, and a dog began to bark. These noises began to fade as I climbed upward through the dense brush. Box and all, I was hauling myself up through the Hollywood jungle garden, vine by vine, fern by fern, willing my legs to keep chugging along beneath me, higher, up that hill. The wet earth was giving way to dry dirt and gravel now; I was coming out of the trees. I kept moving, but I couldn't help looking up; was Sam still going to be there?

I saw a dark shape up at the top of the ridge; he was there. "Hey!" I cried. I figured it was a good idea to let him know I was nearby; I didn't call him by name, God forbid I should spook him.

There was a shout down below. They'd spotted me—a little black human fly, crawling up the hill. Please, Sam, don't desert me now.

He didn't—he had the truck in gear when I got to the top and it was already, ever so slowly, rolling. I tossed the box with my belt around it in the back seat, hopped up on the sideboard and held on to the door for dear life. And we were off.

Sam was pushing the Ford as fast as it could go; he yelled something to me, but I didn't feel much like talking. I crawled into the cab before we'd even rounded the first bend. When I sat up, I looked back over my shoulder, down at the Tilden estate. We were driving further up the hill now, already a mile or two away from where Sam had parked, and I could see the whole place, spread out down below. The gardens, the orchard, the jungle running up the side of the hill, the enormous jewel of a swimming pool.

What impressed me the most, though, were the cute little lights that were now burning brightly in the bungalow.

6

We didn't go right back to Sam's room. Instead, we went to a dive that Sam knew south of Hollywood; and when I say dive, I mean *dive*, the street in front of it wasn't even paved. Sam had a key; he made a couple of extra bucks a week sweeping it out after closing time.

Inside, the joint was everything I expected and more, it was dark as the pits of hell and smelled like a drunk's undershorts. The floor stuck to your shoes; the only reason I'd let Sam take me there was that I swore that at least I'd get a free drink out of this mess. I grabbed a bottle off the bar while he was busy bolting the front door.

We kept the lights out over the bar, but there was a bare bulb hanging from the ceiling in the empty card room out back. Sam sat down at the stained round wooden table and clapped his hands together. Old King Cole waiting to be presented with his treasure.

I let him have it.

"Cross country I drove, to collect this pile of shit!" I flipped open the busted top of the walnut silverware box so he could see. "Goddamit, old man, you're lucky I don't snap your fucking neck!"

He ran his fingers through the dog-eared pictures, hoping that he was seeing wrong and they were really thousand dollar bills.

"That's it?" he says, incredulous. "A bunch of her old pitchers?"

"What, that's not enough? Not enough of a score for you, you stupid drunken old rube?" I took a pull from the bottle; it didn't improve my mood. "Don't worry, pal, there's a lot more where that came from! There's a whole 'nother drawer full in there, and a pickled frog, besides! We're set for life! We'll live like kings on moldy old photos and a fucking pickled frog."

He couldn't believe it, he rifled through the lower drawer of the box.

"There must be somethin' else in here, somethin' of value—maybe it's got a secret compartment or somethin'—" He banged the top of the box.

"Yeah, and look around for a secret decoder ring while you're in there, don't forget that! Maybe there's a whistle or some Crackerjacks or something—"

"Well, it ain't my fault."

"Whose fucking fault is it, then? Mine? Hers? Yeah, that's it, it's her fault! Let's call her up and give her hell! 'Hey, you daffy bitch, I just risked my ass going to prison to break into your tool shed and all I got was pictures of your ugly old relatives! How about leaving some diamonds out there next time, you cheap bitch!"

"Ya don't have to get all sarcastic about it, there's no call to go assigning blame—"

"Oh, I don't blame you. I blame me. I listened to you." I rubbed my eyes. "I listened to you…" The liquor was starting to kick in.

Sam was holding up the jar to the light.

"Don't look like any kind of a frog I ever saw," he said, frowning. "It's hard to make it out in there with all those little booger thingies and flakes and such floatin' around." He peered closer. "I think it's only got one leg…"

"Well, I hope that doesn't affect the resale value," I said, taking another hit off the bottle. "We're counting on this big score to see us through the Depression."

That got a rise out of him. He put down the jar and looked hard at me for a moment. Then he began to pick through the pile of photographs in front of them, sorting them in some order.

"Well, maybe I'm not the brightest fella in the room," he drawled, not looking up, "but it seems to me that I once recall you sitting next to me on a Greyhound bus and treating me to a big long lecture on how your little information-selling business worked."

I lay down on some boxes in the corner.

"And I distinctly recall you saying that if you follow someone around everyday for a few weeks you're bound to catch them some place they oughtn't to be."

The ceiling was dirty, too. How the hell do they dirty up a ceiling?

"Yeah. So what."

"Well," he continued, "Ain't it kind of the same thing as following somebody around for two weeks, if you got hold of twenty years or so worth of pitchers of that somebody? Maybe one of 'em is a pitcher of that somebody, some place they weren't supposed to be."

I snorted. But I turned my head to look at him; he was making little stacks of pictures on the table, sort of like he was playing solitaire.

"And, come to think of it, if you happened to be the type who now and then get a craving to set and reminisce over some pitchers of your worthless maw and paw, would you keep 'em under lock and key away in a special building out in the back of your house, where no one else was ever allowed to go? Wouldn't you rather keep them handy, in a scrapbook in the parlor, or on top of the piano in the sitting room or something?"

I put the bottle down, and hauled myself up. I told you, Sam was smarter than he looked. There might be something there…

The photos were old and yellow, mixed in with some crumbling newspaper clippings. I reached for one, and he slapped my hand away.

"I mean," says Sam, "what's in here that's so important she's gotta keep it secret? How come she don't want anybody to see—"

"Okay, okay."

I watched him deal out the pictures onto the tabletop. He seemed to be sorting the stuff out in chronological order—Stacey Tilden as a dancer back on Broadway; photos of her in her featured role in a Gershwin show. A *New York Times* review; Alexander Woolcott saying that she was "an acceptable Candida," whatever that was. The biggest pile was publicity stills from her days as part of a nightclub dance team.

"What was the name of the dance act? It said in the magazine—"

"Hayes and Tilden," Sam cut me off; he was trying to concentrate.

He'd thrown his topcoat onto the crates in the corner. I reached into one of the oversize pockets and pulled out the movie magazine, thumbing through it for the article.

I pulled aside one of the older photographs, started a new pile. I laid down the magazine next to it. "That's her Mom and Dad," I said. The photograph used for the magazine article was the one on the table.

"Here's another one of her Maw," said Sam, tossing it over. She took after her mother, who was beautiful; her father looked like a druggist, probably because he was one. I flipped over the photograph. On the back, in fading ink: "1907. Omaha." Sam looked at it, too, then started to turn over the photos in the piles, looking for more handwriting.

"No, no," I stopped him. "Keep sorting them out first." He did.

I started to re-read the magazine article again, paying strict attention to the part about Stacey Tilden's "years of struggle" this time. Born in Omaha, Nebraska. Father ran a drugstore; married a German immigrant serving girl. First child (Stacey's older brother) born a year later. Father had a lifelong problem with heart disease; he died when Stacey was eight years old and mother pregnant again. Widowed mother left Omaha to stay with cousins in Los Angeles; Stacey's little brother sent off to board with deceased father's relatives in another state. Mother used small legacy to open rooming house. Money went to music and dance lessons for Stacey and to support Stacey's brother. Mother dreamed of a life on the stage for her gifted daughter. Poor but happy childhood of Stacey; highlight was singing in choir and once a year visits to little brother on ranch in Colorado. Adored the brother, but the kid ups and dies, heart disease again. Catharsis for Stacey: at eighteen, she decides it's Broadway or bust.

"What's that mean, catharsis?" says Sam, reading over my shoulder.

"It's Greek," I explained, and read on.

Stunning success on Broadway, Hollywood beckons. Turns down Mayer and Thalberg and signs with an independent producer, Jerry Fiske. Fiske is one of these playboy types; the society columns and blurbs in Winchell. He becomes her Svengali; two hit musicals, and then he arranges her debut as a dramatic actress in Olympic picture's adaptation of a Dorothy Parker story, "The Forgotten Woman." Sensation as a jilted mistress; nominated for Oscar. Wins. Marries Fiske; a Hollywood royal wedding. But then her Mom dies on her, too, and shortly after that Fiske and Stacey divorce. She's all broken up, but vows to continue with her art.

"And the rest is history," I read aloud, "There are some stars that shine so brilliantly in Hollywood's firmament that no future heartbreak, no looming disappointment will ever fully extinguish their transcendent glory. Garbo, Dietrich, Crawford, Lombard, Loy—and now, Stacey Tilden; burning, burning bright in the forests of the night."

"What kinda nut writes that hog shit?" snarled Sam, flipping over a pile of pictures.

"Look, there's her little brother," I said, flipping one back over. A baby picture; all babies look the same to me unless they're pinheads or something. But I knew it was the brother from the writing on the back: "Chester Mulgrew—1901". (Stacey's 'real' last name was Mulgrew, you see.)

"Here he is again," says Sam, tossing another photo on top. This one was of the mother and little Chester together; he was a kid and not a baby in this one, a little mug in a sailor suit and short pants, standing at Mother's knee. I thought there was something familiar about the photo. Not surprising, really, since it was just like a thousand other pictures taken of mothers and kids in photographer's studios back then; you know the pose, the Buster Brown stuff. He was a good-looking little kid, too; sad to think of him kicking off at such a young age. Oh, well.

"There don't seem to be any of little Stacey with her Maw, though."

Something made my skin crawl when Sam said that—then it was gone, when my eyes flickered across the table to another pile. "Here's one of them together right here," I said, and laid it in front of him.

"Naw," says Sam, shuffling through the stacks again, "I mean there ain't no pictures of her when she was a baby. When she was little girl."

My skin was crawling again, but now I knew why. I took a photo out of Sam's hand. Here was the brother, Chester, looking about six years old—and in front of me on the table, Stacey, lovely, winner of a dance contest about sixteen or seventeen. I fanned through a couple of stacks of photos. Sam watched me.

"No pictures of her when she was a baby; no pictures of her when she was a little girl." I heard the sound of my own voice, it seemed to come from someone else. "No pictures of the brother when he gets older." I looked for that first picture I'd seen, the Buster Brown pose of the brother at his mother's knee. There it was. Now I knew where I'd seen it before.

I turned back the pages of the *Photoplay* article, back to the opening splash page with the big portrait of Stacey Tilden surrounded by images from her past. And there it was, in the upper right-hand corner. The Buster Brown photo of brother at mother's knee, just like the one I held in my hand—except that it wasn't a little boy in the magazine photo. It was a little girl. The sailor suit, but no short pants this time—a little skirt and stockings. And the kid in the magazine photo had braids, what do you call 'em, pigtails. The caption beneath: "Stacey Tilden, age seven, poses with her Mother for a formal portrait."

But it wasn't Stacey Tilden, was it? I looked again at the photo in my hand. It was the same photo, no doubt about it. The position of the mother's fingers, at rest on her lap, and the position of the knees of the child, turned at an angle, were exactly the same in both photos, right down to the last shadow. The only parts that had been retouched were the skirt and the pigtails; the remainder of the photos were identical; the folds in the curtains behind the posing figures were the same.

I knew what it meant, I guess, but I was thinking of about a million reasons why it couldn't be. She was one of the most famous women in the world, I told myself. No one so famous, no matter how rich, no matter how influential, could keep this kind of thing a secret, not for nearly ten years. She'd even been married, for Christ's sake, to that producer, Fiske. It was impossible.

And, besides, there was no way to do it physically. I mean, she was a celebrity, photographed constantly by the press, the newspaper guys, the cameramen at the studio. Those guys aren't stupid; I don't care if you shave every twenty minutes and you're the most brilliant fag in the history of the world, someone's going to notice something's wrong, eventually. And what about all the people they pay to work on her body? The costume designers, the make-up guys; they'd be sure to know, she couldn't cover up the biology of her own body, not enough to fool those guys. You know, a man's body produces—stuff, stuff to make hair grow, and make your voice deep, there's no makeup and padding in the world that's gonna change that.

"No," I decided. "It's not possible. She couldn't be. She could never get away with it."

But Sam wasn't listening to me. He was holding up the little glass jar to the naked light bulb again, shaking it a bit and examining its contents more closely.

"Boy, that Chester musta wanted to be a movie star real bad," said Sam.

7

I read in this book once where this guy said blackmail should be legalized. It was this professor guy, some kind of economist, and he believed in the free market. (This book was printed before the Depression.) He was arguing that there are all kinds of jobs that exist because of disparity in knowledge—like, you pay a lawyer for legal advice, or a doctor for medical advice—and, at the same time, you also pay for their confidentiality. So this guy was saying that blackmail is the same, like a confidentiality service, and it was fair to charge the marks for protection of the information. He said that there was a 'social utility value' produced by this kind of enterprise. I didn't quite get it, but his point seemed to be that if more people knew they might be blackmailed, they might stop doing the kind of stuff that makes for good blackmail.

I don't know about that. I don't think people are all that rational, to tell you the truth. In my experience, they generally head straight for the very thing that's going to do them the most harm. Then again, maybe it's just my clientele.

I do know this, though: all the stuff they tell you in school and church about self-control and self-discipline leading to success is, for the most part, bullshit. In my time I've made marks of some of the most successful and powerful people in the United States; so I know for a fact that every single one of them was completely out of control, in one way or another. That's why they're successful, is my theory. Ego, coupled with cunning and money, equals either wild success or utter failure. So people who operate that way end up either dead, broke, or in charge. Self-control and self-discipline are qualities you look for in employees.

I'd been kicking around for a few years, doing this sort of thing. There wasn't any decent work for a guy like me back then; I wasn't a college boy with rich relatives. Just a fairly bright young fellow with a few bright ideas, but no opportunities, no capital. I tried working honest for a while; got myself a regular office job, kind of a clerk at a factory. It stunk. It's tough to get ahead working honest, with no education or connections. I finally figured if I was ever gonna get ahead, I'd have to put together a little nest egg of my own. A chunk of dough; then I could buy myself a piece of something—a store, a business, I don't know what I was thinking back then.

All I knew for sure was, I had to get that money.

So I began to nose around at this plant where I was working; looking for information on the owner. You know, going through the file cabinets, correspondence. I was at the office after hours a lot for a few months; I even began to get a reputation as an industrious, dedicated type. Which was true, in a way.

The owner of this plant was wealthy; it was a munitions factory, and people were still buying bullets and stuff, even during a depression. Especially during a depression, I mean. It's one of those businesses that pick up a little bit when other businesses go bad; like liquor stores, you know? So, I figured that since this bird I was working for had some money, he'd probably pay off if I found something good on him.

And I did. I found some stuff that went back quite a few years, all the way back to the War, in fact. My boss, it seems, had been marking up ammunition he bought cheap down South and reselling it to the government. He also had been selling reloaded ammunition as though it were new; to the government for top dollar. Probably kicked back something to the government guys he dealt with, though that was speculation on my part.

This was very old dirt—it was so long ago that even if I blew the whistle on him the law couldn't touch him; statute of limitations and so forth. But, if I sent the dirt along to some unfriendly congressman's office, or to the local newspaper, it would probably get a lot of ballyhoo, because this guy was fairly prominent in the community. And then his sterling reputation would be shot. And that reputation was worth something, to him.

Also, I hated the s.o.b. He was paying us practically nothing; he considered that we were lucky to have jobs at all. A lot of the employees probably agreed with him about that. The pay was peanuts, nothing; but there were so many guys around waiting in line for any kind of a job—I knew that if I so much as squeaked about getting a nickel more a week out of this guy, I'd be out on my ass.

I'd seen it happen to a couple of fellows. This German guy from the shop floor organized a little meeting at a local barbershop one night. He talked about a union. He was canned the next day; one of the guys must have finked on him and gotten a couple of bucks for his trouble. The German showed up back at the plant to apologize personally to my boss—he had that Kraut thrown out into the street, and I mean *thrown*! These two goons who hung around the big office did it.

So, I figured that this guy, the owner, had it coming to him anyway. It would be a shock to him, though; he liked me, as much as he liked any of his employees. He thought I was honest and hard working and never complained; I admit I look like a clean-cut, all-American type. The type you like to have around a business office; polite but manly, courteous, big smile, straightforward, right to the point. Boy, did he have me wrong!

He smiled and lay down his fountain pen when I arrived in his office for my appointment. Glad to see me.

"Hello, Mellon," he said. (That wasn't an insult; that was the name I was going by when I got out of reform school.)

"Come in, sit down. Oh, you might want to close the door behind you."

When I'd made the appointment to speak to him privately, I'd been very polite, serious. He probably thought I was going to ask for a raise. He wouldn't fire me straight off just for asking; I'd kissed his behind sufficiently in the past few weeks, talked about his golf game with him, you know.

"You have a very concerned manner, Mellon. I assume you wish to discuss money?" He smiled.

"Yes, sir."

"I like you, Mellon. You're very capable; and you make a contribution to this enterprise. But, as you know, the business climate doesn't permit me to raise anyone's pay at the moment. Not even my own."

He let that sink in. Not even his own—golly!

"These are difficult times. I don't envy young men like you. When I was your age, if a bright young fellow didn't like his wages, he could just walk down the street and find himself another job at better pay. In those days, employers had to compete for the services of capable men.

"But these days are not those days. I'd be sorry to see you go, of course, but I suppose it wouldn't take long to replace you. It's got nothing to do with my respect for you personally—it's the market. It would be irrational to raise anyone's salary right now. You understand?"

"Yes, sir, I think I do."

"I thought you would. Now, bearing all that I've said in mind, do you still wish to make the, the—" he gestured towards the folder I'd brought in with me "—presentation you were going to make?"

"Presentation?"

"Yes. Sometimes when young men pitch this 'raise' business to me, they come in with a small arsenal of arguments about why they deserve or need more money. I assume that's what you've got in your hand there."

"Well… I suppose you're right, sir, I guess in a way that is what these papers represent."

"I thought so." Big beefy smile. He leaned back in his swivel chair; it groaned. He was a fairly large guy; he told me all about how he'd played football back in his Ivy League days.

"But, in light of my little...explanation, Mellon—perhaps we can skip the arguments, and return to work. What do you say?"

"Well, if you don't mind, sir, I do have a couple of items in here to show you that might change your mind."

He seemed disappointed that I hadn't gotten the "hint"; he gave me a dark look, and said nothing for a minute, considering. I like to think that at that particular moment he had decided to fire me. Just for irritating him.

He made a gesture; inviting me to place the file on his desk.

I smiled gratefully. "It's pretty self-explanatory, I think," I said, spreading the folder out in front of him.

It was pretty self-explanatory. Purchase orders from the War Department for ammunition; purchase records from the resellers where he'd acquired the ammo at a discount; the transaction records showing his markup; the falsified accounts of the costs of manufacture... I'd gathered this stuff from different departments in the company over the past month or two; when you put it all in one place it made a pretty awful picture.

I watched his face as he looked it over. Annoyed at first; what was the relevance of a bunch of government contracts from more than a decade ago, why was I showing him—

Then it clicked, and he understood, and his eyes looked up at me with the same expression I've seen on so many men's faces since.

Anger? Disgust? Kind of a weird mixture. As though *I'm* the one who's done something wrong.

"What is the point of this." Not a question.

"Well, it just seemed to be something that ought to be called to your attention. It appears, from these documents, sir, that you were overcharging—"

"I—I—don't think that you..."

"Yes?"

Now he was getting angry. Enraged, actually.

"You're a petty little… I'm calling the police."

And he actually picked up the phone. My heart jumped, I admit it. I was pretty new to this blackmail stuff, remember.

But I said nothing, just watched as he put the receiver to his ear. He looked at me for a while, and then he put the telephone down.

"Thank you for bringing this to my attention, Mellon. I can raise your salary five dollars a week."

I couldn't help myself. I whistled. "Five bucks?"

His face began to turn purple.

"I have a better idea, sir. You are going to pay me two thousand dollars. A bonus."

"You're obviously mad. You're fired, get out."

I rose from my chair and pulled the open file towards me, closing it; he lunged across the big desk, faster than I'd thought he could move.

"Give me that!" He'd missed grabbing it by a hair, and started around the desk towards me.

"No." I didn't move from where I was, I waited for him to reach me.

He put his big hand on the folder, and I was sure he was going to hit me. He was about twenty years older than me, but, like I say, a big athletic type, and a head taller than I was.

"Those are internal documents, and belong to this company. You're fired. You're not leaving here with them."

"Fuck you, fat boy."

It was obvious that no one had ever said anything like that to him in his entire life. He was momentarily stunned, stopped in his tracks. So I kicked him in the shin, as hard as I could. (Which is pretty hard, and I was wearing my black Oxfords, from Montgomery Ward.)

It's a schoolyard move, but it usually works. He shrieked and went down. I took a few steps back, and tucked the sheaf of papers under my arms. He looked like he was going to puke.

The intercom buzzer went off on his desk.

The secretary; she'd heard him gasp and howl.

I pressed down the intercom button. "Yes?"

"Is everything all right, sir?"

The boss was in no shape to answer, so I took it for him.

I pressed the speak button again and said "Yes, fine," imitating his voice. It was a pretty bad imitation, but it seemed to satisfy the secretary, because she didn't buzz again.

I walked around the desk and spoke to him. The color had started to come back into his face again.

"I'm going downtown, now, sir. I'll be in the lobby of the Merchant's Bank by two p.m. I'll ask to see the bank manager at that time and I'll tell him that I've come to pick up two thousand dollars in cash. It's going to be drawn from the company account and is being paid to me personally by you as a bonus. And then I'm going to be leaving town. If the bank manager doesn't have the money for me, then I guess I won't be leaving town."

He didn't look at me; he puffed, staring at the floor, a string of spittle hanging from his mouth.

I walked to the door of his office, but before I left I turned around, like I'd just remembered something.

"Oh, by the way. Sir?"

He looked up at that.

"I quit."

8

Sam kept shaking up the little glass jar, trying to get a better look at the contents floating in the cloudy yellow liquid. I finally had to take it away from him. Our financial future was in that jar; I didn't want him to accidentally splatter it all over the back room of a bar.

As I put it back in the drawer of the silverware case, he asked me: "So how much you figger?"

"Hard to say," I said, grabbing the rye again and pulling up a chair next to him. (Now I was drinking to celebrate.) "One of your movie magazines said she pulled in about two hundred and fifty grand for her last couple of pictures." (Notice: I was still calling her "she," even though we knew what we knew about her. And Sam referred to her as "she" and "her," too. It was impossible to think of her any other way; try thinking of Carole Lombard or Lana Turner as a "he" for more than five minutes straight—you can't do it.)

"And then there's her house, the Bel Air place," I went on. "She could mortgage that, if she couldn't pay off in ready cash. And who knows what she's got in investments. Not stocks, but real estate. These movie stars like to buy up land, beat the taxes and stuff. You might find yourself owning a little piece of downtown, or the San Fernando Valley, Sam."

His tiny little bird's eyes had grown rounder and wider while I was talking.

"You're funnin' me."

I was puzzled by his surprised reaction to my figuring. "No, I'm not."

"I was thinkin', maybe she'd pay ten, twenty thousand—"

I sputtered. "Be serious! Sam, it's not how much she's willing to *pay*, it's how much the dirt is *worth*. She's the big star at Olympic, maybe their only real star. Like Marlene Dietrich at Paramount or Greta Garbo at MGM. If we go public, she's finished, and not only that, her studio's finished. Who's that guy, her boss, the one who runs Olympic Pictures?"

"Jack Roth."

"Right. How much do you think he'd pay to keep this quiet? Even if she won't pay us, you can bet your wrinkled old ass he will." I felt a big grin spreading all over my face and the whiskey was warming me; I was happy.

"She's huge at the box office. And she's got another picture coming out real soon, right? If she keeps going the way she's been going, she can bring in millions for Roth and Olympic for years to come. But if we tell, they all go broke. So they'll pay." I was getting excited; jeez, I think I was almost getting a hard-on at the thought.

"In fact," I went on, delighting in evil, "If Roth so much as squeaks at paying anything less than one million, I'll take that little jar across the street and sell it to MGM! Shit, they'd love it! Didn't I read somewhere that Mayer and Thalberg hate this Jack Roth character?"

"Everybody does," says Sam.

"Right! So here's their chance to ruin Roth and pick up his bankrupt studio—and his theater chain—for peanuts! That's probably Mayer's wet dream."

"Yeah," said Sam, but he looked down at the table. "But Roth'll come after us. He's an awfully mean fella."

"He can't. Okay, he'll try to scare us off, we got to be ready for that. But he can't touch us as long as he knows we've got the jar and the photos." I tapped the lid of the jar. "That's our life preserver. Tonight I'm drivin' out of town to one of those places you were telling me about, where you used to do your wrangling."

"What, the movie ranches? Up in the Valley?"

"Yeah. I'm gonna take that box and bury it somewhere, out on one of those movie ranches."

"Which one?"

"I don't know yet, and I'm not going to tell you when I do know. You're better off not knowing. Safer for you that way." He looked at me; I looked at him. "Unless you don't trust me, Sam, I'll tell you if you want—"

"Naw, naw, I trust you enough, I guess."

That made me feel good, for some reason.

"You gonna keep it buried out there until they pay?"

"We'll keep it buried out there forever, I hope! If it goes like I think it's gonna go, we'll never set eyes on it again. They're gonna pay us to keep quiet, not to get this stuff back. And they won't lay a finger on us so long as we've got it and they don't."

"But what if they flat out refuse to pay?"

"Sam, they won't. It's not just Roth and Stacey Tilden that are screwed. Everybody in this town would get hurt if this came out. The most famous woman in the movies is a man, or a freak, or whatever she is these days, how do you think the audiences would react to that news? They'd lynch the Jews who run the studios and start accusing Gary Cooper of being a bull dyke. Christ, you think Roth and those other producer guys are ever gonna let that happen? They probably still get the shakes thinking about Fatty Arbuckle."

I smiled at Sam, the first time since coming to town.

"We got it made, cowboy."

He stared back at me.

"A million dollars," he said, softly.

"Easy." It was fun to see the old guy enjoy himself.

And his little marble eyes started to get all teary in their old crevices. He was crying softly, in spite of himself. It was kind of moving to see.

"Excuse me, son," he said, dabbing his eyes with his sleeve. "I can't help it. My life has been kinda hard since Emma left me, and givin' up the drink and all… I just can't believe…" His voice caught in his throat, and he buried his face in his hands, sobbing silently.

I slapped him on the back, hearty. "That's okay, old man," I said. "I guess you're entitled to a break. I know I am."

His big red beak was beginning to run, he wiped that on his sleeve. "I'll be alright in a moment," he said.

"Sure you will," I said, and stared at the innumerable water stains in the tabletop. One was perfectly round, a glass had been set down in that spot, many, many years before. The edge of the roundness was ragged, like the sun behind the moon during an eclipse. As I stared down at it, Sam snorfled quietly. I was feeling poetic; but it was probably just the liquor, I guess.

"Okay," I said, rising and setting the bottle down on the table. "Buck up, old friend. We're hittin' the trail. I'll drop you off back at your dump so you can get some sleep, and then I'm off to bury the box. I should be back at your place early this morning."

He nodded and rose. "Take my truck, it won't look so funny out there in the canyon in the middle of the night. And there's some tools in the basement of the rooming house, I bet there's a shovel down there you could borrow."

"Good. Let's blow." I shut up the silverware box and started to pick it up, but Sam stopped me and took me by the arm.

"One thing I gotta say before we go, though," he said, facing me and looking me straight in the eye. "I've lived and worked in these parts for more than twenty years straight now, and I thought I'd seen every sort of degenerate, lowlife behavior a man could engage in. But, son, you have got them all beat. You have actually broken into a man's home and stolen his balls. That's a new low, even for Los Angeles. Can I shake your hand?"

I let him.

I drove west out of Hollywood after I dropped off Sam. To the coast and then up into the Santa Monica

Mountains; yes, they're very pretty, those stars. When I looked back, I could see the whole city of Los Angeles, lit up, and it looked like starlight was shining from below, too. On the way down the other side was a black valley. Must have been full of orchards; I could smell orange blossom.

It was a ways out there, quite a drive, and I should have been dog-tired after the night's experiences, but it was a lovely night and I had an excited, Christmas-y kind of feeling—Sam and I were about to pull off the score of a lifetime, certainly the biggest score I'd ever made.

I was out here looking for a movie ranch, one of the ones that Sam had told me about. A movie ranch is a spread out in the San Fernando Valley that the studios used to film locations for Westerns; cowboy pictures. They were big and wild and mostly overgrown; the movie people left them rough and undeveloped so they'd look more 'authentic' on film.

Sam sometimes mentioned these places when he reminisced about his stuntman days. I made a mental note of the name of one in particular; and that afternoon I'd figured out the address from looking over a tourist map and a phone directory. Because once I decided to go in with Sam on this Stacey Tilden thing, finding a nice, safe, off-the-premises spot for incriminating evidence was key. Otherwise, how are you ever gonna get a good night's sleep, right?

There weren't many other vehicles out this way, especially at night, so no one spotted me after I turned off onto a dirt road. I drove on it a mile or two and came to the place I'd had in mind—you couldn't miss it, even at night; place must have been pretty grand in its day. The gate was formed of great big spars with the ranch's name spelled out in logs hanging over the top.

The place was abandoned or neglected, just as Sam said. I cut the headlamps of the truck and stepped out. I got the gate open and drove the truck in. I didn't go very far onto the property, only about a hundred feet or so. I wanted the box to be easy to find again if there was an emergency. I was able to make out a large rock on the right side of the road; it would be a good marker.

I worked in the dark with the spade; it took me less than a half hour to dig three feet down; the ground was hard and I kept looking around, just in case.

I needn't have bothered; there was no one there. I packed the box down into the earth and covered it back up. I hoped that nobody would come along and move that rock.

I drove out, closed the gate behind me, and headed for the highway. The sky behind me was beginning to glow orange and purple; first light coming up. And now, I really was tired.

Tired, but happy. Sam was snoring away when I came in; I got him up and told him to beat it, he'd had enough sleep and the bed was a single. He got up and puttered around for a bit, but I went out like a light as soon as I hit the pillow.

Hours later, I was shaken awake, Ma trying to get me up for school. My first thought was that Ma had gotten uglier, and then I realized it was Sam, shaking me, waking me up, yelling something. He started batting me with a folded up newspaper; why do that? It was annoying, loud, obnoxious, like the sunlight streaming in through the window.

"Look. Look here," he says, unfolding the newspaper and laying it on my chest.

"Sleep," I said.

"Sleep, nothing!" He was all anxious. "Look at this, the morning paper."

"NAZIS REOCCUPY RHINELAND," said the headline, and I thought, gee, that's a tough break for the Frogs, but why wake me up? Then I saw his bony claw was tapping at a little blurb of a headline at the bottom of the page:

"Fire at Star's Home."

I sat up as best as I could, and read:

"A small blaze destroyed a building located on the palatial Bel Air estate of motion picture actress Stacey Tilden last night, according to local police. The fire was already burning in a small building at the rear of the estate when Miss Tilden, star of the upcoming Olympic Pictures release, "A Woman Scorned," returned to Bel Air after spending the weekend at her ranch in Mexico. 'Miss Tilden notified us immediately and we attempted to save the building,' said Captain Arthur T. Mitchell of the Bel Air Volunteer Fire Department. 'Unfortunately, we were too late and it was completely destroyed.'

"No persons were injured by the blaze, which apparently started shortly after midnight. The building, a small bungalow originally built to house servants, was located a significant distance away from the main house and there was no appreciable damage to any other portion of the property.

" 'It was a very pretty little fire, but not much of a loss, really,' a smiling Stacey Tilden joked later. 'I'd intended to tear it down, anyway.' The bungalow has been unoccupied since Miss Tilden purchased the property in 1930. 'I used it for storage, mostly," said Miss Tilden. "There was nothing very important in there, just some old junk with a little sentimental value.'

"Miss Tilden received the Academy of Motion Picture Arts and Science's Award for Best Actress of 1931 for her performance as 'Dora' in the Olympic Pictures production, "The Forgotten Woman." She was recently named as the number three box office attraction in the United States in a poll of motion picture distributors and exhibitors."

I handed the paper back to Sam and rolled over. I tasted the rye from the night before.

"You didn't tell me you burned the joint down," says Sam.

"I didn't." I kept my eyes closed.

"Then who did?"

"She did," I said.

"What—what did—"

"She's scared, pissed off, don't worry about it," I said. "Go to sleep." And he shut up, though I knew he was still worried.

I thought I'd go out like a light again, but I didn't. Actually, something was bugging me, too, though I couldn't quite figure out what it was. Unusual for me to worry, once I'm sure I've got something really good on the mark. It's getting that first part together, the setup part, that makes me nervous. After that I figure the mark is the one with the problem, not me.

But this time was different; something was keeping me awake. I felt the invading sunlight growing stronger on my eyelids. Had I missed something important? Left something undone, or forgotten something important that could screw things up later?

Maybe I was worried because this was the 'Big Job'; bigger than anything I'd ever dreamed about. Maybe I wanted it too bad. If so, I'd have to keep a close eye on myself.

I hadn't been there to see it happen, of course, but it was as clear in my mind as if I had been there. Maybe the reason I could picture the scene so clearly was that I knew her face and form so well from the movies—you know, the way you can picture Clark Gable or Bette Davis in your mind's eye, instantly, though you've never seen them in person.

I was sure she'd burned the place down herself.

What had she felt when she'd seen the window broken and the box gone? It couldn't have been pretty. Fear and rage at being found out by a stranger, a criminal. That response is typical with most marks.

Shortly after that, she'd decided that the thing to do was to burn down the bungalow, with her past still inside it. Or maybe she ordered the servants to burn the joint down. The firemen didn't get there 'til the little house and everything in it were practically rubble and ashes. Stacey must have taken special care to make sure the place was good and blazing before she let the servants call for help.

What kind of a person does something like that? It's not very rational, is it? It's like they're thinking, "This place betrayed me, gave away my secret to some outsider—so I'll destroy it." And I could see it: her standing there in the night in front of the inferno, lit up by walls of flame that went shooting up into the black sky, reflected in the pool beside her. She would have stood there and watched and made sure that the inside walls were consumed and gave way, and then fell into a blazing pile; her childhood going up like it was matchsticks. Then the shingled roof would collapse in great sections, falling into the heart of the fire, a million sparks—and her not moving; the famous, lovely face in the firelight, feeling the tremendous heat, making sure. What was she thinking about, right then?

I couldn't stop playing the scene in my mind. I'd seen her do that kind of stuff in movies. Playing the "vengeful mistress," the "wronged woman" who takes revenge. It was kind of her specialty.

Jeez, I thought to myself, I hope she's not like that in real life.

9

When I woke up that afternoon, I was a bit on the ravenous side. Sam took me to a greasy spoon near the rooming house; this place featured two angry little fellas in white jackets and paper hats behind the counter, shoveling out hamburger sandwiches and baked beans. When I asked one of them if it was too late to get some ham and eggs, he looked at the clock—big hand on the twelve, little hand on the five—and glared at me like I was some kind of Red agitator. But he made them, and they were pretty good, as was the coffee.

Sam had stepped out to get the *Examiner*; it also had a little something on the fire at the Tilden place. Basically the same rundown of the facts, except at the bottom of this article there was a phone number, and a request that anyone who knew any information about the cause of the fire call the number.

"Whaddya make-a that?" says Sam.

"I'm not sure. The cops, or the fire department?"

"Not at that telephone number," he says. "It's a different exchange, that ain't in Bel Air."

I put down my fork and got off the diner stool. There was a phone booth in the corner.

"You gonna call 'em?"

"Why not?"

He couldn't think of a reason, so I went into the booth, dropped in my nickel, and got the operator to connect me.

The voice that answered was a woman's. She said:

"Olympic Studios."

I said nothing, I was thinking.

"Hello? Olympic Studios." Pause. "Hello?"

I hung up.

Sam was standing outside the phone booth looking in at me like he was the faithful dog.

"It's the studio," I said to him. "Not the cops."

"So what does that mean?"

"I'm not sure, but I think it means they know. Or maybe it's Tilden, taking messages there instead of at home." I thought for a moment about the best way to handle it. Then I was rustling through the pockets of my jacket; empty.

"Give me another nickel, Sam."

He did, and I put in another call to the number.

"Olympic Studios."

"Hi. I'm calling about that little fire out at Stacey Tilden's place last night."

"Do you have information for Miss Tilden?"

She sounded bored, she'd probably fielded a hundred crank calls that day.

"Yeah, I do. Write this down. 'Miss Tilden—I know that the cause of the fire was a box for keeping silverware which was kept out in the bungalow.' "

"Silverware?"

"Yeah, silverware. And write down: 'a single window was broken in the back when you got there.' "

"What does that mean?"

"She'll know, just write it down."

"Just a moment, please." She was talking to someone else at her end of the line, but I couldn't make it out—probably had her hand over the receiver.

She came back on: "How can Miss Tilden get in touch with you?"

The trap snaps shut, I thought. "I'll meet her tomorrow morning, eight a.m." That, I figured, was early for a movie star; she'd show up for the meeting tired, scared, and hopefully hung over. "Eight a.m. sharp, tomorrow, you understand?"

"I understand," said the woman's voice. "Where?"

"Tell her she should run a classified in tomorrow morning's paper," I said. "Tell her to name a public place for us to meet in the ad, and tell her to use the word 'Silverware' in the ad, so I know she'll be there."

"Silverwa—"

"—And tell her it's just me and her, nobody else, or I'm gone. I won't have the goods with me."

"How—"

I hung up.

I came out of the booth and turned to Sam.

"Looks good."

"What do we do now?"

"Nothing. We wait for her to get back to us."

"We just wait?"

"We're done for today, until tomorrow's paper comes out, anyway." I looked out the window of the café at the sunny street; was it always this nice out here? We had some time to kill before sundown.

"Say, why don't you show me around town?"

Sam looked up at me.

"You know," I said. "Gimme the tour, a little history."

"Cost ya a buck," he said, defensive.

I stared at him, incredulous and disgusted.

"Well, I-I gotta pay for gas, dammit, don't I?" he blithered, embarrassed. "I didn't make a nickel today, nor yesterday, neither, I gotta pay the rent—"

"Okay, okay, keep your shirt on." I reached into my pocket and brought out a crumpled single. "There you go."

"I'm sorry I have to take it from you," he said, looking down at the floor as he slipped it into his trousers. "Makes me feel kinda small."

"Don't worry about it," I said. "Just make sure I get to see Myrna Loy's place."

"That's not on the dollar tour," he said. Then he put on his hat and walked out of the café ahead of me.

It was nice driving around; the sun was high and white but it wasn't too hot. I got to see a lot. It's hard to believe, but Los Angeles still had a bit of a small town feel back then.

Some of the roads weren't paved and there was no shortage of trees and greenery. The air smelled fresh as we headed out Santa Monica Boulevard towards the ocean. We saw the Pacific, almost as big as the sky, but more turquoise, and there was this amusement park out there, real Coney Island stuff. Then we turned back towards Beverly Hills and Hollywood and began the tour proper. On the way, Sam pointed out a couple of nightclubs that would be swinging later in the evening. Out of my price range at the moment, of course, but not for long.

I got my buck's worth. Sam drove through Beverly Hills and showed me the stars' homes, and also some places that he passed off as stars' homes to customers who would have been disappointed by the real thing. We saw Pickfair, which is where Mary Pickford and Douglas Fairbanks camped out. Also the Chaplin place—very grand. Joan Crawford's house was out a little further west in another neighborhood; nice, but pretty modest for Joan Crawford, I thought. Two little blonde kids were sitting out on her front lawn, staring at us; a little girl and a little boy. I asked Sam if they were Joan's; Sam said so far as he knew Joan didn't have any kids. I decided they couldn't be hers; they were too nervous-looking.

We drove off, and Sam started in again with the stories about the old days; about D. W. Griffith and Valentino and Tom Mix. I liked just listening to him and not having to talk. I think he was enjoying himself, too, because he got to talk all he wanted without being interrupted; and he didn't have to clean up his best Hollywood stories, as he did for the little old ladies from Des Moines. He was telling me all the dirt he'd ever heard about anybody whose house we passed by, and it was pretty filthy, believe me.

We saw Howard Hughes' operation downtown; he was still pretending to be a big movie producer in those days. I wondered why a guy with that much money didn't want a big place up in the hills; Sam said it was because Hughes was some kind of a damn nut, and "a damn nut from Texas is a damn nut indeed."

Sam told me about the spots around Los Angeles that he loved only from afar, these days; the places way out of town that he used to go to all the time when he worked in movies. Not like the movie ranch out in the Valley, where I'd buried the stuff; he was talking about the real thing: the little cow towns and the old ranches out beyond the city, in the desert. He used to spend a lot of time out there when he was riding; some of it was still pretty wild and it reminded him of when he was a kid. He couldn't afford to stay out there now, but when we got paid off (if we got paid off), he promised to show it to me.

"Then again," said Sam, turning on to a side street, "I guess it's all different these days. Probably not how I remember it."

Where we were looked just fine to me; the sky was getting darker now and turning sapphire, the light breaking into different layers like curtains rising, one after the other. The sun cut a red and orange gash through the whole thing; my kind of evening. But Sam was still missing his desert:

"Yeah, I bet it's different out there, now. Lotta new roads goin' up, minin' companies fencin' stuff in. Sometimes it's best just to remember."

We turned for home just after the sun went down. I thought we should take it easy that night, get to bed early. (Sam got the bed; I got the floor and a couple of Mexican blankets.)

When the alarm woke me up the next morning at six, Sam was gone; out to get the papers, the greedy old bird.

I'd deliberately failed to tell the operator which newspaper to place the ad in. Why? Because I wanted to see how nervous my new mark was.

She was very nervous. Because when Sam returned to the room with two coffees and the morning papers, we found that she'd placed an ad for us in the classified section of each of them. That put a smile on my face. This was looking better and better for Sam and me. The ads all read the same:

'Grand Central Airport. Control Tower. Time is what you said. Silverware.'

"She's bitin'," I said to Sam, folding up the last paper.

"Grand Central Airport, that's just north of Griffith Park. Think it's smart to go see her in person?"

"I'm not too worried about it. I'll just hang around the airport, and if I see her, we'll talk."

"Think maybe she'll have the cops down there to meet you?"

"I doubt it. It's not gonna help her career any to have me put in jail. And they can't do much to me, even if I do get arrested; it's not like we stole the Lindbergh baby or something."

"Kinda gives me the jitters, a bit."

"Well, that's crime for ya."

"Whatcha gonna say to her?"

"I don't exactly know. I guess I'll try to sense her mood. Make a little small talk, weather, I really liked your last picture, then I'll sneak it in—'Stacey, it's gonna cost you a million bucks to get your balls back, how's that grab ya?' "

Sam really was edgy, he started picking up stuff around the room; kind of aimless.

"Now don't get yourself into a state," I said. "Doesn't help."

"I guess I ain't as used to this kind of stuff as you are," he said, folding blankets. "What if the cops *are* there, and you don't come back?"

"I won't rat you out, don't worry," I said.

"I ain't worried about that shit," says Sam, annoyed. "I'm worried about you goin' to jail, and neither of us bein' paid."

"Part of the game," I said. "You're playing for the big money, you take the big chances. Me, I'm looking on the bright side. I'm thinking she might even show with some dough on her. Maybe I can get us a thousand or so, on account, that'd cheer you up, wouldn't it?"

"If that fella, or gal, or whatever the hell she is, is crazy enough to cut off his own balls, she's crazy enough to do anything."

"That's probably right, but here we are."

"I don't like that she's got the studio involved, either," he went on. He'd folded the blankets about eight times, by now. "Olympic Studios, that Roth fella, he's the biggest skunk in town, and this town ain't nothin' *but* skunks."

I sipped my coffee.

"No foolin', son," he continues, folding his socks. "The fellas who run these studios are mean. They got their own studio cops, and connections to some genuine bad-asses. Goons who bust up unions and stuff. They can get pretty tough, if they don't like you."

"Then I guess it's a good thing I never told you where I buried that box."

He looked pretty mournful. "Yes," he said. "I admit the less I know about it, the better."

"Sam," I said, "There's no guarantees with something like this, but I've dealt with some pretty mean guys before and I always got paid. We might have to skip town pretty fast when all is said and done, but that's fine with us so long as we leave rich, right?" I looked at Sam's alarm clock. "Is it far to the airport?"

"I can get you there pretty quick in the truck, not even a half an hour."

"Okay. Then you go out this morning and set up your little tours of the movie star's homes' lemonade stand, or whatever it is, just like usual—just do whatever it is you do on a regular day. Then come straight back here and pick me up when you think we oughtta be shoving off. I'm gonna stick around and do a little figuring and come up with a number to throw at Stacey."

He went, silently, but he didn't look very happy.

10

The airport was a good choice for a meeting place: sunny, open, a few employees around, but no crowds. I walked out onto the airstrip when the clock in the waiting room said eight. I spotted the tower easy, you couldn't miss it; it was one of those new streamlined jobs, real 'mo-derne.'

I didn't see anybody waiting for me there as I got closer, but that didn't worry me. They were probably watching from somewhere else on the field; I expected she'd pull up in a big limo or a little foreign sports car once I reached the tower. I was a little excited, and not just at the prospect of the money. I'd never met a movie star before.

I stood in the shade at the foot of the tower. No sign of anybody, yet. Some chumps were rolling a little plane out on to the runway at the other end of the field; it looked like hot work.

"Silverware?" said a man's voice, behind me.

I nearly jumped out of my skin. He was a big, skinny goop in coveralls. A pilot type, with squinty eyes and a great big hooter in the middle of his face, like a hawk or something. Probably ex-Army Air Corps.

He was squinting at me, waiting for an answer. When none came, he looked down at the metal clipboard in his hand and said, "This says there's a guy named Silverware waiting for me at the Control Tower, I'm supposed to take him to the Tilden place in Mexico. You him?"

I looked at him. "Let me see that."

It was some kind of order sheet, or form, or something. The date was today; something about Mexico was scribbled on the page, a phone number, and at the bottom was written "per S.T." I made a mental note of the phone number.

I handed back the clipboard. "Who are you?" I said.

"My name is Riggs," he said, holding out his hand.

"I'm a pilot; I fly Miss Tilden and her friends down to her Mexico place sometimes."

I ignored the hand, so he withdrew it. "I was supposed to meet with Miss Tilden," I said.

"I don't know anything about that," says Riggs. "She's waiting to see you down in Mexico."

"Did you fly her down there?"

"No," he said. "But when I got here this morning she'd already called from there and left instructions. Look, do you want to go, or not? I'm supposed to go either way."

I was leaning against the tower, sizing him up. He seemed like a fairly honest guy.

"Mind if I make a phone call before we leave?"

He looked at his watch.

"I'll give you fifteen minutes," he said, and he turned and started walking away, headed along the bleached concrete runway. For my benefit, he pointed to the metal plane that had been wheeled out. It was a little job, like a kid's toy; like that guy Wiley Post used to fly.

I walked back over to the building with the waiting room and asked to use the phone. I called Sam's rooming house; he wouldn't be home yet but I wanted to leave him a message. I didn't want him getting nervous if I wasn't back in time.

"Message for Sam in Room 24," I told the desk clerk at the other end of the line. "Tell him it's Hart, I'll be calling him again later, and not to worry, everything's fine. Okay?"

It was okay, and I walked back out onto the airstrip again to meet up with my ride. He'd started up the engine and taxied into position for take-off.

As I got closer I had to hold onto my hat; a hot breeze came from the propeller. The noise was tremendous.

I could see Riggs at the controls through the glass. He wore tinted spectacles now and he motioned me to hurry up. I didn't. He scowled at me as I climbed in, slow and awkward. I was making him late.

He reached across me, locking my door. Then he worked his magic with the controls, bumping up the engine and rolling forward, gaining speed. I ignored Riggs' boorish attitude and I tried to appear blasé. But secretly, I was a little bit excited about the whole deal.

After all, I'd never ridden in an airplane before.

After you fly out of Los Angeles, it's nothing but red mountains and desert, and then more desert. Then gray and brown mountains, like crumpled burlap beneath you. I saw ocean, though, that was something—all brilliant silvered blue to our left the whole way. We were headed south; I guessed we were headed down what they call Baja California, the part of California that Mexico got to keep when the U.S. took the rest. You know, that big long peninsula part that kind of hangs off the west coast of Mexico.

I could see why the U.S. didn't want it; from the air it seemed like nothing but a great big stick made of sand and rock, stuck out in the middle of the ocean. A few spots of green that I could see; oases, I guessed, though I never heard that word used in connection with western deserts. The rest was all weird mountains and canyons, like on the cover of one of those science fiction magazines. No sign of any people; I couldn't even make out a paved road down there.

We were flying along at a pretty good clip, I guess—a hundred and twenty or so; and I was enjoying myself, and trying to figure out where this place was we were going: let's see, due south about an hour in the air so far, along the Pacific.

Couldn't make head nor tail of it.

"How much further?" I shouted at Riggs, over the engine.

"Not much," he says. He noticed that I was doing up my jacket buttons, it was a bit chilly up there. He reached under his seat and brought out a vacuum flask.

"Take some of that," he said; I nodded my thanks. Riggs was starting to warm up to me. It was good coffee, laced with good brandy, which took me by surprise. Very warming.

I only took one swig, though. I had to stay awake and on my guard. This whole deal smelled like a dead rat; why was she taking me all the way down to Mexico, if all she wanted to do was talk? She wouldn't kill me or have me killed, because she probably figured on me having a partner running loose who would share her dirty secret with the world if I didn't come back. But a guy can get into all sorts of trouble once he leaves the States; there aren't as many laws to protect you, it's tougher to talk yourself out of a jam, and, as they say, 'accidents will happen.' I might have been more worried than I was if I didn't have Sam's revolver tucked inside my jacket.

This was an old pistol that Sam kept in his room. I'd swiped it that morning without telling Sam before we left for the meeting at the airport. I didn't want to let Sam know it, but he'd rattled me a little with his talk of studio security and labor racketeers. I didn't need any broken bones, that's for sure. I don't care much for guns. But I know how to use one; and, anyway, better safe than sorry.

"Get ready," shouted Riggs. "We're almost there."

Good, I thought, I have to take a wicked piss. I looked down. "I don't see the house."

"It's not down there," he shouts, "It's not on the Baja. It's across the bay." He jerks his thumb off to his left out the window. I tried to look, but he pulled back on the stick and banked the plane slowly to the left. We were heading east.

I saw the blue strip of the bay below slipping away. Then it was gone, nothing but red and gray and yellow desert again. The descent was slow; it was twenty minutes before he started pulling switches, preparing to land.

He pointed towards my window. "Look down and to your right!" Far away were blue mountains, but down below us was a trail cut into the desert. A white speck on the trail that grew bigger and closer as we descended.

A car.

A sedan, I thought as we whizzed by, and Riggs said, "Hold on." To what, I wondered, and we touched down. Pretty smooth for a bush pilot. We coasted and I twisted in my seat, but I was unable to see the car behind me. After we slowed to a stop Riggs began a long, slow turn so that we faced the car in the distance. It was tooling along, heading our way, leaving a little trail of dust.

Riggs reached across me and opened my door. I got out. (Smart, right?)

I watched him through the open door of the cockpit as he fiddled with buttons and switches, and then I turned to squint at the car, getting closer. It was a limousine, white, cloth top on it, looked like a big one. A Duesenberg, maybe. Now that's real money, there; keeping a Doozy all the way down here in the desert, just because you want to impress the—

The cockpit door slammed behind me. I spun around, tugged at it. It pulled away from me, and as the engines got louder I realized with a sick feeling that Riggs was leaving.

I suppose I could have pulled out the pistol and fired at him, but that seemed kind of extreme, and I didn't want to scare off my approaching limo. So as the plane rolled forward I just stepped back away from it, so I wouldn't get bowled over by the wings on the rudder.

Riggs kept going, a little faster, then real fast—and then the plane was shimmering through the heat as it took off into the sky.

I turned around. The Duesenberg was still about a hundred yards off. It must be going very slowly. Actually, I realized, it's not going at all. It's stopped; it's not kicking up its little cloud of dust anymore.

I was getting that bad feeling in the pit of my stomach. It was the middle of the afternoon, and it must have been about a hundred and twenty degrees out there. I took my hat off to wipe the sweat off my head, and put it back on right away; the sun was like a slap on the forehead.

Very funny, Stacey, I thought, starting for the car. Make me come to you, in this heat. Very humiliating, a little revenge. You'll pay for it, you fruit.

It was so hot I was having trouble breathing, and I'm a fairly healthy boy, normally. The car was still too far off for me to see who was inside; my sole consolation was that it must be hot for them in there, too.

Then I realized that the car was moving again. Backwards, away from me. The driver had put it in reverse, and was cruising away as fast as I was walking. For a moment I thought I made out the face of the driver—the chauffeur—but the glare made it impossible to—

"Hey!" I yelled. But I already knew what was going on.

Without thinking about it, I was running, running to catch the retreating car. It was like running through a burning building. My heart leapt when I saw the car stop, only fifty yards or so ahead of me, but the driver was just changing gears. He put it into first, spun it around, and took off as fast as he could, kicking up sand and dirt in his wake.

I stopped running. I was getting as angry as I was scared. I pulled out the revolver and fired two shots at the limo. I doubt even one of them hit; I hadn't taken aim and the heat made everything hazy. The car just kept on going, faster, getting tinier.

I stood and watched it, holding the stupid, useless revolver. Then I looked behind me. Empty sky, Riggs long gone—not that he ever cared anyway. The last hint of a town I'd seen anywhere was from the air, hundreds of miles back.

The only tracks on the ground were the ones left by the limo.

Uh-oh.

I stood there a moment, feeling really screwed. I could keep moving, or I could stay here. If I stayed where I was, the

Duesenberg might come back for me, and it might not. Slowly, I started to follow its tracks. I couldn't think of anything else to do. The good news was, I didn't have to pee anymore, I'd already sweated it out in the five minutes I'd been in the heat.

I must have been walking for more than two hours. In that heat. I wasn't even sure it was the way; for all I knew the tracks led away from the Tilden place.

In fact, it was looking like that was the case—because the tracks veered off the road and out into the desert. Whoever it was had driven up this far ahead of me, apparently, and then doubled back down some trail. They were probably going to lead me in circles, until I dropped.

The sun was high; it was hardly noon. I looked where the tire tracks left the road. I could see a long way, but there was nothing out there that looked like it might save my life. Just more bush, a couple of outcroppings of rock and hill, and mountains, many miles off.

I left the road and began to follow the tracks into the desert. I figured that if I stopped moving I'd just dry out like a raisin and blow away.

After an hour or so I heard the horn. It was coming from up above my head; I thought I was imagining it at first. No, there was the car; the sun shining off the chrome. Up on the side of an outcropping, about three hundred yards or so off the road. The driver had parked it facing me, on top of this rock mound, a butte, I guess they call it. Keeping an eye on me.

I shielded my eyes with my hands. I thought I saw a tiny figure by the passenger side of the car; then it was gone.

Did they want me to walk over there? Climb the butte? My head ached; the sun came right through the hat. They were a long way off; I decided to go towards them. Maybe they'd come looking for me—

I'd gone a few steps when I saw a little geyser of sand and rocks shoot up ahead of me—the sound of the shot didn't come until a second later. I looked up in the direction of the car and stared for a second.

There was another shot, and I scrabbled behind a bush like I was a little rabbit or something. It really wasn't any cover at all; from the top of the butte the shooter could have put a bullet in my back or my leg without even trying hard. I thought again of one of the pictures in Sam's magazine; Stacey posing with the hunting rifle. The sportswoman. I was sure she was using a rifle, probably with a scope.

There wasn't any place around here to run to. No cover for a mile or so; all sun, no shade. So why didn't she finish me off? I thought about that one as I lay there in the sun. Like I say, it wouldn't have been any trouble for her to hit me; one bullet, bang, the end. And I then I understood.

She didn't want to kill me herself, she wanted the desert to do it for her. She'd just keep me pinned down out here 'til I was good and tired, and then all she'd have to do is come back and check on me every few hours, until I was done. If anybody ever found my body out here (which didn't seem likely), she'd just say that I'd been coming to visit and had gotten lo in the desert.

How cruel. Now I wished I had told Sam where I buried that box; at least then this fucking fruitcake would pay for sitting up there and watching me fry to death.

Something was being taken from the car and set up on the hill. I couldn't make out the figure moving the something and the haze didn't help. It was taller than the car—and it popped open suddenly.

A parasol, or beach umbrella, being set up near the limo. She was going to sit up there with a Japanese houseboy or two, like it was a catered picnic. Sipping iced champagne, with the rifle handy, enjoying the sight of me dying on my belly before her very eyes. That's so cold-blooded! I thought. If she got bored or I tried to make a break for it, she could always put one in my thigh to break up the monotony. Catch me on the hop. Not that there was anywhere to hop to.

So I stayed where I was, breathing dust and alternating between cursing and panicking. It had been some time since I'd left Los Angeles. Sam was a worrier, but I'd left that message for him not to worry. And anyway, what could he do? He didn't know where I was, and I doubted that his first guess was going to be "lying behind a bush east of Baja."

I wasn't going to be rescued. I would have to get out of this one on my lonesome. There was the gun in my coat pocket, four shots left, but what was I going to shoot at? Myself, if it got any hotter. Maybe they'd come for me if I played dead, and I'd get the drop on them, like in one of Sam's westerns. I doubted it. I shouldn't have panicked and shot at the car; that tipped them off about the revolver. I didn't have any surprises for them.

Maybe it would get cooler if I laid here a while. Maybe, but if it did, that would be the first time in history.

My brain was boiling. I was getting hazy, too hazy to be properly scared, even. It seemed like a good idea to go to sleep, even if it wasn't a good idea. I remembered Vera's old man, how I'd left him out there by the side of the road in Arizona with two broken legs. He'd been rescued, hadn't he? Poor guy, I never appreciated before now what I'd put him through.

I must have fallen asleep, or passed out, because when I woke up, the sun was further down in the sky, and it had actually cooled off to a hundred and ten or so. I looked up through the branches of my new home, the bush, and saw that the car wasn't parked up on top of the butte anymore. I rolled over on my back, and things and bones and stuff inside me complained and ached.

No car, anywhere. I got up, and I felt lighter, a little less burdened by the heat; maybe I'd sweated off a few pounds—

The revolver was gone. Christ, how'd she do that? I looked around on the ground beside me; nothing there, it was gone. Must have sneaked up on me while I was napping. I felt stupid, for so many different reasons. I stood there and it wasn't so bad, just standing there; the only thing was, I couldn't seem to muster up the strength to take a step forward.

C'mon, pull yourself together, chum, I said, and made myself walk forward, thinking about water. I knew I was walking, but I wasn't sure that I was going anywhere. I promised myself that I'd pull over the first time I saw anything that even remotely looked like shade, but I wasn't quite sure I'd recognize it even if I saw it.

Something moved, off in the haze, crawling across the desert far in front of me. Her car, I knew, but it was very far away, and maybe not even there, really. My legs started moving towards it, carrying me along.

It was there after all. Parked not more than fifty yards or so ahead.

The passenger door opened up, and this little guy got out. A man in black trousers, with a white jacket, and a black bowtie, I think. A waiter?

He was taking a silver bucket out of the car. It shone in the sunlight, and I was sure there was ice in it, or water, or both, because he had it wrapped in a cloth, (with another one thrown over his arm for show)—and he was setting it out on a folding table by the side of the car.

I watched him pull a clear glass pitcher out of the bucket, and from somewhere else he produced a water glass and he set them beside the pitcher. I was stumbling towards him without thinking about it.

As I got closer I could see that he was an Oriental, but my attention was on that glass pitcher, reflecting back the sun like a bowl full of diamonds. Ice in the pitcher.

The waiter held up the glass and poured icy water from the pitcher into the glass; holding it up to the light so I could see it. I had to stop myself from reaching out for it. The waiter set the glass down on the folding table. He put the pitcher of ice water back inside the silver bucket, and then he slid back into the car. The Duesenberg turned its wheels and trundled off, slowly. I didn't really watch it; all I knew was I had to have that glass of water, sitting there on the rickety little table, shining in the sun. What if the table blew over before I got there? What if I was so tired that I couldn't hold the glass, and spilled it onto the ground?

I reached the table, and to make sure I wouldn't knock it over, I got down on all fours, approaching it like it was a bomb that I had to defuse. I reached up and wrapped my palm around the glass, carefully.

It was real, and it was wet and cold.

I put it to my mouth; my lips were cracked and dry and I forced myself to sip, rather than gulp.

Gin.

It burned at first as it went down, but it was cold, they'd kept it so cold that it was freezing and syrupy. I was still sipping, but something was telling me to stop, to draw the liquor away from my lips. Some argument struggling to get to the front of my brain.

"Gin." I said it out loud, reminding myself.

I knew what was wrong. If I drink this, I thought, I will die. If I drink all this, I pass out here, in a coma, and the heat will kill me. If you lay down here drunk, I told myself, you'll never get up again.

I thought about it, my brain frying under the sharp white sun.

I lost the argument and drank down the gin, protesting inside as I did it.

I put the glass down carefully on the rickety little table. I knelt, thinking I might vomit, but decided I didn't have the strength.

And then, feeling sort of ashamed of myself, I lay down in the dirt so I could die.

11

I woke up wishing that I *was* dead. My brain felt like somebody had taken it out with a monkey wrench and put it back in with a rubber mallet.

The bed was nice; though. Beats the floor of Sam's room, I thought to myself. The sheets were cool on my naked back—silk, had to be.

I pinched a fold of cloth between the fingers of my right hand before I opened my eyes. It was still daylight, but the room had been darkened and was a little breezy. I didn't feel up to turning my head yet, but I could see the yellow light of the sun cast across the room in front of me, turning the wall gold. Still in Mexico, I thought.

I was in the bedroom of a woman. I saw the vanity and the mirrors. A rich woman, because the bedroom was large, though it had a low ceiling. There were many folding doors for closets. A fan hung from the ceiling, making silent circles.

I tested muscles and bones; nothing seemed broken, but I felt horrible. My head— I tasted gin, and then I remembered the desert, and then Stacey Tilden and her waiter, or houseboy, whatever he was.

She hadn't left me out there, after all. Why not?

I rolled my head around on my neck, it felt like a load of bricks. I began to haul myself up, and I realized that my skin was burning, in spite of the cool silk—the sun had done that. Also, I was naked.

I looked at my hands, burned bright red, and then at my elbows, fish belly white, protected by my clothing. I noticed I was clean—my body had been washed.

I sat up, now. Next to me on a night table was a clay water pitcher and a drinking glass. I put a finger into the pitcher and tasted the contents—water.

It was sweet and fresh. I drank two glasses, deliberately taking them slow while I looked around the room.

There were palms in the corners; red flowers grew in a window box, the desert glowed brightly outside beyond the curtains. So this was Stacey's country place; the hunting spread. From the light outside I guessed it was about five or six in the afternoon.

Telephone. I looked at the nightstand, and then at the one on the other side, and then at the vanity. No telephone.

I slipped out of bed, looked for wiring at the foot of the wall. There were marks there by the bed; both the phone and the wire had been removed.

The tile was cold beneath my feet as I padded towards one of the closets. The door folded back—the closet was full of lingerie. Nice stuff, too. Smelled terrific, but not what I was in the market for.

I opened another closet; towels, and a couple of bathrobes hanging on hooks. They were pretty small, but I couldn't be particular. I put one on; it was some kind of white material; easy on the skin, thank God.

I looked around again. Bookcase, tapestry on the wall. Ugly-looking animal skins on the tiles for rugs; was this one a cougar? Yeah.

Not very feminine, Chester.

I went to the nightstand again, opening its drawers. Pencils, notepad, earrings tossed aside—Christ, they were diamonds. Brilliant. I slipped them in the pocket of the bathrobe.

But the real prize was in the lower drawer. A little black phone book. I thumbed through quickly; a woman's handwriting—I looked up the name "Tilden"—no entry; the name "Roth," no entry, but the initials "J-R" and a number—Jack Roth, Stacey's boss at Olympic. The book was worth a fortune to someone like me. I put it in the bathrobe pocket, too.

I took out one of the earrings again and examined it; it seemed real, but I know nothing about jewelry. I glanced at the vanity. When opportunity knocks—

There was a string of pearls in the upper right-hand drawer; real oyster-choking size. I tasted them; they felt rough on my teeth—does that mean they're real or fakes? Who cares, I thought, and they went in my pocket. A couple more drawers: some turquoise-looking stuff, skip that; a brooch, with what looked like rubies, that's a keeper—and the jackpot, the crackerjack prize: a velvet box that opened up and said "Tiffany's" to me. It contained an emerald-cut diamond that you could read a book by if you didn't happen to have a night light.

Things were looking up—

I heard a voice coming from outside. A man's voice. He was calling to someone, not me. I slipped the velvet box into my overburdened bathrobe pocket and moved to the window. I couldn't see him out there, but I could see some of the other buildings that made up the ranch—low stucco with plain white facades, red tiled roofs. An estancia, they call it. Off in the distance was a corral; I saw a single horse, sunning itself.

The man's voice again, calling out. In a foreign language. Japanese.

I smiled. My waiter pal.

If he was outside, calling to someone, chances were that that someone was outside, too. So, there's at least two other people here, both of them outside.

I opened the door, slowly. A long, darkened hallway, crossed with rays of sunlight. Big heavy black beams holding up the ceiling. Some heavy wooden furniture, made of some really dark wood—'Mission' style, I think they call it.

There was a chair near the door; on the floor next to it was an issue of *Time* magazine and an ashtray with a few butts. The Japanese, probably, had been on guard at the door—he was outside now, taking a break or catching up on some work.

I looked around for a gun. After all, it was supposed to be a hunting lodge, right? Sometimes they hung them on the walls, for display—

Not this time. I looked up at a blank spot on the wall; there were a couple of empty mounting hooks where a rifle or something used to be. These Japs are careful, I thought.

I closed the bedroom door silently, and began to sneak down the hallway. I had to go careful, like a movie burglar, because the walls were pierced by these Roman arch kind of windows or bays, to let in light and air to the house—someone passing by would spot me easy. The whole house was like that; getting out of here was going to be a pain in the ass.

I arrived at a kind of a great hall or parlor, done up in low, red leather furniture. There was a rifle hanging on the wall above the huge fireplace, but it looked like it was about a hundred years old. No good. There was a display rifle case, but of course it was locked; I'd have to smash out the glass to get one of the shotguns inside, and that would bring my waiter pal running.

I thought of the kitchen, wondering where it was. There might be something useful in there. I looked around the doorways off the great hall—a dining room, with a banquet table that would have been okay for King Arthur and his crowd, except it wasn't round. The door at the back should lead to the kitchen, and now I really would have to go slow, because if there's one place you're sure to find servants…

The door leading from the dining room to the kitchen had no lock or handle. They never do, in rich people's houses; that's so the serving people can enter and leave silently, without disturbing the guests. I swung it open a crack, listening for movement.

I opened it a little more, and peered inside. Nobody in sight. I stepped in; it was hotter than the other rooms, full of sunlight, and the stove was lit. Something was bubbling away on the top of the stove—beans in a cast-iron pan. I was starving, come to think of it. There were fresh tortillas on a napkin lying in a bowl by the stove. The bowl was sitting on a wooden serving tray with a setting for one. I realized that this was my lunch in the making.

I heard the kitchen's screen door open behind me.

He was standing there and smiling at me, nice as pie. The Japanese who'd served up the gin in the desert; a good-looking young fella. He didn't have on his jacket, because he'd been doing a little work around the joint, but he was immaculate in his white shirt, suspenders, and sharply pressed pants. He still wore the bow-tie. He wiped his hands with a rag.

"Good afternoon, sir." He bowed.

"Good afternoon," I said. I smiled back at him.

"Miss Tilden will arrive shortly," he said. Born in America, it sounded like. "She's on her way down from Los Angeles to join you at the moment."

"Uh-huh," I said, looking out the window of the kitchen. There's at least one more person hanging around here besides me and this guy, I was thinking. Out back was a big old well, you know, like a wishing well. Beyond that was another building, one-story stucco job.

"I hope you're feeling better," says the domestic, very sincere, and he slipped by me to stir the beans. He took a pinch of something from a dish near the stove and sprinkled it on top of the bubbling beans.

"Miss Tilden instructed me to tell you that the episode in the desert was the result of a misunderstanding. She regrets the incident."

I didn't reply; I was still looking out the window. No one in sight.

"Miss Tilden now wishes to do business with you in good faith."

"Is there a phone around here?" I asked him.

He nodded and opened a cabinet on the opposite wall; inside was a telephone and a bunch of telephone stuff. He picked up the receiver and asked, "Would you like me to make a call for you?"

"Yeah," I said, "Call Tremont three, three, three, three three, in Los Angeles." I pulled the wooden spoon out of the pan of beans and blew on it. Tasted pretty good.

He smiled at me, and then he turned to the wall and started talking Spanish to the operator, earpiece in one hand, phone in the other.

I picked up the pan with a potholder that lay near the stove. I pulled out the back of his pants with my left hand, and I shoved the pan and the boiling beans way down into his shorts with my right. His hands were busy with the phone and he'd been concentrating on getting his Spanish right, so it took him a second to realize.

He screamed, very loud; must have blown out the operator's eardrum, I thought. The legs of his trousers were cut tight, so the pan and its contents were stuck good down there. He dropped the phone and started doing a little dance around the kitchen, going from bad Spanish to frantic Japanese.

Probably saying something rude or coarse about me, I thought, so I hauled off and socked him in the mouth as hard as I could. I heard the pot inside his pants clunk against the floor when he fell. He wriggled on the floor like an upended beetle.

He's just doing himself more damage that way, I thought, keeping an eye on him as I picked the phone up off the floor.

I set the phone back in the cupboard and picked up the receiver. "Ho-la!" I said, "Ho-la? Ko-mo es-Ta, usted?" A voice was squawking angrily in Spanish as I looked out the window, watching the courtyard, hoping to spot whoever came running to help my screaming waiter pal on the floor.

And there he was, rounding the corner of the little stucco building across the courtyard: middle-aged guy, also Oriental, sprinting towards the kitchen at top speed. I kept an eye on him through the door as I hung up the phone. He was naked from the waist up, but he had on jodhpurs and boots—a chauffeur, I realized. In one hand he carried a rag, the other was empty.

There was a butcher block next to the counter, with a bunch of knives stored in slots. I reached for the biggest handle and drew out a large chef's knife. I held it casually behind my back, out of sight, and ducked behind the cupboard.

I heard the screen door slam again and the sound of boots thumping into the kitchen. The waiter had passed out on the kitchen floor before he'd gotten his pants halfway off. The pot and spilled beans lay cooling off on the tiles of the kitchen floor; it looked pretty awful.

The chauffeur crouched down over him and shook him. He yelled something at him in Japanese. Gee, I thought, this guy's older than I thought.

I bent down behind him, and put the edge of the knife along his throat.

"Don't move," I said. He didn't.

I drew him up slowly, until we were both standing.

"Is there anyone else in the house?"

He began to answer in Japanese.

"Shh!" I said, twisting his arm behind him and pressing the blade for emphasis. "If you can't speak English, Pops, that's just too bad, because I'll have to slit your throat."

"I speak English," he said. "There is no one else here now."

"Where's my clothes?"

"The laundry," he said.

"Where's that?"

"Outside—"

He raised his hand slowly and pointed out the window of the kitchen towards a building. It was maybe forty or fifty yards off.

"Okay," I said. "Let's go."

I stuck close behind him, keeping the knife at his throat. He was much smaller than I was, so it was easy to control him. Until we stepped outside, and my bare feet touched the hot stones of the courtyard, and began to fry like Dover soles. I started to hop and prance like a flamingo. It was a good thing the old guy had his back to me; if he'd seen that, it would have undermined my authority.

"Wait a minute," I said, forcing him to bend over forward.

I climbed up on his back, keeping the knife at his throat. "Carry me!" I hissed. "Go on!"

He said something in hoarse Japanese, but he slipped his old arms under my bare legs and hitched me up on his back, playing horsie. No mean feat, since he was at least sixty and I had at least fifty pounds on him. But it didn't matter to me if he got himself a little tuckered out.

He staggered a bit at first, but then he hit his stride and we made progress quickly across the big, dusty courtyard. We got past the well when he started to lose his grip on my legs and I felt myself slipping down. I drew the knife tighter; he gasped as its edge bit deeper into his throat and found the strength to hitch me back up.

Inside the laundry room it was nice and cool, tubs of water and one of those old hand-wringers. I could see there was another door inside- open. It led to some kind of garage setup.

And there, hanging in the corner, was the suit I'd borrowed from Sam's Chinese friend. It looked fresh as a daisy, pressed and laundered; a new white dress shirt was also hanging out for me, and my shoes had been shined. Jeez, even my hat looked like it had been blocked.

I didn't let the old guy put me down, though I was fairly uncomfortable by this time, too, you know. I told him to pick up the suit and my shoes and not to let anything get wrinkled. He did, puffing and clasping the suit and shoes to his chest. I grabbed my hat and put it on my head, and I took my shirt and held it up by the hanger; I didn't think it was fair that the old man should have to carry everything. Then I told him to take me back outside.

He was blowing like a whale now. I told him to take me around the front to the garage. As we (slowly) rounded the corner of the building, I saw the great big Duesenberg parked outside. There was a bucket of soapy water nearby; the old chauffeur must have been washing the car when he heard the houseboy scream. The sun had already burnt it dry; must be hell keeping that thing clean out here, I thought. I felt kind of sorry for the old guy.

Inside the garage were two other vehicles—a beat up old truck for doing ranch stuff, and a sporty little convertible number for show, a Bentley. *Very* nice; cherry red with spoked spare tires mounted on the back and the sides; those little rocket ship-style duct pipes sprouted out of the sides of the big hood and vanished down into the undercarriage. Stylish; I always wanted to drive one of those.

I told the chauffeur to start it up for me. He stumbled over to a workbench at one side of the room, carefully hung my clothes on the handle of a vise, and then took out a set of keys from his pants pocket. He stuck one in a padlock on the door of a big metal locker at the rear of the garage, and opened it up. Inside were more sets of keys hanging off pegs, very neatly organized. He selected a key from a peg, and then we began to stumble back over to the Bentley. He was giving out little muffled cries of agony under his breath, now. I don't think it was attitude; he couldn't help himself.

He reached into the car and slipped the ignition key into the lock on the dashboard, and then he gave out beneath me, with a kind of death rattle. It took me by surprise; I just barely got the knife away from his throat in time. He lay on the floor, heaving, looking about ten years older than when we first met.

I stuck the knife in the top of the workbench and went through his pockets; there was a five-spot and some driver's stuff and identification, all of which I took. Then I got into my duds quickly, keeping an eye on him as he lay puffing like a beached fish.

Boy, even my socks felt brand new, and I could practically see my reflection in the shoes when I did them up. I hopped into the seat of the Bentley and stepped down on the starter; nice quiet motor, hummed like a top. I unlatched the hood and folded it open; looked over the radiator and checked the oil. I shut the hood and checked the gas. Full.

"Okay, Pops," I said to the man on the floor, wiping my hands with a rag, "Everything looks pretty good. Let's get you squared away." I picked him up; he was limp as a rag and light as a feather. I wondered how he ever managed to get me off the ground.

He protested a bit, but I got him into the metal locker without any real trouble; he didn't even try to stop me from closing the door. It slammed shut; the padlock went on with a neat click, and that was the end of his workday. I noticed a couple of spare cans of gas sitting in the garage; I put these on the passenger side of the Bentley. Might need 'em later.

Then I went over and pulled the big chef's knife out of the workbench, and began to slash all the tires on the truck. They were still hissing away when I went outside and started in on the Duesenberg's tires. I didn't want them following me; they might have a couple of spares around the place, but why make it easy?

I'd just made a huge gash in the right rear tire of the limo when I heard a familiar, unpleasant noise—a loud, angry bang. I looked up in its direction—the wishing well, over there in the sun in the middle of the courtyard, and crouched down beside it was—

I ducked back behind the car before I completed that thought, and beat the next shot. The houseboy, of course, but he had a goddamn rifle with him this time.

I sprinted around the front of the garage to the Bentley and hopped in, moving like Red Grange. The engine was still running, and I took off the brake and put it into gear, expecting to see the kid come round the corner any second now and put a bullet through the windshield.

But he didn't; as I pulled out, I figured either the burns on his ass and legs had slowed him down or he was just the cautious type. The Bentley roared and I spun the wheel to the right.

He was a good shot, I remembered, as I rounded the corner of the garage. And that thing probably had a scope on it—he'd have plenty of time to put a bullet through a tire or my radiator or through me, even, as I drove away from the ranch.

So, instead of driving away from there as fast as I could, I cut the wheel again and drove around the other side of the garage, circling it—and coming up behind him.

As I rounded the last corner and sped up, I could see him lying there ahead of me by the wishing well. He was flat on his stomach with his pants off, his little naked legs splayed out behind him, aiming his rifle like an infantry sniper. He had me pinned down in the garage, or so he thought. I have to say, he cut a very sorry-looking figure. He'd put his white serving jacket back on, but his undershorts and bare legs were still horrible with the dried caked beans.

He heard the Bentley, of course, but it was only at that last moment that he realized that the roar of the engine was coming from *behind* him. I'd thought about swerving at the last minute to avoid him, but I couldn't take a chance on him hitting a tire or something as I sped away. Better safe than sorry, I thought, pressing down the gas pedal.

He twisted his head around to look at me, and I would describe his expression as "surprised" when he disappeared beneath the wheels of the car. I was going pretty fast when I went over him, and when we connected he raised the right side of the car, ba-bump, ba-bump; but the suspension in the Bentley was good, it wasn't any worse than rolling over a dead log in the middle of the road. Didn't slow me down a bit.

That oughtta spoil your aim, I thought, as I sped away from the ranch and into the desert. Any punk can be tough if he's got a gun and the other guy doesn't. The hard thing is to be tough without a gun. I'm the type who can be tough without a gun. (If I'm in a car doing sixty and the other guy happens to be laying down in front of it.)

I just kept going, not looking back, and once I joined up with the road north I really opened it up. This road was all dirt and sand, but I was flying now, outrunning my own dust. I hoped there was a map or two in the glove compartment; I could check once I got well away from the ranch.

As the desert flashed by in a blur alongside, I wondered if the old chauffeur knew of some way to get out of that locker. It was going to get pretty close inside there. I remembered that there were a lot of keys inside the locker with him, but the only ones that would do him any good were here in my pocket. Maybe that houseboy would perk up after a while and crawl in there and help the old guy out. If he wasn't too busy scrubbing tire tread marks out of his white serving jacket.

He had said that Stacey Tilden was on her way down here; if that was true, she'd probably come to their rescue. Maybe. I'd been kind of rough with those two, I guess; but they'd played rough with me, right? It was kind of a coincidence, too, because I'd just been reading in the paper the other morning how tough it was for the Japanese working for Californians these days.

It was all academic, really, I thought to myself, watching the blue mountains turn to gold as I closed in on them. Those guys had their problems; I had mine. After all, they'd never really cared about my needs, had they?

Why should I be the only one to suffer?

12

I spent all that evening driving north in the Bentley. It was a little rough for the first few hours, but then I hit a main road and went across the border.

I hoped the guard at the gate wouldn't give me a good going over; according to the driver's license in my pocket, my last name was "Nakamura." If there was a problem, I figured one phone call to Stacey or her studio would straighten it out; they had a vested interest in my return to Los Angeles.

"Nice car," says the guard.

"Thanks," I grinned.

"He ain't no Okie if he's drivin' that, eh, Nick?" This to the other guard.

We all had a good laugh at that one, and then he waved me on through.

When I got to San Diego I found the bus station and parked the car a few blocks away. I figured the bus station was the best place to put in a call to Sam at his rooming house back in L.A.; I didn't want him worrying about me and doing something stupid.

On the way over to the phone, I noticed a few folks lying around between buses—a salesman, snoring away and hugging his sample case; two old ladies traveling together and scaring local sailors with their faces; a young fella, sharply dressed, sitting on the other end of the long wooden bench. He grinned up at me knowingly as he folded back his evening paper—pimp, I thought instantly, and gave him the air as I went to the phone booth.

The operator connected me long distance, and I waited while the desk manager called Sam to the phone:

"Hello?" He sounded scared.

"Sambo."

"Is that you?"

"Yes, it is."

"Shit-fire! Where are ya?"

"Not far. I'm on my way up to Los Angeles."

"You get the money?"

I felt the pearls and diamond ring and stuff in my jacket pocket.

"Sort of. How's things your end?"

"Did they tell you I called?"

I thought a moment.

"Did who tell me you what?"

"I guess I shouldn'ta done it," he said, "But I got worried when you didn't call by the end of the afternoon, and I called the studio and left a message for Stacey Tilden." He was whispering now. "I told 'em that if you didn't show by tomorrow morning, I'd drop off the goods at the Hollywood Reporter and tell 'em the whole story."

"But you didn't tell them who you were, did you?"

"Naw, what do you think I am?"

"Okay, okay."

"Did I screw things up for you?"

"No. No, that was good. They—" (How to put this, over the telephone?) "—They tried to get rid of me, but after you called they must have decided against it."

I thought for a moment.

"Look," I said. "I don't think I should come back there, not right now."

"Okay…"

"They know what I look like, and they're plenty pissed off. So it's better for both of us if we stay split up for a while. You trust me for your cut, don't you?"

"Yeah, sure."

"Okay, then. I'll try to wire you a few bucks pretty soon. Check the Western Union office in your neighborhood in a couple of days, the dough will be under your name."

"Okay."

"Don't call anybody anymore."

"Okay. Cop trouble?"

"No, no, nothing like that. Just a little trouble closing the deal. I'm gonna smooth everything over as soon as I get back to town."

"Okay."

"Anything else you got to tell me?"

"You owe fifty cents for the towels you used while you were here—"

I hung up. I took Stacey's earrings out of my pocket and looked at them; I think I even sighed. I bet they cost at least about two thousand, the pair of them. But it was late and I was tired and I had four dollars and fifty cents left.

I walked across the waiting room of the bus station and sold them to the pimp for fifty bucks. He was certain that they were fakes and I was cheating him; as I walked away I told him he'd never get that lucky again in his life.

I hoped.

I stayed in San Diego that night. Crummy joint; but the bed was okay. Still, I'd been in too many crummy joints in my short life. I promised myself I'd do better, next place I stayed.

So when I woke up the next morning, I had a bath and dressed and went down the hallway to use the phone. A lady with a face like a startled ferret was talking to her sister in Kansas City or some place. She finally got upset with me staring at her and hung up.

I called Los Angeles again. I'd decided to stay at the Ambassador. Sam and I had driven by it a couple of days before; I figured it would be an okay place because he said they used to hold the Academy Awards Banquet there, in the old days.

"Ambassador Hotel," said the educated voice at the other end.

"I want to reserve a suite," I told him. "The name is Hart, William Hart."

"Yes, sir."

"One with a view, private bath, the works."

"All the suites have baths, sir," he says, frosty. Oh, great, a wise guy.

"When will you be arriving, Mr. Hart?"

"Tonight."

"Of course, sir. And how will you be paying for this, sir?"

"Charge it to the account of Miss Stacey Tilden."

"Stacey—"

"The movie star, you know her, right?"

"Well, yes, of course, sir, but I'll have to—"

"Look, I'm coming in tonight; you can call her house in Bel Air. Just leave a message; she'll call back and okay it. Tell her the suite is for Mr. Hart, her houseguest in Mexico who had to leave all of the sudden."

"Mr. Hart, if Miss Tilden is responsible for the room, I'll have to get a letter of credit or some form of—"

"Look, chief, do I have to speak to the manager to get this taken care of? What's your name, chief?"

Silence.

"My name is Herman."

"Is that your first name or your last name, Herman?"

"It's my first name, but—"

"What's your last name?"

Pause, again. "Herman Colman."

"Really! Any relation to the actor Ronald Colman?"

He simpered a bit at that and softened, saying, "No, sir, but—"

"Actually I don't care who the hell you're related to, Herman. Just get that suite ready for me by five p.m. today. Either that or put the manager on so we can straighten this out without you."

Icily, he says: "I'll have to call Miss Tilden, sir."

"You do that. She might still be down in Mexico, but I'll give you a bunch of numbers, you call them all until you get her. Do you have a pencil handy?"

"Yes, sir."

"I knew you would." I gave him the number of the Mexican place, the Bel Air address, and Jack Roth's office number.

"One of those should work. Oh, yeah, tell them there's supposed to be some money, waiting for me at the desk. She should leave it with you, but in my name. Hart. Straighten this out for me and I'll take care of you, Herman, okay?"

His ice voice again: "I'll do my best, Mr. Hart."

"Miss Tilden and I would appreciate it if you did. I'm on my way over right now, so try to spruce the place up a bit before I get there, empty a few ashtrays, make sure the sheets on the bed are clean, okay?"

Silence, then: "Yes, sir."

"Ta-ta, then!" I said, and hung up.

The drive up to Los Angeles was kind of boring, but the Ambassador was nice. Big place; lovely pool. Girls in swimsuits hanging around, grinning idiots doing fancy dives to impress them. The girls weren't impressed; they seemed more interested in the little fat guys in shorts and dark glasses who lay in the sun and took telephone calls from trays presented by bowing Mexican waiters.

Inside it was lavish; lots of people running around the lobby trying to impress each other with their commitment to service, or being served. A fat lady with a Southern accent was having a heated argument about her cocker spaniel with a patient, priestly-looking manager; she was practically wilting the carnation in the poor bastard's buttonhole. The bell captain looked up from his desk book and eyed me unappreciatively; I didn't look like much of a tipper.

"I'm here to see Herman Colman," I said. Always pays to have a name when you go into a strange place, especially if you know you're wearing the cheapest suit in the house.

"Mr. Colman," he nodded and smiled. Probably thought I was applying for a job. He dings his little bell, and a pink gibbon in a red jacket and cap appears from out of the cloakroom.

"Charles, take this gentlemen to see Mr. Colman."

I followed Charles across the vast and magnificent Persian Gulf of a carpet, and he made me wait outside a walnut door while he rousted out Herman.

Herman turned out to be a little balding guy in an immaculate morning suit, with a carnation as fresh as a baby in his buttonhole. He looked about ten years too old to be a chorus boy, but he still had the winning smile.

"I am Herman Colman. How can I help you, sir?" he says.

"I'm Hart, Bill Hart, we spoke on the phone this morning, remember me?"

I reached for his hand, he extended his automatically; it was a damp rag. The smile never faltered, though.

"I remember you very well indeed, Mr. Hart. Welcome to the Ambassador." He showed a couple of teeth.

"Well, thank you for having me. I trust you got through to Miss Tilden?"

"I did indeed, sir, and she has instructed us to see to your every need while you stay with us, Mr. Hart. Incidentally, I feel I should apologize for my abruptness on the phone, but naturally, when a guest wishes to engage a suite on such short notice—"

"Now, let's forget about all that stuff, and start all over, you and me. Did she—did Stacey happen to leave any, uh…"

"Oh, yes, yes," and he whirled around and scurried back through his walnut doorway, and scurried out a couple of seconds later with a lovely, big fat white envelope in his hand. He offered it to me, taking a little bow.

"She instructed me to give this to you personally, Mr. Hart."

I nodded, and peeked inside the envelope. It looked like there was about a thousand bucks or so in there. In new fifty dollar bills. Things were looking up.

I took out one of the fifties and handed it to Herman.

"Thank you for your trouble, Herman," I said, watching him make the bill disappear like he was Houdini.

"THANK you, sir," he said, hoarsely, ducking his head like I had suddenly turned into the Prince of Wales. (You have to remember, these were the days when guys like Herman counted themselves lucky if they took home forty bucks a week.) "Do you wish to see your rooms, now, Mr. Hart?"

"Yes, I believe I will," I said, tucking the envelope inside my jacket pocket.

"I'll escort you personally," said Herman, and I knew that from that fifty on, Herman was a friend for life. He clapped his hands together; it was like the crack of a bullwhip. Another beardless bellboy appeared at his side, like a genie. "Take Mr. Hart's luggage to his room!" snaps Herman at the kid.

"Actually, I haven't got any luggage," I said. This disappointed him a bit, so I added, "It's being sent." That brightened him up again. I took out my car keys and jingled them in front of the bellboy's nose. "You can take care of the Bentley, if you like," I offered.

"Of course, Mr. Hart," says Herman, "Go on, Donald. This way, please, Mr. Hart."

Herman started across the huge lobby to the elevators and I followed in step behind him; we must have looked like a vaudeville dance team. The crowd parted before us and every head turned as if on cue; who was this slightly shabby, handsome stranger who rated being taken straight up to his suite by one of the natty little managers?

We stepped into a waiting elevator, and Herman muttered something at the operator who straightened up and grabbed a brass handle. I took off my hat and gave the gawkers my winningest smile as the boy closed the elevator door in their faces.

This was more like it.

I like hotels. You don't have to clean up after yourself.

And the Ambassador was a good hotel; the suite was nice. Maybe it was a little "powder puff" around the edges here and there, but I could see the pool from the window, and watch the babes from a distance. With every minute that passes, I am closing in on you, dolls.

"Is this satisfactory, Mr. Hart?"

"It'll do just fine, Herman." I threw my hat on a credenza. Herman immediately picked it up, straightened the brim, and opened a closet next to the door; he set the hat on the top shelf like it was the crown jewels.

"I can have some refreshment sent up, if you wish, sir," he said.

"No, thanks, I think I'll take a little nap before I eat dinner," I said, yawning. "Stretch out, relax a bit."

"Yes, sir. Would you like a massage?"

I looked at him; it's amazing what a guy will do for fifty bucks in this town, I thought.

"I mean, Mr. Hart," he coughed, "—that I can arrange for a masseur to come up to the suite and give you a rubdown. Some of our guests find it very refreshing."

"Oh," I nodded, and sat back on the couch. "Thanks, but no thanks." I felt my face. "I'll tell you what though, I could use a shave. Haircut, too, I bet."

"I'll have the hairdresser sent up at your convenience, Mr. Hart."

"No hurry. Why don't you send him around six or seven. I'll freshen up then; I may go out on the town tonight."

"Between six and seven. I understand, sir."

"And if you've got a cute little gal who can do my nails, send her up with the barber. I'm due for a trim," I said, inspecting my fingers.

"Miss Pierce is our manicurist; she's very presentable."

"Good, send her. And that's all I can think of, right now."

Herman could take a hint; he nodded and went for the door. As he went out, he turned, inclined his head again, and said: "And I hope you enjoy your stay with us, Mr. Fifty."

And with that, he shut the door, silently. A moment passed, and then there was a timid knock on the door.

"Yes?" I said.

He opened the door and stepped in, horrified. "I'm terribly sorry about that, Mr. Hart, of course I know your name, I don't know what—"

"That's okay, that's okay," I reassured him, patting him on the shoulder and sending him back out the door. "You just take care of me and see that I have a swell time while I'm here, and you'll be seeing a lot more of me and Mr. Fifty."

I closed the door behind him, loosened my tie, and kicked off my shoes. I took a peek in the envelope again, did a quick count—nine hundred and fifty dollars.

Then I sighed, and looked around.

"This is the most beautiful room I've ever seen," I said to myself. Out loud.

13

A quick bath, and then into the best bed I ever had; slept like a rock. No dreams, no deserts with buzzards. But now there was a ringing, the ringing of a telephone…

It was still daylight, and the clock on the nightstand said three-thirty—who knew I was here? Stacey. It better not be Sam, I thought, picking up the receiver.

"Yeah?"

"Herman Colman, the day manager, Mr. Hart."

"Yeah?"

"I'm so sorry to disturb your nap, Mr. Hart, but I thought you ought to know—the bell captain just informed me that two men are on their way up to your room."

"Huh?"

"Two men, two little men sent by Miss Tilden. The bell captain said they were very agitated—"

"Why did you let them come up?" I was already up and putting on my pants.

"As I said, sir, they went upstairs without my knowledge or consent, of course the hotel detective is on his way up, too—"

I hung up on him, glad I'd made it a fifty instead of a twenty.

I'd gotten into my shoes when I heard the knock on the door of the front room. I looked out the window of the bedroom; no help there. There was a second knock, more emphatic.

I went out to the front room and looked through the glass peephole built into the door of the suite.

I didn't know them. There were two; Latin types, moustaches, black suits, watching the door intently, waiting for it to open. It was hard to make them out; the peephole was one of those fisheye lenses that made their heads look about five times the size of their bodies. Each of them seemed to be holding something in their tiny little arms, at waist level, pointing it at the door, maybe. Waiting for me to open it—

I hopped back from the door, off to one side. I figured I'd tiptoe back to the bedroom and call Herman; should I tell him to get the cops?

Then there was some kind of argument out in the hallway; I heard one little voice that sounded Italian and then another, bigger voice that growled back in English. A disagreement.

I took the chain off the door and opened it. There was a large ex-palooka type, obviously the hotel detective, digging his fat finger into the skinny little chest of another guy, who might have been an Italian undertaker, while a second little Italian undertaker tried to interrupt him, shaking a pair of pressed dress pants at him.

"What's the beef, fellas?" I said, through the chain.

"Sorry to disturb you, Mr. Hart, I'm Jim Benson, the house detective," says the palooka. He grinned at me with his best teeth and took off his hat. (Herman must have told him about the fifty.)

"These two guys," he says, disgusted, "—snuck past the front desk and bell captain, they said they had to deliver something to you—"

This set off the Italians again. I unchained the door.

"Please, signore," says one of the undertakers, and he slides right by me into the front room before the house dick can grab him. "We are sent by Miss Tilden, Miss Stacey Tilden, the famous movie star." From beneath the pair of pants on the hanger, he whips out this little cream envelope, like the society debutantes use to write thank-you notes.

I opened it up and read while the house dick threatened the undertakers. It was handwritten; a fancy kind of handwriting, like it was the Declaration of Independence:

'You are a little stinker, aren't you? Sneaking out of Mexico before I could fly down there and get my hands on you. The servants are still talking about you, you know.

'Well, you'll have to be punished, that's all there is to it. These boys are here to fit you out in respectable clothes so you can take me to dinner at the Cocoanut Grove this evening. The table will be under my name; I expect you to be there at ten p.m. sharp. I'll be in shortly after. And I promise we'll do nothing but talk business the whole evening—That's all you deserve!

'I understand you got the little something I sent up to tide you over; hope you're enjoying the Bentley and all those other little trinkets of mine while you can. By the way, how did you like the desert? I wish you could have stayed ever so much longer. I promise to have you back there again, real soon.

'Don't worry, baby, there's plenty more where that came from.

'Love you to death,

'S.'

Hmm, I thought, as one of the Italians wound his measuring tape around my neck. She sounds kind of pissed.

Herman entered with his usual quiet dignity and parted the house detective from the other little Italian like he was Moses.

"So sorry about this disturbance, Mr. Hart," he began.

"That's okay, Herman," I said, tucking the envelope into my pants pocket. "These guys are just here to fit me for a suit. I forgot Miss Tilden was going to send them over. Just a minute." I went to the bedroom, dragging one of the tailors by his tape in my wake, and when I returned I held up another fifty and handed it to Herman.

"You split that with the detective here," I said, "—and thanks to the both of you for doing such a good job of keeping me posted about visitors and stuff. Keep it up, fellas."

Herman did his disappearing bill trick again and nodded; the detective put his hat back on and grinned, "Gee, thanks."

Before they could say "Will there be anything else?" I'd hustled them both out the door and closed it behind them. And then the two tailors were on me like mosquitoes.

"So, you work for Miss Tilden?"

"Miss Tilden, Mr. Powell, sometimes Mr. Gable, whoever got the money, we work."

"Whoever pays, we work," affirmed the one at my knee.

"So what do I wear to this Cocoanut Grove joint?"

"You wear what everybody else wears, you wear a monkey suit."

"A tuxedo?"

"That's right, a tuxedo, a white tie." He jerked something around my neck.

"Hey, fellas, listen." They said nothing. "You guys make other kinds of suits besides tuxedos?"

"We make any kinda suit," says the one at my elbow, through the pins in his teeth.

"Can you make a business suit?" I shook them off and walked to the closet; I pulled out my suit jacket and showed it to them.

"Can you make a suit like this?" I asked.

"No, we can't make a suit like that," says one of them, grabbing me by the elbow again and starting to measure. "That's the only kinda suit we can't make. You want another suit like that, I got an uncle back in Milano, he can make a suit like that. He's blind and retarded." He took the jacket and hanger and tossed them across the room. Then he put the pins back in his mouth and began to measure the small of my back.

"Listen, fellas, I'm in kind of a spot. I landed in town to visit Miss Tilden and I didn't bring any clothes with me."

"That's tough."

"Yeah, well, how about if you guys make me a business suit, could you do that?"

"We're very, very busy right now. Lotsa big stars, waiting around for clothes."

"Well, how much would you want for a nice suit?"

He told me, and I blinked back the tears. The most expensive suit I ever owned in my life cost twenty-five bucks; I got it for my father's funeral.

"Okay," I said, "You bring me back one of those tonight with this tuxedo you're fitting me for."

"That I cannot do. Very busy right now, maybe for fifty dollars I have a sport jacket—"

"Look," I said, taking a hundred bucks out of my envelope, "You charge the suit to Miss Tilden's account, you keep this hundred for you and your brother or whatever he is, and you bring it back here tonight by eight p.m."

He looked down at the hundred, and then he looked at me, serious. As he took the hundred and put it in his jacket pocket, he stared at me and said, "I like you. You're not one of these bullshit guys." He clapped me on the shoulder. "Okay, you got yourself a suit, we're gonna charge it to Miss Tilden."

His brother started to snap something at him in Italian; he snapped back. Then they both continued working in silence for a minute and then he said:

"He's afraid Miss Tilden's not gonna pay."

"She'll pay, go ahead and call her first if you're not sure."

"Oh, I'm sure, I'm sure," he says, a bit annoyed, and nodded at the little guy adjusting my hems. "It's my partner, he's not sure. We'll call Miss Tilden. You want her to buy you some shoes, too? We only got tux shoes, here."

"Sure, why not."

"Okay. You're gonna look very nice; like a movie star. We got a tropical weight suit, it's light, very nice white suit, very stylish. You sure Miss Tilden's gonna pay?"

"Call her."

"No, no, you're okay, mister, but we gotta get paid."

I took another two fifties from the envelope, and held them up to him.

"Look, if I give you two hundred, can you make me

look like Clark Gable?"

He pointed to his partner. "For two hundred dollars, I can make *him* look like Clark Gable."

He took the bills, and they worked away like little elves.

I got the rest of my nap after they left. Herman woke me up at seven p.m. sharp; he was watching me like a hawk. So was the hotel detective; it would be hard for anyone else to get by them after that last fifty.

The next visitors were the barber and the manicurist, who was 'very presentable,' just like Herman said. I had her order me a club sandwich and a glass of milk while the barber gave me a going-over. She polished my nails for a while; I asked her what it was like being a pretty little manicurist in a great big hotel. She told me, and I sympathized. I think the conversation made the barber pretty nauseous, but that was his problem.

The waiter arrived; he brought up a bowl of fresh fruit along with my snack, compliments of the management. He also told me that I had a delivery waiting for me in the hotel checkroom; it looked like clothing, did I want it sent up? Sure I did, and I sent him down to get the stuff with a fifty dollar bill in his hand—for change, this time, I couldn't grease the whole town with fifties, for Chrissakes. Not yet.

The waiter returned a few minutes later with the finest threads I'd ever seen in my life. He hung them up on the jacket stand and set out the two pairs of shoes on the floor so we could all admire them. We all did, and then I thanked everybody and dismissed them all with a five spot, which made their eyes bug out. Except for the manicurist, whose goodbye smile was a French novel. I was already famous in this town. At the Ambassador, at least.

There was a note pinned in the buttonhole of one of the new jackets; it was on billing stationary with the letterhead "Ricci." It said:

'She paid.

'We charged her for the shirts and the sport coat, too.

'Mille grazie,

Ricci.'

A double-breasted linen suit, top of the line. Very becoming. Two white silk shirts, proof against the chilly Southern California evenings. Silk neckties. Two pairs of shoes; they looked handmade. Very nice. The sport coat was cashmere; it felt like a woman's backside. I'd look good in that, too. (The sport coat, I mean.)

And here was the tux. Very Adolphe Menjou. I always wanted to wear one of these things, but I figured I'd have to get married. My sunburn was starting to feel awful, even after the bath, but vanity and curiosity won out and I got into the tux.

The brothers had slipped some shirt studs into the pocket; but it took me a while to figure out the tie. I got it more or less right the third time around, and looked myself over in the full-length mirror.

The Ricci fellas knew their stuff. With my hair slicked back and with that tux on me I looked debonair out the wazoo. My shoulders looked about three inches wider than they actually were and the razor-sharp cut of my trousers said "Let's get dancin', ladies." I could see my reflection from another angle in the shine on my new shoes, and I looked very happy.

I didn't even feel like going out tonight, I just wanted to stick around, admire myself in the mirror. Maybe invite that little manicurist back up for a gander. My face was kind of red from the sunburn, but that could be passed off as the blush of false modesty.

The phone.

"Yes?" I even sounded taller.

"Good evening, Mr. Hart."

"Good evening, Herman."

"Miss Tilden asked me to call you when your table at the Cocoanut Grove was ready this evening, Mr. Hart."

"Thank you, Herman. I'll be down presently."

I hung up, took my wallet out of my old jacket and put some twenties in it. The wallet was beat up, I'd have to replace it soon. But it looked much better after I put the money in it.

Down in the lobby, I made a phone call. Sam was in; the rooming house manager went to get him. He sounded tired when he got to the phone.

"Got some money for ya, pardner."

"Yeah?"

"Yeah. You know where the Ambassador is?"

"Uh-huh."

"You come down there this evening, about a half an hour from now, ask to see Mr. Colman, Mr. Herman Colman. He's the manager at the desk. Don't mention your own name. Tell him you're there to pick up an envelope he's holding for Mr. Hart. Tell him that Mr. Hart's signature is on the envelope."

"How much?"

"Don't be crass. Three hundred bucks, how's that sound, is that enough to get you off your fat ass and down here to the hotel?"

"Don't get sore—"

"I'm not sore. Listen, it's not fifty-fifty, I got more than that from her so far, but it's not enough and I need it to keep operating. Okay by you?"

"Yeah, yeah," he says, impatiently. "But what time—"

"A half an hour or so. And, remember, don't call me here at the hotel, I'll leave messages for you."

"Yeah. How's it goin'?"

"Hard to say. I'm meeting her tonight."

"Watch out, now."

"Yeah, don't worry, I'll dress warm. Bye bye, Grandma." I hung up and smiled at Herman; he'd been coming up close behind while I was on the phone, clasped hands, not listening, but dying to listen, you know?

"Mr. Hart," he inclined his head slightly.

"Good evening, Herman," I said.

"How is your stay with us so far, sir?"

"Oh, it's lovely," I said. "Listen, I've got a little favor to ask—"

The smile vanished and he was all serious attention; the pink ears seemed to prick up like a Doberman pinscher.

"An old friend of mine is dropping by the hotel this evening to pick up something from me; some cash." Herman nodded. "I'd like to leave it at the desk for him, but this guy's a queer old duck and he insists on picking it up from the hotel manager personally, would you mind?"

He did not mind at all, and he took me back into his microscopic office and handed me an "Ambassador" envelope. He watched closely as I put three hundred dollars in fifties in it and licked the envelope shut; he seemed sorry that I wouldn't let him lick it for me. I borrowed his fountain pen and wrote the name 'Hart' on the front. As I signed, I told Herman that my friend would give my name instead of his own when asking for the envelope and that was fine by me. I handed the envelope to Herman and he asked me if I wanted a receipt; I gave him a deprecating, "don't be silly, old boy" look and clapped him on the shoulder.

"Anything else I can do for you this evening, Mr. Hart?"

"That's all for now, Herman, thanks." We stepped back into the lobby together and I was watching some of the late night folks make their way across the floor towards the hotel's nightclub. The women looked gorgeous, glittering gowns of many colors wrapped tight around the bodies of babes who wanted to make it in pictures. The men were sharp, too, in their tuxes; almost as sharp as me.

For some reason, I thought of my old checked clown suit, hanging at the back of the closet in Sam's rooming house. I made a mental note to give it to charity; perhaps to some poor person.

14

Stacey picked the Cocoanut Grove because it was in the hotel; probably didn't want me sticking her for carfare in addition to everything else. Or maybe not—the Cocoanut Grove was the place to hang out, if you were a movie star, or hoped to be. Very lush, very chic; sort of a Coney Island for ambitious degenerates.

The room itself was a great hall in the Ambassador, filled with, what else? Palm trees. Not real ones, of course; that would have been in bad taste. These were fake palm trees left over from one of Valentino's pictures back in the twenties; the club's owner picked them up for a song when the film was finished, so he decided on a kind of tropical "*ambiance*."

Wedged into the jungle were all these round tables draped in linen. They had night lamps on them; so you could read if you didn't feel like dancing, I guess.

The band was already swinging when I showed up—on time, like a sucker. Ten o'clock was way too early; nobody who was anybody would get here for at least another hour or so; it was crowded, but crowded with people who didn't count. Out-of-town millionaires, and a few studio writers trying to get their starlet dates drunk before the real celebrities showed up and cut them out.

So it didn't surprise me that the headwaiter was patronizing. Herman had probably put in a good word for me, but he had me and my red face figured out. He'd obviously pegged me for some kind of junior oil money goofball, in town to throw jewelry at the movie stars. When I asked for Miss Tilden's table he acted surprised; at first I thought this was part of the "nose in the air" routine, but later I learned that the surprise was due to the fact that Miss Tilden was on her way to the club at all. It turned out that Stacey Tilden was notorious around town as a 'sensitive artist' type; she didn't 'do' the club scene if she could help it, and she outranked most of the movie stars who did.

Anyway, the maitre d' was suddenly impressed—he spat a whole bunch of rapid-fire questions at a junior partner with a reservations book; then snapped his fingers for a waiter and whispered in his ear. From watching this little scene, I concluded that Tilden's arrival was something of an "event" around here—in a club that never had any shortage of celebrities and top-rank stars.

Not that that raised the maitre d's opinion of me; to him I was still an All-American nobody, even if I was Miss Tilden's date for the evening. He gave me a quick smile, said "follow me, please" in the same voice he used to talk to the help. I followed him, a bit meek; it always amazes me how headwaiters, of all the people in the world, can instantly smell out my lack of standing in this life. The fact that I arrived early, without Miss Tilden on my arm, probably only confirmed his judgment of me: "Rube *avec* money."

He tucked me into my chair at the table Stacey had reserved. A little guy sneaks up behind us and fills a glass with ice water; then the maitre d' snapped his fingers again—another one shows up with a wine list or menu or something. I waved it away and said, "Gin and tonic," he nods and disappears. (It was weird, but I actually developed a taste for gin as a result of my desert experience.)

"I hope you and Miss Tilden have a pleasant evening, sir," says the maitre d', like he's talking to a two-year-old boy in the barbershop for his first haircut. He was getting on my nerves.

"Look, I'll tip you at the end of the evening, if that's okay with you. Run along now, why don't you? Waiter."

That took the cheesy smile off his face, alright. I bet I wouldn't see him for the rest of the evening, and that was fine with me. I'd have a fine old time without him; this was a good table. It was in a corner, private; surrounded by its own trees, but with a good view of the dance floor and the stage.

Impressive: Stacey was a recluse, by Hollywood standards, and rarely showed her pretty face in the nightclubs—but she was so big in pictures that she rated this kind of table at this kind of place, any time she wanted. All she had to do was ask. That's juice, boys and girls.

The band was Gus Arnheim, a black tie outfit. A bit too sweet for me, but I figured the night was young; they'd get to playing the hot stuff once the real party started. I took another look around—there were arches and columns beyond the palms; a little stone gallery or balcony or something across the room on the other side of the dance floor, more palm trees beyond. Every other woman was a blonde in a slinky gown cut low in the back; the men looked as horny as they were rich. Some couples were dancing already; there was still room on the floor for the slick ones to do a few fancy moves.

White-jacket returned with my gin and tonic; I twirled the ice cubes with my swizzle stick and kept my eyes on the floor—it was interesting to watch, like watching the animals at the zoo. I could see some predatory types at the tables near the dance floor; men and women both—the prey were the attractive or important men and women on the dance floor. Every so often a predator would take a glance in that direction, looking for an opportunity.

It was easy to tell who was an aspiring what. The actors and actresses were the ones who were either beautiful or striking; they laughed loudly so that you could hear them over the noise of the band. They were table-hopping, courting potential connections, flitting like butterflies, laying on hands and pecking cheeks. The ugly old women with expensive jewelry were either studio executive's wives or columnists. The young starlets fawned on them and the handsome men bowed. Prince Charmings courting powerful dames who might do them some good.

There were younger men who weren't so good-looking; they seemed like greengrocers or cops or schoolteachers done up in evening dress. These guys would be junior executives or writers from the different studios. Sam had explained the employee hierarchy to me; so I figured that I might be able to tell the writers from the junior executives by looking at their dates. The writers' girls would be just a little bit shabbier.

The band kicked into a tango and the lights changed; dimmer but somehow hotter at the same time. A buzz went around the room—it wasn't audible over the music, more of a general feeling in the place. You know how, when there's a traffic accident or something and you know that there is, but you don't know exactly where to look to see it? It was like that.

Because someone famous was here, finally—Charlie Chaplin; I could see him come in across the hall, grinning broadly and waving to one of the tables. The girl on his arm looked even younger than my lost love Vera; here's to you, Charles. A handsome guy without the tramp getup, I thought; and his tux is even better than mine. But I'm taller, I thought to myself, as I took a sip of the gin and tonic. Much taller.

Everybody in the club seemed to relax a little after Chaplin's entrance; their evening of fun had now been officially validated by the arrival of at least one celebrity. The appearance of Chaplin seemed to rub a bit of celebrity off on them, gave them the license to have a good time now. A couple had appropriated the dance floor and was struggling to keep it all to themselves; their tango was hot and choreographed, with lots of good moves and low dips—the stalking, then he grabs her, a violent twist, and then a kind of ballet-type falling away at the end of a phrase, which I thought was a nice touch on an old routine. She was cute; a Spanish-looking babe in red organdy.

The band was helping them out, now; the sweetness that had annoyed me earlier was giving way to a more sinister feel. The real sex stuff. The couple's embraces became more fervent and desperate; they were building to the big finale. But their grand finish was spoiled by another wave of excitement, starting up at the other end of the room. Another movie star…

I could tell where the crowd's attention was by looking at the turning heads; like nail filings pointing in the direction of a magnet, they tipped me off to the relevant location. A little man, surrounded by larger men—and on the little man's elbow, a blonde, encased in chrome, a shimmery dress that hugged the curves. The maitre d' sailed ahead of this group like a herald, navigating the tables. Behind him, the little man did a sort of a 'royal wave' kind of routine, acknowledging folks at the tables as he passed. The chromium blonde on the guy's arm was nodding and grinning at everybody, too. But they mostly ignored her.

I watched them make their way across the floor, up to the gallery. The guy slapped an important back here, shook a fat hand there. At one table he wagged a disapproving finger at a gigolo type and looked angry. The look on the gigolo's face after the little man left his table told the whole story: the little man wagging his finger was a producer, or studio head, or maybe both. Only a guy with that much juice can ruin a ladies' man's evening so quickly.

I wished the light was better; there was something familiar about him. Who was he? Louis Mayer? Too late to figure out now; his back was to me as he climbed the stairs to his table in the palm gallery. The wiggle in his blonde's behind reminded me of Vera. I wondered where she was tonight?

And then they were gone; swallowed up by a black tide of junior executives and agents. No one had seen the tango couple leave the dance floor; the important arrivals were fairly steady now and there was no time for anyone else. There was Frederic March, an actor I always liked—that was Gloria Swanson, geez, was she still around? I thought she married some Count or something.

I nearly spilled my drink, startled, because she looked up at me at just that moment, the terrifying eyes of a movie star. Did she hear what I'd been thinking? Then I figured it out; I'm sitting at Stacey Tilden's table. Gloria's been told Stacey's coming; she's just looking my way to see if she's in yet. I smiled and nodded at her, but she wasn't impressed; she turned away, smiling like a shark at a young man who rose to greet her.

It had started out hot in here and it was getting a lot hotter; the heat of a party, now. I could smell the smoke of expensive cigarettes and the perfume of the women; it was kind of exciting—but then again, maybe it was the liquor, or the prospect of big money, which I always find exciting.

She must have been standing next to me for some time; and the crowd hadn't seen her come in, obviously, or there would have been another of those silent uproars. She was standing next to a palm, and for a moment I thought she was a more exotic part of the décor, like a statue of a goddess.

Then she moved, and that illusion went bust. She was smaller than I'd thought she'd be; but when she turned her head to look at me it seemed like she was the only other person in the room. (If you could count her as a person.)

The face of a goddess, alright; the goddess of sex. The eyes glittered like green jewels, even in the shadows beneath the palms. Lesser jewelry glittered on the whiter-than-ivory throat. The hair was dark and lush and red, and I wondered how it would feel if I ran my hand through it.

I don't know if you've ever run into a famous person in the flesh; there's something about it that throws you for a few seconds—if you've only seen someone in the movies, part of you won't accept that they are here, on the same plane of reality with you. Especially if they looked like this; too lovely to be real, but right here before you.

But how could I think of her that way, knowing what I knew about her? Him, he, she, whatever it was? You had to be there. The face and shape were perfect, and as real as I was. There was no illusion to be taken in by; she was the woman I'd lusted after in those movies.

She turned to face me, size me up. Before she even said a word, I knew she hated me—well, why shouldn't she, right? All my marks hated me, I reminded them that they could be brought down, lose everything. But with me it's an honor, earning the hatred of someone that powerful, or this beautiful. It's like knighthood or something. I suddenly felt like I'd made it into the big leagues of crime. Being despised by a bunch of headwaiters and small time businessmen and hotelkeepers is one thing, but when you've earned the deep and abiding hatred of an idol—that's really something.

Then the lovely perfect mouth curled a bit, became the famous cynical smile that I'd seen on the screen before; the knowing smile of triumph over an enemy lover. Played for me only, tonight. Why was she giving me that smile?

Because, without thinking about it or knowing I'd done so, I'd stood up. She was right; it was kind of funny. There couldn't have been more than three or four people in the world who knew her secret, and I was one of those people. And in spite of that—in spite of myself—I'd risen from my chair to acknowledge the presence of a beautiful woman, the most beautiful woman I'd ever seen in my life.

15

"Well?" she said.

Words wouldn't come to me; not right away. Normally, I'm a pretty cool character, but it took me a second or two to get my bearings. I was star-struck.

"Well, what?" I said, stupidly.

She looked at me coldly now. "May I sit down?"

The spell was broken by the question—remember, kid, she's not a real woman at all, she's some kind of crazy powder puff in drag, that's all. She sure looked like a woman, though—

She sounded annoyed now.

"I said, may I sit down?"

"It's your table," I said, trying to be masterful. My voice sounded strange to me, and her voice was a beautiful woman's voice. Not affected or false at all. Like on the screen—full of promise, very sexy, very bedroom.

Then I realized that she was waiting for me to hold her chair. I just smiled at her and sat back down. I had to regain the upper hand, show her who's boss.

It pissed her off.

"You're not a very clever man, are you?" she said, as she seated herself. "There are more than a hundred people in this club who will be studying us very closely all evening. Is it really in your best interests to make them wonder why you're not showing me all the ordinary courtesies a gentleman shows a lady?"

"Well, they'll probably figure that I'm no gentleman," I said, "Or that you're no lady." I laughed at that. "And hey, they'd be right, wouldn't they, Chester?"

She looked up like I'd slapped her across the face, and for some reason I was sorry I'd said that.

"A cruel and stupid little man."

"Well, being stranded out in the desert makes a guy a little rough around the edges." I still couldn't take my eyes off her...

"What shall I call you?" she said, taking out a gold cigarette case. "Besides all the things I've already called you, I mean."

I took a lighter out of my pocket; I thought it might cool her down a bit if I played along for a while. (I always carry a lighter even though I don't smoke; it's for girls, or when I have to set something on fire.)

"You can call me Hart," I said, giving her a light.

"How appropriate," she said, and she blew out a little cloud of smoke and smiled that smile. "And what are you, Mr. Hart? Some racetrack tout or petty thief with big ideas? Or am I to be your sole means of support from now on?"

This was gonna go nowhere fast if all we did was sit here and insult each other all evening. Anyway, I didn't have anything against her, personally. So, I said:

"You know, I gotta hand it to you. You really are very beautiful."

She didn't quite know what to make of that. She'd heard that a million times before, of course, but from a guy who knew the real score? Besides, it was true; in spite of what I knew, she was the loveliest thing I'd ever seen.

She put her elbows on the table and gave me 'the look.'

"Don't you think it's a little late in the day to try and turn on the charm?"

"Just stating the facts," I said. "Fag or no fag, Chester, you're the most beautiful whatever-you-are I've ever seen in my life." I lifted my glass and toasted her.

"Don't call me that," she snapped.

"Don't call you what? 'Fag' or 'Chester'?"

"Don't call me either of those things. As a matter of fact, I'm not either of those things. Anymore."

"Well what the hell are you, then?"

"What I am and what I do and how I live my life are none of your goddamn business."

I smiled. "I gotta box full of photos and a little glass jar that says different."

A waiter appeared at the table.

"Would you care to see the wine list this evening, Miss Tilden?"

Her manner changed instantly; her smile came easy and radiated warmth. "Not yet, Tony, just bring me a gin and tonic, too."

"Yes, ma'am."

"How are your children?"

The waiter was polite, but he seemed about to bust with pride.

"They're fine, Mrs. Tilden, thank you for asking." He disappeared.

"How come you can't be sweet like that to me?" I said to her.

"It's easy to be nice to people who don't matter," she said.

"And I matter?"

"Oh, you do," she said, leaning back from the table, folding her white arms across her chest and lifting the cigarette. "What is it that you want from me, little man?"

"Well, how about a million bucks?" I said. I admit I felt a little ridiculous, saying it out loud.

"You must be mad," she said, looking at me like I was mad.

"Why not?" I said, as confidently as I could. "You've got it, it's an easy number to remember, sounds good to me. A million, you get your stuff back, I get lost."

"You're serious," she says.

"Sure, I'm serious," I said. "You knew I'd want money. You already tried to kill me, that didn't work. So you're stuck with me."

She smiled again.

"For a while."

"Look, you can threaten all you want, and you can try your luck again. I'm not bulletproof. But killing people can get kind of messy, and I'm not the only guy you'd have to kill to keep this quiet."

She was listening now.

"This isn't my first time doing this kind of thing. We thought this over very careful. If you're taking home as much per picture as the trades say you are, you can afford it. You're on top of the world, and you could lose everything. You can't afford not to pay."

"You're… absolutely mad…" she said, and looked away.

"You already said that. And I'm no crazier than you are, that's for sure. I know that even if you don't have a million ready, you can raise it easy. That castle you've got out in Bel Air, I've been there—the income from the movies, and I guess you've got some other property, real estate, the serious jewelry, and so forth. Worse comes to worse, you could borrow it from the studio."

"Impossible," she said.

"That's a funny sort of word for a guy like you to use, Chest—" I started. But I stopped talking when she laid her soft white hand on top of mine, gently—she smiled graciously at the waiter as he set down her drink in front of her and floated off. I was looking down at her hand; it was a woman's hand, long and gentle and as perfect as the rest of her. Then the hand flew away from mine like she'd accidentally touched a snake.

"And how would you like this million you're dreaming of?" she says, stirring her drink. "Would you like it in cash? Shall I write you a check?"

"Don't get all hoity-toity again," I said. "You don't have to pay me a dime, in cash. Here's what you will do, though. You'll buy up a bunch of land. Downtown, and some out in the San Fernando Valley. Good land. I'll pick it out for you, over the next few months or so. I'll be your silent partner, your purchasing agent. You can buy it on credit, if you want, but you'll pay it off, and fast, and you'll turn over the deeds to me. Sign them over. We could cut you in if you want. It would be like an investment."

She stared at me. There was curiosity in the deep emerald eyes now. "You and your partners have… some sort of syndicate or something?"

"Yeah, that's right," I said, wondering what she would say if she saw the other half of the 'syndicate' sitting on a folding chair out on Hollywood Boulevard, selling maps to the stars' homes. "We'll buy property for you, too; that would make the whole thing look better. But the money for that would come out of your pocket, not ours."

"Of course."

"Anyway, I figure that if I do this over the first few months, I'll have started a little, artificial 'boom', you know, in land prices. And then I'll be able to unload some of the land I bought during the first few months at a higher price than what I bought it for."

"And the rest?"

"I'll keep it. Depression can't last forever; folks are coming to town all the time. I read that this place is already twice as big as it was ten years ago."

She said, mocking, "Such impressive plans. Such an ambitious young man. A baby Napoleon."

"Maybe. Hey, if you can be Josephine, I can be Napoleon."

That made her smile, which made my heart start beating faster. And I don't care what you think, fellas; your hearts would have beat faster too, if a woman who looked like that liked one of your jokes—even if you knew she wasn't a woman.

I recovered and started talking again. "This isn't some kind of smash-and-grab, take-the-money-and-run kind of thing. I need some serious dough to get myself started, so much dough in one chunk that I can't miss. Shaking you down is gonna be the last time I ever do anything like this again, if I can help it. I'm doing this to you so I can get something together for myself. Like you did, except I'm keeping my balls."

She looked away, and I couldn't tell if it was to laugh or because she was embarrassed. Neither, I saw when she looked back at me. All icicles.

"No offense, darling," she said. "But you aren't anybody, really, are you? It sounds lovely when you tell me about it, but why should I believe in the financial acumen of a man who runs up my bill at a tailor's shop just so he can get himself a new suit and an extra pair of free shoes?"

"Well, I hate to bring this up again, but it's not like you have a choice about believing in me or not," I said. "You either play along or you're through, right? The reason I'm offering you a cut of the future is to sort of, sweeten the blow, you know?"

She was appraising me now. Then she said:

"I feel a little sorry for you. I figured you'd turn out to be a cheap crook, looking for drug money or a gambling stake. But it turns out you're a bit of a dreamer. Like I was."

"What's wrong with that?" I said.

"Nothing," she says, putting her elbows on the table and resting her face on her folded hands, and looking at me as though she'd just fallen in love with me. "Except that I can't pay you your million dollars. Because I don't have it. In fact, I don't have a dime to my name."

I stared at her for a moment. Oh no, I thought to myself, I've heard this shit before from too many different customers. I hate it when people lie to me.

I got mad, and I started to get up. "I didn't come here to kid around," I said. "Come looking for me when you get serious."

"Sit down," she said, like she was talking to a dog.

I thought about it for a moment, but I sat down.

"Did you really think you were the only man in town who knows about me?" she said.

I waited for the rest in silence; my stomach didn't feel so good.

"You say you know all there is to know about me. Very well, then you know I could work at any studio in town; I could have my pick. Tell me, then, why am I working for this awful man, Jack Roth, at his pathetic little Olympic Studios? Turning his B pictures into A pictures for straight salary? Why am I not at MGM, or Paramount, where I could work with the most talented people in the industry, at practically any price I named?"

"Roth knows?"

"Of course he knows. He's known for years. I've been his daily bread and butter this last two years and he knows that, too." She laughed. "Jack Roth is more interested in keeping my secret than I am." Then she turned to me, smiling the sly little girl smile. "Do you know what he'd do to you, if he found out you knew?"

"No, what?" Was she trying to scare me?

"Ever hear of a man named O'Brien, works for Roth?"

"No."

"You *are* new to town. Ask your partners, whoever they may be, about Mr. Roth and Mr. O'Brien." She was looking over the dance floor for someone or something.

"Alright, skip that, what about the money you get from doing the pictures?"

"It's in a bank, under my name. I deposit a few thousand each and every week, and I'm not allowed to touch a cent of it. Not one cent. If I do, Mr. Roth will send Mr. O'Brien to break my pretty little fingers for me. And there's nothing I can do about it." She took a drag on her cigarette, and let the smoke trickle out. "Because Roth knows."

"But you've got that house, and—"

"The studio owns the house. I get an allowance, if I behave. And whatever jewelry I can get my hands on; gifts from aspiring lovers. I couldn't raise much more than twenty thousand on my own, and Jack knows that. He'd also know if I was trying to raise it. My personal life fascinates Jack."

"What if I went to him for the money?"

She laughed again. "I wouldn't advise it, darling."

"What, this guy O'Brien would come after me?"

"Let's just say that you'd end up wishing you were back in the Mexican desert with my Japanese gentlemen." She took a sip of her drink. "Jack has the money, and he has me. And when I stop making money for him, he'll get rid of me."

"What does that mean, he'll get rid of you?"

"He'll find himself a new prima donna, or steal himself one from a bigger studio. And pay her with the money I've made for him."

I only half-believed that, but I was curious. "And what happens to you then?"

"I didn't know you cared, darling." She rested her hand on mine again; she was a little high now. "Well…" she began, and then she stopped for a moment. She turned her head and stared across the floor of the club into the gallery beyond. "Jack isn't about to let me wander off the Olympic lot so I can write my memoirs."

She looked back at me. Her sexy smile was a little *too* crooked, now. "I have an idea that he's going to fix it so I 'commit suicide'."

I must have had a strange expression on my face, because she shrugged and went on: "I've considered it from all angles, and that's the conclusion I've come to. He's done that sort of thing before. A pregnant mistress, that juvenile under contract who couldn't kick the heroin. Jack is a bit of a gangster. O'Brien fixes it up for him afterwards; he used to be a policeman or something." She signaled Tony the waiter.

"I suppose that if it happens to me, it will be tied in to my last picture somehow—another one of these, Tony, please—the grosses from my pictures begin to flag, I'm on my way down. So he'll cast me in some sappy tearjerker; not the lead, the floozy he'll replace me with will get the lead. But I'll get a standout secondary role where I can shine. 'Best Supporting Actress' stuff." She said it real sarcastic. "We'll finish filming my scenes, and then—my sad, lonely death, in all the papers. The picture should make an extra ten, fifteen percent, depending on how his press people handle it."

"And then Jack will deliver a very moving tribute to me at the Awards Banquet."

I should have felt sorry for the little fruit, I guess. But I was picturing my own empire melting away in front of me like an ice cream castle in the middle of that Mexican desert.

There was still a straw to grasp at.

"You say you might be able to raise twenty grand on your own?"

She turned the beautiful green eyes on me; they were drunk and full of contempt. "Yes, I could. Or, I could just tell Roth about you, and then he'd tell O'Brien about you, and that would be too bad for all of us, because O'Brien would fix it so none of us would ever be seen on this earth, again. For the good of the studio, you see."

I pondered this. "You sound kind of bitter," I observed.

"You're so perceptive, darling," she said, staring down into her next drink. "On the other hand, I may be able to fix it so that things turn out very nicely for both of us. If you're as smart as you seem to think you are, that is."

What was that supposed to mean?

"You see," she said, and the gorgeous face looked kind of strange in the light from the lamp on the table, "I know a few things about *Jack*."

16

The maitre d' snuck up on us; he addressed Miss Tilden, turning his back on me. Pointedly, I thought. "Mr. Chaplin sends a bottle of champagne to your table with his compliments, Miss Tilden."

"Oh, isn't that sweet," I heard her saying, as a kid in an usher's outfit laid down the bucket and the setups on her side of the table. "Where is he, Raoul? Over there?"

"Hey, Raoul," I said, tugging down sharply on the maitre d's coattails, "Get your ass out of my face, I want to see Charlie Chaplin."

He turned and stared down at me, loosening his collar. "Your pardon, sir!" he said; it came out more like "Screw you, too, buddy!"

"That's okay, just stay out of the way from now on," I said. Then, to the busboy: "Hey, sonny, take this gin and tonic and put it in a doggy bag for me, I'll take it when I go. And put a glass of that bubbly stuff over on this side of the table, too, she can't drink the whole thing by herself. Try as she may," I added. The kid grinned as he set down a glass in front of me. I took a buck out of my pocket and handed it to him. "Here, split that with your grandpa," I said, indicating the maitre d'. "Tell him to buy himself a new hairpiece with his half."

The maitre d' stalked off, and the kid looked away so we couldn't see his face as he disappeared. They'd be laughing about that one back in the kitchen for months to come.

Stacey wasn't amused. "Bullies the help, too," she said. "Such breeding."

"Well, it's hard to get good help these days," I said. "You gotta keep 'em on their toes. How is your domestic staff, by the way?"

"Hospitalized."

"That's too bad. I'll have to send them some flowers, or a bottle of gin, or something." I sipped the champagne; it was fine. "Do those guys know, your servants?"

"No," she said. "Anyway, they're very discreet gentlemen. Very loyal. They'll be very hard to replace."

"Sorry," I said. "As long as we're getting personal, can I ask you something else?"

She didn't answer; just glared.

"You've been married," I said. "To that guy, that producer, what's his name."

Her crooked smile. "Jerry Fiske."

"Yeah," I said. "I mean, how'd you pull that off, wasn't he, surprised, or something when—"

She laughed. An amused, easy laugh; perfect and perfectly feminine.

"He was very surprised, when we first became lovers. Surprised and delighted, in the end."

Then she laughed again; at the expression on my face, I guess. I've always prided myself my ability to maintain my deadpan in the strangest situations, but there were still some things that could shock even me, back in those younger days.

"You mean he—"

"Some people have very, very complex inner lives," said Stacey, dead serious. "I would have thought that someone in your 'profession' would have realized that. Jerry as it turned out, is complex. So am I." She looked up at me. "Are you?"

"I'm not *that* complex," I said.

"Then you're probably simple," she snapped back, and she got out another cigarette. "Anyway, Jerry was in love with me, and I wanted him. My 'secret' only made everything seem more delicious. Anyway, I'd always wanted a church wedding, and his mother was crazy about me."

"So why'd you ask for the divorce?"

"He betrayed me."

"He found sombody else like you?"

"No, you jackass, he didn't cheat on me, he betrayed me. He sold me out to Roth. Jerry owed money, gambling debts, and he got Roth to cover it for him. In return he told Roth about me, and I've been in Roth's back pocket ever since. I told Jerry to get lost, or some night I'd do to him what I'd done to myself."

"Wow."

"He still works for Roth; he's vice president in charge of Stacey Tilden." She took a drag on the cigarette. "He's also executive vice-president in charge of kissing Jack Roth's behind. There he is now."

I looked down at the dance floor; it was crowded now but I was able to pick him out because I'd seen the photo in that movie magazine. The eel with a pencil moustache; a tall, skinny eel, as it turned out. He was taking a turn on the floor with the cutie pie in the chrome dress; the hot blonde who'd turned heads when she shimmied up the stairs with that little producer type—

"Roth's here, you know," I said to Stacey.

She inclined a bit and looked over her nose across the room into the dark gallery at the other side of the club. "Of course he is. And that's his calling card out there on the dance floor. A bleach blonde chippie. Little cow can't even dance."

"Who is she?" I asked, watching as Fiske dipped the blonde.

"Nobody," she said, and took a sip from her champagne. "She's supposed to be Jerry's date, but she's not, of course. Jerry's as queer as a three-dollar bill. He's crazy about men, that's why we never got along; I wasn't man enough for him. Jack's married, so Jerry escorts his women around town whenever they need an airing. When did they come in?"

"Not long before you did."

Then she drank off the rest of the glass and said: "Alright, come on; let's dance." She started to get up, and, involuntarily, so did I.

"You're kidding," I said to her.

"I need to get us invited to Roth's table."

"No, I don't think I can dance with—"

"It will seem very odd, if you don't," she said. I still hesitated and the eyes turned to green hate. "Louella Parsons is watching us!" she hissed, as if that would clinch it.

Stacey put her hand on top of mine again, gave me the loveliest sincerest smile I've ever seen anywhere, and began to dig her sculpted nails into the skin on the back of my hand. Those nails were like knives. I started to draw my hand away, but she was stronger than she looked. "You fool, I've turned down German princes who asked me to dance with them," she said under her breath. "You're not in the 4-H club anymore, come on, let's go!"

I gave up, she was right; it was no good starting a scene in front of everybody, better dance with her. She slipped her arm under mine and began to steer me gently through the palms down towards the dance floor.

Well, she was pretty hot, you know. The prettiest gal there, in a room full of babes. There we were, out on the dance floor, and I must have looked pretty funny with my sunburned face and dazed expression. And suddenly in front of me is Jean Harlow; she squealed and broke away from her partner to give Stacey a peck on the cheek, and whisper something that Stacey laughed at—then Harlow looked up at me and winked and flashed a smile and I saw those amazing breasts bounce beneath the nearly invisible white lace of her gown and time seemed to stand still for a second—and then she was gone, back with her partner. William Powell, the lucky prick.

And now Stacey had me by the arm of my monkey suit, forcing up my elbow into the air and pulling me close to her (she smelled terrific). She shouted angrily above the band: "Wake up!"

And there I was, swinging her around the floor of the Cocoanut Grove. (Yes, I led.) And Stacey was right about us being the center of attention whether we wanted to be or not. I could feel all these eyes on me, like when I was in the school play or something. It made me feel kind of self-conscious.

But she was used to it, of course. She wriggled authoritatively in front of me and did a fancy turn; and then I figured, hey, the band is pretty good, you're already out here, so why not make the most of it? I did a Victor Sylvester move; Stacey smiled approval, brilliant and lovely. A flashbulb went off. I was thinking, geez, kid, here you are quick-stepping with a *guy* around the Cocoanut Grove, in front of all of Hollywood society, and that guy is the most attractive woman in the place. And a better dancer than you.

What would that fellow Freud make of all this, I wondered.

"Here comes Jerry," says Stacey, when we moved in close together again. "I may have to ditch you for a few minutes."

"You're breakin' my heart," I muttered. Then Fiske was tapping me on the shoulder. "Excuse me, friend." His breath was minty. "Mind if I grab a dance with my ex-wife?" he yells over the band. "You can dance with my date, if you like; she's pretty cute, too, you know."

He pointed across the floor, and I looked, because I remembered that he was squiring that hot little blonde for Roth. The one decked out in the chromium nightie. And there she was, all by herself on the dance floor, smiling and waiting for me to ask for the next dance.

Vera.

17

It was a slow number, so we got to talk over old times together.

"Where the hell's my hundred and fifty bucks?" I said, holding her close. She smelled like heaven; no cheap perfume, this time.

"What's the matter, honey, aren't you glad to see me?"

"Surprised, is more like it. You get around a lot for a girl your age."

"I told you, lover, I've got plans."

"Yeah, I remember you mentioning—"

"Oh, look at you, you're all sunburned, you poor baby…"

"Suddenly you care what happens to me?"

"I'm sorry I cut out on you like that, honey, I hope you're not all sore at me."

"I oughtta knock your teeth out, you're nothing but a common thief."

"Don't be mean and spoil everything, not now. I hardly knew what I was doing. I mean, one minute you're telling me you're a deacon or something out buying Bibles for Negroes, and the next minute you're hoppin' all over me like a rabbit. And then you rolled over and went to sleep with a great big ol' smile on your face, and there I was, all alone, lying awake and feeling all guilty, worried about my future—all of the sudden I just had the strangest feeling that when you woke up, you were gonna try to sweet-talk me into turning tricks for you—"

"Hey—"

"And that's no life for a young girl. And then I thought about your wallet sitting there in your coat pocket, looking all lonesome in there, and I thought, well, why not."

"Yeah, why not?" I said.

"I knew you couldn't stay mad at me. I'll pay you back, real soon."

"Sure. How's your Dad?"

"Now isn't that funny, I talked to him long distance the other day and he asked about you, too!"

"I'll bet he did. So I guess he lived, then."

She scanned the tables for celebrities while she talked. "He'll be in a wheelchair for a while, though."

"Kinda tough, trying to catch speeders in a wheelchair."

"He sounded a little bit down-in-the-mouth. Now you tell me something, 'Deacon Bob'—how did you go from sneaking underage girls across the border to taking Stacey Tilden dancing at the Cocoanut Grove in less than two weeks?"

"Clean living." What kind of perfume was that?

"Tell me, what's she like?"

"Who?"

"Stacey Tilden, silly, who else? I just love her, she's just the most glamorous woman there is! What's she really like?"

I thought about that one. "She's not what you'd expect." I wasn't exactly sure why, but I added: "I'll tell you what, though, why don't you and I get together later and I'll tell you all about her. I've got a suite here at the hotel—"

"Me, too!"

That stopped me. "How—"

"My new beau is putting me up here, while I get my movie career started. He's a very important man at Olympic Studios."

"I'll bet he is," I said. "Boy, you really are the ambitious type, aren't you?" I was looking at a bracelet on her wrist. Those were big rocks.

She drew her hand back down, and pulled away from me a bit. But the blue eyes were shining, proud.

"Like you said, I'm not your average girl."

"So this guy is gonna put you in the movies?"

"Isn't that exciting?" Her blue eyes glittered. "I knew I could do it! I'm in a movie! It's a picture about these Romans and gladiators and Jesus and the Christians."

"Which one do you play?"

"Well, it's not a big part or anything. I'm one of the Emperor's slave girls. But I've got a line!"

"Yeah, I know, I fell for it."

"No, really! I say, 'Mighty Caesar wakes!'"

I had to smile at that.

"I knew you were talented. Hey, why don't you come visit me up at my place later and I'll help you rehearse?"

"Honey, you know I'd love to come up and see you, but my new man is just so jealous. You really ought to try and find someone closer to your own age. Oh, by the way—thanks for that donut."

And she turned and danced away from me, wiggling her little silver-plated behind.

The band had gone from a slow torch song right into a hot jazz number. That, I guess, was a cue for Vera: she spun across the dance floor a few times by herself, perfect pirouettes.

The singer for the band smiled and gave her a hand up to the bandstand, and she took her place at the microphone like it belonged to her. Then she froze, real dramatic, like she suddenly had stage fright. That was a cute trick because it guaranteed that every eye in the place was on her when she put on a great big smile and began to sing.

It was a tune that Bunny Berigan's band used to do; it was called "Ten Easy Lessons." A funny number, and catchy; the lyrics were about how a guy who was a flop with dames could learn to be a Casanova in 'just ten easy lessons.' Vera's voice was good, and she looked like a little doll up there—hot stuff, but with lots of personality.

Then the lyrics part was over and the band came up. She began to dance, solo; very slinky, very sexy. The wild clarinet and the muted trumpet were warming things up for her, but they didn't need to: she was plenty hot, real good on her toes. And now she was back down on the dance floor, still doing her routine; you could tell this crowd was liking her and the number. Her dance was like something you'd see in Harlem; where the hell had she picked that up in Arizona? She could move, alright, and all any of us could do was watch, everybody gave her plenty of room—until this one skinny little balding runt steps out from the crowd to take her on…

He tapped out a few steps, she answered back with a few of her own—and then they were off, almost as though they'd rehearsed it. And they hadn't, of course; that was what made it so great. I realized then that the bald guy was Fred Astaire.

A few more fancy turns, the orchestra reached a crescendo, or whatever you call it—and she practically flew through the air, with him guiding her, coming down for a landing in his arms as the band hit that final chord.

And I found I was applauding like hell, like everybody else in the joint. And you were going to work her in the old badger game, I thought to myself, a bit ashamed. She pecked Fred Astaire on the cheek, exchanged a pleasantry with him, and then she turned and strode triumphantly back—towards that snake Jerry Fiske, who took her in his arms. He'd already dropped Stacey like a hot potato; Vera was the one to be seen with at this particular moment.

But Stacey came up fast and swiped him across the back of the neck with a perfumed scarf; she was scolding him. Fiske turned to Stacey again and bowed; now he was introducing the two of them.

Stacey had class, but right then she was looking at Vera as though Vera was yesterday's garbage (which to Stacey she was, I guess). Vera didn't seem to notice; she was so thrilled to meet her idol in the flesh that she grinned like a dummy and blabbed flattery.

Stacey didn't answer. She just looked at Vera with mild surprise, like she hadn't thought her capable of speech; then she said something to Fiske like Vera wasn't there. Fiske nodded; Stacey turned from them and started across the floor towards me, with poor Vera gaping after her like a fish. Fiske took Vera's arm and they left the floor, heading for Roth's personal corner of the jungle. Now I felt Stacey's arm slip into mine; but I was still watching Fiske and Vera. I saw Vera glance back at us—Stacey had spoiled her first moment in the spotlight.

"You know her?" Stacey was pissed; but not at me, this time.

"I know lots of people."

"I thought that might be your type," she said, "Cheap trash wrapped up in tin foil so you don't notice the smell." Then she smiled down benignly at one of the tables we passed, steering me back the way Fiske and Vera had gone.

"Where are we going?"

"To Jack Roth's table. Jerry invited us."

"You think that's smart, to introduce me to him?"

"It's necessary," she said, tightening her grip on my arm. "He'll have found out all about you by tomorrow morning, anyway. He pays people to spy on me, which means that they're spying on you, too."

A wall of guys in black tuxes, their backs to us, sealing off a round table from the rest of the world, heads inclined respectfully. One little guy in wire spectacles pops out, smiles at Stacey, tugs the sleeve of the guy behind him—and then the wall of tuxes parts in front of us, admitting us to the inner circle. A guy jumps up to offer his chair to Stacey, and that's when I see him: Jack Roth in all his glory, cigarette in hand, trailing silver smoke, raising his eyes to acknowledge the arrival of his leading lady.

Vera was seated next to him, and Jerry Fiske, officially her "date," was leaning across her, talking at Roth over the music. Roth wasn't listening; he was studying the two of us together. The eyes were hard but humorous, the face tan and tracked with crow's-feet. Sharp dresser, and still fairly handsome for a guy his age. Very trim; almost too healthy-looking. An old guy trying to stay young.

Vera looked up when she saw us, then lowered her eyes quickly. She fixed her hair and wouldn't look at us; whatever Stacey had said or failed to say to her still smarted. She sat close to Roth, but not touching; she knew the rules, obviously. I grinned at her, and then I nodded to Roth, very friendly and respectful. He was trim, sure, but he looked weird next to Vera. There was something corrupt about seeing all her soft white skin so close to those liver-spotted hands. Vera's hair was blonder these days and her dresses were more expensive—he was the one who'd done that; changed her to fit some pattern in his head. It made me a bit uncomfortable.

Fiske glanced up and saw Stacey, affecting delight. He made his way around the table and gave her a kiss on the cheek, which she received patiently—divorced, but still great friends, and isn't that civilized. There had been a chorus of greetings and wisecracks from the studio executives when we arrived; Stacey answered these with gracious smiles and polite laughter as she took her place at the table. A flunky seated next to her saw that she wasn't going to disengage herself from my arm, so he finally gave up his chair so I could sit down, too. He was grinning, but I'll bet inside he was cursing the day I was born.

I noticed that Roth was the only guy at the table who hadn't risen from his chair when Stacey appeared. That was cute: he knew, and was reminding Stacey that he knew. Subtle torture.

"Well, how's my favorite movie star?" says Roth, stubbing out his cigarette, never taking his eyes from her.

"Couldn't be better, Jack darling," music in her voice. "And how are we, this evening, your majesty?"

Chuckles all around from the yes men.

"You don't have to call me that when we're not at work, Stacey," he says; more chuckles all around. (It must be great carrying your own private audience around wherever you go so there's always somebody to laugh at your witticisms, I thought. I'll have to try that when I get rich.)

Roth gestured to Vera without looking at her, a wave of his cigarette. "This is Miss Vera Martin, Jerry's latest discovery."

Vera 'Martin'? Just a week ago her name was Vera Honecker. She looked up quickly at Stacey, her idol; but then down at the tablecloth again, humble.

"The ladies have already met," said Fiske. He sounded pleasant but he shot Stacey a warning glance.

Stacey was smiling beatifically at poor little Vera; smiling like a beautiful crocodile. "Such a darling child," she said. "So talented."

Roth ignored her tone; he was above all that show-biz sarcasm stuff. He said: "And who's this lucky young fellow, there next to you?"

"This is Mr. Hart. Mr. Hart, Jack Roth, president of Olympic Studios."

"Charmed, I'm sure," I said, rising a bit and reaching over the table to slip my hand into his. His hand was dry and calloused, like he'd been doing hard work. How could that be, I wondered? I nodded at Vera, grinning. "Miss Martin." She didn't blush; she smiled right back at me and nodded. Me, she could handle.

"You an actor, Mr. Hart?" said Roth, as I sat back down.

"No," I said. "I just like actresses, that's all."

And the boys gave me a little chuckle of my own; a courtesy chuckle out of deference to Stacey. From the way these guys standing around the table were reacting, you'd think we were all George Bernard Shaw or something. Vera was looking at me now. Watching me to see how I'd do with 'the great man'; or maybe she was trying to make Stacey jealous, get some of her own back.

"Everybody loves Stacey Tilden, Mr. Hart," says Roth, very gracious, and fervent agreement was mumbled. "She's a very popular young lady these days, isn't that right, Jerry?"

Fiske smiled. "I've always been fond of her."

"Not always," says Stacey.

"Now, now, children," says Roth, wagging his fatherly finger at them. "I'm sure we're all glad to see you out having a good time with a nice young gentleman, for a change, Stacey. You've been working too hard lately, and you lock yourself away in that big old castle all by yourself at the end of the day, like, like that…that princess in the story—"

"Rapunzel," said Fiske, studying the back of a matchbook.

"Yes," said Roth. "Rapunzel." He got thoughtful. "It's good to work, and it's good to work hard, but what's the point of working at all, if you can't enjoy life?"

The men around the table all seemed to be impressed with this novel observation; they nodded their agreement. They ordered some more drinks to demonstrate their enthusiasm for the studio's new "joie de vivre" policy.

"What line of work are you in, Mr. Hart?" says Roth, sounding like he didn't care. He might have been a bit more curious, I thought, given the fact that he'd just seen me dancing with his latest mistress. He drew a cigarette from the gold case and two lighters appeared in front of him instantly. "What do you do for a living?"

"I'm a cowboy," I said, without thinking. And then I grinned straight at him, wide as I could. Roth looked up at me over the cigarette that was being lit for him. From the corner of my eye I could see that Vera was smiling and looking away. Someone kicked me, sharp, under the table; that would be Stacey.

"A cowboy?" said an incredulous voice in the crowd of executives.

"Yeah, I thought you might do something outdoors," says Roth. He seemed genuinely interested, now. "You got quite a bit of color there."

"Yup," I said, warming to the theme, "I spend most every day, out there in the sun and the fresh air, ropin' and ridin'."

"That's good, hard work, isn't it?"

"Yup," I said. I saw Vera cover her face with her hands for a moment, and I glanced at Stacey next to me. She was trying to look bored but I knew that inside she was seething.

Roth didn't notice. "I make a lot of pictures with cowboys in 'em, but I don't think I've ever met a real one 'til tonight—and here in the Cocoanut Grove, too, how about that, boys?" General sensation among the boys.

"Well, I guess I never met no movie producer before either," I said, and they all laughed to beat the band. Except for Stacey, who leaned over as if to tell me a secret and hissed, "Stop being an ass."

"What kind of horse do you ride, Mr. Hart?" says Roth, pleasantly.

"A grrreat, big one," I said, and I sucked down my glass of champagne. That remark didn't get much of a laugh; the boys all knew Mr. Roth preferred straight answers to straight questions. Stacey kicked me once more, and I felt some blood starting to seep into my sock. But I was having fun, now. I wasn't sure what the point of all this was, but I was enjoying it.

"No, really, I'd like to know, what kind of horse?" said Roth. "I'm something of a horseman myself, in my small way. I'd like to know what you cowboys ride. I ride a quarter horse, myself."

"Well, me, I ride the whole thing," I said, and before Stacey could kick me again, I made a show of reaching for the champagne bottle across the table while stomping my shoe down on top of her slippered foot as hard as I could without actually getting out of my chair. She took a sharp breath, involuntarily drawing in the smoke she'd just exhaled from her own cigarette. (And several surrounding cigarettes, besides.)

Which started her on a bit of a coughing jag. It was ladylike and suppressed, but heartfelt. The studio flies acted all concerned and offered her solicitous pats on the arm, helpful hints to ease her discomfort.

Me, I grabbed the bottle from the ice bucket and poured myself another glass of champagne. Then I slapped her so hard on her bare back that her head snapped forward. "That's it, honey, bring it up—here, spit it into my hanky, yonder." I tossed my white silk handkerchief on the table in front of her, while I topped off her glass of champagne.

Roth wasn't happy, anymore. He was beginning to suspect something was up. "I think that maybe—"

"A palomino, Mr. Roth," I said, looking up at him and squinting. "A big old palomino, that's what I ride." I toasted him. "Your health, Mr. Roth." All hands reached for glasses to join in this toast; no one would miss a chance to toast the health of Mr. Roth. Vera raised her champagne with both hands and drank with the rest of us. She smiled at me from behind the glass; I was funny.

Mr. Roth nodded and received the salute graciously, but I knew he didn't like me much. Then he said, cool:

"A palomino. Really. I would think that would be a little small for cowboy work."

"What the hell is that supposed to mean?" I snapped, suddenly loud and offended. The group went silent as death; no one ever spoke to Jack Roth in that tone of voice; it just never happened. (It was just like a scene in one of his westerns.)

"I didn't mean anything by it," replied Roth evenly, not taking his eyes off me. "I just thought that you might need a bigger horse for ranch work."

"Oh, well, that's okay then," I said, and smiled; the tension melted away. "I thought you were saying something bad about my horse, Brown Thunder. And that's one thing I won't stand for from any man, Mr. Roth."

Stacey started to drag me up from the table; she was a bit off balance because of the bad foot I'd just given her.

"Come on, darling, this is my favorite song, let's dance," she said.

"You can say what you like about Miss Tilden, here, Mr. Roth," I went on, serious, "—but I won't stand for any rude remarks about my horse. Brown Thunder is a palomino, and I'm a pal of hers. And I have to be careful to close the gate of the corral at night, or I'm Appaloosa."

More silence; and well-deserved, I thought. Stacey was tugging me as gracefully as a lady could. Fiske was now at her side and was whispering something urgent in her ear.

"Of course, for short trips, I use a Shetland pony," I called back to Roth as I straightened my tie. "Or I take a cab. So long, toots," I said to Vera, and I whinnied real loud as I turned on my heel and took Stacey by the arm, off to the dance floor again.

18

We danced another two dances, some Latin kind of thing and then another slow torch song; I think it was "Smoke Gets In Your Eyes." And maybe it was the wine, but I had practically forgotten Stacey's true nature, or whatever you want to call it. She smelled like a girl, and she sure felt like a girl. Whatever she was, she was a lot more feminine than any of those nuns that used to beat the shit out of me once a week back in Catholic school.

"You nearly broke my foot," she hissed in my ear.

"Well, my ankle doesn't feel so good," I whispered back.

"I should have left you out there in the desert," she said.

"Let's not dwell on the past, babe," I said. "So I met your friend Roth, so what?"

"Not here," she said. "Let's go back to my table."

We did. I held her chair for her this time, by the way.

She ordered champagne, and then she turned to me. "What do you think?"

Took me by surprise, sort of. "What do I think of what?"

"Roth, stupid. And Fiske."

"I didn't care for either of them," I said. "What did you ever see in that guy?"

"Well, for one thing, he's a better dancer than you."

"Well, since we're being critical," I said, "I don't feel myself getting any wealthier than when I came in tonight…"

"Whether or not you end up wealthy depends entirely on whether you're as brave and as bright as you pretend to be."

"How's that?"

The favorite waiter came back with the champagne, fixed us up, and disappeared. It was spooky how these guys seemed to drop in and out of the palm trees.

Stacey watched him go, and then she asked me: "What do you know about safes?"

"What, you mean like, a safe, with a combination?"

"Yes."

"Not much," I said, truthfully. "Nothing, actually, it's not really in my line."

"What about your partners? Your friends, like the one who rang me up and told me not to leave you out there in the desert. Would they know anything about—"

"Maybe." I said. I kept her going, I wanted to hear the rest. The champagne sparkled gold in the glasses. I liked champagne; hadn't had it much before.

"'Maybe' isn't going to do it. We need someone who can get into a safe."

"We?" I said.

"Yes, we. Because Roth has a safe, at his home out in Beverly Hills, and inside it is something that can make all your little dreams of empire come true."

I said nothing.

She folded her hands in front of her. "He owns an estate; a big place, like mine. One of the rooms in the house is used as an office when he's out there. In that room is a wall safe, and in that safe are some business records."

"Records of what?"

"Records of illegal transactions. Jack has been involved in some very serious crimes. If the records were discovered, he could go to prison, or worse."

"What's worse than prison?"

"Did you ever hear of a man named Cornero?"

I shrugged.

"Or Siegel, Bugsy Siegel?"

I said nothing. Sure I'd heard of him, but what was he to her?

"Or a man named Lansky? There's another man; he lives out here. He has an Italian name, Drag-na—"

"What's this got to do with Roth?"

"You asked me what could be worse than prison." She took a sip of champagne.

"Roth is mixed up with Siegel and Lansky?"

She raised her eyebrows, and looked out at the dance floor again. Every crook who's ever set foot in Manhattan knew Bugsy Siegel and Meyer Lansky; the Bug and Meyer mob. The other names I'd never heard of; locals, probably. But I knew that Siegel and Lansky were strictly New York; they had nothing to do with Los Angeles, so far as I knew. This was all beginning to sound like bullshit to me.

"Look," I said, and I leaned over the table at her. "This 'mysterious' routine of yours is not going to cut it. I could forgive you for trying to have me killed, that's over and done with, but one thing I will not forgive is you trying to jerk me off with some crazy story—"

"Don't talk to me like that," she snapped, but this time I wasn't having it.

"I've put up with your pansy b.s. as long as I care to," I said, tossing my napkin on the table, and rising from the chair. "I want to see some serious dough out of you by tomorrow, or you're all over."

"If you walk out now, you get nothing," she said. "If you stay, you have a chance to be the big man you think you ought to be. You can expose me if you like, but then we'll both be finished. Because Roth will have you killed."

I'd stopped to listen to her again. If anybody was looking at us, they probably figured we were having a lover's spat.

"I'm not frightened of you, Mr. Hart, or anybody else in the world. I've lived my entire life on a tightrope. I don't scare anymore."

She sounded like one of her movies. Was this acting?

"I can prove what I say is true, if you let me," she said. "You and I will go on a little ride together after we leave this club. And when we come back, you'll be convinced that what I've told you is true."

I stood there making up my mind—and suddenly a whistle blew, and all hell broke loose. Every woman in the club seemed to be screaming all at once; screaming in delight. Every man (except me) seemed to be scrambling for the nearest palm tree. What the hell was this, a raid or something?

I watched, unbelieving, as the men in ties and tails leapt up onto tables, upsetting and shattering glasses, trying to gain height. Their girls jumped up and down in ecstasy, watching them and hugging each other, shrieking with laughter. Some of the men crawled onto the backs of men who were already scaling the tree trunks, using them as human ladders.

Now I saw what the men were after—descending from the palms at the top of the trees, were monkeys. They were big stuffed monkeys, like you might win at Coney Island if you knocked over the three milk bottles with a baseball. They had been rigged to shimmy down the palm trees at some signal from the management, and obviously the object of the game was for the male patrons to get one of these monkeys. And then to present the monkeys to their dates, judging from the fervent cheering coming from the skirts in the audience.

Two playboys burst through the bush near our table and scrambled up the tree behind Stacey, clawing their way up the side. One of them got shoved out of the way and jostled her—he stopped, bowed courteously by way of apology, and then turned again and ripped his companion's tailcoat straight up the back. He grabbed both ends of the coat and tore him off the tree like he was a piece of loose bark. Then he started up the tree himself and managed to seize the monkey by the tail. But his friend had recovered and was already biting him on the leg, the back of the calf, to be exact. The first guy screamed and relaxed his grip a bit, which enabled a third little playboy to reach through the fronds behind him and grab his monkey. Then things got ugly.

It looked like a pretty rugged go down on the club floor, too; I saw one guy snatch down a monkey by the tail and swing it triumphantly from half way up the palm tree. He looked too fat to be doing this kind of stuff, and his shirtfront had popped up. Then he was dragged down by the crowd, and I saw him sink under a wave of suits, monkey and all.

The lights had come up to help the folks riot more accurately; balloons and paper streamers filled the air, and the band blared. I thought to look across the room to Roth's table in the gallery, all lit up for the moment. He was having no part of this, wise fellow; he was simply sitting there smoking, chatting friendly with pretty little Vera, who seemed to be nodding and agreeing to his every word. A wreck of an accountant stumbled up to the table and handed Roth a monkey; Roth nodded his thanks and then turned and presented it to Vera, who hugged it to her chest, delighted.

Jesus H. Christ, I thought. I turned to Stacey, who sat back in her chair, looking fashionably bored. Behind her on the floor, the leg-biter and the suit-tearer were wrestling, trying to kill each other.

"Alright," I said. "Let's get out of here."

Stacey flicked her cigarette ash on the floor and looked up at me, a cat trying to look innocent. "Aren't you going to get me a monkey?" she asked.

"You've already got more monkeys than you can handle," I said, taking her by the elbow and hauling her up out of the chair.

We strolled out of the madhouse, arm in arm.

19

She went to fix herself up in the powder room; I told her I'd meet her in the lobby. I was getting sober now and I started thinking about Roth and Vera; there might be something useful there…

I felt a hearty hand clapping me on the shoulder.

"Mr. Hart!"

It was the hotel detective, greeting me like a long lost brother; a rich one.

"Oh, how ya doin'," I said, forcing a grin. "Your name was, ah, Munson?"

"Benson."

"Right, sorry, Detective Benson." (Cops, real or no, love it when you call them by their title.)

"That's quite alright, sir. A friend of yours was in here earlier, Mr. Hart. He picked up the envelope you left for him, and he left a package for you, too." He went and got it out from behind the desk; a large brown paper parcel.

I put it up on the desk and tore open the butcher's paper—it was my red-checked 'clown' suit. Very funny, Sam. He was trying to remind me not to get above myself, staying here at the fancy hotel and throwing our money around.

"Have a boy take this up to my room, willya, Benson?"

"Sure, Mr. Hart."

I had an idea. "Oh, by the way—I need somebody to do a little police work for me tonight, can you help me out?"

"Well," he says slowly, "That depends on what it is…"

"Oh, nothing bad, nothing illegal." He nods his head at this, approving. "There's a young lady staying here, her name is Vera Martin." He smiled at the name. "You know who I mean?"

"Sure, I do, every guy in the hotel knows her—" he corrected himself real quick—"I mean, no disrespect or nothing, not 'cause she's a—'cause she's a real looker, you know—"

"I know exactly what you mean," I said, reassuring, clapping him on the back. "The thing is, I kind of want to find out something about her, and I don't quite know how to go about it."

"What is it you need to know?"

"Well, she's out there in the club right now, and I need to know when she leaves—"

"The club usually breaks up just about now," he says, looking at his watch—

"—And who she leaves with, tonight."

The eyes got a bit beady, cop's eyes. He said nothing.

"You know, sorta keep an eye on her as she comes out of the club, see whether she goes straight back up to her room, she's got a suite up on the fifth floor—"

"Tenth floor."

"Oh, yeah, right," I said, making a note of that info. "Anyway, I wanted to find out whether she goes up to her room after she leaves the club, or whether she goes out on the town again, with anybody."

"Somebody from Olympic Studios," he says. Wise guy.

"Maybe. I'd like to know who, what time—the make of the car, if she leaves in one. You could leave a message for me at the desk. Anonymous, of course. Could you do that for me?"

I looked him in the eye, man to man, and grasped his hand firmly in mine, shaking it, so he could palm the bill.

He took off his hat and glanced down in his hand; and then he smiled at me through his yellow choppers and said, "Sure, why not?"

"Thanks, Benson, you're a pal." He was staring at something behind me, like he was hypnotized. I turned.

The Queen of Hollywood, back from the powder room. Waiting for me.

The Bentley was out front; I held the door for her this time and she got in. It still felt funny to feel all the eyes on me; admiration spilling over from Stacey to me. The late night crowd staggering out of the club and into the street; a couple of funny-looking fat ladies with autograph books were still around. The doorman had done a little blocking for us, and we managed to get out of there without talking to anyone.

We drove out into the night. "Where are we going?" I shouted above the Bentley's engine.

"San Pedro," she shouted back.

It sounded familiar, but I didn't know how to get there.

"You'll have to give me directions."

She said nothing, but when I turned my head to look at her she nodded 'yes.' She wouldn't look at me, she just stared straight ahead. She was concentrating on the road, or maybe on something else entirely. Every so often she'd tug on my sleeve and show me where to turn; pantomime, sort of.

All I knew was we were heading south; away from the studios and the nightclubs and through the low rent residences—well-groomed cottages and bungalows, planted among groves of palm trees and oil wells.

Yeah, that's right, oil wells. They were all over the town back then; you could see them up against the blue night like black skeletons, competing with the tall palms for a piece of the sky. There was oil all over Los Angeles, Sam had told me; you'd even see the wells on studio lots, sometimes. One house we passed had one on the front lawn, towering over the bungalow like it was the owner's very own Eiffel Tower.

I lost track of where the city began and ended. The neighborhoods were endless, and at night you couldn't tell one from another. This place we were driving through now might be a different town altogether. I was wondering if we were lost; we'd already driven a good twenty miles. And then there was a sign: San Pedro. I smelled water in the air, somewhere close by—and then I remembered: this was where Sam had said they kept their yachts. The movie people, I mean. A rich kid's marina. We passed another sign that said "P&O" The P&O wharf, some kind of big dock or something. It didn't look like much in the dark; long and flat and black, with rows of telephone poles that stretched along the road between us and the sea.

Then I saw the shapes of long sailboats, and sloops, and, who am I kidding, I don't know jack shit about boats. But they looked private and expensive, sitting out there in the dark water. Stacey told me to slow down. The lighting wasn't very good and I began to get a little queasy again; what if this was another of Stacey's setups? I got a grip on myself and decided it wasn't; she wouldn't have come in person if it was. It didn't figure she'd try to kill me again so soon; she couldn't get her precious little jar back without me.

She pointed out one of the smaller rows of boats and told me to park. I did, and took a look around. There was the small dock in front of us with a few boats tied up; off to our right were the bigger docks. There didn't seem to be many people around—some fellas loading or unloading something by the light of a lantern on the big dock farthest away.

Out on the horizon, across the water, was a long row of lights. It looked like a far-away highway, built out in the middle of the black ocean. There was nothing beyond, just night; that didn't make sense, the lights had to be sitting on something... Then I got it; it was a seawall, a barrier, to protect the inner harbor against the big waves or storms or something. A boat was rounding it; a fishing boat, maybe.

I turned and saw that Stacey was gone. I looked quickly around; she had already walked out onto the small dock and was waiting for me, watching me impatiently. She looked very out of place there; the evening dress and the wrap and jewelry and all.

When she saw that I was following her again she turned and went on. We passed some docked sailboats and went out to the end. She didn't look back again. What's that Greek story, the one about the guy with the harp who leads his bride out of the underworld, without ever looking back? It was like that, only in reverse—there was nothing but empty blackness out at the end of the dock.

I caught up to her. I heard her rustling keys in her tiny evening bag. Then she stopped, and held the keys out to me. I took them, and she pointed at something behind me, all imperious, like the wicked queen.

I turned and saw it, tied up at a big post—a little boat, a motorboat. Well, not that little, really; it was a launch, or a runabout, with a compartment in the back for passengers and an American flag hanging off a pole at the back. Real fancy. (I must confess, though, I was a little disappointed; I'd been hoping we were headed for one of those big fancy movie star yachts.)

"Untie it," she said. The big rope around the post was tight, but a few tugs and it came free.

"Now get in," she said. And I climbed down the little wooden ladder and tried to get my balance on the side or the gunwall or gunwale of the boat or whatever you call it. It wasn't easy, the thing rocked like hell and the wood was slick and varnished as shiny as my shoes. Real high class stuff, but totally impractical.

Still, I made it into the driver's compartment okay. I sat down in front of the wheel and grinned proudly up at Stacey where she stood looking down on me from the dock.

"Help me down, you idiot," she snapped at me, and I rose quickly, a little embarrassed that I'd forgot she was coming along. I tugged on one of the smaller ropes that still held the boat to the dock—it was secure, so I kind of guided Stacey down as best I could, taking her gloved hand while trying to keep my balance.

At the bottom rung of the ladder she stopped, and she looked up at me, angry; like I was supposed to know what to do next. I obviously didn't, so she said:

"Pick me up, you fool! Carry me!"

"What, into the boat?"

"I've got heels on!"

Well, I guess it would be tough for anybody to do this in heels, so I picked her up—she was light as a feather, she probably never ate a thing—and I swung her into the boat, nearly dropping her on her head when the boat rocked suddenly. She plopped down flat on her ass in the seat next to me, and she gave me an awful look; I guess her Japanese guys did it better.

"Cast off," she said.

I knew what that meant, anyway. I crawled out over the windshield and onto the 'hood', and undid the smaller ropes. We began to drift off into the choppy little waves off the dock. The tux didn't seem that warm to me out here on the water; I wished I'd brought a sweater.

I jumped like a startled cat when I felt the roar of the engine beneath me; Stacey had turned the key in the ignition.

We were in "neutral", I guess you call it, but the boat was spinning a bit. I scrambled back over the windshield and into the driver's side again.

"Have you ever driven a runabout?"

"Who hasn't?" I said, all carefree, spinning the wheel around.

When nothing happened, I felt her gloved hand guiding mine to something in the middle of the floor between us—the gearshift, or the throttle, maybe. I pushed it and we went forward, with a lurch and a splash, but then slow and steady, once I figured it out.

We picked up speed, and Stacey was doing her "pointing routine" again—out beyond the seawall, she seemed to be telling me. We were going at a pretty good clip now, still in the harbor for the moment, and I smiled—I was tired, but this was kind of fun; at least as much fun as the Bentley. I'd have to get myself one of these babies, too, when Stacey finally paid off. She reached across me without taking her eyes off the black water ahead, and flicked something on the dashboard—electric running lights.

I felt pretty good now, getting my second wind from the fresh air—let's see what this baby will do, I thought, and I gave it full throttle as we started to close in on the end of the sea wall. The tip of the boat was forced up out of the water by speed and the rushing air, and we seemed to be skating along with only the rear engines in the water, flying across the harbor in the dark. Stacey didn't like that, I felt her pounding me on the arm, lady-like but insistent, trying to get me to slow down—

And then we hit the open sea and the big waves, and the boat got tossed up into the air like a bushel basket of apples—we hung dead in the air for a split second; my ass left the driver's seat—and then, bam! we came straight down onto the water like a safe hitting the pavement. The engine cut out, and I felt my back teeth almost come loose.

I didn't think that Stacey could come up with any more dirty looks to give me, but there it was—I guess that's why she gets the big money. The splash from the landing had soaked her wrap, and she took it off, muttering something under her breath.

"Sorry," I said.

"Can't you be just a little bit considerate?" she snapped. "Howard Hughes gave me this boat."

"Stop name-dropping," I said, turning the key in the ignition. It choked, but it started again, and I raised my eyebrows in triumph, looking at her. She wasn't amused.

"Lead on," I cried, and she pointed off to our right, directing me to follow along the outer side of the seawall.

I took it slow. We chugged along, keeping a fair distance from the lights on the wall. I kept looking out at the horizon—the night was clear and I could make out the lights of a boat or two: trawlers, I guessed. I took a look at Stacey, and I saw that she was keeping an eye on the wall, alongside us. She's counting the lamps, I realized.

She turned, saw me watching her, and brushed a lock of hair away from her forehead. She said:

"There's an anchor stowed in the back. I'll take the wheel. Climb in the back and drop the anchor."

I did as I was told, crawling over the partition between the compartments to the back of the boat. Men's evening wear was definitely not the right attire for this kind of work; my shoes felt tight and slippery at the same time, and I had to take off my jacket to free up the anchor.

But it went over the side easy enough, and it didn't seem to sink very far before the line went slack—it wasn't all too deep, here.

I was downright chilly. I slipped my coat back on and climbed up into the front again. Stacey had already cut the engine; she was the one who watched the horizon, now.

"What happens next?" I asked her.

"We wait."

"What are we waiting for?"

"Money," she smiled, and she looked at me, knowing I'd react. Boy, she had me pegged, alright.

"Keep your eyes open," she said. "They'll be coming soon."

We sat there in silence for a moment, and she lit a cigarette. She saw me studying the moon.

"You enjoy beautiful things, Mr. Hart?"

"Yeah, I guess."

"But you can't afford them."

"The moon belongs to everyone," I said. "And not all of us can be rich and beautiful, right?"

"I didn't start out that way," she said. "As you well know."

"No, I guess you didn't," I said, and I toasted her. "You're a self-made—whatever you are."

That stung; she looked up at me, giving me movie actress look number one-hundred-and-eighteen: "You've wounded me, sir—but I can take it, and nobly, too."

"I must seem comical to you."

"No more than anybody else. I try to see the humor in everybody. Else."

"It's a very evil way of living. The ones who don't know seem stupid and unappreciative. The few who do know are petty sadists and blackmailers, like yourself. The illusion is practically impossible; I can never let my guard down, not for a second. I probably should have gone insane years ago. Of course, I would have gone insane, anyway."

This last comment was interesting to me. "What do you mean by that?"

She kept her eyes on the dark horizon. "Some people like me talk about being women trapped in the body of men. But I am a woman; I've never been anything else. Why should some stupid, superfluous flesh make any difference? There was never a moment of doubt. My mother knew it; my father was the one who didn't understand. He wasn't cruel, but he told me that God doesn't make mistakes. He tried to change me, but he failed. After he died, I began to work on this illusion"—that word again, I noticed—"so that the world could accept a fact that my mother and I had already accepted."

So you cut your own nuts off? I thought to myself, but I didn't say it out loud. I wanted her to keep talking about it; she might spill something useful. Also, I was curious—I still didn't quite believe it myself, especially now that I'd met her in person.

"My mother was beautiful, and she taught me how to be beautiful. It was very difficult; it's a profession, or an artistic discipline. Your body is the canvas; you learn how to design for it.

"That's why I feel sorry for all those stupid, fat little housewives who go to see my movies and write me all those silly letters. They've never realized that you can't just *be* what I am; you have to make yourself that way. Every day, make yourself into something that men will admire and want to own.

It's not something that you can get out of a makeup kit or a diet or a dress designer. Those are only the pieces of a craft.

"You have to study, and criticize yourself, and watch, and never relax for an instant, and feel every eye that's watching you, and know what they're thinking. And there is actual, physical pain. A kind of self-torture, like foot-binding..."

She looked at me. "Do you know what castrati are?"

I'm well-read, I gave it a shot. "Some kind of, a, a singer—"

"Boys who sing," she said, looking away again. "A long time ago, after the Renaissance. The boys would be castrated, so that they could always sing like angels. Their voices were perfect, superior to the voices of women. They were the most prized possessions of the European royalty, rich and sought after.

"I was very young when I decided that I would recreate myself as a beautiful woman. That would be my art. And I would be an actress, a great actress—because if I was artist enough to create this reality, the reality of a beautiful woman, then I could create any reality that anyone desired.

"My cheekbones were wrong. I wrapped a lead pipe in some newspaper and broke them. I told the doctor what I'd done and that I'd do it again if he didn't set them higher, give my face some definition. He did it.

"And the other thing. Why should I let two ugly little sacs of flesh at the end of my body inhibit my performance? They weren't ever really a part of me, anyway, except physically."

I was staring at her, and I heard myself saying:

"But you still have your dick, though, right?"

"Of course I kept my dick, what do you think I am, crazy?" She stubbed out her cigarette. "I feel sexual pleasure, anytime I want, probably more than you or any woman does. It's just of a different quality, that's all."

"But who with?" I said. I figured it was okay to ask; she'd raised the subject, after all.

"I can have my pick of any man in the world," she said, matter-of-fact.

"But what difference does that make?" I said. The champagne was sneaking up on me again. "I mean, sure you're a doll"—I saw her smile when I admitted that—"but as soon as you get undressed, well, the cat's out of the bag, right?"

"Feeling the fullness of a woman's love is not simply a matter of dressing and undressing."

"But what about when a guy wants to, you know?"

"Minds like yours are the reason I had to escape the middle class," she says.

"But, I mean—"

"Oh, if you must know.... I give the best head in Hollywood, alright? Now do you understand?"

Wow. That's quite a claim. But I pressed on:

"But no guy ever asks you to—"

"This will surprise you, Mr. Hart, but a man who is fortunate enough to be on the receiving end of the best oral gratification he's ever had in his life, from one of the most beautiful women in the world, doesn't tend to ask lots of questions."

She had me there. Kind of a conversation stopper, though. I thought it over for a moment, and then I asked: "But what do you do on the second date?"

"There never is a second date." She flicked her cigarette over the side of the boat. "After Jerry betrayed me to Roth, I swore I'd never let any man get that close to me again. They aren't worth it."

Now she was just talking to the night. I found myself staring at her again. Her profile, lit up by the soft lights of the dashboard; glowing like a studio portrait.

She sure was pretty, alright. It was kind of creepy. To be completely honest, I did want her. But it was so creepy, because it wasn't like being with a real woman or a real man.

Or a real anything, for that matter. Sitting there in the moonlight, the boat gently rocking in the water, and next to you is this unreal being, like a spirit or a vampire or beautiful monster or something—and you want her sexually.

I don't think I can exactly explain it. But it was creepy; my flesh crawled because I was repelled and excited by her at the same time.

A bell tolled nearby, and I looked, but couldn't see anything.

"Saved by the bell, Mr. Hart," said Stacey, and I realized she'd known what I was thinking about her while we were sitting there in silence. It was kind of scary to me, for some reason.

20

She pressed on the dashboard. An electric horn; two sharp toots in response to the bell.

In the black, two spotlights leapt to life, bright and white; maybe a hundred yards off. Another boat. I saw Stacey's lovely face, looking a bit worried.

"Who are they?" I asked. She didn't say anything; she was scrunching herself down in her seat, trying to hide below the dashboard. It must have been tough, in that tight dress.

"Where are you—"

"Never mind," she said. "They mustn't see me with you. I usually send my servants to do this errand for me, but you've incapacitated them."

I half-rose in my seat and looked out at the boat, practically invisible behind the white lights.

"Should I—"

"Just stay put and keep an eye on them," she said, from below.

I watched, but I couldn't see anything. Then I heard it; an enormous splash, something large and heavy had been tossed over the side of the other boat.

The spotlights went out. All was dark again, except for the light coming from the beacons on the seawall behind us.

Stacey hauled herself back up into her seat and reached for the wheel of the runabout. She turned the key and the starter screeched; the engine jumped and the boat chugged forward, barely in gear.

"Keep an eye out for it," she said.

"For what?"

"A box," she said. "A large wooden crate."

It didn't take long to find it. She flipped a switch and a little searchlight came on; it was mounted on the front of the boat and it scoured the choppy water in front of us.

I saw it first. A big wooden crate, like she said; kind of like the boxes you pack for shipping stuff overseas. She cut the motor and spun the wheel, pointed the boat towards the crate.

"There's a hook in the back," said Stacey, watching the crate like it was her very own child. "Get it and use it to drag the box into the boat."

"Why me?" I asked, for no particular reason.

"You're the one who wants to be rich."

True, I thought, as I climbed into the back and felt around the floor and the sides of the compartment. I couldn't see it but I could feel it; a heavy metal bar. I carefully pulled it out—a longshoreman's hook, I think it was.

Something banged against the mahogany side of the runabout; I looked over the edge and there it was, scraping the boat, running alongside—

"Hurry!" said Stacey. I stood and swung my arm over and sank the big iron hook into the wood; it splintered and stuck.

"Can you manage it by yourself?" she said, but I already had the crate up the gunwale; it was goddamn heavy, but my adrenalin and my curiosity were up now. I used my body weight to pull it up over the side and into the boat. I let it drop onto the carpeted flooring.

Stacey cut the motor and the searchlight, and she was swinging her little self over the partition to come into the rear of the boat with me. "Go on, open it," she said.

I was tearing wooden slats off of it—inside was some kind of rubberized canvas cloth, made to repel water. I fumbled with it for a moment; then she brushed my hands away and reached under a fold—I heard something rip, and then it opened, spilling out from the bulging tear in the wrapping paper. It was dark, and I couldn't see it, but I knew that smell. Money.

The bills were bound into tight little stacks, hundreds and hundreds of little stacks, overfilling the case. I held a stack right up to my nose so that I could read it in the reflected light from the seawall—fifties, maybe an inch thick of fifties—

I hadn't been able to pay attention to what Stacey was saying until just now.

"...Roth is partners with some gamblers; men from Chicago and New York. They finance these gambling barges; floating casinos that do business out at sea off San Pedro."

This was a thousand in fifties, this one little stack right here in my hand—

"Every evening, a launch leaves a gambling barge with the night's proceeds. A 'drop', they call it."

"You do this every night?" I asked; I couldn't take my eyes off the stack of fifties; at least a thousand in this one stack, and there were hundreds of stacks—

"Roth uses different people, all over town. Different points for the drops. I'm one of the people he uses."

"Why you?"

"He knows I won't talk. The police don't bother celebrities, and they wouldn't suspect someone like me of doing gamblers' dirty work for them." She looked at the seawall, drifting closer to us, bit by bit. "I send my servants out to pick up the crate once or twice a month, when the phone call comes in."

"What happens after you get it?" I picked up two more stacks; a stack of twenties, another bunch of fifties...

"I fly it down to my ranch in Mexico," she said, bored. "Then a Mexican gentleman arrives at the ranch and takes it from me. And then it comes back into the United States. Processed as foreign box office receipts by studio accounting." She lit another cigarette and watched me going through the stacks of cash, counting and estimating. "Sometimes the barges drop the money in Mexico and I fly it back up to Los Angeles, and Roth keeps it. A straight skim."

"Whaddya mean, 'skim'?" I said, sufficiently recovered to converse again.

"Skim, isn't that the word?" she said. "I mean that Roth and his partners don't split it with the gentlemen back in New York and Chicago. They take it off the top."

"You're kidding," I said. "Roth is stealing dough from Siegel and Lansky?"

"You have heard of them, then," she said.

I sat back on a seat cushion, a stack of fifties grasped tightly in each hand. I couldn't bear to put them down. But I was beginning to understand, now.

"You want to rat him out," I said.

I couldn't see the expression on her face; her back was to me. "No," she said, "I want *you* to 'rat him out' for me."

"And why would I do that?" I said, kind of suspecting the answer.

"Because you can blackmail me, and perhaps get twenty thousand, and perhaps get your neck broken by Roth's goons," she said evenly, "Or, you can blackmail Jack Roth, who will pay you the million you're after, in cash and land. To keep this little secret of his a secret."

I was looking at the dark piles of money, spread out over the floor of the boat now.

"You think he'd pay?"

"He's a coward, as well as a thief," she said, sounding like her movies again. "He's terrified of those men in New York, but he needs the cash to run his precious studio. He'll pay you, if you can keep him from killing you."

"Why don't you try and shake him down yourself, then?"

"Oh, darling, that would be so bad for my career. Besides, I'm rather inexperienced at this kind of thing. You're the professional."

I thumbed one of the stacks, a beautiful rippling noise over the sound of lapping waves. The sea was considerably calmer now.

"Well?" said Stacey Tilden.

I leaned back. "I'll have to think about it."

"Oh, yes, you must think about it."

And then she turned her head, and I could see that the goddess was smiling again.

She knew it; I was hooked, alright.

21

We motored back around the wall and into the bay again, and sat there for a half hour or so while she explained things.

Roth had a wall safe out at his place in Beverly Hills. It contained many precious items, including business papers that would prove that he was laundering this gambling money for those gangsters back East. On two separate occasions in the past year, Stacey had been ordered to bring the cash straight to Roth's place. Both times she'd talked her way into his study, ostensibly to talk movie business and beg for a bigger allowance.

Actually, she hung around because she was curious about what Roth would do with all this cash on hand. As he lectured her, he'd separate the evening's take into piles and make entries on a legal pad; when he was all done the cash and his notes went into a wall safe. It was concealed behind a big painting of Roth's family, which hung on the wall behind his desk. (Roth had seen this safe-behind-the-painting setup in one of the old silent thrillers he produced; he'd thought it very original.)

Did he open and shut the safe himself? Yes.

Stacey said the safe also held documents that proved her original gender; Roth had shown some of them to her one night when he was feeling particularly sadistic. Stacey wanted those back.

Of course, she wasn't naïve enough to think that destroying the stuff would protect her from disclosure; she was sure there were copies somewhere else. But the file on Stacey also included information about Fiske and proved the special understanding they'd had with each other during their marriage. Stacey wanted to destroy Fiske; the stuff in the safe would enable her to do that. I opined that she'd be smarter to use any dirt she got on Fiske to shake him down for more money. I understood that she hated him for selling her out to Roth, but after all, business was business. Then she explained (without looking at me) that during their marriage Fiske had taken photos of her while she slept—naked. I understood a little better, then, why she hated him so much.

We motored slowly back to the pier. I kept shooting sorrowful glances over my shoulder as Stacey was gathering up the cash. I wanted to know more about Roth, but she couldn't tell me much, really. She knew that Roth and his older brother had started out as bookkeepers in New York; they'd built the studio up from a chain of nickelodeons they'd bought before the war. Roth was married and had a few kids, but he kept the wife and family out of town as much as possible. The only time he saw them is when he needed to have a picture taken to sell the public on the studio's 'family' image. That figured, a wife and kids here in town would cramp his style; the guy thinks he's a ladies' man.

While I was tying the launch up at the pier, I wondered out loud if his family represented a weak spot; if there was something there we might use as leverage. Stacey didn't think so. She'd met the wife once and she had seemed scared to death of Jack; just like the folks here in town.

I got the money up the side of the pier from the boat; Stacey didn't see any need to help out with the heavy lifting. Wouldn't be ladylike, I guess. She did pull up the Bentley onto the pier so that I could stuff the box in the back; it brought a lump to my throat to close the trunk on all that fresh, untraceable cash.

We drove back into Los Angeles. It was getting very late, and Stacey said we had one more stop to make tonight before we were through. We had to stop once to wait for an endless freight train to trundle by, crossing the tracks in the road in front of us. I wanted to know more. I asked Stacey more questions about the money in the back of the Bentley.

She'd said that Roth kept her on a really tight leash, financially; I asked if she'd ever considered sneaking an extra couple of thousand out of the weekly take before handing it over to Roth. Would anybody really miss it?

She looked at me and smiled that incredible smile. "Are you asking for me, or for yourself?"

"Both of us, I guess."

She looked up at the train, sliding by in the night, the low rumble of a dinosaur parade. "You wouldn't be stealing from Jack," she said. "You'd be stealing from his friends back East, and in Chicago. I told you, technically Jack's just a, a 'bagman', I believe that's the term. The gamblers do the real accounting, over the telephone and by wire. The rest of us are just beasts of burden."

I got the point; if money was missing from the evening's take, the gangsters would come after Roth, who'd come after Stacey, who'd fink on me, or on anybody else who took so much as a dime out of the kitty—so I'd better just forget about the whole thing. This was too bad, I thought; I had a whole family of hotel managers, bellboys, and hotel detectives to support back at the Ambassador. They'd be very disappointed.

The last car went by, and we were free to go again. We were headed north, now, and I realized where we were going: the airport. The one where I'd gotten my lift down to her place in Mexico.

There were lights still burning in some of the offices when we rolled up onto the tar. I pulled up to park, but Stacey stopped me and made me pull out onto the runway.

Then I saw it; that pretty little airplane, waiting for us at the end of the runway. "Flash the headlamps," said Stacey, watching the plane. I did, and the plane put on some little lights of its own. That big-nosed pilot was probably sitting there in the cockpit, waiting for the evening's delivery. A bang, and an electrical whine from the plane: he was starting up the engines, getting them warm.

"I hope you're not expecting me to get on that thing again," I said, slowing down a bit.

"I wouldn't dream of it, sweetie," she said. "I know how you hate the country. What are you doing?"

I'd stopped the car; we were still quite a ways off from the plane. It occurred to me that the pilot or someone else in that plane might have a gun.

"You can take it from here," I said, hopping out of the front seat. I opened up the back of the Bentley and hauled out the crate; I dropped it onto the runway.

She got out, too, and she was pissed. "And what am I supposed to do, walk the rest of the way with that on my back?"

"Why don't you toodle on over to your airplane and get flyboy to help you? Oh, that's right, you're wearing heels. Here, I'll make it a little lighter for you." I knelt and pulled out one thick stack of fifties from inside the crate. I waved it at her and slipped it into my jacket pocket.

"You're insane," she said. "Roth will kill you if he finds that much missing."

"No," I said, closing the trunk and walking back around the car. "He'll kill you, because you're not going to sic him on me—if you're really serious about us pulling off this safe job together." I slipped in behind the wheel of the car and patted my chest, where the money was. "I got expenses, too, you know. I'm a big tipper."

"You're a bastard!"

"Yeah, well, you're a sissy. If you find yourself running a little short this week, just do what I always do—sell some more of your jewelry."

I put her car in gear and spun around on the tarmac, leaving her standing there to admire the coming dawn. Or maybe she watched me go; I didn't look back.

I couldn't bear to say goodbye to all that cash for good—the little stack in my pocket was warming my heart, but I could tell that it was already lonely for its departing brothers.

22

It's tough getting money out of a woman. Y'ever notice that? Any kind of a woman; even a "woman" like Stacey. They're tight-fisted, and that's not a very appealing quality. Of course, men have their faults, too. But most women are cheap, let's face it.

I left the car in front of the Ambassador with one of the guys at the door. The sun was starting to come up and I was yawning; the doorman gave me a sly wink as if to say, "you devilish young playboy, you, sir." I winked back; no reason to burst his bubble.

The lobby was pretty empty at this time of morning; a few cleaning types puttering around, some Southern-sounding guy disputing his bill. I didn't see any familiar faces behind the desk; the hotel dick had called it a night and Herman wouldn't come on for a while yet, being the day manager. Too bad; I had more work to do. I was pretty tired, but there's no rest for the wicked.

"Any messages for me? The name is Hart."

The sleepy-looking desk clerk went back to the mail slots. He returned with a couple of notes from the switchboard.

The first was a call that came in at about eleven p.m. the night before: "Thanks for the dough." Unsigned; that would be Sam. Didn't know he was so hoity-toity, writing thank-you notes like that.

The next note was also unsigned, but this one was typed; I knew immediately that it was from Benson, the hotel dick I'd asked to keep an eye on Vera. He'd typed the note because he didn't want the management to spot his handwriting; it's not nice to spy on hotel guests, even if it's for other hotel guests. The style told me that Benson was undoubtedly a former cop:

"Your young friend left in a chauffeur-driven silver Rolls Royce at about one-fifteen a.m. She was accompanied by the owner of the Rolls and his employee; both of whom are associated with O.S. The chauffeur was interviewed prior to the threesome's departure. The chauffeur revealed that their destination was the owner's home in Beverly Hills; he also asserted that your young friend would not be returning to the Ambassador this evening because she would be spending the evening with the owner of the Rolls."

Perfect. Thank you, Benson, that's another *Jackson* for you. I walked across the lobby and picked up the phone.

"Ambassador Hotel."

"Yes, I've got an important message for Miss Vera Martin, she's staying at your hotel."

"Who is calling, please?"

"This is Wilfred—" I looked around the lobby, then up at the ceiling—"Wilfred Chandelier, I'm a director at Olympic Studios, she's doing a picture with us up there."

"I'll ring her room, Mr.—"

"No, no, no! Heavens no, don't wake the poor girl, she needs all the sleep she can get. I just want to make sure that she receives a very important message before she shows up at the studio this morning."

"We can deliver the message to her room and slip it under her door—"

I went silent on her for a moment, and then—"Oh, well, I suppose that will have to do."

"How do you spell your name Mr. Chandelier?"

I spelled it, as best as I could.

"And what is the message?"

"Tell her—are you writing this down?"

"Yes."

"Tell her that her line has been changed, it's no longer 'Mighty Caesar wakes!' It's now 'Mighty Caesar sleepeth!' Have you got that?"

"Sleep-eth?"

"Yes, sleep-eth!" I spelled that, too.

"See that she gets that at once, will you?"

"Yes, sir, Mr. Chandelier, I'll send it up to her room right away."

The hotel dick had let on that Vera's rooms were up on the tenth floor; I took the elevator up and waited. It wasn't long before the elevator stopped there again and a bellboy got off, bearing a silver tray with a card on it. I fell in silently behind him and followed him down the hallway, noting the numbers on the doors of the rooms we passed. He stopped at a door ahead of me; didn't knock, just knelt, took the message off the tray, and put it under the door. I didn't stop; I just kept on going down the hall to pass him without looking back. He probably noticed me when I went by, but since I didn't turn around he wouldn't have a face to go with the suit.

I rounded a corner and waited. A moment went by and I heard the elevator door close. I gave it another minute to be sure, but it was tough being patient: This floor was quiet now, but people would be getting their wake-up calls soon.

The lock on her door was nothing; I was through it in less time than if I'd had the key. I closed the door behind me, not bothering to put the chain on—I felt pretty safe; Vera and Roth had had a late night and they'd be sleeping in together somewhere out in Beverly Hills this morning. She wouldn't be back for a while. All I had to worry about were chambermaids, and they wouldn't be around for a while.

I was a little miffed; Vera's suite was nicer than mine. They'd given her a bigger fruit basket, too, how did she rate that? She hadn't slipped Herman a fifty for it, that's for sure. I read the card: "Eat fruit and stay young and beautiful -- J."

J for Jack. How nice, how fatherly. I put the card in my pocket. There was no signature, but it might be helpful if I had to copy his handwriting sometime.

The suite was messy, stockings on the floor, shoes and clothes scattered about—housekeeping wasn't one of Vera's talents. But that was okay by me; it would make it harder for her to figure out that someone had gone through her room. And that was what I was there to do.

I started with the bedroom, the phone by the bed. This is where people take quick messages and write themselves reminders when they're sleepy and off-guard. There were no notes on the hotel stationery next to the phone, but there were a couple of crumpled up names and phone numbers in the wastebasket next to the night table. These would be numbers Vera had scribbled down the night before, since the wastebasket was emptied every day.

Like every other actress I've ever met, Vera read the movie magazines. These were scattered around the room; one lay on top of the bed. I picked it up and flipped through it, and sure enough, there was a scribble in pen on one of the pages. People do that when they're talking on the phone and don't want to get up to find paper. I grabbed a piece of paper and copied the number from the margin.

Next I went through the drawers by the night table; always a good place to find good stuff. A couple of ladies' things, creams and disgusting ointments—I stuck my finger in one jar of oily stuff and wiggled it around. Sometimes people hide gems or rings in there, and I knew that Vera had been getting little presents from Roth recently. All I got for my trouble was a slimy finger.

But here was an address book, which is solid gold for a guy like me. I went through it quickly and copied out some numbers and addresses on hotel stationery.

It took less than five minutes to get the numbers I thought would be helpful—her family back in Arizona, Roth's private line at Olympic, his number and address in Beverly Hills, Fiske. I also got the initials of a couple of people who seemed to live out in Beverly Hills. She'd obviously bought this address book since she got into town; there were very few Arizona numbers.

Maybe I should explain; I wasn't planning to use anything against Vera, herself. (Unless she made trouble for me.) I was looking for stuff on Roth, and any other Romeo that Vera might have hooked up with during her 'meteoric rise.' Vera, remember, was no older that seventeen; and she wouldn't have bothered to inform Roth or Fiske or any other suitors of that fact. Tying Vera to the guys in her address book was a kind of insurance policy for myself: if things went sour for Sam and me at some time in the future, I could hang the threat of a statutory rape charge over the heads of the chumps listed in Vera's date book. That would be a good way to win friends and influence people in a hurry.

I tossed the book back into the night table drawer; the list went into my pocket. Now for the next drawer: there were some letters in this one. I knew she wouldn't be keeping anything really juicy in such an obvious place. But I looked them over anyway, because I'm thorough.

It was kind of touching; they were love letters, from a kid back in Arizona. They'd been written about a year or so before; Vera must have gotten them when she was still living with her folks and taken them with her when she hit the road for Hollywood. Apparently she'd attended school with this boy and he'd been stuck on her something fierce. Puppy love, you know. The letters were full of moony kid stuff about how beautiful she was and how he wanted to marry her after graduation, once he started working full-time at his dad's store. A couple of the letters included some romantic poetry he wrote to her. I'm no Shakespeare, but my advice to him would be not to use cow imagery in a love poem.

The dates on the more recent letters ran right up until the week that Vera ran off for good. It was apparent from the boy's whiny tone that Vera had never answered him. But she'd hung on to his letters; even kept them handy, by her bedside—late night reading when Roth didn't need her and she was feeling lonely. Maybe she figured that the kind of life this kid promised her was not for her; but these were little trophies—"I could have had that if I wanted to." Or maybe she had other reasons for hanging on to them.

This was getting maudlin; I still had stuff to do and I was dead tired. I noted the kid's name and put the letters back; there was nothing else of value in the drawer. What I was hoping for was a diary, with entries, that would put Vera at certain places with particular people on definite dates; that would be all the insurance I could ask for.

I started to look in all the usual places—under the bed, under the box spring, behind the radio, between the heavy furniture and wall, any place that the chambermaids wouldn't normally clean. (Hotel rooms are easy.) But there was nothing, so I started in on the closets.

She'd dumped the cheap little traveling bag that she'd taken hitchhiking; there was no luggage in the closets. The round hatboxes looked promising but came up empty. Vera had lots of new clothes; sometimes babes stuff things into shoes or in the pockets of dresses—not Vera.

The drawers of the bureaus I usually search last; a person wishing to hide something good would be unlikely to put it in a bureau drawer, the most accessible place in the room. But, you never know, so: underwear, silk stockings, underwear, a couple of negligees folded neatly—the smell of Vera's body on them, mmm.

No jewelry, though. Disappointing, but not surprising. This was a hotel, after all; and Vera was smart. She'd have the pricey stuff on her; either that or keep it locked up in the hotel safe downstairs.

More underwear, jeez, how much underwear does she need? It was good stuff, though; French and lacey—I was getting jealous of Roth, the old lecher.

The bottom drawer was sweaters and sensible clothes—boring, but thick fabrics are good for hiding things in—nothing. I was wasting my time.

The bathroom, next. The bathroom is good, because you can find out about a mark's medical history—if he's got heart problems, if he's addicted to drugs, if he's got the clap. My guess was that Vera was in the pink, but who knows, maybe Roth spends the night once in a while and leaves some pills around—

There was makeup, and the usual ton of crap that women think they need to get along in life—lotions, oils, different flavor soaps, all of that. And the usual bag of cotton swabs and junk in tubes, and stuff to shave your legs with. But no pharmaceuticals.

I looked in the cabinet under the sink. Nothing, just hotel stuff for the occasional cleaning. I reached back up under the U-joint plumbing and felt around behind the big old sink, because sometimes people hide— Bingo. I grabbed and pulled down; it came out easy.

A small, black, soft leather bag, like you'd use to stow stuff for the golf course or tennis club in; only smaller. I unzipped it.

More underwear. Jeez, is that it? Couldn't be, you don't hide underwear back behind the plumbing. Then, a brainwave—this was not the sexy French underwear, like the stuff in bureau drawers. This was plain old cotton girl's underwear, the kind Mom orders through the mail—for her kids…

Ribbons and bows, like Shirley Temple might wear in her hair. At the bottom of the bag, a pair of shiny patent leather shoes—Shirley Temple again, but these were big. Big enough for Vera's teenage feet.

Here was a wooden paddle—like for whacking bad little boys and girls on the ass. It wasn't very big, but it had round holes shot through its surface at regular intervals. From my days back at Catholic school I knew that this was done so that wind resistance would not soften the blows against your bottom. A little extra pain.

And something else, that jingled—a pair of handcuffs, polished as bright as the chromium dress that Vera had been wearing on the dance floor last night. The little key was stuck in the lock of the cuffs; I turned it and they sprang open—they worked; they were real. The key was kept in the cuffs in case there was surprise knock on the hotel room door, I guessed.

Because all of this stuff was obviously meant for playing weird 'little girl spanking games' with Roth, obviously. Who spanked who, I wondered? Now I'm not a prude, but when it comes to sex stuff, I'm pretty much a plain vanilla cone with no sprinkles. First Stacey; and now Roth turns out to be a weirdo, too. Was everybody in this town some kind of freak?

The bag and its contents were very incriminating; especially given Vera's age and the nature of the perversion. Olympic Studios made pictures the whole family could enjoy; even Bible epics, like the one Roth had cast Vera in. The news that Roth was dressing up underage starlets as little girls and giving them a darn good spanking would not play well in the sticks, as they say. It might ruin him; and from what I'd heard so far the heads of the other studios would be delighted to help out.

That's a good morning's haul, I thought, as I slipped the handcuffs and one pair of cotton underwear into my jacket pocket. The rest I put back pretty much the way I found it; stuffed back up under the U-joint in the cabinet. Vera and Roth would find out that the cuffs were gone, of course, but that didn't matter. What mattered was; someone else *knew*.

I hadn't quite given up on the diary possibility yet. Vera seemed like the type who'd keep one, and it would help me nail Roth down good and tight. So I took a last look around, up behind the curtains and in all the unlikely places; I still had time before the chambermaids would show. I hadn't looked behind the drawers of the nightstand near the bed; that was a possibility. I pulled out the drawer full of love letters and reached into the back; I came up empty.

Maybe there was something in one of this rube's letters that I'd missed, though—Ah! One mentioned Vera's birthday coming up, and here was one that talked about graduation from high school next year. These would come in handy against Roth, I'd have to take them with me; Vera would miss them for sure, but I needed them—

Sometimes you know that someone is in the room with you even though you never actually hear or see them come in. You know how that is; the gravity or the feeling in the room somehow changes, and it makes you look up and realize, hey, I'm not alone.

There was Vera, standing silently across the other side of her bed from me, still wearing the chromium evening gown, big blue eyes trying to burn holes of hate right through me—me, with my grubby paws all over her tear-stained love letters.

23

"What the hell are you doing here?" I said.

She tossed a little bag on the top of the bed as she came towards me. It looked like the one I'd found under the bathroom sink; I wondered what kind of game was in that one.

She said nothing for a second; then she burst into tears.

She grabbed at the letters in my hand, wailing, "Give me those! Give me that!"

"Okay, okay," I said, embarrassed, and I held them out to her at arm's length. (She had sharp nails, I remembered.)

She crumpled them up in her hand, without looking at them; it wasn't the letters she'd wanted, she'd just wanted to stop someone else from contaminating them by reading them. I was really sorry, I hadn't meant to upset her; I liked her, kind of.

"Get out!" she said.

I looked at her for a moment. I didn't want to hurt her, but I had things to do, and I needed to talk to her before I did them. And I didn't want her calling Roth and letting him know she'd found me in her room.

"I have to talk to you about something."

"You get out of my room, right now!"

"I'll talk to you for five minutes, and then I'll go."

Sniveling, she picked up the phone by the bed. She listened for the switchboard operator at the other end of the line, but she didn't say anything into the phone. I knew she wouldn't. She couldn't afford to get tossed out of the Ambassador for having a man in her room.

I sat down in a chair near the window, and waited for her to pull herself together. She wouldn't look at me, but she put the phone down. I watched as she walked out of the bedroom; I got a little antsy when I realized she was headed for the front door of the suite, but I relaxed when I heard her close and chain the door. She came silently back into the bedroom, still not looking me in the eye. She sat down on the bedside facing me, and clasped her pretty hands in front of her in her lap, holding the crumpled letters.

"What do you want to talk to me about."

I handed her my handkerchief, and she cleaned her face up a bit. Then I said.

"I need to know some things."

"Like what?"

"I need to know some things about your boyfriend."

She seemed a bit surprised. "Jerry?"

I shook my head. "Your real boyfriend. Roth."

That seemed to scare her a bit. Maybe she'd been expecting me to ask about something else entirely. "I can't tell you anything about Jack."

"I know that you went to his house in Beverly Hills last night after you left the club. Why did you come back so soon?"

"I can't tell you anything about Jack."

She still looked scared.

"He's not a very nice guy, you know."

She was listening.

"He's mixed up with gangsters. He's done some pretty bad things to a lot of different people around here. To girls like you. Did you know that about him?"

Her eyes were red; she was tired, too. Like me. Light was coming in through the curtains.

"I have an idea that I'm going to take a lot of money off of Roth, in the very near future. It might even happen sometime this week. I need you to help me." I pulled back the edge of the curtain and looked down at the street below, the morning traffic starting up.

"Are you interested?"

"No," she said, quickly and quietly.

"I'm not in this alone," I said, looking at her again. "I've got important partners, and we've got what we need to pull this thing off. I'm talking about a lot of money. Enough to keep you in style for life."

She was just looking at me.

"Or, if you want, you'd be able to get something besides money. Roth will have to do what we say for a while. We could make him give you the lead in a picture or something. You're a good dancer."

She was waiting for me to finish and go. I was getting annoyed with the silent treatment.

"We don't need you to pull this off," I said. "But Roth might decide to get tough, and it would be good to have somebody close to him. To distract him or at least to keep an eye on him. That's all you'd have to do."

"I wouldn't do that to Jack."

"Why, cause he treats you so swell?" I wanted to mention the handcuffs and the paddle I'd found, but I decided against it. "Look, Vera. I know you think you've come a long way already. I also know you don't think much of me. But ask around about Roth. He's a mean guy and he doesn't have any use for anybody who might put him in a jam. I figure he doesn't know your real age. Don't get me wrong; I'm not gonna tell on you. But if he should find out and get the notion that he's looking at a statutory rape charge because you lied to him, that would be very dangerous for you."

"You said five minutes."

I was a little angry with her, now. I was spelling it all out for her, and she was ignoring me. Christ, she was more concerned about her goofy old letters. I got up out of the chair, and walked out of the bedroom. She followed me, making sure I was going.

"You might change your mind," I said, "Leave a message for me at the front desk."

She just unchained the front door and let me out.

"He's a dangerous guy—" I got in, just before she closed the door. I stood out in the hall for a moment listening to her chain it up from the other side.

I turned and walked back down the hallway, towards the elevator. I wasn't worried about her telling Roth about me; not that much. She was loyal to him, okay; but she'd just gotten her first role in a picture and she was still Roth's lady-of-the-month. She wouldn't want to piss him off by admitting she was somehow connected with a shabby little crook like me. She wouldn't say anything. But she wouldn't play along with me, either.

Too bad. I was sorry for Vera; she'd been scared and embarrassed. It was like I'd caught her doing something wrong. I hadn't meant to, but I'd humiliated her. Not because I'd found the little bag under the sink full of weirdo stuff; the underwear and the paddle and all. That didn't matter; she wouldn't be ashamed of the sex stuff. That was just her way of getting along, getting a break.

What she was ashamed of was those letters I'd been reading. That stuff was private; she hadn't wanted anyone to know she read those letters. (Especially the kid who wrote them, I bet.) Now, because of me, it wasn't private anymore. I'd ruined it. It was going to be a long time before she'd forgive me for busting up that fantasy.

So, as far as the master plan was concerned, Vera was a write-off, thanks to my crummy timing. She might have come in handy, and made herself a small fortune, besides. But it was no good trying to reason with her, what did she know? She was just a baby, anyway.

24

Back in my own room, I slept sound, no dreams. I didn't get my usual eight hours in, but I felt pretty good when I got up, considering the crazy night I'd had. And it's always reassuring to wake up with a big fat stack of fifty-dollar bills next to my nose. Thanks again, Stacey.

There were no messages when I called down to the desk, and I was glad of that. I needed a quiet day to myself, after all that excitement; and what better place to take it easy than the local public library?

I like hanging around libraries; it's a nice change from the speakeasies, bars, diners, and whorehouses where I usually go to work my dirty little deals. Everything is calm and quiet and civilized inside a library. It's soothing; sometimes being in a library made me wish that I'd been a good boy back in my schooldays and studied hard. Of course, if I had been a good boy and studied hard, I might have ended up as a librarian: making $1100 a year, getting flirted at by women who looked like my grandfather, and getting laid off every time they cut the city payroll so they could make a new job for another one of the mayor's idiot brothers.

I knew how to use a library, though—I knew how they indexed and cross-indexed stuff, and how to read and find government documents, and lots of other good stuff. This comes in handy for figuring out how much a mark is actually worth. If I'd done the proper legwork before I tried to shake down Stacey, I might have figured out that she had no real money of her own; that the studio owned her house and the rest of her stuff. Knowing all that in advance could have saved me a trip to the Mexican desert.

Never assume, was my new motto.

I was here to check out Roth.

It was easy; Roth, like Stacey, was a national celebrity, though not nearly so famous. Any movie star had any movie producer beat in the fame department. But Roth was doing okay for himself; he must have had a good press department at Olympic, because the profiles in the slick fan magazines were all pretty flattering.

The local trade magazines were slightly sour on him, though. By 'trades', I mean the magazines they print for the people who are actually in the business; the *Hollywood Reporter*, stuff like that. Movie people read them because they loved to read any kind of dirt about their bosses. Everybody hated the guys who ran the studios. There was the occasional exception, like Irving Thalberg, the boy genius who ran MGM; some people liked him. But he was definitely an exception; most of the studio heads were about as popular as the sores on a leper's willie.

And Roth rated pretty low even among this competition. The articles on him included comments about him by peers and former employees; snide comments about deals gone bad or promises that never came true. Nothing overt, because these magazines wouldn't print anything overt. The reader was supposed to read between the lines.

You might read these insinuations about Roth and write them off as just the usual carping by losers about winners. But there was a difference in tone: for example, the stuff the trades printed about his rivals, Mayer of MGM and Zukor of Paramount, indicated that those guys were feared. But the articles that dealt with Roth suggested that he was feared and hated.

For example, these show biz papers covered his various charities and benefactions; but they also gave you the impression that this was all just good public relations on his part. You might get the idea that the donations were conscience money, except that nobody seemed to think that Roth had one.

The business items on him were kind of byzantine; Roth often seemed to buy and sell projects, actors, and enterprises almost simultaneously. One notorious episode involved his announcement that he'd signed Clark Gable for Olympic; this was soon exposed as a lie, but the public stock of the studio soared on the news—I imagine Roth got some kind of kickback from speculators soon after. He retracted the announcement, saying it was the result of a misunderstanding.

The financial stuff on Olympic was very interesting; what little there was of it. The company issued a report to its investors and some of the figures from the report were there in the finance pages—I knew that this stuff didn't mean jack shit, really; this was before the Securities and Exchange Commission really got going. A company's report to its stockholders bore about as much resemblance to reality as a Mickey Mouse cartoon does to the life of a rodent.

It was the 'Holdings' information that interested me. This indicated that Roth's company was steadily acquiring real property throughout the Los Angeles area, both downtown and up in the San Fernando Valley. (Hey! That's *my* scam!) The studio accountants wouldn't print that unless Olympic Studios was the owner of record, with proper title. I guess the realty acquisitions were there to soothe the more conservative investors: if Stacey Tilden's next three pictures flop, we always have the San Fernando Valley.

Now, this was the kind of information on a mark that shifts my salivary glands into first gear. The guy was a live prospect. But what about Jack Roth, the man? There was no book written about him, no biography or anything. Just the usual studio press handout, rehashed different ways for different publications. But, with this, and the various quotes from his assorted victims, I was able to put together the following picture:

Like Stacey said, Roth and his older brother had started out as a couple of bookkeepers back in New York in the old days. The older brother was a go-getter type; he convinced young Jack that there was money to be made in the nickelodeon business. When a couple of local nickelodeons got into some financial problems, the older brother offered to run them for the owners; he later hired Jack to manage finances. The older brother did what he could to promote and improve the theaters; soon they were showing a profit again. The Roth brothers decided that the time was right to borrow money from various friends and relatives, and buy control of some theaters of their own.

New York City real estate was way too pricey, but there were plenty of failing vaudeville houses and halls for rent out in the sticks—New York State, Connecticut. The older brother would do some figuring and pick out a likely town on the map; then he'd send Jack up there to buy or lease some under-used building in the area. These buildings were then turned into nickelodeons, and they prospered, just like the ones back in Manhattan.

The older brother had a gift for finding new, untapped markets for pictures; he also knew how to promote and polish up the newly-acquired theaters and make them into going concerns. But in the end it was Jack who turned out to be the more ambitious brother. He was the one who got them involved in motion picture production—two-reeler silents, cheap Westerns and white slavery melodramas shot in upstate New York. Made for peanuts, shown in the Roth theaters at no cost to them, rented out to other theater chains that needed product—and always turning a profit.

The Roths had grown up on the Lower East Side and met their share of shady characters when they were kids. These old pals were sometimes useful if Jack was interested in a particular theater and had to convince the seller not to hold out for too high a price. Also, as the business grew, the shady old pals were sometimes a source of capital. Of course, these guys would occasionally ask for favors in return—introductions to actresses, opportunities in theater union management. One article from a 1921 financial journal mentioned that Legs Diamond had received a court order to sell his holdings in the Roth theater chain.

From the chronology and what Stacey told me, I figured that this was when the money-laundering angle really got started—for who's to say how much money a movie really takes in? How could the government tell whether the money collected from the box offices came from ticket sales or bootleg liquor sales? And, although they were now wealthy men themselves, the Roths needed their cut of the dough. Because their little empire was under attack.

On the surface, everything looked good. By the early twenties the Roths were rich, and they'd gone out to Hollywood together to produce their films there. But they were newcomers, and their timing was off. Because when they arrived in Hollywood, the big theater chains were already trying to buy out little guys like them. All the independent studios and all the local theater chains had become fair game for the big theater syndicates and their Wall Street money. They'd circle around their smaller competitors like sharks, waiting for a moment of weakness, a bad business decision, or a little inattention—then, snap! You and your company were gone. Lots of cagey operators, like Samuel Goldwyn, ended up losing their studios to these bigger players. But the Roths were formidable. They'd successfully fought off one takeover by Mayer and his partners. The business journals of the day seemed to think they were likely to survive other takeovers.

What the journals didn't say, though, was obvious to me—the Roths were able to resist the bigger players because they had access to all that lovely syndicate cash they were washing for the Bug and Meyer gang. They even had access to Bug and Meyer, if it came to that.

There were conflicting statements in the press, starting about 1925. Jack was quoted as talking about expansion—then a week or so later his brother would go into print to sort of throw a wet blanket over what Jack had said the week before. It wasn't just my imagination; an article on the brothers at the end of that year commented on the different messages coming out of Olympic and on how it was driving investors crazy. The writer's guess was that Jack was trying to convince his brother that they could be pretty good at this takeover stuff themselves, if they flexed their muscle a bit.

But Roth's brother didn't have any appetite for world conquest. He was the cautious one; kept saying how important it was to stay out of debt, wherever possible. Jack, on the other hand, was sounding like the big spender, making all kinds of shark noises.

Now, this next part of the story I put together myself; deduction, like Sherlock Holmes.

Okay—so the brother didn't want to expand and risk it all; that was clear from the articles. And as the older brother he was, technically, the head of the family. But then Jack must have got his bright idea—if my brother refuses to be one of the big guys, then why shouldn't I sell my personal interest in the Roth theater chain to the other big guys, all on my lonesome? He knew they lusted after all those lovely New York and Connecticut Roth movie houses; Jack could get practically anything he asked for—a studio of his own, an iron-clad distribution deal for whatever pictures he turned out, and a huge pile of cash besides.

The only thing standing in the way of this sweet deal was his older brother—so, his brother had to go. Jack must have strung him along for a year or so while he prepared—Jack's big-mouthing in print about expanding stopped completely. He had to be conning his brother, figuring that he'd never go for the idea of selling off everything he'd spent his life building. This was necessary; if everything seemed fine, the brother and the other investors wouldn't bother to take any preventive measures.

Through brokers, Jack began to acquire a small stake in other studios, the ones drooling at the prospect of taking over the Roth theaters. Jack knew that this secret buying would eventually get the attention of the big studios, and that they'd realize what Jack was contemplating. They did—the 1928 papers were full of rumors about the Roths. I imagined hostile studios beginning to compete with each other, sending bids to Jack in secret, outdoing each other with increasingly fabulous offers guaranteeing his wealth and independence in return for the theaters. I also imagined Jack Roth, looking his older brother in the eye and swearing that there was nothing to what was in the papers.

When the right deal finally came in, Jack was ready. The final battle was outlined in a *Wall Street Journal* article that appeared years after the fact. The theaters of the Roth chain were nominally owned by various family members—the brothers, their wives, cousins, in-laws, and so forth. Jack must have been scribbling away in secret for months, transferring as many of these theaters as he could into his wife's name. When he finally told the rest of the family that he was selling out to Warner's, the family was left with one of two choices: they could go along with Jack and sell out at a decent price, or stick with the older brother, and try to survive as a microscopic independent theater chain. With no movies to exhibit (and no secret mob funding). They all knew the score; if they chose the older brother they'd be run out of business within a year and then bought up for peanuts.

Of course, they chose security and went along with Jack's deal. And, of course, none of them ever spoke to or of Jack again. Which was fine by Jack. He was an independent force in Hollywood now, producing high quality pictures, winning awards, making money for himself, no strings attached.

The *Journal* article did not mention what happened to Jack's older brother after the sell-out. But an article in the *Examiner* told how he'd suffered a heart attack and been admitted to a local hospital in the middle of the night.

Another article appeared a few months later in *Variety*. It said he'd had a nervous breakdown, and mentioned his financial troubles. Financial troubles? You ain't kiddin', pal.

My guess is he was bankrupt, as well as unemployed and dispossessed. If he'd had no inkling of Jack's plan to sell him out, he'd probably had every dime he owned tied up in the Roth theater chain, which no longer existed.

He must have tried to commit suicide during this nervous breakdown, because an article appearing a week later indicated that Jack had managed to have him committed. The brother had been shipped off to an asylum in upstate New York. His wife and kids left Hollywood, too; they were moved to a town near the hospital. So they could hold Pop's hand during visiting hours, I guess.

Jack still sent them a check every month, according to the most recent profile of him I could find. This was from an article appearing in *Collier's*. Compared to all those other articles, this piece was a real love letter to Jack: "Roth's older brother Stanley, an industry pioneer, fell seriously ill after making a series of poor business decisions. He finally retired to upstate New York to spend more time with his wife and children. Roth continues to send his brother a percentage of his own profits from his Olympic Studio ventures. 'Of course, I take care of him and his kids,' says Jack, 'We had our disagreements, but my entire career was built on that man's back. And, listen—there's nothing more important than family.'

What a sweetheart.

25

I got an invite that same afternoon; raised gold script on rough ivory paper, with Roth's signature. Delivered to my room at the Ambassador by a studio messenger, no less.

Stacey's idea was to get me into this birthday party Roth was throwing for himself that evening. I would go as her date; she would show up with the combination to Roth's safe and then steer me into the study where the safe was. After that, I'd be on my own; but that should be okay because this party that Roth threw himself every year was always held outdoors, under the stars, by the man-made lake behind the mansion on his estate. Apparently this yearly affair was a spectacular blowout, complete with fireworks, brass and swing bands, Civil War veterans in wheelchairs, and human sacrifice or something. Roth and his guests would be busy getting entertained; the staff would be preoccupied with their duties. Stacey's Japanese pals (both back from the hospital, glad to hear it) would be running interference for me up at the house so that nobody would walk in on me.

So all I had to do was walk into the study, twirl the dial, and walk out with a few million bucks worth of dirt on Roth.

Oh, sure.

The whole thing stunk like last month's fish. Stacey had introduced me to Roth at the club; and even if I hadn't wised off at his table, he was no businessman if he wasn't having me checked out by his studio bloodhounds. Stacey was his biggest moneymaker; he had to make sure she wasn't going to compromise the studio or her career by getting herself romantically involved with some cheap gigolo or grifter (moi). And, of course, Stacey knew that Roth was having me followed, or at least checked out. I had to assume that. They were probably already down in the lobby or out in the halls; asking questions and getting answers from Herman the desk manager, the hotel detective, the rest of the staff. The Olympic studio toughs would be threatening them or trying to out-bribe me. Stacey knew that, too; she'd practically painted a bull's-eye on me by introducing me to Roth and Fiske the night before. Why, then, was she proposing to hand me over the combination to her boss' safe, with all these studio goons buzzing around me thick as flies?

It had the word "SETUP" written all over it in ten-foot-high neon letters, blinking on and off every two seconds. And the only thing you can do when you're being set up is to run away, fast as you can.

On the other hand—God, how I wanted that money.

First, it was there to be taken—Roth was by far the richest guy I'd ever had a crack at; I wouldn't get this close to a guy that rich for a long, long time if I did the smart thing and walked away from this one.

Second, as far as setups were concerned, I kept telling myself that Stacey's proposed deal (that I take Roth instead of her) didn't change a thing between Stacey and me. Stacey had tried to kill me out in the desert, but it only took one anonymous call from poor old Sam to convince her that I was part of some "gang" that would forward her little jar of memories to some sleazy little newspaper reporter if anything bad happened to me. If I went down—caught in the act while trying to open the safe, or with a bullet in the back of my head after I'd gotten the stuff out for her—Stacey had to believe that she would go down, too. In flames. So, why should she set me up for something nasty? I couldn't think of a reason.

And, finally, I could be wrong about the setup thing, totally wrong. I'd been wrong about people before, and there was the slim chance that Stacey was telling the truth about the safe and its contents. Especially since it turned out she had been telling the truth about being broke herself. I'd checked her story out after my trip to the library; I drove out to Bel Air and went into the local Registry of Deeds. (Tailed, no doubt, by studio cops; but it didn't matter at this point.) I did a title search on her Bel Air home, and sure enough, Olympic had bought the estate two years before. The studio held the property in trust for Stacey, and her ex-husband Fiske was the trustee. So maybe it was all on the level.

Like hell it was.

I had to get in touch with Sam. Hey, I may be stupid and greedy, but I'm also suspicious and cowardly. I was damned if I was going safecracking all alone.

I called him from a pay phone down the block from the hotel. I didn't spot anybody tailing me, but that didn't mean anything; according to Sam and Stacey, the guys who gumshoe'd for the studios were very good. I dialed the chophouse across the street from where Sam did his tour business.

"Listen, are you standin' near the front window?" I said to the kid who answered.

"Yeah," says the kid, cautious.

"Look across the street. Is there an old fat guy with a moustache sitting in a lawn chair, fanning himself?"

"Yeah," says the kid, "He's always there. Who's this?"

"That guy will give you a buck if you take him a message for me."

"What message?"

"Tell him to knock off work about an hour early, and meet me at the place we used to eat breakfast in." For Sam, that meant about five p.m.

"You want him to know who called?"

"He'll know. And tell him I said to give you a buck."

I was at the diner at five on the nose. Sam was already there, and he was mad as a Greek with rabies because the kid from the chophouse had gotten five bucks out of him for delivering my message.

"Never mind that," I said, and I pressed an envelope into his hand. He peeked inside; a thousand bucks in cash. That cheered him up considerably, and I had to tell him to put his eyeballs back into his head and take a look at the back of the envelope.

I'd drawn up a little ground plan on the envelope, based on what Stacey had told me about Roth's place. I explained all about Stacey's "New Deal" and how we were going to take Roth for millions. He was doubtful, but he heard me out.

"She doesn't know about you," I said. "If she is setting me up, I want you there with me so I've got a hole card to play. You're gonna be there that night with your truck, in case I have to get out fast."

"I ain't been invited."

"You're the king of valet parking, remember? Find out who's working the parking for the Roth birthday party and get yourself hired."

He considered. "I guess I could."

"Sure you could. Offer to kick the guy back a few bucks if he hires you, anything, just be there. I'll look for you when I show up around eleven p.m. Make sure you're at the front gate. I'll be driving a Bentley."

He raised an eyebrow, not too sure about the whole thing.

"I'm supposed to do the job in the study at midnight, when the fireworks are going off. You be outside the study with the truck then, you see that X there? You can't miss the room, it's a wall of windows, big French doors that open up onto a patio. You park in front of the patio, when it's dark, headlamps off, understand?"

He nodded impatiently. "How long should I wait for you?"

"I'm not sure," I said. "Stacey wants me to get everything I can out of the safe and just waltz out the front door with it. I think instead I'm gonna take the stuff out onto the patio, and hand it off to you. Then you can drive it out of there in the truck. Bring a tarp or something to put the stuff in. Bring tools, too; we might have to bury it somewhere later."

"But the parking fellers will know it was me that took the stuff, if I just light off like that."

"They'll know anyway. They'll know you and me and Stacey were all in on it. The thing that keeps us alive and out of jail is the fact that you have the stuff from the safe, see?"

He mulled that one over.

"So I gotta get outta there pretty damn quick."

"That's right. And you gotta get yourself lost for a while, 'til things cool down and they give up the idea of trying to get the stuff back without negotiating for it."

"Where should I go?"

"How should I know, Sam? You tell me. You're from here. Isn't there some place around town you could lay low for a few days? Jeez, whatever you do, don't go back to that flophouse you live in, they'll nail you in a heartbeat."

He thought a moment. "I got a friend out in Santa Monica, I guess he'd put me up—"

"Not good enough," I said, "You've got to start running and keep on running, they'll be looking for you, they'll be checking out entire states. So keep moving, and don't get on a train, they'll be checking the trains."

"I could drive the truck to—"

"You can't take the truck," I said. "They'll spot you for sure if you're driving that truck. You leave the truck behind, with the stuff on it. Keep it stuffed under the seat or wrapped up in a tarp, or whatever. You drive the truck out of town that same night, north up to Glendale. There's a little motor court I stayed at in Glendale." I wrote down the name of the place for him; it was the place where Vera had stranded me after our night of love. "Park out back, so no one can see the truck from the street in the daytime. Leave the keys under the front seat. Then go to the office and wake up the manager and rent a cabin. Book the cabin for two nights. Sign in under a different name."

"What name is that?"

"I don't know, whatever you want, just make up a name so I know it's you."

"How about Dell?"

"Dell?"

"Yeah."

"Dell what?"

He looked down at his coffee cup.

"Dell Coffey?"

"Brilliant," I said, "Sign in under the name Dell Coffey and tell the manager you've got a partner joining you the next day. That's me, by the way."

"Then what?"

"Then you can spend the night in the cabin, if you want, but the next morning you've got to get out of there. Leave the truck where it is and call a taxi. After that, you're on your own. Get a Greyhound or something out of Glendale."

"What happens to the stuff from the safe?"

"I'll be out the next day to get it out of the truck."

"Seems like a lot of trouble. You don't want me to hide it, instead? I know some places I could park it awhile—"

"No, it's like with the jar, Stacey's jar. The less you know the better, because they'll be able to find you easier than they will me. You've got a real name and address, you're gonna be working the party parking cars. I don't want you to be able to tell them anything, if they catch up to you. That's the only thing that's keeping us alive, is them not knowing where the stuff is."

"You think they're gonna catch up to me?" He was looking pretty worried.

"Yeah," I said. No point trying to bullshit him; Sam was a bullshitter himself. "You could get pretty far on what's in that envelope, but they'll spend more than that in one day just to find us. You told me yourself that these studio guys are serious characters. They may catch you, and they may try to scare you a bit, rough you up."

Sam looked old when I said that.

"But they probably won't hurt you bad, not until they know where Roth's stuff is and how to get it back. There's a skinny chance you might be able to duck them altogether if you just keep on moving and never use the same name."

I let that sink in. Then I asked him: "Still game?"

He looked up at me. A light rose in the bloodshot blue eyes.

"Shit, yes."

I slapped him on the shoulder, "Attaboy."

"When can I come back?"

"You meet me right here, on the first of next month. Five p.m., just like today. If you have to get a message to me, don't call the Ambassador, I won't be there. Send a wire to the Western Union office over on Fairfax Avenue."

"Western Union, Fairfax," he mumbled.

"I'll be staying around town somewhere, but I'll check in there every so often. I'll get back to you within a day or two if you leave a number. But don't even do that, unless it's real important."

He nodded, getting old again.

"That about it?" he said.

"Yeah," I said. "You want me to go over it again?"

"Naw," he said, picking up the envelope. "I got it. Midnight. Drive the truck to that motor court. Dell Coffey. Book a cabin, two days. 'My partner's gonna show tomorrow, it's okay if he wants to use the truck.' Get a nap, then get the hell out of town, and keep on goin'. Meet here first of next month, same time. Western Union on Fairfax, but leave a number only if it's an emergency."

"Good. You want something to eat?"

"No thanks," he said, picking up the envelope, rising from the booth, careful of his back. He shook the envelope at me. "Thanks for the dough."

I shrugged. "Your share."

He nodded. "I'll see ya at the party, I guess."

"We're gonna be rich, Sam," I said, seriously.

"Yeah, I know," he replied, looking like a Bassett hound. "I have to go lie down now."

And he hobbled away, bowlegged.

I watched him go, sipping my coffee and thinking, Jesus, we're all doomed.

26

I drove out to the Roth place by myself that night; I went through the hills, the long way 'round. I wanted to scout out the roads near the house; the need for a quick exit was a definite possibility.

My first glimpse of the place was from quite a ways off; I had stopped and parked on an adjoining hill. Across the valley I could see it shining in the dark, near the top of the next hill. And it really was shining; it was lit up for the party with arc lights, the colors of a Roman candle.

The house itself looked like some kind of temple. I've seen those photographs in travel books of Egyptian tombs; it was like that. Not the Pyramids; the other kind, the long, low walls of pillars and recesses, built into the sides of hidden valleys out in the desert. Roth's house was made like one of those—like it was carved out of rock along the top of the hill. My guess was that it was at least as long as a football field; it was fronted by about a hundred columns or pillars or whatever you call them. Private roads leading to it had been cut into the side of the hill.

I could see the lights from cars crawling up the hill towards the place; early arrivals, like me the night before at the club—nobody important. Stacey would arrive later, on her own. Nominally, I was her "date" again; but she wanted to join up on the grounds, after the party was well under way. That was when she'd give me the combination, and send me on my way to fame and fortune.

I watched those first cars make it to the top of the hill, the grand entrance to Roth's "temple"; they parked there for a moment or two, and then they continued on down the hill, back towards the gate at the bottom. That would be Sam and his valet pals, relieving the arriving guests of their cars.

The night was quiet and the band had already started

up; I could just hear slight little horns coming from somewhere on the hill, like music from a tiny gramophone. The food and the band and the dancing would be outdoors; important because that would draw people away from the main house, where I'd be working on the safe.

The farther away the better, I was thinking, peering through the dark at the outline of the hill. I was wishing for a pair of binoculars when I saw them: more lights, coming up from behind the trees down the slope from the main house. These were colored, too—pink and green and pastel orange; they highlighted the groves of palms that surrounded them. Roth's very own private Cocoanut Grove; no imitation trees here. There was a glittering strip along the foot of the grove, a long thin slice of moving reflecting light that bordered part of the palm forest. Water; too big for a swimming pool—that would be the artificial lake Stacey had mentioned.

The exact distance between the main house and the brilliant grove was hard to gauge from where I stood; but it was significant, and I felt a little better about the whole deal as I climbed back into the Bentley and took off. The main action at this party was going to be down in that grove.

I kept an eye out for Sam as I pulled up to the great stone gate at the bottom of Roth's hill. I was damned if I was going to go through with this if Sam chickened out. This place was a fortress, and I'd need help to get out of here, combination or no.

There he was; I could see him under the lanterns that were mounted into the stone gate. Sam looked funny in his valet parking outfit; he was giving a little salute to a geezer with a blonde in a long cabriolet as he hopped up on the running board to guide them up the hill. He didn't seem to notice me as I rolled by them in my car. I kept going, because I wanted to make sure that Sam was the one who parked the Bentley. I drove a little ways up the road that wound around the estate, taking my time.

I passed other cars coming around the hill the other

way: beautiful lemon colored Lincolns and black Cadillac sedans; a few sporty foreign jobs for the smart set. The party was starting up in earnest now; I'd better get inside. There was Sam again, coming back from the top of the hill. I gave him a toot on the horn and cut off a crummy Nash that was trying to attract his attention. He spotted me and waved; the next minute he'd hopped into the passenger seat and we were headed through the gate together.

"Listen," I said. We were taking our time, winding up the hill; the trees at the foot of the estate giving way to a lawn that stretched out in front of the great house at the top. "Don't park this one with the other cars," I said, nodding at the rows of limos they'd organized at the edge of the clearing, nearer the gate. "I might have to leave in a hurry."

"Where, then?" he asked. I thought he sounded nervous.

"Park it across the street, in front of the gate. I saw a big clump of trees and stuff growing down there; leave it there. Leave the keys under the front seat, make sure they're easy to find."

"Okay."

We were coming up on it now; jeez, it really did look like an Egyptian temple or tomb or something; the mugs in tuxes and babes in evening dresses on the big steps out front looked out of place.

"I want you there with the truck right on time," I said to Sam, "You know where you're supposed to be?" I pulled up and handed him the keys.

He nodded. "Took a drive up there earlier this evening," he said. "Big windows out back, with a big old porch in front of 'em. I'll be there."

We got out of the car, and he walked around and took my place behind the wheel. He started it up, and put it into gear.

"Good luck," he said.

"Thank you," I said, not thinking, and I realized that I

was as scared as he was. Scared-er, maybe.

I had a right to be, this was the biggest thing I'd ever tried to pull in my short career. I mean, I'm pretty good at sneaking around hotel rooms and snapping pictures of people having sex and stuff. But this cat burglar jazz was not in my job description. I'm sure I looked suave, mounting the steps casually, taking all the Hollywood smiles that came my way as my due—but my mouth tasted like old socks and my stomach felt like I'd swallowed a Mexican hat dance.

I didn't want Roth to spot me; he might be greeting people. So I hung around outside for a while, between the pillars, taking deep breaths and trying to fight off panic. I temporarily recovered when Carole Lombard walked by with some society heel on her elbow; the nod and the smile she gave me as she sailed by took my mind off my worries. I watched her as she went in through the main door and got a grip on myself. That's the stakes you're playing for, kid; don't blow it by being scared.

I took a look through one of the twenty-foot windows that flanked the main door; I scanned the crowd, hoping to spot Roth (so I'd be able to duck him). The front hall looked like it was about two hundred feet tall. In the torchlight I saw some kind of mosaic or something inlaid all across the ceiling. There was Bette Davis, sipping champagne by one of the pillars inside, leaning against it like it was a lamppost. The pillars held up the roof. Unlike the ones on the porch, they were covered with carvings; for all I knew, they were authentic imports. More light came from lamps hidden somewhere within the walls; soft golden rays fell between the columns and cast huge shadows of laughing, talking guests across the room. There were statues in there, too—black stone figures on top of huge granite blocks, standing watch over the beautiful crowd below; gods with the heads of dogs.

I think Roth made the place look spooky on purpose; the guests were obviously meant to get a drink, say hello, and then move on outside to the real festivities down the hill. The echo in the hall made the crowd's chatter sound raucous. The guests were a lot like the bunch I'd seen at the Grove last night, except more sober and with bigger diamonds.

Another difference in this crowd was that there were some older guys present. Short little guys with white hair or bald heads. Some stood erect and dignified, others sat quietly on the rectangular, modern furniture. Their tuxes were cut in a conservative, old-fashioned style. They stayed well away from the younger crowd, but they watched them carefully, keeping an eye on all the lovely creatures they owned: these were the heads of studios, come to pay tribute to Roth. They spoke to each other once in a while, bending or leaning over so that old ears could hear; zookeepers discussing the health and prospects of their menageries. The other guests seemed to avoid them; the only intrusion was an occasional waiter offering food or champagne, which the old men usually refused.

One of the men looked over his shoulder and spotted me peering through the window; I ducked away fast, feeling like I'd been caught doing something wrong.

Just in case, I sort of attached myself to an arriving party of five or six guys and gals and went inside with them, pretending to laugh along with all the rest at some joke I hadn't heard.

27

It was darker inside than out because of all of that "mood" lighting; but I found that comforting, for some reason. I grabbed a glass of champagne as it sailed by on a tray and retired behind a pillar of my own, back in the shadows.

I was still trying to get a feel for the layout—Stacey's map had been pretty sketchy, and I'd have to get around by myself once the other guests headed out. There must have been at least two hundred people in the hall, but small groups were already drifting down to the far end, towards the huge gated glass doors that opened out into the night. They were gradually being herded that way, lured by the sound of the band. But some hung behind to chit-chat or flirt or take care of business—my quintet of old studio guys was still there, relaxing a bit now that the kids were leaving the room.

I strolled by in the general direction of the exit, slowly, staying as near the west wall as I could. You would have thought I was looking for someone, not counting the doors that led out of the main hall and into the west wing. One was open in front of me, a uniform walked out carrying a tray; okay, that led to the kitchen—not relevant. There were two more doors beyond. I walked to the next one and tried the long handle; locked. I went on to the last door, nodding to a group of older ladies in expensive dresses who were definitely not movie stars; they smiled back, it looked awful.

This door opened; and out popped a tall, lovely creature with sapphire eyes and a necklace to match. She slipped by without looking at me. If she wasn't anybody famous, I thought, she should be.

I looked down the dark hall beyond the open door: a long gallery, flooded with moonlight, because the wall facing north was all windows. A shaft of yellow light opened up in the wall to my left; a door opening; two women gabbing to each other as they returned to the hall to rejoin their dates. That would be a bathroom, since two women were coming out of it together. I nodded at them as they passed; I was a young man waiting impatiently for his date, still holed up in the ladies' lounge. I looked away and stood modestly by a window, pretending to watch the city lights.

I was getting warmer, I knew: Stacey had described this gallery full of windows. According to her, the study and the safe would be directly ahead of me, at the end of the hall. Of course, the door might be locked, but there were ways of dealing with that—I had the cat's paw tucked in my left pants pocket. And, in another pocket, a gun, in case I had to make somebody open the door for me. God forbid. This was a little Colt pistol I'd picked up in a pawnshop back in town; back in my hotel room I'd filed down the numbers on it and sawed off some of the barrel to make it smaller. I had it folded up in a piece of newspaper and stuffed inside my jacket, so no unsightly bulges would ruin the line of my suit.

I looked back down the gallery behind me before I tried the door to the study. I turned the handle of the door—and it opened. I guess Roth figured that nobody would dare steal from him, bless his tiny little heart.

The study, like every other room in the joint, was huge; high ceilings, more pillars, and another wall of windows to my right. This section of the house looked down over Los Angeles proper; beyond the glass was a soft aura of white light running the whole length of the black horizon of the hills. The effect was a little compromised by the moonlight, but that was okay with me, because in the glow I could make out the long, low desk at the end of the room, and the shape of the huge portrait, hanging on the dark wall behind. This was it.

Fine, I'd found it, but I was way too early, and anyway, I didn't have the combination yet. No sense in hanging around. I padded back across the carpet the way I'd come in, and grabbed the inside handle of the door. I wanted to take a peek down the gallery before I slipped back into the party.

There was a horrible click that came from behind the handle as I turned it; I felt the vibration run all the way through my palm and up my arm. I knew that sound; somehow, some way, I had locked this door. So I was trapped in this room.

I tried the handle again immediately, rattling it; it wouldn't give a fraction, and I was suddenly furious—it didn't make any sense, a door handle that locks by itself, from the inside, and, Christ, where was the catch, or the lock, or the release or whatever, how the hell do you—Then I was aware of all the noise I must have been kicking up with all my rattling and cursing under my breath. I froze and listened at the door. It wouldn't do if one of the dolls at the other end of the hallway heard me scrabbling away and told the rest of the party that someone had locked himself inside Roth's private sanctuary.

I heard nothing; that was a reprieve, anyway. I was sweating; I felt in my trouser pocket for the cat's paw and drew it out. I'd brought the goddamn thing in case I had trouble getting in; I certainly hadn't anticipated having to use it to get out, before I'd even stolen anything. And supposing the door is somehow wired? I couldn't see any wires coming out of the door in this darkness, but that didn't mean anything, the installers were really good at hiding that stuff these days, and, my God, what if it's a silent alarm, and I've already set it off by locking the door or rattling it—

Okay, take it easy, now, sucker. Just pretend this is all happening to someone else and you're just acting it out, and you'll be fine. Look, there's a couple of glass doors over there, with moonlight and freedom just streaming in all through them, why don'tcha try those, genius?

I walked quickly across the thick Turkish rug to the wall of glass. The doors mounted in it had a wrought iron frame and they opened onto that porch or terrace or patio, outside. The handles of the door were heavy iron, and they had keyholes; but, hallelujah, there was a little mechanism above one of the keyholes, and turning this with my sweaty fingers opened the deadbolt that held the doors shut.

Still, I had trouble getting even one of them open. All that iron and glass; they must have been at least twelve feet tall. I leaned my weight into it and it gave, and I slipped out on to the terrace outside. At the edge of the terrace was the sea of light in the valley below, the endless white grid glowing under the low mist over the city. Thin rays broke the mist and raked the sky. Searchlights advertising a premiere; somebody else's career was on the line tonight, too.

To my right was blackness; the dark surface of the inevitable swimming pool stretching out across the back of the house. It wasn't quite as big as Stacey's, but this one had a bridge running across it, joining the house to the hillside below. I could make out tiny colored lanterns, lighting the way down to the party for Roth's guests.

I stood and thought it over. The moon was bright, but it was dark here on the terrace. Also higher than the rest of the surrounding grounds. The study behind me would stay pitch black, of course. Not bad—after the guests had all left the main house, I'd be able to work in peace up here all by myself for a while. Unless a stray servant or two wandered in on me.

I closed the glass door and kind of skittered across the flagstones of the terrace on my fancy shoes and went down into the bushes below. I figured it was time to find Stacey.

I continued to wade through the bushes that ran along the edge of the terrace. There was a broad stairway leading down, but I didn't want to use it—someone might spot me coming down from the direction of the study. I was weighing stuff in my mind as I stumbled along: it was a break that I'd accidentally locked that study door—if it was still locked when I returned later, I could be fairly sure that no one had been by to check on the room. And I knew now that I could get back in through the doors on the terrace—provided, of course, no one came by in the meantime and locked them from the inside. If that happened, I'd have to bust out a section of glass near the door handle and reach in to open the deadbolt. If I could open the deadbolt. If I had the combination. If there was a safe behind that painting.

A path of stones appeared, leading down through the ornamental garden. I made for it as best I could in the dark, keeping an eye on the bright colored lights beyond, following the music. I was doing pretty good, like Jungle Jim, when all of the sudden I stepped on something big and soft and squishy, like foam rubber. It writhed and screamed underneath me and I leapt through the air like a gazelle, scared out of my wits and landing in a crouch on the stones of the path. Hunched down like a runner, I turned to look behind me. There was an inhuman squeal and gasp and something huge moved beneath the bushes.

"What the hell was that?" A man's voice.

"Someone stepped on my ass," a woman's voice hissed. "Who's out there?" She sounded scared and outraged at the same time.

I was going to crack wise, but decided against it. I didn't want anybody recognizing my voice later.

"Sssh, quiet!" said the man's voice; urgent, throaty.

"There's someone there!" she squeaks back at him. I just straightened up and turned my back on them, strolling away down my stone path, saying nothing, slightly offended. It's not even eleven o'clock yet, for Christ's sake; what are these people, animals? I wondered what she looked like, though.

I reached the bottom of the path and stepped out onto the lighted way, straightening my tie.

28

I made my way down the lanterned stairway. The majority of the guests were meandering down the huge stone staircase that led from the rear of the big house to the lights and music below. Steps that ran long and wide like the New York Public Library.

Couples paused to chat or catch their breath near the marble fountains that were set on the stairs at regular intervals. Women hugged and kissed each other, delighted to see their pals had been invited, too; the men smoked and struck attitudes—one hand casually in the hip pocket, the other waving a lit cigarette. The fountains had lights mounted beneath the surface of the pools; colored rays shot up into the night.

And then I turned the other way and headed for the big bash itself, down on the "Midway"—well, it looked like a Midway at a state fair, anyway. It was as big as one, with more flashing lights and better music. Actually, once I was in it, it reminded me of Bourbon Street down in New Orleans on a hot Saturday night; combination circus and orgy. Roth had turned it into a sort of thoroughfare; he'd built a temporary brilliant avenue down here and it was pretty wild up at this end. All the music and carnival lights; places to stop and get a drink, dance, whatever. At the end of the way the lights petered out and emptied into the dark—the lake I'd seen at the end of the grove.

The guests, and there were hundreds by now, would wander down this avenue with their drinks and dates, taking in the spectacle. The sides of the avenue were flanked by booths; mountains of food and liquor on display and various weirdoes pulling stunts to amuse the crowd. Here was a young fellow in a tux, his hair cut too long; he was up on a platform and had managed to draw his own little audience. His specialty was doing nasty imitations of the more famous guests; when I got there he was doing Katherine Hepburn for Katherine Hepburn. She didn't seem to find it too funny, but her friends thought it was a riot. The guy had a string of slightly smutty jokes, most of which I'd heard before.

Something fluttered down on me—and then there were thousands of these things, fluttering all around me like tiny bats. Flower petals, falling like snow, floating down on us. Scattered from these great silken or gauze sheets by dancing girls, about twenty of them in harem get-ups. They moved into the crowd in this kind of burlesque parade formation, leaping and dancing and showing skin. I thought these might be the slave chicks from Roth's Bible picture, the one he'd cast Vera in—a little advance publicity for the picture, here at a party for insiders. Vera didn't seem to be among the dancers; but then Roth probably wouldn't have his current girlfriend working the entertainment end of his birthday bash. That would be in bad taste. She was probably around somewhere, though.

Here was a bunch of people, eating, laughing—I was hungry, so I wandered in through them to get to the food. I found myself standing in front of this kind of altar of ice, nearly ten feet tall, glowing as brilliant as a diamond. When I got up close I could see that its surface was covered with an endless sea of—bugs, or big insects or something. No—they were shrimp; cooked, pink shrimp—and up top, floating in the middle in a pool of water carved into the apex of this monster, was a midget, a naked white girl midget with a tiara. She was ladling out shrimp with a silver dipper and telling people where to get the lemons and the cocktail sauce. A "shrimp" bar, get it?

Well, that killed my appetite completely. It seemed a bit excessive and, anyway, I never eat anything with a midget in it. I wandered further down, headed for the music. The band was hot and loud; Roth had good taste in that, at least. It was a Negro outfit, playing jazz. I got a better look and saw that some kids were already dancing; doing clever routines on the slick floor set down in front of the bandstand. The guy on the sax was good; it was just possible that Roth had spent the dough to import a Kansas City outfit for this bash, and I was a big fan of—

And then I nearly peed in my pants as two lions—real lions—crossed my path. The nearest one was less than two feet in front of me; I practically tripped over him. It took me a second to recover and realize that these lions were held by chains, like dogs—by a tall Negro woman wearing a leopard skin. She was quite a sight, herself. The leopard skin didn't hide much; she had long legs and beautiful brown breasts that bobbed a bit as she drew the lions back.

A few of the other guests had seen me jump and thought it was hilarious. The lion lady was laughing, too, perfect white teeth, and laughter full of doves.

"It's okay, they won't bite."

"What are you, their agent?" I said, trying to recover some dignity.

I liked looking at her; I stayed and talked to her about lions for a bit. Actually, I couldn't take my eyes off her; even the stupid headdress of orange feathers couldn't spoil a face like that one. Those lions cramped my style, though—one was sniffing my hand suspiciously; the other sat himself down on the grass, eyeing me and waiting for me to make a wrong move towards the mistress.

"Actually, they're very friendly," she was saying. No accent at all, was she American? "Besides, they're so doped up they probably think you're a lion, too."

I knelt down to take a closer look at one of these doped-up lions, peering into the big golden eye that was trained on me. He nosed up to me, too, checking me out; and I reached up (slow) and put my hand behind his mane, stroking the fur at the side of his head. He liked that and the girl laughed again, softly. I looked up; those beautiful naked breasts, the confidence with the animals. I smiled at her, and

I'd finally thought of something clever to say, when over rushes this babe in a silver fox fur piece and swoops down on the other lion like a harpy, squealing, "Oh, look at the pretty kitty!" She reaches to grab him, and my lion turns quicker than I'd thought possible, and growls. Suddenly I'm back up on my feet, backing away.

The babe in the fox fur was plastered, at least as doped up as the cats; I could smell it coming off her and I was standing almost ten feet away. Her husband, or whatever he was, took her by her arm and pulled her away, snarling something; she yelped "I wanna see the lions!" And the lions wanna see her, too; they moved slowly towards her and my jungle goddess had to yank that chain pretty hard to discourage them.

I left that scene and moved on. With some regret; I thought I might have been able to make some time with that gal, maybe get a phone number. Oh, well. My watch said that Stacey ought to be here pretty soon. A waiter headed in my direction with more champagne, but it was crowded down here now and the tray was empty by the time it got to me. Just as well.

Beyond the bandstand were rows of –monoliths, I guess you'd call them. There were six or seven of them and they were two, nearly three stories tall—their walls were made of great sheets of ice and fires blazed inside. Somehow, the fires had been dyed to different shades; each monolith had its own color, and they glowed like red and green and golden coals, monuments of burning ice—and encased inside each of them was a girl. Stark naked, you could see, when the light from the fire below her was right.

But the girls were alive, because their limbs would occasionally writhe with the music before they froze in place again. How did they do that? The fire inside kept the girl from freezing, I guess, but how did they breathe?

The crowd looked up at them, exchanging few words; even this bunch was impressed. They wandered among the monoliths, gawking like tourists. Looking up at the girls, trying to make out their features and their Asian gestures through the ice—I think it soothed these guests, some how. Here was someone as beautiful as you were, but with a worse job: standing naked inside the melting ice to honor the boss, and to amuse you.

I went on to the end of the avenue. Here was the lake I'd seen earlier this evening from across the valley. Roth had carved or excavated it into this level of his hill; engineering it so it would hold water here, way up above the town. I couldn't see the end of it from where I stood; it curved around a bend and was ringed with trees. There were palms, but also a grove of sculpted pines or something; like the pictures I'd seen of Roman gardens. A broken pillar had been planted here and there on the shore to add to the effect; imported ruins.

The main attraction, though, were the thousands (or tens of thousands, maybe) of lotus blossoms on the lake. They drifted on the surface, shifting slowly with the wind. And there were swans; they glided across the lake, cutting trails in the blossoms, then the blossoms patiently closed in on the trails.

Some people seemed to find it romantic. A few couples were walking together by the shore, holding hands. I watched two girls exchanging a passionate kiss on the bank opposite me; I wondered if they were guests or if this was part of the show.

I thought it was all pretty romantic, too; until two of the swans glided by and I noticed how they glittered in the moonlight. I stepped closer to see; swans don't sparkle—and then I saw. The birds had been painted; covered with some kind of glittering silver paint or gilt or something. I wondered how they would get that stuff off those birds tomorrow, or if they would even bother.

That was all the romance I could stand for now. I turned to go back up towards the main drag again. In the distance the band struck up a hot number; it sounded faint and tinny. Then I heard a gentle voice behind me.

"Enjoying yourself?" said Stacey.

29

She was even lovelier tonight. The dark and lush red hair, the white skin, an emerald evening dress. Smiling up at me, wicked.

"You look good," I told her.

"Oh, that silver tongue of yours. You're sweeping me off my feet." She closed in for a hug, and whispered in my ear, nuzzling it: "I couldn't get the combination."

My heart sank into my trousers, but people were watching me now because she was with me; so I forced a smile and followed when she took my hand and suggested a walk.

The other guests were polite; they kept their distance as we took our walk in the moonlight, holding hands like lovers do.

"What does that mean, you couldn't get the combination?"

"I should think it's self-explanatory, darling."

"Well, what the hell am I supposed to do now, yank the thing out of the wall with my teeth?"

"That's entirely up to you. One of my Japanese friends will be playing the lookout for you. He'll be in the house from a quarter to midnight 'til a quarter after, if you still feel like giving it a try."

"Giving what a try? There's nothing to try any more, the whole thing's off, I can't open a safe without the combination."

"Calm down."

"It's over, you're back to where you started, you're gonna pay me yourself, and I don't care how you get the dough, or who you have to—"

"Did you ever know a man named Boswell?"

That stopped me. "Who?"

"A banker? From Boston? From a very respectable

old family, I understand."

She sure knew how to get my attention.

"I had a very interesting afternoon," she said, and she turned and strolled along the lakeside. "Jack called me into the office. His goon O'Brien was there, too. Jack decided to have you checked out after that amusing performance you gave at the Cocoanut Grove the other night. He told me so much about you."

"Like what?"

"Well, O'Brien found out that you were new to town, and asked some questions about you at the Ambassador and so forth… He traced car registrations and made a few calls to some old friends of his in the F.B.I. And he formed this theory that you were somehow connected to this poor Mr. Boswell, who jumped out of a twelve-story window one afternoon."

"Never heard of him," I said, a little too loud.

"Of course you haven't." Oh, that smile. "By the way, did you ever go by a different name? I mean, Hart isn't your real name, is it?"

I was having trouble swallowing; I stared out at the flowers on the pool of still water.

"Well, my name isn't really Stacey Tilden either, there's no shame in that, sweetie. But Jack and Mr. O'Brien have got the idea that you were going to try and extort money from me. They wanted to warn me about you, isn't that hilarious? Watching out for me, like a couple of big brothers.

"By the way, Jack knows that you were toting that blonde chippy with you when you arrived in town. And he knows that she's underage, and he knows that you brought her in across the state border. So, he's going under the assumption that she's been working with you all along, to put him on the spot. So I don't think much of her chances for a long career in films." She pronounced the word "films" as though it had two syllables; I hate people who do that.

She turned, very graceful, and took both my hands in

hers.

"Penny for your thoughts."

I should have pushed her in the fucking lake right then, but I had to hear the rest.

"What happens now?" My voice sounded distant.

"Well," she said thoughtfully, "that depends on you, really. We can call the whole thing off, like you said, and you can go back to your nice warm bed at the Ambassador. And when you wake up tomorrow morning, you'll be in the trunk of O'Brien's car, with two bullets in the back of your head." She was enjoying this way too much, I thought.

"Or, maybe Jack will go easy on you. Maybe they'll just let the Boston police know where to find you. Of course, the federal people will also want you for that Mann Act violation. And then there's always the California law; they'll take you for statutory rape. You'll be very popular, Mr. Whoever-You-Are-This-Week."

She put her hand on my shoulder.

"But don't worry so much about all that, sweetheart. Chances are they won't let you go to prison. You might talk, and Jack hates loose ends."

She turned away and sighed.

"The trunk of O'Brien's car is what I'd be worried about, if I were you."

I stared at the water and the painted swans. They made me feel kind of sick.

She was looking at them, too. "I suppose the best thing is to just go ahead as we originally planned. You get that safe open, take what's inside, and then we'll have at least as much on Mr. Roth as he does on us. Then maybe he'll leave you alone."

"That's crazy." The band started up. A slow number.

"Not really. Jack and O'Brien don't know anything about our plans for this evening. They think that I'm on their side. If you do manage to get those records out of here, they'll be afraid to give you up or do you in. At least until we've all come to some understanding."

"I can't." My voice was a little squawky. "I don't know how to crack a safe."

"Get me a flower, will you?" she said. And I did; I knelt by the lake and picked out a pretty one and stood and handed it to her.

"Darling," she said, taking it. "If I were you, I'd devote the next twenty minutes figuring out how to 'crack a safe.' These are the most important twenty minutes of your sad little proletarian life. The dizzying heights of success, or... " she sniffed the flower, "... spectacular destruction."

"I can't do it."

"But you have to. Isn't it exciting? You could run, but you wouldn't get very far before O'Brien and his boys caught up to you. A word of advice: If you *do* decide to make a run for it, don't go to Mexico. That's the first place they'll look. Not that it matters where you go, really. They'll get you anyway, and sooner rather than later."

And then she turned and began to walk away slowly, leaving me standing alone in the moonlight, by the sea of blossoms. "I'm sure you'll think of something," she called out softly, without turning around. "You're so clever."

30

Off in the distance, someone fired a cannon. Wild, faraway cheers from the crowd, in response.

I was back up inside the house, standing alone in the dark study. I was doing things mechanically now, because I couldn't think of any way out. I could see okay; the lights of the party down the hill were blazing brilliantly and they cast dim red and green beams around the walls of the room. I was looking up at the painting of Roth's family, the one that concealed the wall safe.

Stacey was right—Roth's kids were ugly. The wife wasn't, but the sons and daughters had the same smarmy grin as their father; the painter hadn't tried to hide it. I worked the big gilt frame of the painting with my fingers, looking for a catch or handle—something that would swing it away from the wall and expose the safe. I couldn't find it; Stacey had gotten this part wrong, and I began to curse her, quietly as I could.

And I still had no idea how I was going to get this safe open, once I got to it. Sam would be along any minute; I'd have to be here to meet him or he'd panic. Of course, when I told him I didn't have the combination, he'd probably panic anyway.

Fuck this ugly painting, I said to myself, and I took the iron cat's paw out of my pants pocket and plunged the sharper end of it into the canvas. It ripped, and I began to tear across the bottom of the frame. If I was gonna leave this place empty-handed tonight, the least I could do was vandalize Roth's bad art.

I guess I was getting a little hysterical, but it worked—tearing the canvas gave me access to the safe. I could see it in there now, mounted in the wall, a big old steel-faced job. It had a dial on it, and a heavy L-shaped iron handle, so you could swing the door open easy after dialing the combination.

If you knew the combination, that is.

I was mad and I kept ripping. I hopped up a foot or so into the air, grabbed a handful of canvas, and removed Roth's youngest son and the family dog from the portrait. Now I could see the face of the safe. I peered into the bottom of the frame and found the catch inside; the do-hickey that I had so much trouble finding. I felt the fluttering of rose petals in my stomach; the catch was wired, running into the wall. If I'd managed to find it and opened it the wrong way, or forced it open with my little baby crowbar, the joint would have probably lit up with bells and alarms like it was the Chicago fire.

And then it got darker in the study and things got quieter—they were dimming the spotlights down the hill and someone was speaking on a microphone. Making an introduction; or a speech, more likely. Congratulating Jack on his birthday, or Jack thanking his guests, maybe. It was during this relative silence that I heard the put-put-put, drawing closer and closer, coming from outside the window. Sam and his truck, right on time. Right on time for nothing, Sam, because I can't open this thing. I stared at the safe again; it stared back.

I heard the engine idling now. I walked over to the big window and took a look—the headlamps were off, but I could make out the outline of the truck, sitting there on the lawn at the end of the wide flagstone patio. Down the hill, the green and blue and red and gold lights of Roth's party had started up again.

Sam sat waiting, and I had nothing to give him but an explanation. I unlocked the latch of the huge glass door and trotted across the patio.

I couldn't see Sam's face inside the dark cab of the truck, but I guessed he was sweating, too.

"Bad news," I said.

"Which is?" he said, like he'd been expecting bad news.

"She didn't get the combination."

He looked away, into the distance, pondering our fate

for a moment. Then he turned to me again, and asked, "Anything we can do about it?"

"Not much," I said. "I found the safe, it's behind that painting, like she said. But that's as far as I got." I knew the answer, but I asked anyway. "You know anything about cracking safes?"

"Naw. You?"

I shook my head. I was looking down at that party; it seemed very far away, like it was in another state or something.

"How much time we got left before folks start headin' up to the house again?"

I held my watch up in front of my face.

"Maybe ten minutes. There's gonna be fireworks. Some folks will probably want to watch from up here."

He pulled the parking brake and started to get out of the cab.

"May as well take a look at her, anyhow." He walked around the front of the cab, and together we went back up the steps of the patio; I'd left the big glass door open.

Inside, our feet were silent on the carpet. I motioned him to follow me into the dark. We stood together a moment, looking at the ripped canvas and the face of the safe.

I leaned forward, placing my hands on the edge of the desk; I thought I might be sick. There it was, right in front of us, in front of me; a way out of this crummy, fucking life of shakedowns, hopping freights to get out of town, running away from cops—

"Look at this," said Sam. He had walked around the desk and was trying the iron handle of the safe, twisting it in his hand. Jesus Christ, had Roth left the thing open?

No, of course not, it was shut tight as a nun's asshole; it didn't budge an inch as Sam tested it.

"Look at what?"

"That's purchase."

"Purchase? What the hell are you telling me, we got about seven minutes—"

"Purchase. I got that chain of mine out in the back of the truck, I could tie it up to this handle."

"And then what? You and me are gonna yank it outta the wall?"

He nodded at the big windows, the beautiful wall of glass that looked out over the night landscape.

"Could back the truck up in here," he said.

I got dizzy for a second; it wouldn't pay to think about this too much.

"Let's go, come on!"

I raced over to the glass doors and started pushing another door open; I barely noticed old Sam trotting by me, out onto the patio. Like I said, these doors were about twelve feet tall and framed in ornamental iron, and I don't know if you know this, but tempered glass is kind of heavy. So I had a little trouble getting them both open as wide as they would go, all by myself. I really didn't stop to think about whether the truck could make it through them or not.

I was putting all my weight on the second one when I noticed Sam's truck stumbling up the patio steps, and crossing the flagstones. He was going pretty fast, considering; he almost clipped me as he tooled on by, driving straight through the doors into the dark cavern of the study.

He aimed the truck straight across the vast Persian carpet, away from the safe. I nearly called out to stop him, but then I saw his plan—he was going to back it up, so that the tail end faced the safe. He put it in reverse and started back towards the wall. I started to giggle uncontrollably, as I sometimes do when things get out of hand.

His years of valet parking experience paid off handsomely. He inched the truck backwards until it finally jammed up against the mahogany desk, which was still between him and the wall.

I ran up to the cab. "The desk, you're hitting the—"

"It's okay," he says, his tortoise head craning back out the cab window, eyes fixed on the safe. "We'll need something to take the weight if we do get it out of that wall. Get that chair out from behind the desk!"

I didn't know Sam could be such a take-charge kind of guy. I ran around the desk and rolled the huge leather movie producer's chair out from behind the mahogany. The desk was beginning to creak and protest; it finally gave, sliding a little, then a little more as the truck pressed up against it. I bet that desk weighed about a half a ton; I hoped the Ford could take it.

It could. Momentum and strength won out over friction and Roth's carpet—when the back feet of the desk hit the marble part of the floor, the thing practically sailed over that last few feet—flush, secure, and wedged in tight between the truck and the wall.

Then Sam pulled forward, just about a foot or so—so we'd have room to tie the chain to the back of the truck, I realized. I hopped up onto the desk and into the truck bed and started hauling out the chain. It was heavier than I expected; when I'd seen Sam using it to admit cars at the front gate, I'd assumed it was just for show. But it was the real thing, a serious piece of hardware. I found one end of it and skipped across to the top of the desk again, and began to loop the chain around the metal handle on the face of the safe. I hadn't paid much attention to it before; the handle was a long teardrop-shaped shaft, about an inch and a half thick, solid steel, designed to fit into the palm of your hand. It was joined to the face of the safe by a steel bend of the same width. I looped a couple of links over and through and around the handle, and around the bend in the shaft.

Sam was beneath the back end of the Ford; I could hear chain clinking on metal—tying it to the axle? I hoped not; this safe looked like it was in a lot better shape than his Ford.

"Make sure it's on tight!" he wheezed at me from under the truck. "Then feed me all the slack you can!"

I pulled on the handle at my end and then I began slipping the difference in slack down under the truck to him.

"How's that?"

He didn't answer. I looked at my watch; I guessed we had two or three minutes left.

Sam crawled back up from under the truck; he was clattering leftover chain into the flatbed.

"Okay, here goes."

He hopped into the cab. I hopped, too; off the table, and back to the open doors to the terrace. The music from the party was coming loud and strong—and was that somebody coming up the hill, towards us? No. It was two somebodies. Still far away, but definitely starting up the hill, towards us.

31

The sound of the truck having a heart attack made me turn around. Sam was rocking it back and forth—the engine roared as he went through gears, and the chain, already taut, seemed to be stretching a bit like a rubber band. I stepped into the room to take a closer look at it; I thought I could actually hear it humming from the strain. Then I realized that the chain or the handle on the safe or both might snap and I'd end up with a face full of links. So I backed away outside again.

Sam must have been worried about that chain, too—he wasn't gunning the truck forward, he was just playing with the gears and the accelerator pedal, trying to work the safe loose from the wall. It was really in there—its handle didn't break off, but it didn't budge out of the wall, either, and I began to think we ought to just hightail it out of there—

The two figures coming up the side of the hill were closer now, a little more than a hundred yards off. They weren't running or coming fast, which was good; it meant they didn't have a clue about what was going on up here in the study. But as they passed a light down in the garden, I could see that it was two men, wearing suits, not evening clothes. Which meant that these two guys on their way up were not guests. They were on the estate tonight because they were on the job. Which was bad.

I took the pistol out of my jacket, tore it out of its newspaper wrapping and broke it open. The bullets were in my pocket; I loaded them into the chamber, checked the hammer and took off the safety. I kept peeking at the two men; soon they'd be close enough to hear the truck engine grinding away inside the house.

And then, like a muffled bolt of lightning, there came a loud crack from the study. I ducked back in to look at the safe—it hadn't given way, but the wall had. A long, jagged crack, visible even in the dark, had appeared in the polished wood surface of the wall around the safe; a fissure that ran from the top of the safe all the way up to the ceiling.

The metal lip around the front of the safe now protruded an inch or two from the surface of the wall. The truck was still going, but Sam had backed it up an inch to put a little slack in the chain. Then he put it in neutral and hopped out of the cab to inspect his progress.

He didn't seem happy. "It must be bolted into the beams," he said to me. He noticed the gun in my hand. "What's that for?"

"There's a couple of guys on their way up the hill," I said. "Is it gonna come out?"

He glared at it and said, "Gimme a hand."

He got up onto the top of the big desk and started undoing the chain from the handle. I hopped up after him, helping him to untangle it. I noticed that the strain of the truck had warped the handle a bit, but it was still stuck solid to the door of the safe.

Then Sam began to loop the chain around the perimeter of the exposed lip of the safe; I understood what he was doing. That exposed lip was cast, part of the safe's frame; nothing on earth was going to separate it from the rest of the safe. With more of the chain gripping the safe, the beams holding the safe into the wall would give before the lip did.

Sam tied down the chain with some kind of weird cowboy knot; then he hopped off the table and headed back to the cab.

Then the lights of the room came on.

Someone had come into the study and hit the switch.

"What the devil is going on here?"

The butler, or major domo or whatever he was, was standing by the light switch, staring at us, outraged; with a face like a puffing carp. Boy, was he pissed; look at what we'd done to Mr. Roth's wall, with this truck we'd parked on Mr. Roth's carpet!

Sam was nonplussed for a second; but I was cool and calm, standing there on the table top. This, I could handle—I drew the pistol, smiled, aimed, gave the butler a second to take it all in—and fired.

He had pretty good reflexes, for a butler. He was already gone when the bullet struck the limestone molding near where he'd been standing. I hopped off the top of the table and hit the carpet, running after him; the sound of the shot unfroze Sam and he slipped into the cab and gunned the engine.

I flicked the lights off and began to pistol-whip the Bakelite switch. Those lights would stay off. We didn't want a repeat of that last little incident. I took a quick look down the hall after that butler; he was still running, so I dashed across the room to the open glass doors—

I already knew what I'd see once I was out on the terrace: sure enough, my two little suits were jogging up the hill towards us as fast as their strike-breaking, knuckle-cracking legs could carry them.

I took aim and fired.

These boys had been in the service; they knew what to do when you hear a gunshot—you get down, flat down on the ground, and you stay there 'til you figure out what the hell is going on.

The engine of the Ford roared like an angry lion; and when I turned and looked back inside, I saw the truck leap forward like it was trying to break free, almost reared up into the air—

The wall screeched and groaned like it was giving birth— which it was, in a way, because the Ford was slowly drawing the safe out of it, spilling splintered wood and cracked plaster. The safe was monstrous; and it collapsed on top of the desk like it was exhausted, splitting the desk beneath it. It looked like a miniature coffin made of blackened iron and steel.

Sam slid out of the cab and I ran back inside; then we

both jumped up into the back of the truck and did our damnedest to shift the safe onto the truck bed—it was like trying to shove over a bank building, but our hearts were pumping and we felt like we could do anything, now.

The corners of the box had these big, steel bolts welded to them; at least two inches thick and jutting out at right angles. These had been sunk into the wall beams, to hold the thing in. We used them as handles, and between the two of us managed to tip thing over on its face—then we pushed it over. It hit that truck bed like a bomb going off, and I felt the wooden boards crack under my feet. But they held; the safe lay on its back in the truck, and Sam was in the cab again before I could catch my breath.

I nearly fell off when Sam jerked the truck into first gear. I caught myself on one of the rails, and when I looked up, I saw it.

A figure in the glass door in front of us, silhouetted against the night sky. It was a "shadowy figure," just like they say in the pulps, hard to see; but it unmistakably had something in its hand, something mean, with a barrel—

I aimed to kill this time—because, hey, we were playing for keeps now. But the Ford was turning around the carpet, and that spoiled my shot—the glass beside the shadowy figure exploded, and he spun around and back out onto the patio, through a rain of diamond fragments.

I laughed; Sam was still spinning the wheel towards the open glass doors. "If they get in the way, run them down!" I screamed—not because Sam needed to be told, but because I wanted those guys to hear it.

I got down as we hit the doorframe; and when I say "hit," I mean "hit," because Sam's aim wasn't any too good in the dark. You can't blame him; he was all excited. I kept my face covered and my head down behind the rails, and I heard a shot, not one of mine, as we splashed through the glass and out onto the patio. When I finally dared to look up, I saw that we'd made it out. I was being shaken like a baby's rattle—

those steps leading down to the lawn—I had to grab a bolt on the side of the safe to keep from being thrown off the back of the truck.

Another shot, but it went wide; we were running on the grass now, steady enough for me to get my bearings again. I could see one of them; he'd stuck his head up over the low wall running around the patio. That was a stupid chance for him to take; on the other hand, I didn't want to waste a bullet.

From somewhere inside the house a burglar alarm came on; a screaming bell going off as we rumbled away from the house. But we were lucky; there was a hell of a racket coming from down the hill by the lake now. Fireworks, explosions, the cannon again. It was just past midnight; it was now officially Jack Roth's birthday. The alarm would be lost in the commotion; if anybody noticed it they probably figured it was all part of the act. The tinny music of the band hadn't even stopped. So nobody at the party had a care in the world. Except me and Sam. And those guys who were after us.

32

Sam had that accelerator jammed down to the floorboards. I held tight to the railings hoping he wouldn't get distracted and hit a bush or a servant or something. He took the corner of the house at something like forty miles an hour—that sent me ass over elbow across the bed of the truck, and I nearly broke my hip on the safe as I went.

I crawled up towards the cab, wondering whether I should tell Sam to slow down. Now we were crossing the wide-open mall of the lawn that stretched out between the main house and the front gate. It was long, but way up ahead I could make out the stone wall and the gate that had been built into it. It was flanked by neat little rows of parked cars; you couldn't miss it in this moonlight.

We must have looked pretty conspicuous under all that moonlight, too. I took a peek back in the direction of the house and didn't see anyone following, but that didn't mean jack shit. Those mugs I'd shot at were on the phone now for sure, calling for reinforcements. Jeez, for all I knew, there might even be a phone up there at that front gate—

"Sam!" I yelled into the cab, through the glass rear window. He couldn't hear me, or was pretending not to. I rapped the glass to get his attention; too hard, it turned out, because it cracked. I yelled again; this time he looked over his shoulder, acknowledging my presence but still aiming straight at that front gate, full speed ahead.

"We might run into some trouble at the gate!"

I felt the accelerator ease up just a fraction at that; he was listening.

"You drop me off up there, and then keep going with the truck!" I yelled. "I'll hold them off for a while, give you a head start!"

"How will you get out?" he says. It was funny; he

sounded kind of like a crow when he shouted, I'd never heard him do that before.

"Don't worry about it! Just go when I tell you!" The gate was already rushing up towards us. A few valets and a couple of chauffeurs were hanging around watching the fireworks and enjoying a smoke. They stared in the direction of the Ford as it bore down on them, but they didn't seem alarmed or agitated. I could see that the big iron doors of the main gate were closed.

"Pull up when we get there," I shouted at Sam. "I'll hop off and get the doors open! Then take off and don't stop for anything, just keep going!"

"Then what?"

"Stick to the plan!" By now, I'd completely forgotten what the plan was, but it sounded like good advice. I felt the truck slow down, and I hopped off the back, losing my balance as I hit the soft grass.

When I got up, dusting myself off, I was looking at two of Sam's valet parking pals, who looked back at me in astonishment. "Hi, fellas!" I said, walking towards them. They didn't answer, they were waiting for some explanation. "Open the gate, willya?" I said, as pleasantly as I could.

They just stood there, like a bunch of dummies. Sam had stopped the truck behind me; I turned my head and saw him chattering away with a kid who stood with one foot on the running board. The kid probably worked for the estate or the groundskeeper or something; he listened to Sam's yammering, but he wasn't impressed and he wasn't moving.

There was a little office type of building that had been built into the stone wall next to the gate. I heard a telephone start to ring inside it, and then a guy in a uniform came out into the open from behind the big shrubs—he must have been taking a piss back there; he looked like a watchman. He stared at me as he walked out into the open, and then he looked over at his booth, where the phone was still ringing—

I drew the pistol and fired it at the glass window of the

booth; it shattered loud and pretty. The phone kept on ringing, but no one cared anymore: I didn't even have to tell them, everybody had their hands up in the air and was frozen where they stood. Even the guard.

The kid who'd been listening to Sam was staring pop-eyed at me. He seemed the most intimidated, so I told him to get that gate open. He started to do so while I kind of shepherded the others over away from the rows of cars.

I didn't even see Sam drive away, I was too busy watching my new prisoners and the big house in the distance behind them. I saw something like a tiny black beetle moving fast around the corner of the big house; then two tiny white lights appeared on the 'beetle.' My stomach turned; another car, headed down the mall towards us as fast as it could go—towards me, actually, since Sam was gone. The headlamps were getting brighter and angrier; the car had a kind of 'pissed off' air about it.

"You!" I shouted, dropping my voice an octave or two for authority. All of them shook visibly. "Start one of those cars!" I pointed my pistol at the head of the nearest fat guy and aimed it right between his eyes.

"Which one?" he peeped. I wondered if his voice usually sounded like that.

"That Lincoln!" I said; nodding at the biggest, blackest limousine.

He got into the Lincoln. He didn't have to look for keys, thank God; Sam said they always left the keys in the cars at these big parties.

"You!" I said, all Wallace Beery, to the remaining mugs. "Down on the ground, flat on your bellies, keep your hands out where I can see them." I wasn't really that worried about these guys; I realized now that the one guy in uniform was a chauffeur, not an armed guard. But I had to give them something to do, and they did it, obediently.

I jumped up onto the running board of the Lincoln as the beams of angry headlamps hit the gate and the walls, closing in. It looked like the oncoming car was a Packard; Roth paid his goons well. I took careful aim and fired a shot just above and between the headlamps, guessing. The lights spun away suddenly—maybe I hadn't hit anybody, but I sure scared the driver. The Packard wheeled off behind a row of other cars, where I couldn't see it anymore.

"Pull up to the gate, slow and steady," I said to the poor fat bastard behind the wheel of the Lincoln, and I reached into the open window and hooked my arm around his neck, holding the smoking revolver up under his nose. To keep his attention.

The big Lincoln turned slowly out of its spot, towards the open gate. The guys in the Packard were pissed, alright. They began to pump bullets into the side of the Lincoln. Popping away, hoping to hit something; didn't even care if they got my hostage by accident, the insensitive bastards. I was riding on the running board on the other side of the Lincoln, thank goodness. A loud bang came from the rear of our car; it shook, and then there was a hissing, like a snake. They'd plugged one of the white-walled tires. Okay by me, fellas, it's not my Lincoln.

I wasn't all that worried about the guns, relatively speaking. It was dark, and anyway the Lincoln was a limousine, black and almost as big as a bus. They couldn't see me, on this side of it. Besides, they needed me alive, to tell them how to get that safe back, right?

But the fat guy at the wheel was worried, alright. He was beginning to give off an awful smell all of the sudden. "Park it across the gate," I said to him. "If you can block the gate with this car, I won't kill you, okay?" I figured that would cheer him up a bit, give him a goal to work towards. I felt him nod his wattles; showing me he understood.

I noticed that the kid who'd opened the front gate was still holding onto it, petrified as a lawn jockey. I gave him an encouraging nod as the fat guy angled the limo into place. Another bullet whanged into the passenger side as we wedged it into the sweet spot between the stone posts of the gate.

"Keys!" I snapped at the driver as I opened the door to let him out. He handed the keys to me and I hopped off the running board, motioning for him to slide out of the driver's seat. (He did, literally. I silently pitied the poor owner of this Lincoln.) Then the fat guy took off into the night, faster than I'd have thought possible for a man his size. I went the other way, running down the dark street towards where Sam was supposed to have parked my Bentley.

My legs were saying "Run, run, run!" but my brain was saying, "Stick around, you punk, Sam needs that head start you promised him." I kept my eye on the Lincoln, sitting like a freight car between the two huge stone posts of Roth's front gate. My fat guy had done a pretty good job; you couldn't get a unicycle out between those bumpers and those gateposts. I tossed the keys to the Lincoln off into the bushes and headed for my Bentley.

There it was, in that clump of trees, just like I'd told Sam. I had a momentary panic as I felt around the floor, looking for the keys that Sam was supposed to have left—there they were. I unlocked the ignition, got it started, and left it in neutral with the brake on so I could go back to the edge of the trees to watch the gate. You couldn't see down here from the street or the gate. So far so good, but I had to make sure that Sam had that extra few minutes. I lay down in a bunch of tall spiky ferns, and watched the gate.

It was less than a minute before they got up the courage to come out—first the parking guys, crawling over the hood of the Lincoln. Then came a big, scary-looking guy; one of the suits from the Packard, I guessed. He crawled over the front bumper with great difficulty, snapping orders at the rest of them; his weight actually made the sedan sag a bit. I bet he was sorry he'd shot out that back tire now, but he had the others pretty well organized already. Soon they were a team, pushing together to try to clear the Lincoln from the gate—the kid who'd held the gate was turning the wheel of the car. It had just started to inch forward when I fired.

I aimed for another of the whitewalls, and I think I even hit it. The spokes, anyway. Not a bad shot, in the dark. But of course, my strategy was not to pop out tires, but to keep the guys on the estate pinned down for a bit; scared to come out and move that Lincoln. It worked; they scattered like flies when they heard the shot. All except the big, scary-looking guy in the suit. I could have plugged him right then (and later on I'd be sorry I didn't), but I was down to my last bullet already. And I really didn't see the need to kill anybody now that Sam and I were both out of there.

It was funny how this guy wouldn't run, though. He just turned away from the back of the limo, where he'd been pushing, as if he'd casually changed his mind about where to move it. And then he strolled out to the side of the car—the side facing me, mind you—and he leaned back on it, resting one big foot on the running board. Taking a little break. He was across the street from where I lay and I couldn't really see the face under the hat—but it seemed to me that he was staring straight at me. It was impossible, I was sure he couldn't see me. I was well down in the ferns, laying on my stomach and wearing those dark clothes. In the shadow of a hill, out of the moonlight. But for some reason, I had the impression that he was smiling at me. And it bugged me.

It gave me the creeps, but at least I wasn't worried about him trying to get the boys to move that Lincoln again. Those guys parked cars for a living; they weren't U.S. Marines. They weren't about to take a bullet for dear old Jack Roth, no matter how much he tipped.

The big guy didn't bother to call them back again. He just reached into his jacket—which made my back go up, believe me—and took out a cigarette, if you can believe that, and then he took a lighter out of his pocket and lit up. Knowing that I was lurking out there in the bushes with a loaded gun. Enjoying his smoke, as it were, under the lovely moon and stars. Except he never seemed to take his eyes off me, out here in the dark. Was it possible that he really could see me, somehow?

It was nearly ten minutes since Sam had raced off at top speed with the safe. I figured it was okay for me to make my exit. It would take the big guy at least another five minutes to convince the others that it was safe to come out again and to move that limo. That's as much head start as anybody is entitled to, Sam. This guy across the street was beginning to rattle me. I started to move, crawling backwards like a crayfish among the big ferns.

Then I was out in the clear, back with my beautiful Bentley. It was humming quietly, all warmed up, waiting for me. I hopped into the driver's seat, and kept it quiet as I rolled down out of the trees and onto the street. I didn't look to see if the big man was staring after me; I didn't want to. Anyway, they'd never catch me once this thing got going. I kept the lights off until I'd gone a mile or so. No sense advertising.

Then I stepped down on the gas. I was out of there, and I was alive, moving down the night road at ninety miles an hour. And, maybe, I was rich—you don't build yourself a safe like that unless you're gonna keep something real valuable in it.

But even though things had gone better than I'd hoped, it didn't feel as good as it ought to have felt. Usually I feel confident, once I've actually got the goods on a mark. But that night I was doubtful, for some reason I couldn't tell you. I was still only half convinced that Sam and I would live to enjoy what we'd stolen.

And that guy leaning against the Lincoln—he was creepy. I finally decided he hadn't been able to see me, out there in the dark. He sure was thinking about me, though.

33

I don't know what the hell I was thinking—after all my lecturing to Sam about lamming it, I actually started to drive back to the Ambassador. I was a little rattled by the whole thing, I guess; I was shaking like a dog taking a dump. I was stopped at a traffic light when it finally occurred to me that going back to the hotel might be a bad idea. The Ambassador would already be crawling with creeps on the lookout for me. They've probably just kicked in the door of your lovely little suite, I thought, and they're about to go through every single item in your room.

That would suit them just fine if you strolled in on them. They're just salivating at the possibility, I thought to myself, and I turned back up into the hills again. The San Fernando Valley should be pretty safe for the time being, but I had to ditch this car and the tux. Hanging on to them would be like wearing a neon sign for those guys to follow around.

But maybe, I thought, as I glided through the night—maybe you're worrying too much. That doesn't pay, either, you know. You worry too much, you might end up trying to correct some mistake you didn't make, and that can really screw things up. I wasn't worried about the local law; Roth couldn't call them in without having to answer a lot of embarrassing questions about what was in the safe. It was studio cops that Sam and I had to worry about now. And maybe I was over-estimating them. Stacey and Sam said they were good—but how good was good, out here on the West Coast?

There was a way I could find out. I pulled over at an all-night filling station and used the phone while the kid filled the tank of the Bentley. I called Sam's rooming house; I kept on ringing 'til the manager finally gave up and got out of bed and answered.

"He's not here!" he growled, when I asked for Sam.

"Sure he is," I insisted.

"He ain't come in, damn it, I woulda heard him!"

"Well, check his room can'tcha, this is an emergency!"

"Emergency my ass, you're that bum who was spongin' off him last week, ain'tcha?"

What would impress this guy? "Look," I said, "he won three thousand bucks on a parlay, okay? Bring him to the phone!"

That did it. He set the earpiece down and I could hear him clump away up the stairs after Sam, who, of course, wasn't there. This was all good; it was calming me down considerably, because, you see, it was apparent from the manager's reaction that no one had come down there looking for Sam, yet. The studio cops, if they were good, would already have learned that it was Sam who'd taken off with the safe in the back of his truck. And, again, if they were good, it would have taken them less than a New York minute to get Sam's address and send someone over to go through his room. Obviously, they hadn't been there yet, so there was nothing to—

Then I heard a crash; it was like somebody had turned on the radio and tuned in to listen to 'Gangbusters.' I heard the tinny sounds at the other end of the line—splintering wood, smashed glass, men's voices, and thumping feet like elephants.

Uh oh. I turned around in the booth and looked at my Bentley. The attendant had finished with the gas and was lovingly polishing the windshield. He looked up at me and nodded; I gave him my brightest smile. But I was sick at heart, still listening to all that action on the other end of the phone.

I heard the landlord's voice, hoarse and outraged, but I couldn't make out what he was saying. Something about a warrant. Then there was an awful second of silence, and a horrible, pig-like grunting—also the landlord, I bet. It was, because he was talking again now, but he sounded all serious and respectful now.

There were questions being asked, and I thought I heard the name "Sam" mentioned. Then there was a horrible, meaty sort of sound, a scuffle, and the questions stopped. Then somebody picked up the earpiece and talked into the receiver.

"Hello?"

"Hello," I said cautiously.

"Who's this?" says the voice, all friendly.

"Who's *this*?" I say back, even friendlier.

"I asked you first," says the voice. (At least he had a sense of humor.)

"Gee, I'd rather not say," I said shyly. "I'm calling for a friend, he's bringing my new safe around this evening. Has he arrived, yet?"

That bugged him a bit. "No," says the voice, "He hasn't, Mr. Hart." *That* bugged me. "But if he shows, we'll be sure and tell him you called. Where are you calling from, Mr. Hart?"

"Your mother's house," I said, and then I made a big, smoochy kissing noise into the phone and hung up.

Okay, so these guys were good. I paid the kid for the gas and took off, further into the Valley beyond the hills. I was scared, again. The phone call told me that Sam was still on the loose, but every minute I kept driving this fancy car in these fancy clothes was shortening my life. I had to get anonymous again, and quick.

I got off the highway and went down a county road; back to the farms and orange groves.

It would be dark for a few more hours yet. I pulled the Bentley off the road, and into some kind of orchard or something, and parked it in among the trees. I took out the little valise I'd packed at the hotel. It was full of essentials: my cash was in there, along with Vera's handcuffs and Stacey's address book; also the jewelry and various other good stuff I'd managed to pick up over the last few days.

I felt sad, leaving that Bentley all alone out there in the

middle of a fruit farm. I think I loved that car as much as any dog or woman I ever had. But I left it anyway, and I walked a few hundred yards back to the highway.

I stood among the trees by the roadside, hoping to hitch a ride. A couple of cars went by, but I let them go. It was the trucks I was after; they wouldn't come looking for me in a truck. I figured I stood a pretty good chance of getting picked up, as late as it was; I didn't look like a bum or a hijacker. I bet I was the best-dressed hitchhiker in the San Fernando Valley, that night.

A pair of lights; high off the ground and close together—that was a truck. I dashed out of the orange grove and up onto the road, and stuck my thumb out, jerking it and giving the driver my winning smile. Sure enough, he began to downshift and rolled to a stop about a hundred feet beyond me.

I hopped in, saluting him. He was a Mexican fella, one of these fruit picker types. He nodded to me, grinning. He was probably pretty curious; why was a white man in tie and tails standing out by the side of an orchard in the dead of night, thumbing a ride?

He didn't seem to speak much English. I kind of pantomimed for him: I let on that I had been ditched by my girl (I made the shape with my hands), we had a fight (wagging my finger, yelling), she slapped my face (acted this out), and drove off in my car (I mimed her at steering wheel, ignition, giving me the bird as she drove off).

Well, he laughed fit to bust. I got in, and we tooled off down the road. No cars behind us so far. Then he asked where I was headed for, and I just shrugged, and said "Glendale?"

He shook his head 'no,' and jerked his thumb at the back of his truck: empty fruit crates. "Pasadena," he said. He was supposed to get them somewhere by sun-up, was my guess.

I said I was willing to pay. He understood, but still he

shook his head. I reached into my jacket and pulled out my wallet; I felt his eyes honing in on it as I thumbed through the bills.

I pulled out a ten—I figured that was a week's pay for a guy who did what he did.

He took it from me, held it up to the windshield, and handed it back to me, shaking his head "no" again.

A hard bargainer. I held out two tens. He took them and looked them over. Then he put them in his pocket without looking at me. "Okay," he said.

"Gracias," I said, relaxing a little. I was glad he took the money; he seemed like a nice enough guy and I didn't want to have to get tough and pull the gun or something.

I leaned back, watching the orchards go by in the headlamps as we headed down the Valley. Occasionally we passed another car coming the other way, fast. I wondered which one was out here looking for my Bentley or Sam's Ford.

I was dog-tired, but I couldn't bring myself to close my eyes, not even for a minute. I was worried about Sam. And I was, after all, down to that last bullet.

34

He dropped me off downtown. It was still before dawn and I was headed for that motor court now. I decided to walk, because I didn't want that Mexican telling anyone he'd dropped me off there. It was less than a mile and the fresh air revived me a little.

The office was closed, the manager asleep in the back someplace. I just walked onto the grounds, past the cabins, looking for Sam's truck. I got a little queasy when I didn't see it straight away; there weren't that many cars and it should have been easy to spot, even at this hour. But there it was; parked in back of the cabin he'd rented. Sam had covered up the safe with a big canvas tarp and wrapped the chain around it a few times to discourage peeking.

I opened the truck door and reached under the seat. There were the keys; and the key to the cabin, too. Beautiful, Sam. I went to the cabin, and knocked softly. No answer. I unlocked the door and went in without pulling the chain on the light. The bed was still made up, hadn't been slept in. Good—Sam had done like I said and lit out after dropping off the truck.

I certainly wasn't going to sleep there; those guys following us were pretty impressive. I wasn't going to be caught snoring with that truck and the safe parked out back. If they managed to trace us this far, let them find an empty room and think they just missed us.

I locked the door and got into the truck. I kept the headlamps off and pulled it up around the back of the motor court, way back from the cabins and the road, into some greenery. I parked it up behind some trees. Through the windshield I could still see some of the cabins and the office, off in the distance.

I'd sleep a lot sounder here, stretched out across the

front seat of the truck. Just a few hours rest; I'd be okay for a while. I lay there in the dark of the cab, wondering what I was going to do with this truck. It couldn't stay out here in the woods forever. When I'd planned this thing, I'd thought we'd be leaving the Roth place with a bundle of incriminating paper and maybe a chunk of ready cash; I hadn't planned on having to stash a cast-iron safe and a truck besides. It was a problem.

But I couldn't think about that now. I'd think about that tomorrow. After all, tomorrow is another day… Zzzz.

The sun was already high when I woke up. I took a piss in the woods, and then I drove out of the court. I was now looking for a realtor. My new plan involved renting some foreclosed farm or something, an out of the way place where I could keep the safe and the truck while we negotiated with Roth.

I drove into Glendale and found a haberdashery. The owner had looked at me funny when I strolled in still wearing that tux, but he liked the cash I gave him for a suit off the rack. I wore it out of the store and walked to a realtor's office up the street. The agent was so hungry for a commission that he would have rented me his grandmother, if I asked him.

I followed him out of town in the truck to a property he was listing. It was just the ticket: a farmhouse with a rotten old barn out back that would be perfect for stashing the safe. I parked the truck in the barn and rented the place from him on the spot. Under a phony name, of course; but I paid him six months rent up front, so there weren't too many questions. Not only that, he gave me a lift back into Los Angeles when I told him I might be interested in renting something in town, too.

This, by the way, is a good way to get free rides; just find out what a real estate broker is listing, pick out a property that's near where you want to go, and then tell the realtor you want to go over there to look it over. Chances are he'll drive you all the way out there like he was your chauffeur or something. Then when you get there, you tell him the property's not right for you, the location's all wrong or it smells or something. When he tries to drag you back in the car to show you something else, just tell him to buzz off—tell him you're offended by some crack he made earlier in the day or something. Off he goes, and there you are, within a few blocks of where you wanted to be in the first place, no charge. It's saved me a fortune on taxis, that gag. I've gotten rides as far as fifty miles away from the broker's office; they'll practically take you cross-country if they think there's any chance of a commission. Serves 'em right, I say. Real estate brokers are lying sons-of-bitches, every last one of them.

35

I needed a shave and a shower, but I wanted to see the papers first. Good news: there wasn't anything in the afternoon editions about the theft of the safe; nothing in the morning papers, either. I didn't think there would be; if Stacey was right about what was in the safe, Roth would do his best to keep things quiet. His scary partners back in New York would kill him for sure if his carelessness got them in hot water. (There was an angle I hadn't thought of: if Roth didn't want to pay off when the time came, I'd make some noise about calling New York myself. That would send a chill down his spine, alright.)

His boys probably had to twist a lot of arms and pay a lot out in cash to keep the servants and the press quiet. He had to keep the cops away; otherwise what could he tell them? "Help, help, officer, somebody took Bugsy Siegel's financial statements outta my safe."

It was nearly one in the afternoon. As good a time as any to become a millionaire.

I didn't call first to tell Roth I was coming over; I wanted it to be a surprise. I decided to open negotiations at the studio because I figured that would be a relatively safe place. The Olympic lot would be crowded- full of Roth's employees. I wanted plenty of people around, to see me come in, and, hopefully, to see me go out.

Actually, I wasn't too worried. Roth might be pissed, he might even be howling for my head—but he wouldn't try anything on the Olympic lot. After all, you don't shit where you live, as Shakespeare said. And Roth wasn't crazy; his main interest would be getting his stuff back, intact. Until that happened, he couldn't think about taking me out.

Also, I have a bad stomach; it would be a lot easier on

my nerves for me to go and see Roth, rather than wait around for him to send somebody to see me. So I took a cab out there.

Olympic Studios is in Hollywood, off Sunset Boulevard on what they call "Poverty Row." They call it Poverty Row because the movie companies that are based there don't usually have the bucks to put together big screen extravaganzas or pay the salaries of really big stars. Lots of people in town were puzzled as to why Stacey Tilden stuck with Olympic when Paramount or MGM could do better for her. Her official reason was that Olympic let her choose her own scripts. I knew better.

I gave the name Hart to the guard in the booth at the front gate. I said I was here to see Mr. Roth; to help him recover something he'd lost at his birthday party.

I looked at my watch, and counted the minutes. Two, to be exact.

"Mr. Hart?"

I looked up. A little string bean of a guy appeared before me, big white smile, real friendly. Never seen him before in my life.

"You're here to see Mr. Roth?" He didn't offer his hand and he didn't look like your typical studio type. He was young, but dressed too sharp for an office boy, and his eyes were just piggy little brown spots in his pointy face. I didn't like this kid, whatever he was.

"Yeah, I'm here to see Roth. Who're you?"

"My name is Petey," he said, and the teeth flashed again. The eyes were the only color in his face; he obviously didn't get out in the sunshine much. He turned and walked away from me, onto the lot. He stopped when he saw I wasn't following, and gestured for me to follow.

"This way, please, Mr. Hart." When I hesitated, he said it again. "This way."

The Olympic lot was a bunch of interconnected buildings and long dead-end alleys walled off from the rest of the world. It felt industrial; offices, warehouses for the props and sets and costumes. The shooting stages were housed inside these buildings that looked like giant airplane hangars. I followed Petey along the wide alley between the hangars and the Olympic business offices. I saw all the usual studio bullshit; but it was new to me back then. Painted flats and gazebos and fake storefronts—being hauled around, torn apart, nailed together again. We walked by a miniature medieval city, built to add class to some swashbuckler picture. It was about eight feet tall and forty feet long, with tiny villas and streets and a little model castle up on top. Some fellas were aiming a camera up at it, to get it on film. As I passed I told them that I thought it looked kind of fake. Just a little joke, you know?

Some cowboys and musketeers were across the alley, taking a break, smoking cigarettes, talking about their next job. I noticed that those movie costumes look sort of cheap when you see them in real life. Then we passed a couple of babes dolled up like southern belles; their costumes looked real, it was them that looked a little cheap.

I was surprised to see that we were headed for a low brick one-story building instead of the office building to our right. The name of the building was cut into sandstone over the door: Olympic Studios Film Laboratory. What the hell was this, a tour or something?

Inside looked like a bunch of doctor's offices in an old hospital. It had that funny chemical smell, too. The place was spotless; the floors waxed 'til they glowed. A guy wheeling a bunch of big lights down the hall; a door down the hall opening up and a little girl in a ballerina outfit coming out, followed by a big sweaty guy in shirtsleeves, tapping a clipboard and telling her what she was doing wrong.

"This way, please!" Petey sang out. I turned to see him headed down to the far end of the hall. It was a long way, and we passed a bunch of frosted glass doors with words lettered on them in gold: "Sound," "Synchronization," stuff like that. I could hear activity behind the doors, and the chemical smell was stronger. The stuff they use to develop films, I guessed.

There was a faint, steady humming coming from somewhere, like electricity. I could feel it beneath my feet, coming from somewhere under the floor. Like pressure was building up, slow and steady.

The windows in this half of the hallway had been plastered over. The only light came from bulbs spaced apart in recesses near the ceiling. It was empty, except for Petey and me. Petey was walking quickly ahead of me, passing through sections of artificial light and shadow as he went.

There were no sounds coming from behind the frosted glass doors now. Petey stopped in front of a door that was made of leather, dyed to match the walls, and inscribed with gilt letters that said, "DO NOT OPEN." That didn't discourage Petey. He grabbed the funny-looking handle that opened the padded door, and motioned me to go into the dark room beyond, grinning at me with those big white teeth.

36

I didn't wanna go in there, it looked all dark and scary.

But it was business, so I went. This room, I soon realized, was a screening room; probably one of several on the production lot. You know, one of the private little theaters where an important producer or director can screen movie footage. Rushes, they call them. Louis B. Mayer, head of MGM, was called the "Czar of All the Rushes," get it? Like "Czar of All the Russias?" Heh, heh.

Anyway, it was there so the bigwigs could see how things were going, make sure everybody's actually turning in a good day's work out on the movie sets. I slipped by Petey and took a look inside—it was pretty plush in there, lots of comfy theater seating, but a little claustrophobic. It didn't help that the ceiling was low, so you felt like you were in a cave. The only light in the joint came from a movie being shown on a screen at one end of the room, and the projector showing the movie through a little hole in the wall at the other end.

Petey closed the door silently behind us. I looked at the picture that was being run on the screen. It was some kind of adventure thing; maybe a scene from one of those serials they run for kids at Saturday matinee. A couple of guys wearing sacks over their heads were tying a guy up, villain style. Not my kind of picture. No soundtrack, either, and the projector in the booth was loud as hell.

I looked down the aisle and saw a fat neck and broad shoulders sticking up over the seats, silhouetted by the screen. Petey coughed, and the fat neck swivelled round. He was wearing a fedora, but I could see the face in the beam from the projection booth. Big bulgy eyes behind thick glasses; not pretty. A bespectacled octopus. It was looking over its shoulder and seemed to resent the interruption. Then it spoke.

"Turn it off." The voice was a wheeze.

The ugly face disappeared into pitch black when the projector went off.

"Lights, Eddie," said the raspy voice. Lots of cigarettes and whiskey in that voice.

The lights mounted in the wall came up, soft and dim—and that was just as well, because the big guy rising from the seat was no movie star. He looked more like a bouncer or a cop than a studio chief. The big face behind the glasses was looking me over, daring me to try something.

"You're not Jack Roth," I said.

Petey, still behind me, sniggered at that.

The man started walking up the aisle towards me. It was like watching an elephant get under way—not fat, just big and powerful, overcoming a lot of inertia.

"As a matter of fact," he whispered, "I ain't."

I shrugged my shoulders and turned to go, annoyed. Petey at the door rested one hand on the lapel of my jacket, and shook his head 'no.' He didn't look humorous, anymore.

"You talk to me," says the raspy voice behind me. "You don't get to talk to Mr. Roth. It's bad business for Mr. Roth to be seen talking to guys like you."

When I turned around, he was right there in front of me—or over me, I should say. He was at least a head taller than me, and I'm no midget.

"I don't have time for this bullshit," I said. "The deal—"

He brought a great big finger up in front of me and stuck it right in front of my nose.

"Language!"

I looked him in the eye, as best I could. "You tell your boss to call me when he gets serious."

Then I turned around and shoved Petey out of my way. That was when I saw that there was no inside handle on the door.

"We're all serious, here," said the elephant. He was smiling pleasantly when I turned to face him again. He called up to the projection booth.

"Eddie?"

"Yeah?" The voice came from inside the projection booth.

"Run it back again. Let's all watch it together."

I turned and tried the edge of the door with my fingers; it didn't budge.

"Sit down," says the elephant, and turned and treaded back down the aisle as though he didn't care if I followed or not. "It's an electric door. You don't get out until I let you out. Come on down front here and sit next to me. We'll watch some of this movie together, we'll talk."

He turned and motioned to me.

"C'mon, it'll be fun."

I looked at Petey; he was grinning like a loon again, and he gestured like he was the headwaiter: 'after you, please.'

Okay, what the hell, I came all the way down here. I followed the big man down the aisle.

"My name is Wally O'Brien, ya ever hearda me?" says the monster beside me, stuffing himself back into his chair. The row of seats creaked.

"No," I lied, taking the seat a couple of spaces down from him. The lights were still up, and I could see he had a cauliflower ear. An ex-heavyweight?

"Yeah, I guessed you never hearda me. From outta town, right?" He reached into his pocket, took out a business card and handed it over to me.

"Yeah." I slipped the card into my jacket without reading it; it was dark anyway.

"Everybody in town knows me. I work for Mr. Roth these days. I didn't always. I was his bootlegger back during Prohibition. Then I went straight; Mr. Roth got me a job with the county. Sheriff's Office." He toyed with one of the movie seats between us, testing the hinge, making it squeak.

"Now I'm working for Mr. Roth again. Here at the studio. I'm kind of a troubleshooter."

This was exactly the sort of situation I had wanted to avoid. It was my fault, really; what was I thinking, setting up a meeting here at the studio? I should have made Roth come down to the Cocoanut Grove to talk, or Chasen's, or wherever.

"Eddie!" O'Brien yells, without looking up.

"Yeah?"

"How's it goin' up there?"

"It'll be a minute. I'm havin' trouble with this…sprocket-y projector thing… The film, I can't get it back in the…"

"The thread?"

"Yeah!"

O'Brien turns in his chair, and a whole row of seats groans again.

"Gowan up there and give him a hand, Petey."

Petey hesitated.

"Gowan, it's alright." He turned to me again, and explained: "These boys ain't regular projectionists. They're my boys. Ex-cops, both of 'em. Sometimes a fella has to leave the job, for one reason or another. A studio's a good place to work, good money."

"Look, am I gonna get paid?"

He raised his eyebrows, stopped. Then he lowered the eyebrows again and went on like I'd never spoken.

"The other employees don't like us, though. We give 'em the creeps, I guess. We kinda do stuff like you do, ya know? Follow people around, check up on 'em. Find out what we can find out. The studio and the banks that own the studios, they got a lotta money tied up in some of these actors. So they hire us to watch 'em, and keep 'em out of trouble."

He rubbed his eyes and blinked.

"It pisses a lotta people off when a guy like you comes along and tries to pull a shakedown. I don't just mean the studio heads, either. It's bankers, the Wall Street guys who finance the whole thing. If they smell trouble, that affects next year's prospects. Maybe a big loan will go bad. Lots of people go down."

"So pay up, and I'll get lost."

He looks up at the blank screen. "Something I never knew about this whole movie business, before Mr. Roth explained it to me. The studios, they're hooked up with these theater chains. Movie houses all over the country. That's the way it's been since the business got started. And these movie houses, they're sittin' in prime downtown locations in every city and town in the U.S.A., you follow me?"

Actually, I found this interesting.

"The studios borrow money, big money from these Wall Street guys like Kennedy and the brokerages and all, to buy these theaters. And all that prime downtown real estate the theaters are sitting on. And the studios pay back on these loans each year, with the money they make from showing movies. Exhibition. That's why the big guys need hit pictures all the time, see? They wanna keep payin' off these loans to the bankers, and they wanna pay it off as fast as they can. 'Cause as soon as they pay off these Wall Street guys, they own this prime downtown real estate everywhere, every city in the country. How much you figure all that land is gonna be worth, ten, twenty years from now?"

He looked at me, to see if I could figure it out in my head.

"I figured it out, once," he says. "If these big guys pull it off, they're gonna be billionaires. Big as Rockefeller. That's why things in this town are so crazy all the time. You read about some picture making a million dollars, that's nothing. Nothing compared to what these guys need for their bankers."

The lights in the room went down. O'Brien's voice continued in the dark. "So, a guy like you comes along, some little piss-ant. Okay, it took balls to pull off that job at the party, I respect that, but... when you come along and try to shake down Jack Roth, you're not just screwin' around with Jack Roth. And you're not just messing around with his old pals from back East, either. You're—" he seemed at a loss for the right words here—"You're messin' with a whole bunch of big guys you don't even know about, and if, uh, you interrupt the, uh, income stream… they're gonna step on you."

I started slowly.

"You know, Mr. O'Brien—"

"Wally."

"Okay, Wally. I just had an idea. It might be crazy, but I'll run it by you and you tell me what you think."

"Okay."

"Well, you're trying to convince me I'm in over my head, trying to get this money out of Roth."

"You *are* in over your head."

"Okay, then. Suppose you come in with me? This information I've got—"

He brought his great big hand up. "I don't want to know it."

"You don't know what it is?"

'It's about the safe you took, and it's got something to do with Miss Tilden, and that's all I want to know. It would be dangerous for me to know more than that."

Okay," I nodded.

"I know it could hurt the studio, and Mr. Roth thinks it could hurt the studio so bad that he wants me to fix it. He told me to put all my guys on it. That's all I need to know."

"Okay. But please hear my idea."

Silence.

"I'll bet you're right. I'm not big enough to pull this off. But if you were to come in with me, a silent partner, things might be different, right? You know the town, you know Roth, you know how people do things out here. You could give me advice, and Roth would never know it was coming from you. I'd give you half. Based on what you just told me, what I've got is worth a lot more than I thought, right?"

"Oh, yeah. If it's stuff on Mr. Roth, it's worth a pile to him. Even if it's just stuff about Stacey Tilden, well… You wreck Stacey Tilden, you could wreck the next two years for the studio. Mr. Roth would be out of here, that's for sure. Even if he couldn't pay you to keep quiet, there's a few studios in town that would probably pay you off just so they could ruin him and get a crack at his theater chains."

I didn't like the tone of his voice. Too agreeable.

"So, uh... What do you say?"

"Watch this movie."

37

The film started up; the same scene as before—silver gray movie footage of the deck of a boat. It was nighttime, but the boat's deck was all lit up by offscreen studio lights. Arc lights, I think they call them. One of the men with a sack over his head appeared in the camera frame, holding a big towline. He was uncoiling it on the deck; then he straightened up, and he looked like he was waiting for or listening to someone beyond the screen—maybe the cameraman or director was telling him what to do. (There was no soundtrack, so it was hard to tell.) I noticed he wore a suit and tie, a good cut; but the sack over his head seemed kind of improvised—not a hood, like the Klan, just an old burlap thing with holes cut in it for the eyes.

Another character came on screen; he was wearing the same sort of get-up, the hood and the suit. He took up the end of the towline, and he and the first guy began to heave-ho on it together. They were pulling at something heavy, just off screen.

The movie was definitely unprofessional, real raw. The camera had the boat motion rocking it —up and down, gently, but it got to be annoying. You couldn't see the ocean because the bright lights drowned out the darkness beyond. This wasn't filmed on a studio lot—it wasn't slick enough. It was sort of like home movies. The guys in the hoods looked comical tugging away on the rope like that, coiling up the slack. Not exactly what you'd call drama. And the film ran a little jerky, too..

Then I saw what was on the end of the rope; they'd dragged it on screen. An anchor; a big old iron Popeye-the Sailor-Man-looking anchor. Real heavy—that's why it had taken two of them to drag it into view.

O'Brien was watching the picture, mildly interested.

Now one of the hooded fellows walked out of the frame, then returned, dragging a heavy wooden chair with him. A man was tied into the chair. (I'd seen this part before, when I'd first entered the room.) The man was jerking around, trying to escape, but he was bound by ropes almost as heavy as the towline. Trussed up across the chest, with his legs tied so that they splayed out on either side of the chair. He seemed to be screaming, and the cameraman went in for a closer shot; a big black stain running down the side of his head.

Sam.

The cameraman moved out again and the men in hoods secured one end of the towline to the anchor and ran the other through the back of the chair. Sam was twisting frantically under the ropes, like a worm trying to get off a fishhook. But he wasn't going anywhere; the ropes were too tight, the heavy chair was too strong, and Sam was too old.

I could see he was pleading and crying—and the whirring sound of the projector behind me was somehow more disturbing than if I could actually hear him. He craned his neck and rolled his eyes at the two men in hoods, who were struggling to raise the old anchor up at the bow of the boat. They managed to balance it on the gunwale, and one of the men steadied it on the edge of the pitching boat.

The bigger of the two picked up Sam, chair and all, and tipped him up against the wall of the boat. Compared to the anchor, Sam was a feather.

Then the cameraman started to move in closer again. He went forward, towards Sam. As he closed in (he must have been holding the camera in his hands, it was so unsteady now) I could see that the big black stain running down the side of Sam's head was matted blood. He was screaming at the man behind the camera. I wanted to shut my eyes, but I didn't.

The hooded man hoisted Sam up, and Sam and the chair went over the side. The photographer came forward and tilted the camera down, trying to follow him, trying to catch him on film as he hit the water. But the photographer's lighting pals didn't get the klieg light there in time to catch the splash.

Its beam raked the black surface of the water, looking for Sam. And—there he was; you could see his face, just breaking the surface. The anchor hadn't touched bottom, yet. He gasped and twisted; his hand looked like the white claw of a bird, strapped to the arm of that chair.

He managed to spin around and get his face out of the water one more time. Then he was jerked under the surface and he was gone, like a giant hand had just pulled on a rope and snatched him down below; gone just like that. The camera stared blankly at the bored patch of ocean that had closed over him, you'd never know he'd ever been there.

Then the camera pulled back; the cameraman was backing away from the rail. You could see the two hoods just standing there, facing the camera. They got a little shy now that there was nothing more to do. One of them waved, a little self-conscious.

The film ran out and the screen went white.

"He was a pretty tough old guy," hissed the voice beside me. "But in the end, he told us about the safe. How you got it out of there. And he told us that you buried it somewhere up north. Topanga, maybe."

I turned my head from the blank screen to look at him. I couldn't make out any eyes behind the Coke bottle glasses, lit up by the light from the screen in front of us. The crescent of a smile was cut into the huge, fleshy cop face. "I figured he was tellin' the truth," the hiss continued, "because we'd been working on him for the better part of two hours."

O'Brien began to rise from his seat; it was like seeing a battleship being lifted out of the water. I stood up, too. He was a foot taller than me, easy, and maybe two feet wider.

"He was screaming his head off, telling us everything he knew," said O'Brien. "So will you."

38

Jeez, he was a fucking Frankenstein—I was no delicate flower myself, but I knew this guy could squeeze my neck and pop my head like it was a pimple. Without taking his eyes off me, he said, "Check the door, Petey."

Petey's squeaky voice came from behind me. "It's locked, Wally, d'ya want me to—"

O'Brien's head turned just a fraction in the direction of the voice and I thought, "Now or never." I clawed up at the spectacles on his face and tore them away. Then I leapt back, out into the aisle. The glasses flew off and landed silently somewhere on the carpeted floor.

You wouldn't have thought something that big could move that fast. But he didn't go for me, he went after the glasses.

Petey was quick, too. He was already on me, grabbing me by the collar as he reached inside his coat pocket. I punched him in the face as hard as I could—a short, hard jab. He was stunned for a second; I grabbed the arm he'd been reaching into his coat, took it in both of my hands and twisted. I spun him around, into the seats; he lost his balance and fell back over one of the chairs, with me still holding on to his arm. Bad place to be, Petey.

I pulled his arm over the metal back of one of the seats, and came down on it with all of my body weight (I was almost two hundred pounds, back then). He wasn't a very big boy, small bones; and one of them snapped inside the sleeve of his coat. The scream was awful to hear, bouncing around the inside of that soundproofed room.

O'Brien was still across the aisle, still down among the seats, fumbling frantically—but now he'd found the glasses. He began to haul himself up from the floor, mashing his spectacles back into place with his free hand. And now he was focusing, turning his face up to find me—

Without even thinking I kicked out at him as fast and hard as I could. He had good reflexes; he was already putting up a catcher's mitt hand to block the foot coming towards his face. But I was a little faster; I connected first, and hard. And I had my good shoes on, the ones I'd charged to Stacey's account. I think they called it a Harvard style shoe, you know, shiny hard leather with a toe that came to a point. "Cockroach kickers," the kids used to call them in my old neighborhood.

There was a faint crack when the shoe connected with the glasses. I hadn't been aiming, but I knew I'd broken a lens in his spectacles. Not surprising, since I'd kicked his head like I was trying to make an extra point.

Momentum kept him going; he kept on rising to get to his feet—but then he stopped, and a heavy groan came from somewhere inside him. He covered his face with both hands, and stepped back. He was off-balance, like a big tree about to fall. I hoped.

I felt something moving at my side; Petey again. On his back over the seats, rustling awkwardly inside his jacket with his last good arm. I knew what he was after. I grabbed him by the lapels and he looked up at me, terrified, and yelled: "Eddie!" (The guy in the back room who'd been running the projector, I guessed.)

I punched Petey in the face again; his broken elbow banged against a chair and that was the end of him: he gasped and passed out.

I flipped open his jacket and got out the gun he'd been looking for. It was a little police job, not much bigger than my hand. Suddenly, from behind me, another light; I turned to look at it. The guy from the projection room had stepped out into the theater; he came out backlit by the light inside the booth. I flipped the safety off, raised the pistol and fired in his general direction. To kinda scare him, you know?

Another fast boy; he threw himself back inside the projection booth. I ducked, too, crouching down behind the row of seats. That guy was probably packing, too, and Petey's holler had tipped him off. He might try to take a shot at me from the window of the booth.

I looked across the aisle and saw O'Brien still clutching his face. He was standing over the plush seats like the Cyclops, looking down on me through his good eye. The breath was wheezing out of him, a broken steam pipe. Not from effort, from pain; there was probably some broken glass in the eye and that couldn't feel pleasant. But he wasn't scared of the gun I was pointing at him; he just stared into me through the single remaining lens of the spectacles. He took his hand away from over his bad eye and blood began to spill down the side of his face. All I heard was his breathing.

"Wally!" shouted a voice from up in the projection booth. "You alright?"

"Yeah," said the crocodile hiss.

I was thinking.

"Tell him to come out," I said, still crouched, jerking my head at the projection booth.

O'Brien was thinking, too. "He won't," he said to me.

I clicked the hammer back on the revolver.

"The first one goes in your leg," I said to him, meaning it.

"Eddie!" roars O'Brien. "Come outta there where he can see ya."

You could tell Eddie didn't think much of the idea. "Wally, I could—"

"Come on outta there, now!"

The light at the back of the room reappeared; the door of the projection booth had been opened.

"Turn the lights on, Eddie," I called.

The lights came on. Petey stirred behind me, moaning something about not wanting to go to school. I stayed down.

"Come on down here by me and Mr. O'Brien, Eddie."

O'Brien looked even more horrible with the lights up. The blood had stopped running, but one side of his face looked streaked and mashed; the rest burned red behind the remaining spectacle.

Then he turned his head, sudden; it made me jump a bit. Something had caught his attention at the rear of the theater.

"No, Eddie," he said, very firm.

Eddie had been about to try something cute, I guess. He strolled into view, slouching down the aisle and standing next to O'Brien with his hands in his pockets. He forced himself to smile at me, when he saw the gun in my hand. Teasing me, you know. Punk.

I stood up now, and it felt good. "Take your hands out of your pockets, Eddie, and make sure they're empty."

He raised his hands slowly up in the air, making a big show of stretching his fingers out and displaying his empty palms. Like I said, a punk.

"Wally," I said, pointing my pistol at his chest. "Reach into his coat and get out his gun. Toss it on the floor there."

Eddie kept smiling as O'Brien went into his jacket, but O'Brien was expressionless as he felt through Eddie's pockets. He pulled out a revolver, holding it by the grip with just his thumb and forefinger, so I'd feel secure. He tossed it onto the carpeted floor in the aisle.

Slowly, I knelt down and picked it up, not taking my eyes off them. Eddie grinned as I slipped the second revolver into my coat pocket. He knew how scared I was.

I figured O'Brien didn't have a gun. If he did, he would have had it out before now, right? I got to my feet again and said, "Go on," gesturing up the aisle with the pistol. They got underway slowly, proceeding up the aisle before me.

"Open the door and walk out into the hall," I called to O'Brien. He pressed something on the wall, and the door opened silently. I heard the voices of other people coming from outside, and relaxed a little. Their chatter stopped suddenly when O'Brien and Eddie walked out into the hall; they must have seen O'Brien's eye.

I slipped the gun into my pocket and kept my hand on it as I followed them out. The two of them turned and stood there across the hall from me, facing me like a reception committee. But they wouldn't do anything; there was a gaggle of secretaries and a clerk or two around to cramp their style now.

The secretaries didn't say anything but there was this heavy silence full of meaning: 'who is this man who's done this awful thing to our fearsome Mr. O'Brien?' I didn't say anything, either; I was getting my breath back and feeling kind of sick. I just turned around and started down the hall, getting out of this building and its chemical smells. The little ballerina I'd seen before was still in the hall, with a guy in a gorilla suit; they stopped talking and stared at me as I went by. And as I opened one of the double doors that led to the lot outside, I heard the crocodile voice calling down the hall, behind me:

"See ya around," said Wally O'Brien.

39

So Sam was dead. And I found out that Stacey had disappeared, too. I tried to get her from a phone booth downtown right after I'd got out of Olympic—"Miss Tilden is not available, would you like to leave a message?" I tried calling her at the numbers in Bel Air and at the ranch in Mexico: no dice. She'd skipped. That was bad. She was currently shooting a picture on the Olympic lot; she wouldn't drop out of sight like that unless she'd been scared off.

I couldn't quite figure this out though—why should she feel afraid? Why take a powder now that she and everyone involved knew I had the safe? She knew it was gone, of course; she'd been there at the party and would have made it her business to find out whether the job had come off or not. Stacey was the one who'd said that the safe and its contents were our life preserver; that Roth wouldn't dare touch us until he had it back.

Maybe she didn't believe in life preservers, anymore. Maybe O'Brien had taken her into that screening room too, and shown her that film of Sam, and she'd decided that she'd better fold and get out of town. She could be thousands of miles away already, trying to figure out some way to smooth things over with Roth.

After all, neither of us knew what was actually in the safe; we'd never even opened it. It might contain a lot of good dirt on Roth; it might contain nothing at all. For all we knew, he might have emptied it recently. He wouldn't be scared to kill us if there was nothing in that thing that could hurt him.

Nah—there had to be something good in there. O'Brien certainly wanted it back; he'd killed Sam because Sam wouldn't (couldn't) give it to him. There was something in there that Roth needed pretty bad, alright.

I wired Stacey at the studio and the other places, too—

the wires said that I knew where the goods were, and that she should "contact me with the news." I hoped she'd get my meaning in that last phrase; it meant that she should run an ad for me in the classified sections again, like she had that time before, to let me know how to get in touch with her.

One thing I did know; I was aching to put a bullet in that prick, O'Brien. I would have shot him down right there in the screening room, but I doubt that even Roth could have covered up a mess that big. O'Brien was too prominent a name, on the lot and around town—his disappearance would have to be reported and explained to the cops, and there were a lot of people who had seen me around the studio that day and could identify me.

Still, I decided that O'Brien's life was going to be part of the ransom I extorted from Roth for the return of the safe. Because O'Brien had had no real reason to kill Sam; he knew that Sam had told him everything he could. O'Brien murdered Sam just because he'd felt a little frustrated, that's all.

I'd pitch the idea to Roth—O'Brien (and piles of money), in return for the safe. Roth might go for it, he might not; everything was negotiable. But in the end, it didn't really matter whether Roth okayed it or not—win, lose, or draw, I was going to kill that bastard O'Brien.

These were the pretty thoughts I was thinking as I strolled down the sunny avenues of the business district, looking for a lawyer.

I'd gone straight down to Spring Street after I left the studio. I walked into one of the fancier office buildings and picked the name of a firm off the building registry in the lobby.

The offer of a cash retainer got me past the secretary. The guy I ended up seeing had a nice office and a respectable way of speaking. He sounded East Coast; I bet he went to Yale or some place.

I gave him the bare bones of the truth; I had "stumbled

across" some information that could be very damaging to Mr. Jack Roth and Olympic Studios, and I had been invited by Mr. Roth to his offices to negotiate a confidentiality agreement. When I'd arrived, I'd been threatened and assaulted by "ruffians" apparently in the employ of Mr. Roth, and I wished to get some satisfaction.

Had the police been called in? No, not yet, I thought I'd obtain legal representation first; I wasn't sure whether it was wise to file a police report at this point because of the business angle. ('Very wise,' said the lawyer.) Did I know the names of these ruffians? One of them, was, I believe, a Mr. O'Brien—

And so it went, for almost a half an hour. This guy was good, I thought; he asked lots of questions about Roth and O'Brien and practically none about me. He must have smelled the long green involved, but the important thing was that he knew I didn't really care about suing or anything like that—he understood that what I was really after was protection. Letters and telephone calls from his office to Olympic; a paper trail leading to Roth and O'Brien. Which could be sent to the press if they tried to get tough again.

We shook hands; he told me he'd make inquiries and I told him I'd be available to file a police report later that afternoon. I kept Stacey's name out of it, of course, and I didn't mention Sam or that film. But I left the office feeling better, I'd told him enough to get him started on Olympic and its goons. I decided that I was now safe walking the streets again. For the time being, I mean.

I even felt safe enough to return to the Ambassador. Herman greeted me like the prodigal son; there was an envelope from Miss Tilden waiting for me in his office safe, he said.

So she hadn't forgot about me after all. There was no note inside, though, just more cash; enough to see me through the week in my accustomed style. No other word from or about Miss Tilden, said Herman; the envelope had been delivered to the desk by "an Oriental gentleman who offered no further information."

I lay on the bed in my suite and stared at the ceiling. But I'd have to get out of here pretty soon. The place was crawling with studio spies and hotel employees who were now on the Roth payroll. I was under a microscope, now; I couldn't let my guard down. And these off-the-rack clothes I'd picked up in Glendale felt all itchy and cheap after the nice stuff those Ricci guys had made up for me. I pulled out the tropical weight business number that was hanging in my closet.

While I was changing I started thinking about Sam again. I was still pretty sure I was going to score big from this deal. When it was all over and done with, should I send some of the money to Sam's family? The wife and kids who'd given up on him many years before? It was a moral question, really, and I'm not good at those. What would Sam have wanted? He hadn't spoken to them in years so far as I knew; but he had his sentimental moments. They hadn't done anything to earn a split; but Sam had earned it, the hard way. I wondered what he would have wanted, because I was going to collect for him, dead or alive. I would bleed Roth white—that would be all the revenge that Sam would ever get on him.

I didn't want to rest, but I had to, had to force myself while I had the chance. I stretched out on the bed again, and thought about Vera, upstairs, many floors above me. But maybe she wasn't up there; she might be on the set of that Bible picture she was making for Roth. Slave girl to the Emperor, feeding him grapes.

I must have fallen asleep, because the next thing I remember was the phone ringing.

"Yeah?"

"Have you seen the paper?"

I thought I recognized the voice. A cop's voice. Not O'Brien's, but someone—

"The Times. Today's. Or any of the afternoon

papers."

Click.

I stared at the ceiling again. Who was that? Not Herman—

The hotel dick. Benson. It was him, not giving his name. Why was he getting cute on me now?

I got up and brushed my teeth. It was late in the afternoon. I'd get a copy of the paper and see what Benson was talking about; then a bite to eat. I expected that my new lawyer had gone through most of the necessary preliminaries with Roth's people; hopefully things were back on a business basis between us.

I decided to buy the paper down in the lobby rather than have it sent up; stretch my legs a bit. The lobby was crowded, lots of check-ins. I didn't see Benson hanging around; maybe he'd gone home for the day. I stopped by the desk and checked my messages; just one, typewritten, unsigned. That would be Benson again, not wanting to be identified, but wanting to earn another fifty by keeping me posted. The message read:

'This morning's L.A. Times. Front page.'

That's all. The message said 8:30 a.m.; he'd typed it while I was still out on the road. He'd called me again in the suite just now to make sure I'd see whatever was in the paper.

So I went down to the newsstand and picked up a paper to look it over. I stopped short when I saw it—her photograph, there on page one. The bottom half of the page, but still page one.

Vera, smiling prettily, flirting with the camera. A classy photo, glamorous—probably a portrait she had taken for the studio. The caption read: 'Vera Martin, actress, age 19.' And a smaller line underneath the caption:

STARLET A SUICIDE

40

I read the article. It said that Vera had jumped off the big 'Hollywoodland' sign, the famous one that had been built into the hills that overlooked the town. Vera had climbed up the scaffolding behind the letters of the sign and jumped off the top. The letters were only about fifty feet tall, but they're set into the hill at a steep angle; it's a sheer drop from the top of that sign to the valley below. The paper said that she had probably died instantly.

It also said that she was a new arrival in Hollywood who had recently signed a contract with Olympic. But she was apparently disappointed with her career or a love affair. A note in her handwriting was found on her body by police. It said 'goodbye,' that was all.

She had apparently thrown herself off the sign sometime during the night. Her body was discovered this morning by a local homeowner. This guy had spotted a coyote nosing around up on one of the hills behind his house; he drove it off with a gunshot. He went up to investigate and found Vera.

Olympic had been unable to supply the names of any surviving family; Vera had signed her contract using her stage name and her family's identity and whereabouts were still unknown. The police requested that any parties having information contact them.

Outside, the sun had peaked and was beginning its long, slow slide. I sat in a chair and watched it sink for a while, trying not to think. Finally, I got up and phoned the front desk; ordered up a cab to take me out to Sam's old rooming house.

I needed a car now that the Bentley was gone and my ugly old Dodge roadster was still there, right where I'd parked it when I'd first come to town. I slipped inside the building, broke into Sam's room and got the car keys. Before I left, I took a quick look around to see if O'Brien and his boys had missed anything during their search of the room last night. There was nothing useful; just a stack of Sam's cowboy pulps and some of his old wrangling gear.

I don't know why I drove all the way up to the Hollywoodland sign after I left the rooming house. Kinda stupid of me to go there that same day. Some cop might have been hanging around nearby, hoping someone connected with Vera's death would turn up. A cop would ask a lot of questions; that could have been another mess.

I guess I wasn't thinking too clearly, between Sam and Vera and all that had happened. I parked in the hills, off the road, and I had to hike a good bit to get to the foot of the sign. I went around back of it and looked at the skeletal metal frame that held up each of the gigantic white letters.

I tried to imagine her climbing that scaffolding, climbing it like she was a kid on a jungle gym or something. It must have looked a bit funny; she'd been all dolled up when she died, jewelry and stuff, the paper said.

I walked around the front; looked up at the tops of the great white letters. Then I turned and looked over the valley beyond; Los Angeles in the rich blue of the coming evening, the lights coming on. Down below me, far below, the steep drop, the rocks and dry trees at the bottom. Quite a fall; kill anybody.

What letter had she chosen? The paper hadn't said. "H", I guessed. That was the most prestigious.

It was a pretty day, though; fading away in front of me. I took a seat on a big boulder, and something pinched a bit through my pants pocket. I reached in—ah, the handcuffs, from Roth's bag of sexy games, the ones I'd taken from Vera's hotel room. I took them out and looked at them for a while; and then I put them in my coat pocket.

I spent another half hour or so thinking things over. Then I got back in my car and drove north, down the other side of the hills to the Valley.

Sunset now; a pretty drive out to the movie ranch. Like one of those colored-in postcards; the beams in the fences and the hills above, all yellows and oranges and purples. The sky was full of thunderheads and the road was lined with silhouettes; oil wells, telephone poles, a drive-in in the shape of a crouching monkey. The neon lights on the billboards were coming on as it got darker: "Old Man London—Dry Gin."

The sun was down by the time I got to the ranch and it was getting cold. The posts of the gates looked kind of ghostly now; the scrub and the old wooden building were misted over.

It only took me about fifteen minutes to dig up the box this time, the ground around it was still soft from when I'd buried it. I popped the box open with the shovel and rooted around through the photographs for the jar. I slipped it into my coat pocket, returned the box to its grave, and covered it with the sandy earth again, not taking too much trouble this time. It was real dark, now. I looked at my watch and decided not to drive back into town that night; the next day was Sunday and I'd have a lot to do.

So I drove further down the road to the main buildings of the old ranch. There was no one there, of course; a good place to camp out—under the stars, you know?

And that's what I did. There was a blanket in the back I'd stolen from the hotel, and wrapped up in it was the rest of a bottle of rye I'd bought in town. I built a little fire in the middle of all the old ranch buildings, and wrapped myself up in the blanket and drank the rye. Like an old Indian. I enjoyed watching the fire, and the air was clear. I was tired, too, and I wanted to sleep. I knew I'd sleep better out here because I was sure that no one would find me. I hadn't camped out like that since I was a kid.

I finally fell asleep by the fire; no dreams.

The cold woke me up even though it was still dark. The fire had gone out, and the blanket didn't help much; I was freezing. A bit hung over, too, but I had places to go and people to see. I had a piss over in the corner between two buildings, and then I tossed the blanket and stuff in the back of the car. There was a sip or two of the rye left; I had that for breakfast. Hair of the dog.

The sky was turning from night to morning; cold metal blue as I headed south, back up into the Santa Monica Mountains. The outdoors hadn't agreed with me; when I stopped at a filling station the attendant looked at me like I was just another bum. So while he gassed up the car I used the bathroom to spruce myself up a bit. When I came out he talked to me like I was a person; I tipped him five bucks for filling two extra cans of gas and putting them in the back of the Dodge. When I mentioned I was going cross-country he gave me a couple of jugs of water for the radiator, too. Always tip big; it pays off.

41

I headed up over Mulholland, over the top of the mountains. It didn't take long to find the house with the great big stone gate, flanked by palms. There was a uniformed guard there this morning; an old guy reading the sports section. He straightened up and slipped the paper under the desk as I pulled up to the booth. He adjusted his cap and walked quickly out to the car. I bet he figured I was lost and needed directions; no one would ever come to see his boss in a crappy old Dodge.

"I'm here to see Roth," I said, looking up at him from the car window.

He thought it was a rib. He said: "It ain't even six o'clock in the morning, on a Sunday, for—"

I was holding out one of O'Brien's business cards so he could see it; then I flipped it over so he could read the handwriting on the back: "Let this guy in." (I'd written that there myself.)

"Studio business," I said, no nonsense.

He looked at the card like it was a dog turd, but he took it; then he went to the little booth at the gate. I saw him ringing somebody up on the phone, talking.

We both waited a minute or so for something to happen on the other end of the phone. Then the guard turned to me and motioned for me to go forward, hanging up the phone. I put the Dodge into gear and it rolled in as the huge gate swung open.

He tried to say something to me as I passed him, but I ignored it and kept on. The house looked lovely in the morning light, much more natural than at the party. Very ancient and grand, behind this veil of mist. Like the painted photographs in *National Geographic*; the lost temples.

I drove up along the mall, on the main road that led to

the house. At the end was the paved circular driveway and I parked in front of the main entrance.

The butler already had one of the great doors open for me when I reached the top; he'd dressed in a hurry.

"Hi," I said.

He was trying to place my face; it's hard to forget a guy who once took a shot at you, but then, he'd just got out of bed.

He said: "Mr. Roth requests that you wait for him in the study. He will be with you momentarily."

I nodded. It was a real English accent, I decided, as I followed him down the great hall, the one with the pillars. I looked over the statues, and the carvings in the columns again; maybe they were the real thing, too.

Dawn light was streaming in through the huge glass windows at the far end of the hall. As the butler led me into the study I could see out the windows that the whole sky had turned pink.

"Wait here, please," said the butler, behind me. I didn't hear him leave; I went over to the windows and looked down at Los Angeles. The pink sky had turned the city down below all blue and purple. I watched the light change for a few minutes.

"It's nice, isn't it?"

Roth. I turned; he was standing there in a kind of Japanese bathrobe, hair combed, looking sharp and on his toes though he must have been fast asleep not more than ten minutes ago.

Roth moved forward, towards me, moving silently over the polished black marble. He was wearing slippers; that was why he seemed shorter now than when I'd seen him that night at the Grove. Much shorter; maybe he wore elevator shoes when he was dressed.

"I don't get to enjoy this room as much as I'd like to," he says, joining me by the window and looking down at the city. "Too busy with the studio." He took his hand out of his pocket and pointed, off to our left. "That's Olympic over there, see it? That patch of white buildings. That's why I bought this house."

I thought I could see it; the little white airplane hangar buildings, clustered together. It looked like a postage stamp from up here.

"Every so often, I come into this room at night and look it over," he said. "Make sure nobody's stolen it out from under me when I wasn't looking." He began to walk down the long wall of windows to get a little closer to his studio. I watched him.

"A lot of people tried to take it away from me over the past fifteen years. Thalberg and that bastard Mayer. Kennedy. My own brother, even. It's still mine, though.

"I really oughta use this room more often. It's pretty, this time of day. I'm usually up all night, anyway, 'cause of the pictures." He looked older.

"Of course," he added, lowering his eyebrows and nodding behind me, "I'll have to redecorate."

I turned and looked—the wall where the safe had been was ripped out from under the ceiling, shattered beams stuck out, the carved woodwork was cracked for fifty feet, and a big ugly post had been stuffed under the ceiling to keep it from sagging.

"It's okay, don't worry about it," he said, as though I'd started to apologize. "It's only money, what the hell. You're a businessman, like me. You probably heard about some of the shit I've pulled in my time."

He chuckled and rubbed his face. "You did put my nose out of joint, though, you son-of-a-bitch."

I turned at a noise behind us. The butler, returning to see if we needed anything. He obviously remembered me now; he was looking at me like I was a snake. Roth strolled back towards me; trim black moustache and salt-and-pepper hair.

"You want some coffee or something?"

I looked out the window again, and said, "I'd take a little coffee."

"Evelyn," he said to the butler, pronouncing it 'Ee-ve-lyn. "Bring us some coffee. And squeeze us a couple of oranges, too, will ya? What the hell, bring in a whole tray, we'll eat."

Evelyn was gone, and Roth walked over to his busted desk, and pulled a long stick out of an umbrella stand that sat near it.

"I gotta eat anyway, I'm playing later this morning." He held up the stick so I could see it from across the room; it kind of looked like a skinny croquet hammer, but the handle was much longer. "Polo; you ever play polo?"

I said nothing.

"I ain't making fun, I thought you might have. You look like you mighta been a college boy once. Shit, I didn't play myself until a year ago. I hate golf, and I have to do this society stuff now. It's good for the studio." He laughed softly. "Twenty years ago I used to push racks of coats around the streets of Manhattan. Can you imagine what the guys back there would say if they saw me up on a horse, wearing white pants and whacking a little ball with this thing?" He laughed and dropped the mallet back into the can, and then he sank down into the black leather chair behind the huge mahogany desk. The top was smashed where the safe had hit. He looked strange, sitting in that chair across from me in the pink light; sitting behind his shattered desk, in front of a ruined wall, pretending that nothing was wrong.

"Okay, can we talk a little business now?" He smiled, showing teeth.

I took a seat in an expensive-looking chair that faced the desk. A futuristic, Flash Gordon kind of thing, and it was uncomfortable. I figured that was on purpose, so nobody who came here to talk business with Roth would want to stay too long.

"So," he says, "where's my safe?"

"Let's talk money first," I said.

"Fair enough," says Roth. "That's what you came for.

But hear me out, okay? I'll give you cash, if you want. But I might have something more interesting for you."

I said nothing, so he continued:

"O'Brien is getting old. He's still tough as hell, but he loses his temper. He needs watching, and anyway, some day he'll want to retire. The guys he's got working for him, they're tough, too, but they're strictly muscle. No brains or initiative, like O'Brien, or like you. What would you think about going to work for me?"

I felt myself smiling.

"No, really, think about it. When O'Brien quits he'll be worth about a million. He gets paid good, and he gets his share in the studio profits. He probably makes some money on the side, too; that's okay with me, so long as it doesn't hurt Olympic. It's a good job for a smart kid; if you keep your eyes and ears open you could make a bundle in just a few years.

"Don't misunderstand me," he added quickly, "I'm not asking you to share an office with Wally O'Brien. Christ, not after you kicked the guy's eye out. I mean, you should be our man in New York. Nose around, see what you can find out about our Wall Street guys, maybe turn up something on those finance jerks downtown. They'll *have* to talk to you, I'll make you a studio executive. You get a car, you're on the payroll. Real money."

He waited for a response. When none came, he went on:

"O'Brien will retire in a couple of years, and then you can come back and take over from him. When you're where he is—you can write your own ticket." He scratched his head. "Either way, take it or leave it, you get paid. Think it over a few days, I'll put you up at the, the, where are ya staying, the Ambassador, the Biltmore? I'll move you to a bungalow at the Beverly Hills Hotel, it's better. And I'll give you a down payment. Twenty-thousand in cash, to show good faith."

I stayed quiet.

"I hope this isn't, uh, boring you…"

I waved him off. "No, go on. I'm just thinking about it, that's all."

He smiled again, and nodded. "Thinking, that's good. That's all I'm asking you to do. Think about it."

The rising sun was beginning to warm up the room a little. The butler slipped in through the double doors and wheeled a cart to the desk. It was very nice, linen and silver and fresh flowers.

"Cream with your coffee, sir?" said the butler, handing me a full cup with a saucer. I knew that having to wait on me was just killing this guy.

"That's okay, Evelyn, we can take care of ourselves now, you can go."

Evelyn nodded and padded off.

"So, what's your first impression about this offer I'm making?" asked Roth, as Evelyn shut the doors. He poured himself a cup of coffee and left it on the tray to cool. "Sound like something you might be interested in?"

I was tasting my coffee; it was delicious. "Well," I said, "I'll tell ya. I wouldn't say yes, and I wouldn't say no."

"Well, what would you say, then?"

"I think I'll take my time and think it over," I said. "The part about the twenty thousand sounds good." I sipped my coffee again.

He waved his hand. "We can take care of that today, we can drive down to the studio—"

"Fifty would be better, though."

He looked hard at me. Then:

"Okay. Fifty."

He sipped his coffee. And then he said:

"However—I need something from you."

He paused, all dramatic.

"What I need from you," says Roth, "—is some token of good faith. I don't mind parting with some cash, but I gotta know that we're dealing serious, here. I'll pay you your fifty thousand dollars this afternoon. Now, what are you gonna do for me?" His eyes werc bright.

I sat there a moment, feeling sleepy, and then I reached into my jacket pocket and brought out the little glass jar. It make a loud 'clack' noise when I set it on the broken mahogany desk top in front of me.

He regarded it for a moment, puzzled. Then he realized what he was looking at, and he jumped out of his chair and across the desk, snatching at the jar like it was the brass ring on the merry-go-round. He held it up to the morning light and looked at it—and then he burst out laughing, like I'd told him the funniest joke he'd ever heard in his life.

He collapsed back in the chair, tears were already rolling down his face, and he looked at me, and he held up the jar for me so I could see it. He gave it a big, loud smooch and clutched it to his chest. I must admit, even I had to chuckle when he did that.

"You're the best, Hart," he said. "You're the fucking best I ever saw. Incredible." He looked down at the jar, sighing. "Now you *gotta* come work for me. I'll tell you something funny. When Evelyn told me you were here this morning, I left a message for O'Brien and told him to come straight over here and break your goddamn neck. But you know what we're gonna do instead?"

He stood up and walked around the desk, grabbed the bamboo mallet out of the umbrella stand and raised it over his head. "You and me are going out to the Brentwood Country Club together and you're going to play the very first game of polo you played in your entire life, my friend! And then, a car from the studio is going to pull up and hand you fifty thousand dollars in small bills, and then you're going to eat the best fucking lunch you ever ate, and then I am gonna get us both laid! You know why? Because I love you! Here!" He tossed me the polo mallet; I caught it. It was light, except for the wooden head. "Start practicing!"

He picked up the phone and dialed once. "This is Roth. Get me the studio." He sat on the edge of the desk and crossed his legs, back in his element now.

"This is Roth," he said again, "I want to speak to Humphreys in Accounting." Pause. "I know he's there, if he's not, he's fired. I told him to talk to that, that director on the Alice Faye set this morning. Page him."

He grinned at me while he waited, and shook his head in wonder.

"I can't stay mad at you, kid. You are something else. You shoulda heard what O'Brien said he was gonna do to you. And Stacey—that's the last peep I'm ever gonna hear out of that crazy fag." He held the jar up to the light and shook it like it was one of those snowflake Christmas scenes. "If she's very, very good, she can visit them Tuesdays and Thursdays—Humphreys? Yeah. How much you got in the safe down there? Never mind, how much?"

He listened.

"Okay. That's not enough. We need fifty, cash, small bills." He winked at me. "Who cares if it's Sunday? It's an emergency. I got a deal to do. No, no checks. Call my bookie, borrow it 'til tomorrow. Okay, then, call your bookie, I don't give a shit, just get it. I want it delivered to the Brentwood Country Club under my name; have one of the fellas stay with it 'til I call at the desk. Not Wally O'Brien, though." He looked up at me and laughed; I smiled.

"Okay. I'm at home, I'm having breakfast. Call me here as soon as you've got the cash lined up, you got the number? Okay. Bye."

And he hung up.

He slumped back in his chair and he sighed. "Christ, I wish I was young again, like you. What are you, about twenty-two, twenty-three? You're still a baby. That's the good age, ya know. You can still afford a few mistakes, you still got some time to be crazy, like you are. I can't do the kind of stuff you do, anymore. I got too much to lose. I gotta hire guys like you and O'Brien to do the crazy stuff for me, I'm so old. I just give orders, these days."

He spun his chair on its axis, to face the window. "Your friend, that old drunken cowboy. I'm sorry about that now. I don't like to do that to people, especially an old guy, my own age. O'Brien talked me into it, really. He's a little crazy, you know, he enjoys that kind of thing. But I thought he was right, at the time. I can't cave in to every little hustler that comes along. It woulda been different if I'd known you then like I do now. Too bad for your friend, but that's business."

"And the girl?"

He didn't even hesitate: "The girl was business, too," said Roth. "Sure, I was pissed about her helping you out, but, shit, she lied to me, and I won't tolerate that in a woman. Any woman. That's too bad, too, she was just a kid, and she couldn't have known any better, but that's the way it goes. I couldn't let her sell me out to a punk like you, and have the town laughing at me if I got indicted. How'd she get you in here, by the way?"

"She didn't," I said, watching him.

"What do you mean, she didn't," he said, looking at me.

"I asked her to, but she wouldn't," I explained. "She said you'd been good to her and you'd come through on your promise to get her a part and an agent. So she wouldn't help me."

That surprised him a bit. "No kidding," he said, to the floor. "O'Brien and I figured she steered you guys in here that night. Christ." He looked up at me. "She said I was good to her?"

I didn't say anything.

"Jesus, that's awful," he said. "The poor kid." He seemed genuinely upset. "Well. She couldn't have suffered much, she was already, you know, when they threw her off the sign. She didn't suffer much. What's the matter?"

I guess I'd been staring at him; it seemed to make him uncomfortable. He got up and walked slowly towards his window.

"She shouldn't have kept it to herself, when you asked her to sell me out. She shoulda told me about it, straight away, then I would have taken care of you instead of her." He was standing at the window, sniffling. Was he crying? I got up to see.

"Poor Vera. I really did like her. But there's a lot of pretty girls in—"

The polo mallet caught him on the side of the temple. It made this horrible thwok! noise when it struck, and he slumped to the floor like a sack of wet laundry. And he conked his head again, on that cold marble floor.

42

I was kinda proud of that shot—it was the first time I'd ever swung a polo mallet and I still managed to catch him square on the bean with the business end. And don't believe what you see in the movies and detective magazines; it's hard to knock a guy unconscious without killing him. I had to check to see if he was still alive; his eyes were still half open and he didn't seem to be breathing. I was just about to give up on him when he trembled and coughed up something.

He wasn't too hard to move; only about a hundred and forty pounds or so was my guess, as I hoisted him up across my shoulders. I was slouching out of the room with him slung over my back when the phone on the desk began to ring. Maybe it was his accountant; maybe he'd gotten the money together. I couldn't hang around here to find out. I slipped out between the huge double doors of the study, careful not to bang Roth's head.

Evelyn the butler spotted me as I was lugging him back down the great hall, back towards the main entrance. Evelyn probably heard the phone ringing through the open door and wondered why Mr. Roth wasn't answering, he was horrified when saw us.

"Mr. Roth!" he called out, as he trotted down the hall to catch up to us.

"He'll be okay," I said, "Just needs a little fresh air."

"Is he ill?"

"He's been better, I guess."

"We—we must get a doctor!"

"I *am* a doctor," I said haughtily, and I started nudging the vast front door with my weight. "Help me with this door."

He did, saying "But—but—"

"Go get some clean towels and a box of baking soda," I snapped at him. Best to give him something to do, I thought.

He looked at me for a second, thinking it over.

"Hurry, goddamit, this man's life is in danger!"

That sent him back into the house, pronto. I staggered down the flagstone steps of the entrance. The sun had turned everything to gold by now.

I'd thought of putting Roth in the front seat of the Dodge, but then I realized that you can't drive around Beverly Hills in broad daylight with an old studio head in a kimono slumped up against the car window. People would ask questions.

So, Roth would have to go in the trunk, for now. I set him down on the ground against the rear wheel, while I unlocked it.

Evelyn was back already with a stack of towels and a box of Arm and Hammer. He watched in horror as I hauled his boss up off the driveway and dumped him in the trunk.

I gave Evelyn a glance filled with contempt. "What the hell are you doing there, Evelyn! Put that shit away and go call the Beverly Hills Hospital. Tell them Dr. Schweitzer is bringing in Jack Roth for emergency treatment." I slammed the trunk and walked around the car.

"But what shall I—"

"Just tell them he's got the clap," I said, climbing into the car. "They'll take it from there. You want me to pick up something for you while I'm in town?" I slammed the door and started up the engine.

Evelyn stood there, helpless for a moment. Then he shook his box of baking soda at me for emphasis: "Mr. O'Brien will be here at any moment!"

"Tell him I said 'hi!'" I shouted over the car engine, and I put it into gear.

I got one more glance at the house as I pulled away. Evelyn had run back inside, but he'd left those big doors open; I could make out his little figure lost in the hallway, bobbing and weaving between the dark Egyptian pillars inside, trailing towels, calling "Help! Help!"

It reminded me of that rabbit in 'Alice in Wonderland,' for some reason.

43

I didn't pass O'Brien or his boys on the way out of the hills. I didn't expect to, because they'd be headed from the direction of downtown or the studio, and I was headed another way—northeast. My guess was that O'Brien would arrive a few minutes after I left and would get some kind of hysterical story from poor Evelyn. O'Brien wouldn't have any idea where I was going now, but Evelyn could tell him I was driving a Dodge when I left. And a guy with O'Brien's police connections could run down a Dodge pretty easy. So I had to change cars. I drove straight out to that barn, where I was keeping Sam's truck.

I was on the other side of the Santa Monica Mountains from Hollywood; the north side. I drove down through the hills headed east, down through the San Fernando Valley, again. All the farms and orange groves looked gorgeous in the morning; I'd never seen it in daylight before. It smelled great, too; very fresh, flowery. I remember thinking to myself, gee, this is pretty, I hope they don't spoil it some day by building it up too much.

It was still a little cool when I reached Glendale; it probably wasn't even seven a.m. yet. I kept on down the valley road a while, turning off just before downtown. A mile or two later I was at the farm I'd rented; easy to spot because the mailbox out front had the former owner's name stripped off it.

An empty farm is kind of poetic-looking, to me. I chugged up the drive that ran by the main house, then out back, to the barn. The barn was a rotten old livery sort of a building. Boards were missing from its sides and it needed lots of paint that it would probably never get. I took off the padlock and swung one of the big doors open. And there, in the shade inside, was the Holy Grail: Sam's truck, with that bundle of canvas and chain still sitting on its bed. It looked strange; sitting on the dirt floor, out in the middle of the empty barn like it was an exhibit or something. I guess it seemed funny because, really, this was Sam's tombstone I was looking at, and it was all the memorial he would ever get: the safe, in chains and canvas, sitting on the back of his crummy old Ford truck.

I went back outside for a minute and pulled the Dodge up into the barn, too. Then I got out and looked things over to make sure—I climbed up into the truck bed and peeled away a corner of the canvas tarp. It was still there; Sam had done a good job with the chain, wrapping it tight around the canvas and padlocking it to the frame of the truck. It wasn't going anyplace.

I opened up the trunk of the Dodge; Roth was still out but he was breathing. I took the extra cans of gas and water from the Dodge and put them in the back of the truck. I didn't want us to get caught short with such a big journey in front of us. I thought about putting Roth back in the bed of the truck, too; but he might wake up and jump off. Then I remembered Vera's handcuffs, in my jacket pocket. I felt for them and took a look; the little key was still tucked in the lock.

I lifted Roth out and carried him around the front of the truck; dropped him on the dirt floor outside the passenger side door. I drew up his arm and cuffed one of his wrists. I opened up the passenger door, and snapped the other cuff closed over the metal mounting at the base of the truck's front seat. Roth looked a little funny sitting there on the dirt in his silk kimono, his hand raised up in the air like a student asking for permission to leave the room. I lifted his legs up off the ground and put him into the cab. He sat folded up on the floor there, his bleeding head lolling onto the passenger seat. I shook him a bit; he gurgled but said nothing.

The truck was junk, but it was reliable junk; it started up in one try. I pulled out of the building and rattled down the dirt road, not bothering to close the barn doors behind me. I realized then I'd already made one mistake; I hadn't stopped for something to eat before I took off. This was California way before they built all those freeways and stuff; if you wanted something to eat you had to pull off somewhere at a drive-in or diner or barbecue joint. I sure as hell couldn't do that with Roth chained up on the floor of the cab.

So what, I'd have to go hungry for a while. It would give me something to look forward to later. Besides, I could feast my eyes on the scenery.

Sam knew trucks as well as horses; he'd been taking good care of this Ford. It ran very well once we got to the concrete highway; we were making good time. I didn't push it much past forty, though; it was getting on in the morning and I was afraid it might overheat. I couldn't stop for water with Roth in the front, and I had to save what I had in the jugs. I'd need it later.

I went out through Pasadena, this time. Out to Route 66, which led to San Bernadino and its mountains. I was heading north. Alders grew along a little creek that ran by the road, and it gets kind of twisty, going up a grade, up these slopes.

It was hot by then, and when I made it to the top of the hills, I stopped the truck to let the engine cool a bit and to take a drink of water out of one of the jugs in the back. I got out of the cab and sat up on the back of the truck, leaning back on the canvas that covered the safe. I looked back, down the slope, the direction I'd come from. Blue mountains, green orchards, vineyards. Very inspiring.

You could buy most of that, I was thinking, with the money that Roth would pay you for the safe. Sitting right behind you, in the bed of this truck, is enough dough to make you a rich man for the rest of your life, and then some. It's just a matter of keeping Roth alive until he pays off. Fuck his studio cop job: if he wants to do business, the deal is I take the money and walk. Bye. See ya round.

The water from the jug was warm but sweet; it washed

away the dry in my throat.

And it would be real money, serious capital. Roth wouldn't have that kind of cash on hand of course, but then he wouldn't need cash to pay me off. It could be like I planned with Stacey: I'd have him pay me off in land, a whole bunch of land that I personally picked out between here and that San Fernando Valley, north of town. Take my payment that way, with title to land instead of cash—free and clear, laundered for me by Roth through real estate purchases. I could mortgage that land and buy even more; maybe form a syndicate—a bunch of guys working for me, lawyers and stuff, buying and selling, manipulating prices for maximum payoff on lots I picked up cheap. These days people were selling out for peanuts to big boys who could pay. Between Jack Roth and that safe of his, I could be one of those big boys with the big money.

I watched cars go by. They were headed south and west. People are moving out this way, and they need places to live in and do business in. The Depression won't last forever—when it ends, anything you buy now will be worth ten times what you paid for it. Pretty sweet deal. Not to mention the fact that there's a hell of a lot of oil under Los Angeles County. Shit, they've got wells on some of the studio lots! I'm no geologist, but if I got as much land together as I was thinking about, who knows...

If that happened, I'd even have enough money left over to make me respectable. That's important; keeps the politicians and cops off your back. Donate to hospitals, build some parks, give property to the state for a university or something. Contributions to campaigns. Start voting for Republicans, cursing Roosevelt. Might get into a country club, if I married well. I would never be considered completely legitimate, of course. But my grandkids would, if I ever had any.

And I loved all this blue morning that was filling the sky and the valley; I even liked the heat.

Ah, well. You're young, kid. And you're smart. This isn't the only chance you'll ever have. There will be other days, other chances for you, further down the road.

An animal noise came from the front of the truck; Roth, coming around. I put the cap on the jug of water and pushed it back into the truck. Then I went back to the cab and hopped up into the driver's seat. The engine was still hot; it squawked, but it started. I looked down at Roth; the blood had dried on the side of his head. He was still unconscious, but now he was mumbling, dreaming.

I put the truck in gear and drove back to the main highway. I freewheeled for a while down the other side of the mountain, the dry side.

44

I think I was going through what they called ‘chaparral’, driving out through the foothills—a cowboy movie kind of landscape, hot and sunny. There were some pines, spruce, stuff like that; I guess they held the dirt and grass together and kept them from blowing away.

But that soon gave way to the desert. Long, long ways of nothing, like I’d seen down in Baja. I’d see a chicken coop or pass a filling station every so often—but mostly there was nothing, and nobody. A muddy little irrigation ditch ran by the road for a while and then just disappeared. Not too long after that I saw a sign: “Victorville 25 mi.” I could relax now and watch the sky and the road for a while; I was headed the right way.

Sam had told me about this ‘Victorville.’ I took a gander at it as I drove through (not stopping, Roth was still babbling). It was another place that Sam had recalled from his movie cowboy days. In fact, you’ve probably seen it yourself even if you’ve never actually been there. The Hollywood guys liked to film out there; they used the place as a location in about a million different westerns. Sam’s first big job as a wrangler was in Victorville; he was there in 1915 or so working on a William S. Hart silent. Directors and producers loved the place. Cheap as dirt to film there, and not too far away from L.A. A real old western town, with high desert scenery all around it to boot—perfect for horse operas. Sam said he’d had many wild times out this way; he’d partied out here often with movie folks when a shoot was through. He’d even met Will Rogers in Victorville, once. But Sam said that Rogers didn’t like him.

I recognized the street immediately as I drove in. Has that ever happened to you, that you ended up in some place that you’d never been to before, but you feel you know it anyway? From the movies, or from the photos in books or magazines? It's a funny feeling; you don't trust what you're seeing with your own eyes. This was just like driving into a John Wayne picture; the clapboard buildings with frontier-style lettering, a saloon with swinging doors, the whole bit. I passed two new-looking trucks parked by the side of the dirt street. Probably out here to make a movie, was my guess. Maybe even a Roth picture.

I drove northwest, off the main highway now. There wasn't a real road anymore, just a dirt trail. I bet it was originally for horses. But it had been worn wide by the cars and trucks they'd sent from Hollywood, to film the same landscape, over and over again.

I was getting close, now. It was pretty flat and I could drive pretty fast and make good time, but I didn't want to get lost this far from the main road, or overheat the truck. I used my watch to keep track of my position; I figured if I knew the time I left Victorville, and kept to this trail, and watched my speed, I couldn't get too lost.

It was around noon, and the sun was now officially blazing. The truck kicked up dust the whole way, but most of it was thrown behind us. The real pain in the chops was the haze from the heat of the desert in front of me, and the glare, which hurt my eyes.

At the end of all this flying dirt was a little nowhere, an empty shack. No one was around, but that was good; I could use this place as a marker and it was as good a place as any to turn off: I left the trail and headed northwest into the Mojave.

Now, there was no real road at all. The heat made the air shimmer and it was hard to see; everything went a bit out of focus just a few yards ahead of the truck's hood. It was dangerous, because there was the odd gulley and such every so often. If you couldn't see them coming, you couldn't slow down or steer away from them.

It was only five miles or so before I bottomed out in a

ditch. Way out here, that was a serious event. I got out of the truck and looked things over, checking the tires, the axle. It was okay; God bless Henry Ford, I thought. I also checked the radiator; I figured the water must be boiling in there like a tea kettle.

I nearly gave myself a third degree burn when I tried to open the hood, it was so hot—I needed a rag or something. Inside the truck, Roth moaned, loud. He was coming around.

I poked at the radiator cap and got it loose a half a turn. I had to jump back; it was blowing off steam like a factory whistle. While I waited for it to calm down, I took a look around. I heard a noise, and looking off to our left, I saw it—a large brown bird taking flight, coming out of a depression by the side of the road. I could hear the radiator hiss dying down behind me as I walked over to the gulley, where the bird had been.

A dry wash, with no tire tracks or hoof prints in it. The ground at the bottom looked hard enough to drive on.

The radiator drank up one jug of water, and half of the other. The truck wasn't going to take much more of this heat; I wasn't doing so good myself, it was brutal out here.

I tried starting the truck up again—and it did, thank you, Jesus. We rolled up, slowly. Then I turned off the trail and drove carefully down the side of the dry wash. It was as hard as it looked; as hard as any highway out of Los Angeles. Even so, I kept the truck at a crawl; I didn't want a flat. I wanted to see every single rock before it came up; I bet I never went faster than two or three miles an hour.

Then came a long stretch of nothing—just the walls of the wash, more rocks, and no shade because the sun was still high. I was boiling right through my cotton shirt and trousers, but at least the track was wide down here.

Another mile, and not a sign of water the whole way. I was dying of thirst. We had reached a depression that looked like a dozen others we'd already gone by. I stopped and put on the brake, keeping the engine running. I slid out of the cab, and went into the back to get a sip of water from the jug, and take a look around.

I didn't feel like doing it, but I scrabbled up the rock side of the wash. Nothing, in every direction. The four corners of the earth. Just dirt, dead scrub, and the heat.

I slid back down into the little canyon, all grimy now. I heard Roth babbling again, louder now; you could hear him over the noise of the engine.

I opened the passenger door, and looked at him. He been talking that whole last mile, saying things I couldn't understand. I reached into my back pocket and took out the key to the handcuffs.

They clicked open and I began to pull Roth out of the cab. I dragged him across the rocks, away from the truck. He lay back when I let go of him, like he was taking some sun by his pool back in Beverly Hills. He'd probably never done that; his body was fish-belly white, only the hands and the face were browned by the sun. He lay there, still talking to himself; his eyes were half-open.

I got back behind the wheel. The truck had to hold out just a little bit longer, long enough for this last bit of business: I put it in first gear and gave it a little gas, turning the wheels tight to the left. I rolled it slowly up the side of the wash, a couple of inches at a time, praying the radiator wouldn't explode.

The incline was steep and the wall was soft; never the less, I kept the pressure on and finally managed to get the nose of the truck about a third of the way up the side of the ravine. The front wheels were now sitting up the side, about forty-five degrees higher than the wheels in the back, which still rested on the floor of the wash.

I needed that forty-five degrees; I never could have gotten that safe off the back of the truck without some help from gravity. I put the truck in neutral, pulled the handbrake, and then got out and climbed up into the back as fast as I could.

The sun was making my head fuzzy. I had trouble telling which key on my ring was for the padlock. I had to try them all, but the lock finally snapped open and the chain came loose. Now the hard part: I began to wedge myself as best I could between the back of the safe and the front wall of the truck bed, using sweat and suppleness and body weight to insinuate myself in that small gap… I found I could just get in there, if I folded my legs—I pressed my back and shoulders against the safe, and put the soles of my feet against the back of the cab. Then I pushed with my legs. At first nothing happened, and the blood was boiling in my head now. I was using all of my two hundred pounds, but the safe weighed a lot more…

The angle and the gravity made the difference. Once the safe started to slide, it was gone, off the back of the truck and onto the dirt and sand at the bottom of the wash with a sad thump that shook the earth. I rolled off the truck bed, too, hitting the gravel and almost cracking my head. Roth felt the vibration from the safe hitting the ground and mumbled something critical about the noise. But the sun was too much for him and he became quiet.

I took the free end of the chain and began to wind it around the four welded bolts that framed the safe—the way Sam and I had done when we pulled it out of the wall that night. At least, I was thinking, you won't ever have to move this fucker again. You see, the safe was no good to me anymore. Because the stuff in there was all on Roth, and you can't blackmail a dead man.

I padlocked the chain to itself at the best point; there wasn't an inch of slack. Then I dragged Roth back over to the safe and the chain; he cursed me, even though I'm sure he didn't know who I was at that point.

I took out the handcuffs and slipped one through a link in the chain. I snapped it shut, and checked it. Then I closed the other cuff around Roth's wrist.

I slipped the key in my pocket and checked everything

over one last time. The lock was tight, the handcuffs were good and solid. To get himself out of here, he'd have to drag that safe twenty miles, either that or chew his hand off. He didn't look like he could do either; he looked like a scrawny little white rat of a man, already beginning to turn pink in the sun. There was another six hours before dark, at least. If he came to before then, he'd realize what was happening to him. But even if he never came around, he'd feel it, alright; he'd think he'd died and gone to hell. Which was sort of true, in a way.

I got into the cab and shut the door. I cut the wheel hard; then I took off the brake and let it roll back. I cut the wheel again and put it in first. There was steam coming out from under the hood, but I felt fairly confident; it had held together so far. I let the truck go forward, rolling along the hard bottom of the wash again, back the way we'd come.

I'd only gotten a hundred feet or so away from Roth and the safe when I realized I'd forgotten something. I put the truck in neutral and set the brake again. I fumbled through the pockets of my ruined jacket. It was there; I got out of the truck again and stumbled back across the gravel to Roth.

He lay flat on his back, talking to himself again, but now his eyes were shut tight against the white sun. I knelt and pressed it into his hand; his fingers gripped reflexively and took it. Stacey's jar.

I walked back to the truck; it was hissing impatiently, but I was in no shape to hurry. I turned and looked at Roth once more before I climbed back into the cab.

He'd raised one skinny white knee. He held the jar in the air, gesturing with it like it might stop the sun. I could see the little black mouth moving; opening and closing, but no real words coming out.

Wished I'd brought a camera.

45

As it turned out, the truck made it just fine. It was in better shape than I was, in fact. I made it back into Victorville before sundown. I drank the rest of my water and treated myself to a nap in the back of the truck, pulling the canvas tarp over me for shade.

When I woke up it was already late in the evening—the heat of the day still radiated from the earth, but there was no sun to torture me anymore.

Pretty stars. I took a walk around town. The saloon was for real; I went inside and took a seat at the long bar. I wasn't worried about anybody bothering me with questions; I looked like a bum now in my grimy, filthy suit, and I was still sweating like a pig. Nobody was going to talk to me—the bartender wasn't even sure about serving me until I pulled a ten out of my wallet and laid it on the bar.

I sipped a beer. There were some movie types making a big noise at a couple of the other tables, drinking and laughing like loons. The kind of people Sam used to work with, but young and in their salad days. I tried to picture him there, having a ball, but I couldn't do it. I'd only known him as a wasted old buzzard.

A couple of pretty girls came in, and the party got even louder. The girls were in the movies, too, I bet; they looked a bit too floozy-ish to be real people. They made me think of Vera. I thought of her running her lines and doing a bad job of it; I thought of her looking ridiculous in costume, up there in black-and-silver on the big movie screen with me sitting in the theater, watching her. That would have been something; pretty funny to think of her trying to be an actress. Then again, maybe she wouldn't have been so bad; who knows. She was great when she sang that song and danced at the Cocoanut

Grove. She could have learned to act. Maybe.

I was feeling drunk, and, worse yet, maudlin. I called over the bartender and asked him where I could spend the night; I pulled out another tenner. It was unnecessary; he was a kindly type with gentle, understanding eyes and a big moustache—I could tell he'd been on my side of the bar, too, in his time, and he sympathized. He told me that I could sleep in the back on a table; it would be quiet after closing time, he'd leave me a blanket and a pillow, and there was a toilet. It sounded like heaven.

It was.

The next morning, I took the truck over to the Victorville filling station. The owner looked it over, looked me over, and said: "Been out in the desert?" I admitted I had, and he gave me a quick rundown on what needed to be done; hoses and so forth. I gave him a twenty and said, "Do it," and then I asked him where I could get breakfast while he did the work.

He said there was a local hotel with a café inside, but he doubted I'd get in looking like I did. He was right—my tailor-made suit was ruined, I was unshaven, and I reeked. The hot morning sun wasn't helping any.

I'd seen an old tub by the side of the garage and I asked him if I could put some water in it and clean myself up a bit. He laughed at that and said sure.

The tub was made of steel but it was fairly light; I dragged it around back and turned on a spigot in the back of the building—cold water came rushing out. I thought to myself, what the hell, nobody's looking, and I hopped in the tub, suit and all. It felt great, like a cold beer, and I stripped off my socks and started rinsing them out and wringing them. If I laid them out they'd be dry in no time—the sun was already high and white.

I wondered whether Roth was dead yet. When I turned my neck to look out at the desert behind me, I saw two little Indian kids, a boy and a girl, watching me, laughing. I grinned at them, and started scrubbing under the arms of my jacket. They came closer, still laughing, and I reached out and grabbed my wallet from where it lay by the tub. I held up a dollar bill and motioned the boy over; I asked if he could speak English. He nodded. He looked about nine, a good-looking kid. I told him to go to the store and bring me back some soap; he could keep the change if he came right back.

He grabbed the bill and said something to his sister; then he took off around the garage. She crouched down in the sand to wait for him, about twenty feet off. She looked about seven or so. She picked up a little stick and started to scratch a little something in the sand, blue mountains behind her. Every so often she gave me the once over. She was very pretty.

Her brother was back within five minutes with two different kinds of soap; he tried to give me the change back anyway but I waved him off. He went to join his sister, and I told him to give her a quarter. He did.

Then they both were laughing fit to bust as I soaped up the suit and scrubbed away. I made a big ham production out of it for them; scrubbing my collar and hat, wringing out my tie, and singing an old cowboy song. That brought the owner around back to see what was going on, and the brother and the sister thought that was the funniest thing of all; me in the tub in the soapy suit and the owner standing there with a C-wrench in his hand, each of us staring at the other. Finally he gave up and retreated around the front again. I gave the kids an "okay" sign and began to rinse off.

Then I lay back in the water and just closed my eyes, feeling the sun and thinking. I was having a little trouble figuring out exactly why I had killed Roth. He was worth a hell of a lot to me alive, and I had had the goods on him. A hell of a lot of money to throw away, just to see a man die. Why had I done it?

I wasn't sure. Not to avenge Sam; not really. Sam had known the score all along. He knew the sort of people that ran the movie business, and he'd told me himself that they'd try to kill us if we started screwing around with them. Sam had taken a risk, and lost; he was no innocent victim. So it didn't feel like I'd done it for revenge.

And I thought that it was awful that Roth had killed Vera, she was hardly more than a kid. It had made me very angry, but that wasn't the reason I killed Roth, either. I didn't love Vera or anything like that. And she certainly didn't love me. It didn't make sense that I'd throw away all that wealth and opportunity, to punish him for killing a girl I didn't love.

I stewed there under the sun until I figured it out. I finally decided I'd killed Roth because I would have hated to see him get away with it. Again. Guys like Roth always win; heartless bastards, I mean. I wanted to see one lose, for a change.

It didn't make a lot of sense, and it was very expensive for me to indulge myself like that. If you think about the cost in life opportunities, I'd just thrown away more money than Roth had ever spent or made in his life.

For some reason, I thought this made me better than him. It made me feel as though I had beat a guy like him, one of the big guys. Even though it had cost me dear, it made me feel like I'd won, for a change.

I had killed him just because I wanted to.

Ah, well. Money isn't everything.

I opened up my eyes, and I saw something strange. The two little Indian kids were running, running away from me. Not towards the town, either; they were running out into the desert, like something had scared them. But there was nothing around to scare them—just me, still sitting here, soaking.

And then I felt cold all of the sudden, and I noticed that I was in shadow, which was impossible, because the nearest building was the garage, way behind me—

I'd barely turned to look, when something hard cracked me on the head, and I lost control of my body. The sun was blinding me and I was slipping on the sides of the tub. I felt something crack the side of my head again, and I thought, stop that, that hurts, you're going to kill me.

I saw the shadow now, hanging over me like a mountain, a man-shaped mountain. I couldn't make out the darkened face, but sun glinted off glass where one of the eyes should have been. Then I couldn't keep my own eyes open anymore; it hurt too much to keep them open, the sun was too bright. I wanted to slip down under the water to get away from him, but I was being hauled up, out of the tub, I heard the water running out of my clothes.

And then I couldn't hear anything.

46

And now I was freezing; it was like I was one of those naked girls in the ice monoliths at Roth's party. I opened my eyes and saw brilliant white light; at first I thought it was the sun again, but it was everywhere and all unfocused, like I was cockeyed drunk. And then I felt the cloying wet, all over; and when I opened my mouth there was no air to breathe, only cold water rushing in. I realized I was drowning. I choked and tried to scream, under the water. The scream forced the water out for a moment, but there was no air to breathe back in—only more water. My body was pushing itself up, up from under the water to find air. But something was holding me down, beneath the water; and I couldn't move my arms or legs, they were bound. I wriggled; I was tied to something and couldn't get any leverage—nothing to hold onto, all I could move freely was my neck, and I twisted it wildly. There was a blackness up above the brilliantly lit water all round me, but I couldn't reach it. I was going to die.

Then the water was rushing all around me; I was coming up through the water like a dolphin about to shoot up over a wave. I strained for air and now there was air, finally; freezing night air trying to force its way into me and spill the water out from inside my lungs and throat. I saw stars up above in the night sky for a second, and then my eyes squeezed shut as my body began to heave, spewing the water from inside me.

The water coming out of me was splashing down between my knees, splashing on something hard—cement? I still couldn't open my eyes. I could feel that I was sitting up; sitting on something, tied down to it, and coughing so hard I felt my lungs would break. I grabbed desperate little gasps of air in between coughs to feed my brain, keep it awake.

Through teary eyes, I could make it out, in front of me.

A swimming pool, a big fancy one, like at Roth's party. Was I at Roth's place? I could see the architectural lights, mounted in the pool, just under the surface of the water. Then I began to puke water again; I put my head down, and my body shook.

The air was starting to come back into my lungs now. I began to feel very cold; the night and the wet. The water ran out of my nose and dribbled from my mouth; I was too tired to cough any more. I kept my head hung down like a tired dog and wheezed, the air was whistling back into me. Now I heard men talking behind me, quickly and quietly, an important conversation. I opened my eyes and raised my head a bit, looking over the glowing surface of the vast swimming pool. Above the walls beyond it were black California mountains and the Arabian Nights sky.

This could be Roth's place, I thought. It was hard to tell without all the party scenery and high life going on. I was out in the hills somewhere; that was for sure. And I was tied to a chair, a fancy metal chair like the one in Roth's office—

"Sleeping Beauty," hissed the soft voice of a man. The hissing voice full of cigarettes and liquor; Wally O'Brien.

"Hey, Sleeping Beauty," he says again, in my ear. "It's me. Prince Charming." He cuffed me a couple of times on the ear with his open hand, to get my attention. Not too hard; just school bully stuff.

I grunted a couple of times; you know, to let him know I was paying attention. He grabbed me by the chin and jerked my face towards his own, nearly twisting my neck off its axle. His huge fat face, with a black eye patch now, behind the spectacles with the single lens. A big map of flesh, split with a grin made of huge yellow teeth. The happiest I'd ever seen him. Because I wasn't going anywhere, this time.

"Remember me? Hah?" He squeezed my face between his thumb and two fingers, like I was his favorite little nephew or something. The breath wheezed over me, I smelled the alcohol. He'd had a few tonight.

"Wanna see something funny? Hah?"

Uh-oh.

"You like the Three Stooges?"

Dopey as I felt, I knew something bad was coming. I saw him raise his free hand and hold up two fingers; they looked as thick as broomsticks. Fortunately, I *did* like the Three Stooges, because I guessed what he was going to do and shut my eyes and turned my head down just a bit, just enough to spoil his aim. If I hadn't, the two straight fingers he jabbed at my eye sockets would have popped something out, for sure.

As it was, things went black, and then purple. I was blinded for a second, but I remembered to yelp and scream. Because that might satisfy him for the moment, and he might not hurt me again right away.

"Pretty funny, hah?"

"I thought you said you were only going to ask him questions." Another voice: educated, but full of fear and disgust. Fiske.

"He don't need to see, to answer questions," said O'Brien's voice. It sounded as though he had stood up straight and stepped back from me. And he had: his flat, open-handed smack caught me full on the face—I flew back and up, a few inches into the air, metal chair and all, and tipped over. My head hit the cement, but not too hard; I was still awake. Jesus, this guy slapped better than most guys punch. There was coppery tasting blood in my mouth now; the jaw might be broken or dislocated. It would serve him right if I couldn't talk, the one-eyed prick.

A shoe probed at my cheek, exploring. Not O'Brien's; it wasn't big enough. "He's still dopey, Wally." Ah. One of O'Brien's apprentices. The punk; what was his name?

"Don't matter, so long as he can tell us what we need to know." I could barely make them out, the light coming from inside the house was so dim; they were just huge shapes, watching over me.

"Hurry up, can't you," said Fiske's voice. He stepped around O'Brien to look down on me. "Someone might see us."

"No one around for miles, Mr. Fiske." O'Brien was wiping his hands on something. "Mr. Roth owns everything around here, for miles. This guy could scream his heart out and there's no one to see or hear. Just us."

He picked me up by my hair and righted me on the cement.

"One chance. That's all you get." The bright little blue eye behind the thick lens was burning a hole right through me. "What'd you do with Roth?"

I opened my mouth to speak, but couldn't; nothing came out but bloody spit. Embarrassed, I tried to suck it back in. That infuriated him for some reason, because he reached over me and picked up the back of my chair—and tossed me into the pool like I was a kitten, all six feet of me.

Down I went, it was the deep end. I didn't even struggle this time, just held my breath. No point in trying to get loose; they'd fastened me to the chair with these big leather straps; cinches like they use for horses. I wasn't going anywhere. But I didn't panic; actually, the water made my head feel a little better. I could always panic later, when things looked really bad, like about a minute and a half from now. When I ran out of air. Like Sam.

I touched the bottom; the deep end, and I tipped over and fell slowly on my side. I tried to right myself on the bottom—it was something to do, anyway. I opened my eyes as I threw my weight against the up side of the chair. Because the pool was floodlit, I could make out something new in the water—it was a black shape, flapping towards me like a big bat in the water, leaving waves of beautiful bubbles behind it and kicking like hell. It dived down towards me and grabbed the back of my chair, and began to drag me. I was being hauled across the bottom of the pool, towards the shallow end. I could see I was leaving a little trail of blood behind me as I went; a dark, filmy string of syrup in the illuminated water.

Then we broke the surface, and the punk pulling my

chair was spitting, yelling: "Jeez, Wally, throw'im closer to the skinny end next time, cantcha?

Fiske's snappy little voice was carping at O'Brien, and O'Brien was wheezing back.

"Don't be an idiot, O'Brien!"

"I can handle it, Mr. Fiske."

"Maybe you can't handle it! Maybe you don't understand exactly what is at stake! You have money invested in the studio, don't you? Don't you?"

O'Brien didn't answer. He just stared as his boy dragged me through the water, bringing me up towards the edge of the pool. The punk—Eddie, that was his name— left me sitting up to my neck in the shallows; then he walked up out of the water on concrete steps that had been built into the pool floor.

Fiske was getting a little hysterical. "How much do you think your investment is going to be worth if you kill him and Roth is still missing tomorrow? You'd ruin us all, just to get even with one little—parasite?"

My ears were burning.

"Don't worry, Mr. Fiske. I know what I'm doing."

"People are already asking questions about Roth and that, that girl! There are limits to what I can keep quiet, dammit!"

"Keep your shirt on."

"Just find out where Jack is! Then we turn him over to the police!"

"No."

Fiske was used to yes-men; this 'no' stuff took him by surprise.

"Sorry, Mr. Fiske. We'll find out about Mr. Roth. But after that, this one's all mine."

I couldn't see O'Brien's face from where I was; but I could see Fiske. His face was white.

"That guy is part of my salary this year." O'Brien's voice was gentle, like he was explaining some difficult subject to a child. "Kind of like a Christmas bonus or somethin', you understand?"

Fiske thought it best to say nothing. He just stared; a mouse looking up at a huge snake.

"Don't you worry, though, Mr. Fiske. He's gonna tell us what he knows about Mr. Roth, first. And then he's gonna disappear, easy as pie, quiet as you please. No headlines this time, they'll never even find him. But he's mine. Okay?"

And then he turned slowly away from Fiske and started lumbering along towards me again. Fiske stared after him a moment, and then scurried off to the bar cart at the other end of the pool. I was with him in spirit.

O'Brien stood over me at poolside, his face lit up by the lights beneath the water. He was grinning; and I guess I did look pretty funny, seated in about four feet of water, waves lapping over my shoulders. My eyes were puffing out, too; I could feel something hot and warm running down one of my cheeks, too. Like a tear, but probably not.

"Mr. Fiske is very upset with the way you're being treated."

There was an awful scraping noise as he pulled up a concrete bench to the side of the pool and lowered himself onto it.

"But we both know that you're a pretty tough guy. Just like me. I bet you can take a lot worse if you have to, couldn't you?"

My mouth was full of marbles. "Is that a… hypothetical question?" I tried to say, but the word had too many syllables.

He didn't get me, he just stared for a moment and then went on: "You're gonna tell me where Mr. Roth is. And then, I'm gonna kill you." He let that sink in, and went on. "But not here, out there somewheres." He looked out into the night, beyond the estate.

"There's a lotta guys out there already, you know. In the canyons. That was the spot, back in Prohibition."

He was reminiscing. "It was just last year; there was this guy owed Mr. Roth some dough. He wouldn't pay, not at first. So we took him out there. He was a tough guy, it took me and Eddie a few hours." Eddie was leaning, dripping against the side of a palm tree, smoking a cigarette. "But he finally made out that check. We left him one good hand, so he could write it. And then we had him dig a hole for himself, and then we put him in the hole. But before we did, we made him do one more thing. You know what that was? We made him say, 'thank you.'"

He rose from his bench, and I shook in my chair, under the water.

"You don't look as tough as that guy, though." He started towards me, coming around the edge of the pool, behind me now. I couldn't see him. My teeth chattered.

I felt the top of my scalp coming off, he was picking me up, pulling me straight out of the water by my hair. My cracked jaw hung open and an awful groaning noise came from inside me; he pulled me up over the edge of the pool with water gushing out of my trousers. He set me down on the cement poolside like I was a chess piece.

He turned my chair around so I faced him, and I could see Eddie tossing away his cigarette and skulking back towards the house. He didn't want to see what O'Brien was going to do to me next.

The big red ham of a hand closed over the index finger of my left hand. Then he thought better of that, and grabbed my little finger instead.

"Don't want you passin' out again right away," he explained.

The little finger disappeared into the big hand. My arms were strapped to the chair; there was nothing I could do, even if I had the strength. I felt the little finger go back, back, back, where it had never been before—my eyes were shut tight, but I could see it, in my mind's eye, bending, and a scream was welling up in my throat.

There was a muffled snap! Like somebody breaking a pencil under a blanket. And I gasped.

So did he, but that was his way of giggling. "How's that?" he whispered. "This any better?"

He turned the broken finger, and now I howled, twisting in my chair. Those straps were tight, but you ever see a rat disappear into a hole in a corner in wall, and the rat's much bigger than the hole, and you wonder, how the hell did he do that? I was able to twist, straps or no. And the chair hopped up under my body weight, and I tilted it, and I fell right back in the pool again: anything to get away.

He didn't bother calling Eddie to fetch me out again; this time he reached right in for me, rooted around for a few minutes and then began to haul me up out of the water again by a chair leg. I was upside down. I heard the hissing laugh when I broke the surface of the water again.

"Eddie," O'Brien was saying.

"Yeah?" said a voice from the other side of the pool. He sounded a little scared.

"Go on in the house and get me a poker from the fireplace."

A shadow flickered against the light of the French doors; Eddie going inside. O'Brien was dragging what was left of me and the chair across the cement, around to the terrace at the other side of the pool.

I could see Fiske sitting at the bar there, his back to us. It looked like his head was in his hands. Sensitive type.

O'Brien tipped the chair so I was sitting up again, and then he loosened something at the back. I slid down out of the chair onto the terrace like I was a pile of rags. O'Brien wasn't worried about me trying to get away, now. I was too far gone to be any threat at all to him now. I might as well have been a baby. I lay there staining the flagstones; a tangle of breathing wet clothes. We waited in silence for Eddie to come back with the poker.

Then O'Brien said: "You might want to go inside the

house now, Mr. Fiske. This is gonna take a little while."

Fiske hesitated; then he rose from his chair without turning around.

And then we heard a voice, coming out of the dark palms beyond the edge of the pool:

"No."

A woman's voice.

47

From where I lay, I could only see O'Brien towering over me. There was a glint from his spectacles—I mean, spectacle—as he turned from me towards the direction of the voice. Fiske came up quick as a mouse beside him, looking in the same direction, even paler than before.

My curiosity got the better of me and I writhed on the ground in my wormy way. It was Stacey, of course. She was all dolled up, like she was going out to a party or something; she descended from the palms, glittering in a black evening gown and long black gloves, diamonds. And a silver-plated revolver—she held it out in front of her with very little effort, keeping it pointed right at Wally O'Brien's unmissable chest.

"What are you doing here?" says Fiske, a bit dry in the mouth.

She began to approach, drifting slowly towards us; there didn't seem to be any shoes beneath the long black silk of the evening gown.

"I need him," she said. Me, she meant. "Tell Mr. O'Brien to go home."

"Miss Tilden," hissed O'Brien. "Mr. Roth is missing. I need this guy to tell us where he is."

"You've had your turn, Wally," she said, slightly mocking, giving him that sinister movie smile. She kept the gun trained on him, steady as a statue. She was close, now.

There was a moment's silence. I was wondering whether I should tell Stacey about O'Brien's boy Eddie; did she know he was in the house?

"Stacey," says Fiske. "If I send O'Brien away, will you put that thing down and—"

"You ain't sending me anywhere," says O'Brien, never taking his eyes off Stacey. "I work for Mr. Roth, not you. He's the only one who tells me what to do, Miss Tilden, and he ain't here."

"Then I guess you'll have to decide to leave all by

yourself, Wally," she said, lowering her voice, and clicking back the hammer.

Jeez, I was thinking, this is just like the movies.

Out of the corner of my eye, I could see O'Brien begin to step forward, towards her—but he froze when Stacey said: "You'd better not."

O'Brien looked awful from any angle, but from my angle, laying on my back, he really did remind me of the Cyclops—a grinning Cyclops, now, as he began to step forward again, more carefully.

"Give me that gun, you crazy little faggot," he hissed. (So he knew, after all?)

It was an unfortunate choice of words, that's for sure. The mouth of the gun exploded like the crack of doom, and O'Brien was stopped in mid-step. His grin melted away and he looked down at his shirtfront, disappointed, like he'd spilled something on it. Well, what had he expected, she couldn't miss at this distance.

He took another step forward, still coming towards her—"Faggot!" he hissed, again. That same, ill-advised turn of phrase; O'Brien was a slow learner.

The pistol cracked again.

He was between me and Stacey, now. Still standing, but a bit woozy, like a drunk looking for a place to puke. Then it was all over, for him. He toppled like a falling tower; into the pool with an elephant splash. Some of the water leapt out and hit me where I lay; it revived me, a little.

Stacey stepped over me, to the side of the pool. She was still training the smoking gun on O'Brien's body, just in case he decided to come back from the dead, jump up out of the water and say something rude to her again. I could see her face, in profile. Cool as ice, with maybe just the slightest hint of annoyance; like it was the servants' night off and she'd had to swat a fly all by herself.

Then she spun around and took aim at something behind us, back in the house. And the way she did it; so quick and graceful and natural it might have been a dance move.

I didn't see him right away, but I knew who she was aiming at: Eddie the assistant punk, brought out of the house by the sound of shots. I rolled my head and tried to look; I wanted to see the expression on Eddie's face, if Stacey decided in favor of shooting him, too.

He was ready for her; he'd come out onto the porch with his pistol drawn, all set to defend his boss. But Stacey had the drop on him, and now she was smiling again. She looked like she was enjoying herself.

Eddie wasn't. His face was scared, like a kid who suddenly figures out he's lost in the big department store. Eddie had shown up for an evening of breaking my bones and drowning me in the swimming pool; I was a nobody, I'd never be missed. But now here was Miss Tilden, the studio's biggest star, pointing a gun at him. He couldn't shoot her, could he? And, oh, goodness, there's Mr. O'Brien, floating dead in the pool, already! It was all too much for his little brain to handle.

"Mr. Fiske?"

"Yeah," said Fiske, sounding pretty nauseous.

"What should I do?" said Eddie, his eyes bouncing back and forth between Fiske to Stacey like little bee-bees.

Fiske thought a moment. He'd once been married to Stacey; he probably understood these moods of hers better than the rest of us.

"Just go home," said Fiske.

Eddie still thought Stacey might kill him. She still looked like she might. "Is Mr. O'Brien—"

"Just go home, Eddie," Fiske snapped. "Just go away."

Eddie never took his eyes off Stacey as he backed away, into the house where he'd come from. We heard him when he started running; the fading sound of his shoes clicking on the marble floor inside. He'd lost a showdown with an actress—after tonight, Eddie would always be missing a little of his old pep.

Stacey kept the gun on him until the footsteps faded.

Then she let her arm drop heavily to her side, and turned to look down into the pool again.

We said nothing; the night was quiet and all I could hear was the water of the pool lapping up against its edges. From far away, a car started up and drove off, and now we knew it was just the three of us. And O'Brien, face down in the pool.

I rolled my head on the cement again, and closed my eyes. The night air smelled fresh and electric all of the sudden. Even the cold and the pain in my mouth and skull and my broken finger felt kinda good; how can pain feel good? Oh, yeah—because you think you're going to live, now. I opened my eyes again and stared up at the beautiful night sky, looking at stars that went on to infinity. I had to look at them; I was still flat on my back and I couldn't muster the strength to get to my knees, even. Then I heard her footsteps coming towards me; the high heels, clicking on cement.

"Stacey, don't," said Fiske, but he said it kinda half-hearted.

"I want that jar back." She stood over me, training the gun down on my face.

Best to keep her talking, I thought.

"Hey, Stacey," I whispered. "Can I ask you something?"

She said nothing.

"This was all on purpose, wasn't it?"

It was hard to see her lovely face, way up there above me against the night, but I knew it was looking down on me, unbending and uncaring and no pity in it.

I cleared my throat. "I mean… you had it figured in advance, right?"

"What is he talking about?" said Fiske, quavery. He wanted to keep her talking, too. Not that he cared about me; for all Fiske knew, he was next.

I talked to the sky. "She set it up so Roth and me

would cancel each other out. I had something on her, and Roth had something on her. So she turned me loose on Roth." I paused to spit out a tooth. "She figured either Roth would kill me for trying to blackmail him, or I'd kill Roth to stop him killing me. Either way, she'd come out a little bit ahead. Right?" I said to Stacey.

I heard the smile come back into her voice. "You make me sound so calculating, darling." She adjusted her hair with her free hand. "But I was rooting for you the whole time."

I heard her draw the hammer back on the revolver again; a gentle click. I looked up into the empty black hole at the end of the silver barrel—my destiny, staring me in the face. It seemed as big as a manhole, from where I was. So I closed my eyes, tight. She said:

"Now give me my balls back, little man."

I heard my raspy voice, coming back at her: "I want my money."

"I'll blow your brains out."

There was quiet for a moment.

"Listen, lady. You can get along okay in this town without brains or balls, but you gotta have money."

Pretty witty, considering the circs. Well, okay, it's an old gag; but I said it real natural, with good timing.

And she hadn't fired; not yet, anyway. I made myself open my eyes again and look up at the sexy silhouette. She'd let the gun drop to her side again and her body was shaking; her other hand covered her face.

Then she opened up her mouth and shrieked, shrieked with laughter. It was awful in a way, because it was a man's laughter, loud and long. I turned my head a bit more, watching her collapse into one of the long wooden deck chairs by the pool. She kept the pistol in hand, trailing it on the cement beside her in a lazy way as she giggled to herself and watched the surface of the pool.

"Stacey—" said Fiske—

"Oh, shut up, Jerry," she said, annoyed that he'd interrupted the moment. Fiske shut up, and I heard her sigh. I rolled my head over. She was lying back in the deck chair, toying with the revolver in her lap now.

"The police—" Fiske began—

"That's your problem," said Stacey. "You'll cover it up, some way. You usually do."

That shut him up; I guess he took it as a compliment. Then I looked over at the pool, too. The floodlights under water glowed beneath the huge black shape on the surface, drifting aimlessly. A big black tarantula, trailing long threads of blood behind him in the water as he floated by.

For about a minute, nobody said anything.

It was kind of relaxing, in a way.

"Where is Roth?" said Stacey after a while, getting a cigarette out of her purse.

This, I knew, was addressed to me.

"Gone," I said.

"Forever?"

"I think so," I said. I had one of my inspirations. "Your, your jar, and that safe of his. They're gone, too."

"Where?" said Stacey.

"With Roth. They're gone."

It was Fiske who spoke this time. "Forever?"

"I guess," I mumbled, looking up at the stars again. "You guys don't expect me to tell you everything, right?"

Stacey decided. "Alright," she said. "I'll give you ten thousand, cash. You take it and get out of town, and out of my life."

"What happens if I don't?"

"You go swimming with O'Brien," she said. I could practically hear Fiske shuddering beside her.

I licked some blood off my lips and said, "Make it fifteen."

I heard that sound again; the hammer clicking back on

the revolver.

"Okay, toots," I said, "Ten grand it is. Never argue with a lady. I get to keep the jewelry, though, right?" I asked, hopefully.

"It's yours," she said, tired. "I could never wear it again without thinking of you, anyway."

I rolled over, slowly, so nothing else would break. She wasn't smiling anymore, but the gloved fingers were carefully setting the hammer of the gun back into place. Then she rose slowly from the deck chair; she stretched and yawned, feeling the night breeze.

"Pay him, Jerry," I heard her say.

"I most certainly will not pay him!" squealed Jerry. "That would make us—"

"Pay him." It was an order. "It's petty cash, practically. Anyway, he reminds me of Tom." Tom? Tom Hayes. Her old dance partner, from the twenties. Before she became a star, when she was still a kid.

She'd already turned her back on Fiske and me, and now she was walking away from us; off into the dark palm groves beyond the pool. The reflected light from the water glittered on her gown as she drifted off; it touched on the gun in her gloved hand, swinging gently by her side.

For Fiske, it suddenly sank in: Stacey was walking out, leaving him to deal with the missing and the dead, and sticking him with the check for the whole mess, besides. Horrified, he hopped up and started after her. But his nerve left him halfway and he stopped short.

As Stacey disappeared into the black grove, he called out, pleading with her: "Stacey! You can't do this!"

She didn't answer.

"You can't do this, Stacey!"

She was gone now, but I heard the low, sexy voice one last time, coming from out of the darkness:

"I can do anything I want," said the voice, "I'm a star."

48

By this time, I was thoroughly sick of Los Angeles. Too many weirdoes.

As I lay there in the County hospital, watching my bones knit, I decided that Stacey had the right idea: as soon as it was okay with the doctors, I was getting out of this town, and for good. I'd had enough of this Hollywood crap.

Fiske paid up like she told him to. The money was sent to my ward in a little white unmarked envelope. It was all there, but they didn't pay my hospital bills, which would have been the decent thing to do, the cheap pricks.

I was out in a few days, minus a couple of teeth and plus a little limp, which the doctor said would only be temporary. I was paid up at the Ambassador til the end of that week, so my stuff was still in the closet of the suite when I went back. But, much to my chagrin, I found that the only clean clothes I had left was that goddamn red-checked plaid clown suit I came to town in. I'd ditched my evening clothes out in Glendale, my custom-made summer weight suit had been ruined in the desert where I left Roth, and O'Brien had gotten it all bloody, anyway. I wasn't going to pay for an extra night at the Ambassador just so I could have it cleaned at the hotel laundry. (Stacey was no longer covering my living expenses, you see; anything I spent from now on was coming out of my own pocket.)

So, I left the Ambassador that morning for the last time, sporting the clown suit. And I'm happy to say that I stiffed Herman the desk manager and the hotel detective and every single bellboy I ran into all the way from the front desk to the front door. Good—I got a nice smile from that bunch for nothing, finally. I think I even got a couple of towels out of there, too.

I did have to lay out two hundred bucks for another

car, though. I got a 1927 Chevy coupe at a used car lot downtown. The owner was delighted to have a paying customer and greeted me like an old pal, but I haggled for nearly an hour with him over the price. You should have seen me sweating out there in my red-checked suit, waving cash in his face, and saying things like "This stuff doesn't grow on trees, you know!" Pathetic.

I'd decided against sending dough to Sam's family. His kids were grown up; he'd mentioned the fact that he'd never got any letters from them. His wife hadn't spoken to him in years, but I tried to phone her up, anyway. Anonymous, of course. It turned out she'd remarried and written Sam out of her life. So why cut her in?

And I certainly didn't send Vera's folks any of my ten thousand. No reason I should, right? Vera said her cop dad had regularly beat the hell out of her and her mom had never tried to stop him. Like I'm gonna wire them money? They were ashamed of Vera; I'll bet they didn't even go to her funeral. It was the state that buried Vera.

I wasn't going to throw her a funeral; sorry, but I'd barely gotten out alive myself and I intended to keep my head down until I was well out of Los Angeles. Anyway, I don't believe in spending money on dead people, not even dead friends. That's the least important part of you, the part they bury. I'll bet Vera would have understood that, too, if she'd lived to be a little older. Money is for living people.

So, I ended up with ten grand for all my trouble, minus the hospital bills and the cost of a crappy Chevy coupe. Not the fortune I'd hoped for, but enough to bankroll me for a fresh start in a new life in a new place. I was all fired up to get out of Southern California. The nice weather is not worth all the lunatics you run into. My plan was to head east again and find some real place, with real people. I needed to be around regular folks, people who look you straight in the eye and speak the truth. Those are the kind of people I can make money off of.

So, I turned the old Chevy east, and I took off, going back in the direction I'd come from. (Not by way of Arizona, though, Vera's father the cop might still be looking for me.)

As I began to cross those big deserts again, I thought about Roth, out there somewhere. Probably just a bunch of picked-over bones by now. That would suit Stacey just fine. I wondered about her, too, as I sped along under the sun, not stopping for hitch hikers. Stacey made out best out of this whole deal, I was thinking; she was free of Roth, and me, and at the top of her form, acting-wise.

It turned out I was right, because she stayed on top for years afterwards. Made some of her best pictures. She even decided to stay on with Olympic—that eel Fiske was technically in charge, but I'll bet Stacey was the one who called the shots. Fiske was no Jack Roth: no match for Stacey, that's for sure. She probably made life hell for that guy. I've often wondered if that car crash that killed her in 1940 was really an accident, like they said it was.

It probably was; I doubt Fiske ever got up the guts to kill her, no matter how bad he'd wanted to. She was the only one in the car, and the newspapers said she'd been drinking that night. That rang true; she'd been drinking herself to death for years, right? It began to show in her last few pictures; there's only so much you can do with lights and make up and surgery. If you catch one of those later pictures on late night TV, you can see it creeping into her face, her skin. Killing her looks. The sexy, slightly crooked smile we all admired was twisting into a leer. She was getting old.

And that would kill her, for sure—not to be beautiful, anymore. So maybe it was a genuine suicide. The accident would be kind of like her big last scene, you see; it seemed like something she would do—drunken impulse, the artist who'd lost her status, her beauty. The unalterable decision: she wrenches the wheel, and then the big smash, and the blaze of spectacular burning glory, and all of that smashed glass like diamonds bursting all around her. Like the end of one of her pictures.

I wasn't thinking about all that at the time, of course; that was yet to come. Back then, headed out on the burning highway, I was thinking that this Chevy drove like a milk truck compared to the Bentley. But I had a full tank of gas and cash in my pockets. And now I was far from Los Angeles; for good, I hoped. No more overpaid sex freaks, sadistic gangsters, and crazy, money-mad egomaniacs for this boy. I was going to find myself a regular American town, with regular American folks. Any small town out West would do, really. Just so long as it was normal.

I'd already picked a place out, even; I'd just closed my eyes and put my finger down at random on the road map. There. That'll do.

I even liked the sound of the name: Las Vegas.